The Deadly Talents

Jeffrey Crosby

Published by Jeffrey Crosby, 2020.

Published by Jeffrey D. Crosby

DeadlyTalents.books@gmail.com

ISBN-Printed – 6" x 9" paperback

Amazon: 978-1-7359387-0-7

Draft2Digital: 978-1-7359387-3-8

ISBN-Epub: 978-1-7359387-1-4

ISBN-Mobi: 978-1-7359387-2-1

Cover design: Vibrant Designs

Writing Coach: Jim Surowiecki

Table of Contents

Dedication

To My Wife Marissa
You kept me going when I did not think I could finish.
I love you.

Acknowledgments

THIS IS MY FIRST BOOK and I want to thank my family and friends that put up with me constantly talking about my book and the writing process. Besides my wife, who supported me through every step, I wanted to name some other people whose support and advice helped bring this book to life.

Jim Surowiecki, Wendy & Todd Brown, Marcia Holt, Ranissa & Darnell Scott, Romas Blazys, Laima Blazys, Jesse Stace, Jeff Geraghty, Rebecca Collin, George Gecas, Judy Martin, Josie Hernandez, and Carlos Reyes.

Special thanks to *Debbie Ott* and *Shannon Casey,* who help me resolve some late production formatting and editing issues.

The following people allowed me to use their likeness when creating some of my characters. I have listed them in order of appearance in the book and I will leave it to them to tell you who was who.

Justin Bemos, Jesse Stace, Romas Blazys and Jeff Geraghty.

Prologue - A Godless Gift

FIRE AND MADNESS GREETED Morgan Sumner as he pushed his way through the debris that blocked the door leading to the first-floor nursery. Flame had already engulfed the upper floor, and it was too late to save anyone in those rooms.

Once inside, Morgan found that the debris he had pushed through was the body of a woman, laying face down and holding a baby. The blood coming from her back showed someone had struck her down as she tried to save the child.

Smoke, crying babies and the bodies of what must have been their nursemaids filled the room. Amid this chaos, Morgan saw Chairman Jonathan Lehmann just as he brought a knife down on a screaming baby.

Morgan froze, unable to understand what he had just witnessed. In that moment of hesitation, Chairman Lehmann killed the next child.

"Stop Jonathan! What have you done?" yelled Morgan as Lehmann raised his knife above another crying baby.

Lehmann paused as if seeing Morgan for the first time. "Help me, Morgan," he said, pointing around the room. "These abominations must die!" as he drove his knife down and stepped to the next set of cribs.

Morgan pulled his sword and advanced toward Lehmann until the sword was inches from the Chairman's chest.

Lehmann stared at Morgan. A confused look on his face. His knife held above his head. The heat of the fire reminded Morgan that time was short.

Morgan turned to the sound of movement behind him, and Lehmann brought his knife down. "No!" shouted Morgan as he pushed the blade of his sword forward. Lehmann gasped, then fell backward, his body tugging on the blade of the sword as he fell.

Father Sorren, who had just made his way into the room, joined Morgan.

"Save the children!" Morgan shouted as he grabbed up two babies from adjoining cribs and made his way back to the door. A Shadow Guard met him there and took the children Morgan pushed into his arms.

Morgan ran to another set of cribs. As he lifted one of the babies, he saw Father Sorren kneeling beside Chairman Lehmann. "Leave him!" shouted Morgan over the roar of the fire. "Save the children!" Morgan grabbed the next child. The thickening smoke and the heat of the fire slowed his movement. When he reached the door, an empty-handed Father Sorren joined him. Morgan forced him to take the crying babies he was carrying and tried to reenter the room, but the heat was too great. He stepped back, almost tripping over a body. At his feet was the body of the woman he had discovered when he first entered. The debris that had blocked the door. Clutched in her lifeless arms was a child, eyes wide open, just staring back at Morgan. That is when he realized that the child the woman had carried was still alive. Morgan grabbed the baby and ordered everyone out of the building.

Morgan and the others joined a group of armed men gathered in a circle about thirty feet from the burning building.

On the ground, in the middle of the gathering, Morgan counted five babies.

"Duke Sumner, where is the Chairman?" Morgan turned to see the concerned face of Philip Armon, Captain of the Shadow Guards. Morgan looked toward the burning building, and Captain Armon understood his meaning.

"You are now the ranking member of this expedition, sir. What are your orders?" asked Captain Armon.

"Are there any rebels left alive in the camp?"

"We killed the ones that fought back, which was most of them. A few escaped," said Captain Armon.

"Finish searching the camp. Collect any supplies or information that may be useful and burn this cursed place to the ground."

Morgan turned before the Captain finished saluting and made his way through the group to Father Sorren, who was sitting on the ground studying a collection of documents.

"Explain yourself!" said Morgan.

Father Sorren looked up from his studies as if the Duke was an annoying child, ignorant of the way of things. "Chairman Lehmann was still alive," said Father Sorren. "It was my duty to give him his rites."

"Five children, five!" said Morgan. "We could have saved more!"

Father Sorren looked back down at the papers in his hands and said, in almost a whisper, "Godless Gift?"

"What?" said Morgan, glaring down at Father Sorren.

"Those were the Chairman's last words," said Father Sorren. "I have been looking through these papers he handed me before he ran upstairs."

"I do not care what that madman said," muttered Morgan as he watched Father Sorren move from one bundle of papers to another.

"Maybe you should," said Father Sorren. "If what is written here is true, these children may mean the end to the authority of the Council and my Order of Shadow Guards. It might also explain the action of Chairman Lehmann."

"More madness," said Morgan. "What would present such a threat?"

"The Godless Gift," said Father Sorren. "These papers say the rebels were exploring the possibility that the abilities that give authority to our Seers, and your Family Chairs are not a gift of God, but the result of parental lineage. If that is true, then it's not safe for the remaining children to live."

Morgan's hand grasped the hilt of his sword as he said, "The children live!"

Father Sorren looked from Morgan's hand, clutching the hilt of his swords and back to his eyes. After a few seconds of thought, he said, "You may be right. At least until we have put their theory to the test." Father Sorren watched as Morgan's grip on his sword loosened then said, "Have you thought about what to do with the children?"

Morgan looked back over to the group of men standing around the children and said, "I have not had time to brush the ash from my clothes.

That is a question that can wait until we have dealt with the immediate problem of this camp."

"I would like for my Order to care for them. The Church has experience in these matters." said Father Sorren. "However, I have some conditions."

Morgan gave Father Sorren a stern look. He was not sure he trusted the man and felt that somehow, he was being tricked into something. "What conditions?" he asked.

"First, I must swear everyone here to secrecy. Next, you convince the Council to give us an allowance to offset the expense. Also, you must allow my Order to be the custodians of these documents."

"Agreed," said Morgan. "Anything else?"

Father Sorren gathered the documents he had been studying, then brushed the dirt off his cassock as he stood. He looked over to the group gathered around his new wards and said, "You need to make me the Bishop of my Order."

Chapter 1 - Lost Things Found

ARBIN ADEAN STARED into the crate he just opened, unable to move because of a set of small, black eyes that looked back. They were the eyes of a mouse, a little green mouse. Ones he had not seen in over six years. They were from his favorite childhood story, lovingly reproduced by his mother in needlepoint. A treasure, like many others, that had somehow gone missing. It was one of the memories he wanted to take with him on the day his drunken father kicked him out, disowning him, claiming he was cursed and the reason for all their hardships.

Lifting the little needlepoint gingerly, Arbin stepped away from the crate and his assignment to inventory Mr. Hahn's newest additions to his growing collection. Finding a place to sit, Arbin studied every inch of the little treasure, looking for proof that it was his. A small patch to a tear he made as a child was all that was needed. His mind soon filled with memories of his mother and the time they spent together telling the story that went with the funny little mouse.

After carefully removing the little mouse from the frame it was in, Arbin used the cleanest piece of packing cloth he found to roll it up into a nice little package. He placed it in his pocket and walked toward the warehouse door.

Carl Rupert, the warehouse foreman, was a bulk of a man. He stepped into the doorway, placing that bulk into Arbin's path. Arbin stopped just short of him, giving Rupert time to place his large hand on Arbin's chest, and pushed hard. It took all Arbin's effort to keep from falling to the ground. Before Arbin could respond, Rupert held Arbin by the collar of his shirt with one hand while searching Arbin's coat pocket with the other. It took him only seconds to find the little mouse.

Still holding on to Arbin's shirt, Rupert tossed the little packet back into the open crate it came from. Rupert turned toward the open door and tossed Arbin towards it. Arbin tumbled to the ground and ended up on his side just outside. "You know the rules," growled Rupert. "Nothing leaves this place without my say so. You're done!"

Arbin got to his feet and shouted back at Rupert, "That's mine. My mother gave it to me. I was taking it to Mr. Hahn to tell him about it."

Rupert kept his back to Arbin and waved his hand in the air as if he were swatting insects.

Arbin looked around and saw a couple fists sized stones being used to keep the door open. He picked up one and as he headed inside; he threw it as hard as he could. The stone hit Rupert right between the shoulder blades, causing him to step forward and reach for the impact spot. The force of the strike also knocked the breath out of Rupert for a few seconds. Arbin used those seconds to run to the far side of the workbench in an attempt to grab his keepsake.

Rupert recovered first and with a single hand grabbed the small crate, pulled it away from the workbench, but lost his grip on it. Arbin watched as it crashed to the ground behind Rupert, who looked up from the mess and shouted, "You're going to pay for what you damaged." Arbin looked around for something to defend himself from the advancing Rupert. The only thing handy was a short length of rope which Arbin picked up and threw at Rupert who laughed, raised his hand to block it as he stepped backwards. Rupert's feet found the broken crate and the rest of him followed. Arbin could almost feel the sound of Rupert's head hitting the floor, followed by a lengthy silence. Arbin looked around the workbench at Rupert's motionless body. Nearby was his little mouse. Arbin looked around, not seeing anyone, grabbed his small package and ran.

MIA DIXON SAT ON THE edge of her bed; her hands folded in her lap. Her large brown eyes followed Arbin as he paced back and forth, going on about how his life was cursed. She listened, barely breathing, while the man she thought she would spend the rest of her life with explained why that dream was over.

Arbin was the only person she ever met with the same special abilities as her. When she discovered Arbin three years ago, she believed it destined them to be together.

She fought back the tears, and said several times she understood, but she didn't. She did not understand most of what he was saying after he said he was leaving. She tried to understand what he had done and why he had done it. But no matter how hard she tried, she could not understand why he would not take her away with him. There had been trouble in the past that forced them to move, but the three of them always stuck together. In the past, Jayden, her hot-headed twin brother, was the source of their problems. Arbin had always been the worrier, but once she calmed him down, he would take charge and get them through it. The one thing she did understand, this was not like the past, and she could not stay calm. As she listened to Arbin saying how sorry he was and that it was for the best, she could not take it anymore. She broke into deep sobbing tears. When Arbin tried to comfort her, she pushed him away. Between deep breaths, she yelled for him to go away and that she never wanted to see him again. As he left, she knew that was not true. She laid face down on her bed and cried as hard as she could.

ARBIN DID HIS BEST to relax, trying to clear his mind of Mia's crying that still echoed in his mind. Arbin cared about her and did not want anyone to know he had visited her for fear they might accuse her of aiding him. He needed to 'Fade' and leave before her crying got someone's attention.

The Fade was one of two Talents he was born with in a Fade, Arbin could confuse the mind of most people, forcing them to ignore him or at least not remember important details about him, like who he was or what he looked like.

He focused his mind on pulling that blanket of nothingness around him. Doing his best to block out all noise and smells around him. Soon he felt the calming and coldness that came with the Fade.

During the Great Civil War, over a hundred and fifty years ago, it was a Talent used by assassins. Killers so successful that people believed these Fade users lived in every shadow. A frightened public said these Fades were demons. The evil in every child's nightmare. The Church supported this belief, declaring users of this Talent possessed by evil spirits. To the relief of all, the Church presented a small group they identified as Blessed individuals. Heroes, who with the support of specially trained Shadow Guards, could hunt down and destroy these evil ones, and so started the Great Purge where the Fade Talent was viciously eradicated. Or so they thought.

The Fade was also a Talent he had in common with Jayden, who was the only other person he had ever met with this Talent. It formed a bond that had joined the two men like brothers, but like all brothers they often argued.

It looked like tonight would be no different. Arbin had planned on making his way to one of the nearby docks and, under cover of his Fade, steal a boat and escape. However, Jayden was waiting there, hiding under the cover of his own Fade.

Arbin was not sure why, but Jayden always had difficulty using his Fade on him. He suspected it might have something to do with his other Talent, which was the same as Mia's and those Blessed individuals of old which the Church called Seers. This Seer Talent allowed the user, with the proper amount of concentration, to sense when someone with a Talent was nearby. Both Mia and Arbin could sense Jayden when he was not using his Fade, but only Arbin could resist the effects of Jayden's Fade. Tonight, as soon as he sensed Jayden's presence, Arbin released his Fade, dropped the bag he was carrying, and said, "I messed up. Believe me, I did not mean to kill him."

"Well, maybe you will get it right the next time," said Jayden, releasing his Fade and stepping out from behind the crates where he was hiding. "I have wanted to clobber him a few times myself."

Arbin stared at Jayden, not sure what to say to the welcome news. He let out a deep sigh and said, "I was sure Rupert was dead. He hit the ground so hard and was not moving when I ran out."

Jayden smiled as he walked over to Arbin, gave him a playful shove and said, "You messed him up bad. He's still out. You can bet they will look for you once he wakes up and tells what happened."

Arbin nodded and said, "I understand." He picked up the bag of supplies he had dropped and tossed it into the small boat he had intended to take. He stood looking at the boat for a few seconds, not sure what to say next.

"I talked to Mia," said Jayden. Arbin stiffen at the mention of Mia's name. When Arbin did not turn around, Jayden continued. "I have her packing right now. She agreed it would be best if we left too. She wants to go back home. I told her I would never crawl back there. I said we would see her home, but it's back on the road for me after that. She said she was sorry for yelling at you. She wants you to stay with her but understands if you want to spend time on the road with me."

Arbin turned and looked at Jayden's cheerful face. Even though Mia and Jayden were twins, they looked different. They both had the same raven black hair color, dark brown eyes and the same big smile. Arbin learned that Jayden's smile could leave as fast as it came. His moods were unpredictable. Remembering that, Arbin stepped back and said, "I am not going with you and Mia."

"I think it would be better if we went by wagon," said Jayden, as if he had not heard Arbin. "You know I can't swim, and that boat looks a little too small for the three of us. I'll grab the wagon I drive, and no one will think anything about it. We will have to dump it once we are far enough away. I am sure the horses will find their way back."

Repositioning the small bag, he had hung around his neck and holding on to it like it was some kind of armor, Arbin said, "Jayden, I am not going with you." He paused, then said, "I think you should take Mia home."

Arbin could see the change come over Jayden as his words became clear. Jayden looked around, then stepped closer to Arbin. He leaned forward, pressed his finger against Arbin's chest and said, "I just left my sister crying her eyes out because of you. She begged me..." Jayden paused. Arbin could see he was getting emotional. Jayden continued, "She begged me to bring you back. She said she was sorry for sending you away. I have never seen her like that. Her crying and begging hurt me! Now you and I both know she had nothing to be sorry about. I promised I would bring you back. Get your stuff and let's go!" Jayden stepped back and stood with his arms crossed, glaring at Arbin.

"I care about your sister, that is why I have to leave her," said Arbin.

"What!" shouted Jayden, "That makes no sense at all!" Arbin signaled with his hand for Jayden to quiet down. That only made Jayden angrier. "Three years ago, when we met up with you, I would have been fine with you going your own way. I was against joining up with you, but Mia changed my mind. She said you were one of us. That we could become like a family. I was also against her wanting to marry you. I worried you would hurt her. Silly me, right? Thinking you would do something to hurt her."

Arbin sighed, looked around, then sat on a crate nearby. "When my father kicked me out, he said I was cursed! That my evil Talent caused my mother's death and his poor fortune. At first, I refused to believe him, but in the two years I wandered around before meeting you, I had lots of awful things happen. I hoped, when I met you and Mia, he was wrong. Now, once again, my past returns and with it my curse. I need to go before more bad things happen."

"We don't have time for this! Your father is a drunk, and life is hard. It has nothing to do with our Talent. What happened was an accident. You're running away is what will hurt people. I will not let you do that to my sister!"

Arbin sighed again, stood and positioned the bag around his neck. *He will never understand*, he thought. *Best thing to do is just leave now.* As he took a few steps toward the small boat, Arbin felt a tug on the strap of the bag around his neck. He turned to see that Jayden had hold of it. Arbin let the bag slide off his shoulder and when the strap was near his elbow, he pulled hard on it, yanking it from Jayden's hand. Arbin repositioned the bag while watching Jayden. He could see the anger in his eyes. Arbin and Jayden often roughhoused. Practice, Jayden had called it. There were a few times, because of Jayden's temper and pride, their practice had bordered on being serious. Arbin was not a talented fighter, but he had learned how to dodge.

He had also learned a few of Jayden's tells that signaled he would attack. He saw this one too late.

Jayden stepped forward and drove his fist into Arbin's stomach. Arbin crumbled to the ground, gasping for breath. As Arbin got back to his feet, Jayden grabbed him by the shirt and dragged him saying, "You're going with us!"

Arbin fought back as best he could. Jayden's body was out of his reach, so Arbin pounded on his arm until Jayden lost hold. Before Arbin could react to his freedom, Jayden hit him hard in the face, knocking him down and onto a crate which shattered under his weight.

The punch and the fall hurt. Arbin did not want to get back up, but he knew that once Jayden started something, he did not quit. As he stood, he was surprised that Jayden had not continued the attack. His hand hurt and when he looked at it, he saw some blood from a cut on his arm. He also saw that he was holding a piece of jagged wood. It looked like it was a part of the crate he had landed on. He looked up at Jayden and saw him staring at his hand.

"Maybe Rupert wasn't an accident. Just a clumsy attack," said Jayden, as he pulled out the knife that he always had on him. Jayden stepped forward with his knife in front of him and growled, "You coward!"

Arbin knew he was in trouble. He dropped the piece of wood, grabbed tight to the bag, and ran away from Jayden toward the end of the dock and the waiting river. When Arbin surfaced, he swam toward the center of the river to make sure he was out of range of any thrown objects. When he looked back, he saw Jayden staring at him. Jayden looked at the small boat. The worry on his face made Arbin sure he would not follow by boat. As Arbin swam for the far side of the river, he could hear Jayden cursing at him and threatening to hunt him down and make him pay for what he had done to his sister.

As Arbin climbed onto the shore, he looked back for Jayden but could not see him. *He is coming for me,* he thought. Arbin let himself go into a Fade, then headed south along the river.

Chapter 2 - So It Begins

THE PAIN TODAY WAS getting worse. Just standing still did not help. Chairman Morgan Sumner knew the problem was more than the aches of old age, as his doctor insisted. No matter how much he tried, the thought of his death haunted him. He feared that all his hard work as Council Chairman these last twenty-seven years would be lost if the wrong person replaced him. His plan needed to succeed. It was that need that gave him the strength to face the pain.

Chairman Sumner stared out the window of his office, thinking back over the events of his life as Chairman. The drizzle of an early April morning rain depressed him, and the Nursery fire came back into his thoughts.

"Do you believe in fate, Mr. Bergman?" Chairman Sumner asked as he used his finger to follow rain drops as they slid down the outside of the windowpane.

"Yes," replied Curt Bergman. "If it is managed properly."

"I am sure I can guess your answer, Bishop Sorren," said Chairman Sumner as he continued to look out the window.

"Fate, Faith, the two are often confused," said Bishop Sorren.

The answer brought a slight smile to the Chairman's face despite his mood. He turned slowly to consider his guests; despite the pain he knew would follow. He did his best to mask the pain.

"I am surprised how often actions taken long ago are playing a critical role in our current endeavors," said Chairman Sumner.

"A man that understands his past will understand his future and can plan accordingly," replied Bergman.

"I like that," said Chairman Summer. "I think I will use that in one of my speeches. With your permission."

Curt Bergman, a thin, neatly dressed man of around thirty, smiled and bowed his head slightly. It was enough to allow the Chairman to see the silver sleeve, in the shape of a dragon, that held his long dirty blond hair in a ponytail. Bergman sat comfortably on a small brightly colored sofa which the Chairman's late wife insisted be placed in his office.

The sofa and the family painting over the fireplace were her way of adding some cheerfulness and personality to the otherwise boring office.

Bergman did not visit often, but when he did, he always sat on the sofa. Chairman Sumner noticed how much it suited him, and Bergman said it gave him a comfortable view of the room.

Bishop Sorren sat with his long legs comfortably stretched out in front of him in one of the two expensive leather chairs that had been one of the Chairman's contributions to the office. Just like Bergman and the couch, the black leather chair suited Bishop Sorren, who had found the chair so comfortable he ordered two for his office.

Chairman Sumner's other addition to the room was the oversized dark wooden desk and high-back chair, which he now stood behind. He had kept the rest of the office much the way he found it when he took the position twenty-seven years ago. That was soon after his return from the attack on a rebel camp, and the incident at the Nursery that resulted in the death of then Chairman, Jonathan Lehmann.

Visitors to his office often described it as uninviting because of the limited amount of furniture, which besides the Chairman's personal additions, included an enormous cabinet, a bookcase, two candle stands, a coat rack and a few small tables. They also described it as green, which was only natural, since green was the national color, and the background for the country's flag. The plain white walls only highlighted the dark green curtains on each of the three large floor to ceiling windows. Even the rug under the leather chairs was a plain dark green. Chairman Sumner had taken a lesson from his predecessor and found that the current decor helped to keep meetings short.

"If you are having second thoughts, I just want to remind you, I have confirmed that your son has been meeting with Councilman Darr," said

Bishop Sorren. "There are reports that your son has returned to his old behaviors."

Chairman Sumner placed his hands on the back of his desk chair and said, "I know. I only wish there were some other way."

"We talked about this for a long time, and we both agree that Henry is not the right person to hold your Family Chair on the Council. His death will clear the way for your grandson to be the Heir to your position," said Bishop Sorren. "I can think of no other action we could take."

"We could eliminate Councilman Darr," said Chairman Sumner. "His influence on the Council is growing. I am worried that we waited too long to act. His idea of the country joining the Alliance would be the end of our limited independence. I will resist him no matter the cost, for the good of the country."

"Councilman Darr is just a symptom of the problem," said Bishop Sorren. "There is an appetite for joining the Alliance. These are troubling times with the increasing conflict between many of our neighbors. There is talk of another great war and it scares the people. I fear they no longer honestly believe we can defend them in a crisis without the help of the Alliance. That is why I suggested we use the fear caused by our greatest national crisis and bring back the threat of a Fade. If we show people that together, the Council and the Church can once again defeat a Fade, they will trust us in any crisis."

Bergman cleared his throat. When he had the other's attention, he said, "I think I should remind you, parts of your plan are already in place. It is not too late to stop, but there would be complications. Expensive ones at that."

The Chairman let out a small sigh, looked at Bergman and said, "You are sure our man has received his instructions and will act on it?"

"We have been watching his sister ever since we learned she moved back home, I had someone make friends with their family," said Bergman. "I can confirm that our man got the message and our incentive for him to act."

Morgan paused a few seconds to let that last bit of information sink in and then said, "Incentive?"

"Along with his instructions, we left him one of his sister's fingers, just to prove we were serious," said Bergman.

"Was that necessary? Is she still alive?" the Chairman asked.

Bergman paused, then said, "Yes."

"Where are you keeping her and the children?" asked Bishop Sorren.

"They are in a very safe place," said Bergman. "No one will find them, and it's better if you did not know."

Chairman Sumner looked concerned for a few seconds and Bergman said, "Chairman, you rely on me to handle these things because it's what I do well. I never let you down in the past. Trust me." Bergman paused and then said, "You said nothing about the sister and the children being kept alive after the mission is over. Is that something you want to add now?"

"I think we should reconsider killing the children," said Bishop Sorren.

"If you remember, you are the one that wanted me to kill all the children we found in the Nursery," said Chairman Sumner. "Heresy, you called them. Now you are asking me to spare the children of one of those children of heresy. What happened to your fears of the so-called Godless Gift? You swore that their very existence would destroy the Family Chairs and your Order of Shadow Guards?"

"The risk is real, but time and old age have limited the knowledge of their existence to a much smaller and more controllable group," said Bishop Sorren, glancing at Bergman, who pretended as if he was not part of the conversation. "We now benefit from keeping them alive. I believe we can learn a lot through repeating the experiment with these new children."

Chairman Sumner looked around the office, almost like he was looking at it for the last time. With a sadness in his voice he said, "They are one of those things from my past that has been unresolved too long." He looked at Bergman and said in a more formal tone, "I will leave managing things to you. Use them as you see fit to get the job done. I hope you understand just how critical this assignment is for the future of the country."

"You made that point very clear," replied Bergman as he fiddled with the cuff of his shirt.

Chairman Sumner leaned forward on the back of his chair, focused his attention on Bergman, and waited until Bergman noticed. In a slow and forceful manner, the Chairman said, "Curt, I want you to make sure this part of the plan succeeds, even if you need to do it yourself."

Bergman was a little surprised. In all their dealings, the Chairman had never called him by his first name. Bergman returned the Chairman's gaze, nodded, and in a matching tone said, "It will happen. You have my personal promise."

Chairman Sumner relaxed and there was a quiet, uncomfortable moment that suggested the Chairman considered their meeting finished, but Bergman was still sitting patiently on the couch. Chairman Sumner asked, "Is there anything else?"

Bergman looked over at a package on the corner of the Chairman's desk and said, "With your permission, sir."

Chairman Sumner looked at the package and nodded.

Bergman picked up the package and before he could look inside Chairman Sumner said, "It's all there, plus a small bonus to ensure the job gets done."

Bergman put the package inside the courier pouch he was carrying. He then removed a folded piece of paper from the pouch and held it up between his two fingers. "Here is the name we spoke about. If the plan is to succeed, I need this man to be present when the attack takes place."

Chairman Sumner smiled politely at Bergman and said, "Bishop Sorren will handle that for you. Now if you will excuse us, The Bishop and I have more items to discuss so I am afraid it's time for you to go."

Bergman smiled back, bowed his head to both men in a show of respect, turned and quickly headed for the door, stopping for a few seconds as he handed Bishop Sorren the folded paper.

Chairman Sumner took a deep breath to help with the pain and sat in the large high-back desk chair. He looked over at Bishop Sorren, who was still sitting in his comfortable leather chair.

Despite his first mistrust of the Bishop following the Nursery incident, The Chairman now trusted him and considered him a valued advisor, if not a friend. He enjoyed the Bishops visits and was thankful that he never shied from hearing his worries. This time it was the Bishop that looked worried. "Speak up, what's on your mind?"

"Well, to start with, what do I do with this?" said Bishop Sorren, holding up the folded paper Bergman had given him.

"I talked with the other Family Chairs and they have agreed to fund an increase in staffing for the Shadow Guard," said Chairman Sumner. "Mr. Bergman has done a good job of creating the impression of the existence of a new and troubling rebel group. They have approved adding twelve additional people. That means nine new Shadow Guards and three new Seers. Make sure Bergman's man is among the new people."

"Captain Eustace will want a say in who gets selected," said Bishop Sorren.

"Mix the name in with some political appointments you have been holding on to," said Chairman Sumner. "I am sure the Captain will not complain if you leave him several openings to fill."

"And how do you suggest I get Bergman's man close to Henry?" asked Bishop Sorren.

"I have ordered the Shadow Guard to escort Henry and his family here for the celebration," said Chairman Summer. "I could not convince the Captain not to lead the escort. He and Henry have been friends since childhood. I suggest you tell the Captain we received reports that there will be trouble here in the days leading up to the celebration. Remind him that Henry's own men will escort him, many of which Captain Eustace trained. I am sure you can convince the Captain to leave his more experienced people here to protect the Council. Also, think about which Seers you will send. We do not want our Fade killed before he can do his job."

"You make it sound so simple." said Bishop Sorren. "There is one other thing that has me worried, and that is your health. I can see that the pain is getting worse. How are you feeling?"

Chairman Sumner's shoulders drooped, and he sighed as he leaned back in the chair and said, "Tired. Nothing I do helps with the pain. This weather just makes me cold all the time. I am looking forward to warmer and dryer weather."

"When this thing is over, make a trip to the Springs," said Bishop Sorren. "It worked for me."

Chairman Sumner took a deep breath, straightened back up and said, "If things go as planned, there will be no time for that. Henry's death and Dylan's age will create a power struggle. Everyone will try to get their person appointed as Dylan's Guardian. I will need to work on holding the Family Chairs together so we can get our man assigned as Dylan's Guardian. I hope you are right about our choice."

The Bishop stood and said, "Don't worry. We both know I can keep our choice for Guardian in line. I am sure I will also be able to handle your grandson. Now, I better go see to that request for our additional staff."

Chairman Sumner slowly stood. Bishop Sorren walked over and put his hand on Chairman Sumner's shoulder, closed his eyes and said a quiet prayer for him. Chairman Sumner acknowledged the gesture with a smile, thanked him for his concern, and walked him to the door.

Now that he was alone, Chairman Sumner walked back to the center of the room and stood in front of the family painting. After a few minutes of solemn study, he returned to the window behind his desk. He watched the raindrops splashing on the windowpane, took a deep breath and said, "Heavenly Father, I ask for your blessing and your forgiveness for what I have set in motion."

Chapter 3 - Hiding in Plain Sight

NOOR POINT WAS A TINY village of around seventy families. Located on a low ridge that overlooked the Lorain river and the road that ran alongside it, the village was too small to be recorded on most maps. It was known to the river road travelers since it was positioned near the last bridge across the river before the Grand Divide, a wide lake formed when the two branches of the river met. The right branch brought water that flowed past the Capital city of Leaboro, and the left branch brought things from the mountainous areas near the border. Eight years ago, Arbin Adean was one of those items. Running from his past, he followed the river until it met the catchall of the Grand Divide, and there he rested. Arbin was sure that people were looking for him, so he decided the wilderness of the Grand Divide was as good as any place to camp out while he planned what to do next.

Arbin's travels with his father taught him how to live in the woods for brief periods of time. The first two weeks of his new life were manageable thanks to the few essential items, like a knife and flint, from the bag slung over his shoulder when he jumped into the river. He soon missed the supplies safely stored in the boat he had planned on stealing. Arbin made it a month before hunger, and the weather forced him out of the woods and into the village of Noor Point.

That was eight years ago. Somehow, he found his place in the village and still kept his past a secret. The village was too small for a proper mayor, but Boris Kroner was the closest thing to it. He was a wheelwright and did a business in repairing wagons and housing travelers using the river road. Most of the villagers made a living farming and hunting, but everyone benefited from Kroner's business, Arbin more than others.

Kroner had taken a chance on young Arbin and put him to work. He received room and board for cleaning Kroner's stable, his home, his guest house, the streets and pretty much anything else Kroner needed done. The room being an old shed attached to the back of Kroner's barn. It was small but manageable once Kroner fixed it up enough for Arbin to survive the icy winters.

Arbin found work doing odd jobs for the villagers with a promise of payment when crops came in or they butchered animals. They soon discovered he could read and write. That allowed him to receive extra income from reading and composing letters for those who otherwise could not. He helped where he could, and the townsfolk respected his privacy.

When the day started, he was excited. It was the first market day of the year. A chance for him to collect on a few outstanding promises, like spring vegetables, sheep's wool and sometimes dried meats.

By mid-afternoon, that excitement turned into frustration as he watched the villagers coming and going from a campsite set up on the edge of town. It belonged to a caravan that was forced to stop for repairs to a damaged wheel.

Arbin had been rudely waken late last night as the damaged wagon was moved into the barn. It now sat just a wall away from his little hiding spot and came with its own guards. Two men dressed in the black trousers and dark green jackets of Duke Henry Sumner. The village of Noor Point was in the province under the supervision of Duke Henry. The collection of taxes brought this uniform to the village a couple times a year. Arbin stayed clear of them during these visits because he was not sure if he was still on anyone's most wanted list. Arbin had even seen Duke Henry once when he stopped over after returning home from a visit to the Capital.

The rest of the caravan set up camp in a small clearing just to the south of the village. The path to the clearing led through a small cluster of trees between the village and the campsite. Arbin found a nice perch on the lower branch of one of these trees. Through the sparse early spring foliage, he could see most of the camp.

It soon became obvious that the market day had moved to the campsite where he imagined the villagers selling their goods at crazy prices. As Arbin watched, his stomach grumbled. *Well, there goes any chance for a free lunch,* he thought.

"This is stupid," Arbin muttered. "I need stuff. How do I collect what's owed now?" Arbin noticed Joseph Mercier heading down the path that led to the campsite. Joseph raised rabbits, chickens, a few sheep and was someone that owed Arbin for past favors. Smiling, Arbin thought, *Well, now looks like a good time to collect on those past deeds.* When Joseph was close enough, he called out to him.

Joseph paused for a second, looking around for who called him.

"Up here," said Arbin.

Joseph looked up and recognized Arbin and said, "Can it wait, I was told that one of our guests wants to buy some of my wool."

"I just wanted to know when you could give me the items you promised me," said Arbin.

"I haven't forgotten," said Joseph, "I will get you what I owe you. I will even add some meat if you can wait a little longer. I need this sale."

Arbin knew that Joseph had a large family. He had been true to his word in the past, plus there was the temptation of meat being added to the deal. "Okay," said Arbin. He saw an expression of relief grow on Joseph's face. Arbin looked towards the camp and said, "What do they need with wool when the city is full of it? Are they a merchant?"

"Saddle blankets," said Joseph. "I don't mind selling to Shadow Guards. It's the Seers that worry me."

That last bit startled Arbin so much he almost fell out of the tree. He strained his eyes to study the camp and said, "Seers! How many? Where are they?"

"I heard five or six," said Joseph. "I have seen none in town yet. Good thing. My Mother used to tell me stories about them. She said they could see into your soul and if you were evil, they would haul you away."

Arbin did not respond to Joseph's comment. He continued to study the campsite. Joseph saw his chance to slip away. He waved and headed off down the path.

Arbin knew about the Shadow Guards and their Seers. Everyone knew about them. Stories like the one from Joseph's mother came from a retelling of the days of the great Purge. Arbin knew that most of the stories about the abilities of Seers were not true, but the one authentic thing was, Seers hunted Fades. That is why the Shadow Guard existed, and if the stories of the Purge were true, they were incredibly good at it. Arbin knew he could find Fades, which meant he was sure they could too.

It was getting later, and the light was not as strong, but Arbin made out a few uniformed people moving around the camp. Most of them were the Duke's men. He saw two men on horseback riding toward the camp from the river road. They had light colored or gray pants and sections of light green armor with splashes of gold caused by the reflecting sun. *Those must be Shadow Guards,* he thought. He did not see any other uniforms. He heard that the Seers wore a white tunic with a red crest of a torch on it. That should be easy to spot, but he could not see any.

Arbin climbed out of his tree and headed back towards his little shed. Once inside, he sat on his bed and thought about what he had learned. He laid back and put his hands over his eye. "Seer!" He took a deep breath and then let it out, slowly shaking his head back and forth. *What am I going to do now?* he thought.

Arbin wondered if it would be safe to hide in his room like he had done in the past when Henry's men came to town. He remembered the wagon in the barn just on the other side of the wall. *Do these Seers have the same abilities as Mia and me?* he wondered. *How far away can they sense me?*

It was during his time with Mia and Jayden that he really started to understand his Talents. Just thinking about Mia brought back a flood of emotions, mostly anger. Anger at himself for what happened between them. He had not seen Mia for eight years now. She was part of the reason he went into hiding so long ago. "I wonder if she ever thinks about me. Of course, she thinks about me." He muttered, squeezing the hands on his face tighter. "She hates me."

Arbin continued going down that old road of hating himself, and after delivering himself a few more choice insults, he realized there were bigger issues that needed his attention. *Okay, so what do I do now? Come on, think!*

Seers sense people with Talents. That was how he met Mia. One day, she just found him. He never knew she was there. His time with Mia taught him to always be checking. A safeguard he had let slip without the constant reminder of being near both a Fade and a Seer.

"Well, time to dust off the old Talents and see if anyone is near," Arbin realized he just said that out loud and shook his head. A dangerous habit brought on by his time alone. Arbin took a deep breath and did his best to relax. He tried to remember the sensation he felt when he searched for Mia. Since Arbin had never met a Seer from the Shadow Guard, he was not sure if they gave off the same feeling as Mia. After a few minutes of searching, he relaxed, convinced there were no Seers within his detection range. *Wait,* he thought. *At what range can they detect me? I wonder if they are better or worse than Mia. Maybe the best thing to do is play it safe and leave town for a few days until our visitors leave.*

Arbin looked around at his sparse belongings. He needed to travel light. Arbin collected what he felt he needed for a few days. His most valuable items he kept in a small box wrapped up in an oiled cloth and tucked away in a hole he had dug in the floor at the back of the small room. He made sure it was concealed, took one last look around and headed out. "I'll be back in a few days. A brief stay in the woods might be fun," he whispered to himself.

ON THE WESTERN EDGE of town, there was a small stream and forest that extended for a few miles until it met the foothills. Beyond that were some high plains where sheep grazed.

Arbin had spent a lot of time hunting for small game and fishing in this area in the past. When he first got to town, it was the only way for him to survive. Now he might only go hunting a few times a year, more for enjoyment rather than for survival. He knew of a few places where he could camp out for a few days. The stream and the small wildlife should be able to meet his needs for a while.

Arbin worried about the caravan because these same woods ran along one side of the clearing where it was camped. He would have to make sure he found a place where he could see if someone from the camp was heading his way. *Who knows?* he thought. *The visitors might want to do a little hunting or fishing. I will need to set up a camp where I can cook, and*

*another where I can keep a watch on the Seers. I need to be sure I see them
before they can detect me.*

About a forty-five-minute walk from the edge of the forest was a
cooking camp Arbin had used in the past. The campsite was near a
collection of rocks in a small ravine. It was difficult to reach and hidden
from sight. The site was also far enough from the village that no one should
be able to detect a small fire there.

Arbin headed out for the campsite, hoping he remembered his way
there. The weak light of evening and the fact that it had been a few years
since his last visit made the going slow. He finally saw a familiar landmark
and knew the site was just up ahead. "At last," Arbin said, and he quickly
headed for a small ridgeline and a cluster of trees.

Approaching the camp, Arbin heard voices. He was not expecting
anyone to be there. *It is getting late. Too late to go searching around the forest
for another place to rest,* he thought. Arbin decided the best thing to do was
to see if he could join them for the night.

As Arbin cleared the bushes near the edge of the camp, he found
three strangers gathered around a small fire. Two dressed in what he now
guessed were Shadow Guard uniforms. Their swords leaning against a small
boulder, easily within arm's reach. The other was a thin man with a long
blond ponytail, wearing traveling clothes.

The men spotted Arbin a few seconds after he saw them. Both Arbin
and the men froze in place as they decided what to do. It was clear the men
were not expecting anyone to visit them. The smaller of the uniformed men
said, "I told you we shouldn't have lit a fire." The ponytail man said, "Kill
him!" The two uniformed men paused to grab their swords, giving Arbin a
small head start as he made his way back the way he had come.

Arbin ran through the woods, using what little moonlight there was to
help him make his way through the brush that grabbed at his clothes and
feet. He kept his hands in front of him to help defend his face from the
random low-hanging branch. Arbin was not sure of his location anymore,
but the downward slope of the ground told him he was moving away from
the camp where he had found them.

The sound of yelling and swords crashing through bushes kept him
moving forward. Arbin looked back, expecting to see his pursuers crashing

through the bushes at any moment when he stumbled over a few roots and slid chest first down a small ravine. Arbin paused before getting up, hoping the noise of the fall had not attracted anyone. He glanced around and spotted a cluster of bushes to his left. He scrambled on all fours toward them and curled up in the darkness behind them.

Arbin heard the men searching for him. With each whack of their swords on a bush, his panic grew. Arbin knew that he had to force himself to ignore them if he wanted the Fade to work. It was always harder to get someone to ignore you if they had seen you first or were searching for you. Arbin knew he would need a deep, strong Fade. He took a deep breath and forced himself to imagine he was someplace else, some place peaceful. He concentrated on slowing his breathing. Arbin thought about a time when he was young, about being covered in a safe, warm blanket in the arms of his mother. Soon the surrounding sound faded, and he felt the cool comforting nothingness of the Fade engulf him, calming his panic and blocking out the sounds of the men moving through the brush and the sounds of their swords crashing and slicing through the bushes.

After what seemed like forever, Arbin opened his eyes and looked around. His time with Jayden had taught him that the longer anyone stayed in a Fade, the weaker you got. He felt that strain starting now but did not want to release it until he was sure it was safe. After a few minutes of listening and peering through the darkness, he decided that now was the best time to move. He moved quietly, stopping every few minutes to listen for his pursuers.

After a few moments, he realized he was not carrying his bag. *It must be back where I fell,* Arbin thought. *I cannot take a chance of looking for it now.* Arbin tried to think if there was anything in it that could point back to him but could not think of anything. *I will look for it tomorrow.*

As Arbin continued to move through the forest, he replayed the encounter he had with the three men. *What was that all about?* he wondered. *Why would they be after me? I left long before any of the Seers could have discovered me.* Arbin was sure the men he met were not Seers, but just to be safe he paused and let his senses reach out to search for any Seers nearby. Once he was sure none were near, he continued to move through the darkened forest.

The glow above the tree line and the smell of campfires warned Arbin he was moving towards the town and the visitor encampment. He squatted down behind a cluster of bushes and thought about what to do next. *I do not want to go back to town but staying out here will be hard without my supplies. I need to find some place to spend the night. I will decide what to do in the morning.*

After a few minutes, Arbin remembered a hunting blind he had used before. It was in a small cluster of trees and should be nearby. It should be empty this time of year. With luck, he could spend the night there and head out at first light. As if trying to convince himself that it was a good idea, he thought, *I don't know how comfortable it will be, but without a fire I would rather sleep in a tree than on the ground.*

It took some time for Arbin to find the hunting blind. He was thankful he had the moon to give him some light. The blind was about twelve feet up, had a sturdy perch for resting, and to Arbin's surprise, was just a little closer to the caravan's camp than he had hoped for.

Between the light of the moon and the fires of the camp, he could make out the figures of guards standing post. Most of them wore the dark uniforms of Duke Henry's men. There were a few Shadow Guards, and for the first time he saw individuals in the mostly white uniforms of Seers. That many uniforms made him nervous. Getting out of town was the right choice. He looked around just to make sure the two that had chased him were not nearby. If everyone stayed where they were, he could make it through the night.

After several hours of watching, Arbin found it almost impossible to stay awake. He checked his little nest to make sure he would not fall out during the night and closed his eyes to sleep.

ARBIN WOKE A FEW TIMES because of a nightmare. He dreamed he was in a burning building and unable to move. It was a dream he had several times when he was younger. His mother had always been there to comfort him. He had not had that dream for a while. Waking here, in the tree alone, made him think about his mother. Arbin did his best to fight back the tears.

He took one quick look around to make sure his hiding spot was still safe and did his best to get comfortable again. He was just drifting back off to sleep when he heard yelling from the direction of the camp.

Clouds had reduced the moonlight, and the night was much darker now. Through the darkness and the lights of a few campfires, Arbin saw the campsite had become a hive of activity. People running in several directions, others standing around yelling and pointing. Among them, he spotted the white uniform of Seers. Four of them, with torches, were searching for something when one of them pointed toward the woods and headed that way. Others followed. He was not sure, but they appeared to be chasing someone.

Arbin sat watching the drama. He became concerned when the direction of the chase changed toward the section of woods where he was hiding. Arbin knew he should abandon his hiding space, but he could not take his eyes off the person being chased. He squinted, trying to make out more of the fleeing person. Despite the darkness, something about the person the guards were chasing was familiar.

A quick stab of panic caused his heart to race, and he felt himself slipping into a Fade. "Jayden!" Arbin whispered to himself. It had been eight years since he last saw Jayden. "How did you find me, and why are they chasing you?" he asked himself. "I bet that stupid idiot was using his Fade and got too close to the Seers while looking for me," he grumbled as he watched the chase.

The men chasing Jayden lost track of him at the same time Arbin did. They pushed deeper into the woods, apparently following the trail of broken branches. *I need to get down now,* Arbin thought. Getting caught in a tree was the last thing he wanted, and he worried that Jayden or those Seers might stumble upon his hiding spot at any minute. Remembering the greeting he got from the guards at campsite Arbin thought, *I do not know how these Seers would treat me, but I am sure how Jayden would.*

Once on the ground, Arbin knew he needed to hide. *If I Fade, Jayden will not sense me, but the Seers will.* Arbin heard people crashing through the woods in the distance. *If I run, the guards could mistake me for Jayden and chase me. I think the best thing to do is hide the old fashion way.*

Arbin spotted a thick group of bushes that might give him enough protection. He had just squatted down in them when Jayden ran through them, tripping over Arbin and landing face first. Arbin should have just let Jayden get up and keep running, but he could not stop himself. He jumped on Jayden's back and said, "I do not know how you found me, but this ends now."

The attack took Jayden by surprise, and he was slow to defend against Arbin's punches. Arbin noticed that Jayden was holding a bloodied knife in one hand. Arbin put all his attention into trying to force Jayden to drop the knife. Jayden flung the knife he was holding out of reach into some nearby bushes. The two struggled as Jayden attempted to get his attacker off him. Jayden grabbed onto Arbin and rolled with him away from the knife.

Jayden, who was taller and stronger, got the better of Arbin and ended up on top. Arbin did his best to hold on to Jayden while defending against his punches. It was while Jayden was struggling to break away from Arbin's grasp that he recognized who he was fighting and said, "You! What the hell are you doing here?" Both men stopped fighting and stared at each other for a second.

"Over here" and "Stay where you are!" cried the approaching guards as they smashed their way through the brush.

Jayden looked back at Arbin, spat in his face, allowing him to break free from the surprised Arbin and run off.

Arbin stood up just as the guards arrived. He felt Jayden going back into a Fade and knew it was too late to follow him. Just as Arbin turned to speak to the guards, one of them punched him in the face.

Arbin fell to the ground unconscious.

WHEN ARBIN WOKE UP, his face hurt. He reached up to touch it and discovered his hands and feet were tied.

Arbin struggled to free himself and heard someone shout, "Knock that off or I'll come over and bash you!"

Looking around, Arbin discovered he was inside a tent, just large enough for two cots and a table. Seated at the table were the only other persons in the tent. Two men in Shadow Guard uniforms who appeared irritated at his interruption of the game of cards they were playing. He thought he recognized one of them as the one that hit him. At least his big fists look familiar.

Arbin stopped his struggling and said, "What's going on? Why am I tied up?"

The men glance at him and then return to their card game. Arbin said again, but a little louder, "Why am I tied up? I demand that you let me go."

The bigger of the two guards, the one with the fists, said, "Shut it! You are staying here until someone comes to question you."

"Question me, for what? I have done nothing wrong. You got the wrong guy. You should have gotten the guy I was fighting. He was trying to kill me."

"I said shut it!" said the large guard as he showed Arbin his fist. The threat was simple but effective.

Arbin realized that talking to them was getting him nowhere. He needed to put his efforts into figuring out how to get away. He saw that outside it was still dark. *If I can get away, I am sure I can find a place to hide,* he thought. Arbin knew he could not Fade if he was tied up. He was also tired. Very tired. The effort of using his Fade talent as much as he did and the struggle with Jayden had put more of a drain on his energy than he was accustomed to since he had gone into hiding.

"How long until I can speak to someone?" asked Arbin. The large guard looked up from his game and Arbin added, "I mean someone else."

The big guard gave him a stern look and then returned to his game.

He would learn nothing from these guards, and his head and jaw were hurting. He decided the best thing to do was to relax and wait until someone who could answer his questions arrived.

"I need to get my strength back and be ready," he said to himself.

The big guard shouted, "Quiet you!"

Arbin looked up and realized that he must have said that out loud. He tested the ropes around his hands and feet again and found them securely tied. Arbin took a deep breath, let it out, and did his best to get comfortable. He soon felt the weight of fatigue on his eyelid. Before he knew it, his eyes closed, and he drifted off to sleep.

Chapter 4 - Simple Misunderstanding

ARBIN OPENED HIS EYES. His head was still pounding, and his stomach grumbled. He let out a sigh and moved to get up. The ropes binding his hands and legs were a quick reminder that he was still being held prisoner. The light from the outside said early morning. *I have been here all night? This is crazy!* he thought. *I must get out of here.*

Through the pounding in his head came a strange little tingle at the back of his throat, followed by a shiver. Something like the cross between tasting and smelling when you take a deep sniff of a freshly cut lemon. It was a feeling that reminded him of something from his past. It was a feeling that could only mean one thing. There was a Seer nearby. If he could detect them, he was sure they could detect him.

Arbin looked around the room in a panic and quickly spotted a man, maybe the same age as him, sitting at the table where the guards had been. He had short curly red hair, what looked like the beginnings of a beard, and a broad squarish face. He was wearing a uniform of light green pants, gray padded jacket with a white tunic embroidered with a green and red border. It had a red crest on it that resembled a torch. Arbin knew he was looking at the uniform of a Seer.

The young man, who was drinking from a cup and reading something from a piece of paper, stopped at the sounds of Arbin stirring. He smiled and said, "You are awake. Good. My name is Alexander Keller. You can call me Alex." He paused, then asked, "And your name is?"

Arbin cleared his mind and focused on controlling the defensive urge to Fade that was building.

"How is your head Arbin?" said Alex in a pleasant voice after studying the paper in front of him.

"How do you know my name?" asked Arbin, as he continued to study Alex.

"You are a popular person in town. Lots of people were eager to talk about you," replied Alex. "People are always eager to talk about other people to Seers, but I am sure you know that."

The last comment confused Arbin. "If you know about me, then you know there is no reason to hold me. Untie me and I will be glad to talk about anyone you want."

Alex stared at Arbin for several seconds. He took another drink from his cup, then looked at the papers in front of him. The longer the silence lasted, the more nervous Arbin got.

He knows, thought Arbin. He looked at the ground, expecting Alex to declare him a Fade at any moment. After a few seconds of quiet, Arbin looked up. It surprised him to see a slight smile on Alex's face.

"Tell me about your friend," said Alex. "The one they saw you with in the woods last night."

"Friend, ha!" said Arbin and spat on the ground next to him. "He is no friend. In fact, he is the one you should have tied up in here, not me."

Alex was a little surprised at the anger in Arbin's voice. "Why is that?" he asked.

"Because he tried to kill me! I tried to tell your guards last night, but they would not listen to me," Arbin said loudly.

"They are not my guards!" said Alex with a bit of disgust. "We are part of the same..." Alex stopped himself, paused for a few seconds, then asked, "And why would he want to kill you?"

"He is someone from my past," said Arbin. "Someone I was hoping I would never see again."

"Go on," said Alex.

"His sister was in love with me," said Arbin. "It was about eight years ago. Jayden, that is his name, is very protective of her. One day, Jayden and I disagreed over her. It turned violent, he tried to kill me, I got away and have been hiding ever since."

"If you were hiding from him, what were you doing meeting him in the woods?"

"I was not meeting with him, I was fighting with him," replied Arbin. "Like I said, I tried to tell your guards... those guards. I went into the woods to do some hunting. I was sleeping in a hunting blind when I woke up to the sound of your people chasing someone. I recognized Jayden and figured he had discovered where I live and had come looking from me. He must have gotten too close to the camp and your people discovered him. It was obvious your people could not track him. When he showed up where I was camping, I had no choice but to deal with him. We struggled, but he got the better of me and got away. The guards arrived a few minutes later and here I am."

"My people? What do you mean by that?"

"You know, Seers like you and the one just outside," Arbin said with a sigh.

Alex looked up at Arbin's last comment, then looked over to see if Arbin could see the other Seer standing guard outside the tent. When he realized that Seer Lubin was not visible, he smiled and said, "You are right, we discovered your friend.... Jayden, in the area last night and had some problems 'Tracking' him as you say. There is something different about him, just like there is something quite different about you. Your friend snuck into the heart of our camp, attacked someone and evaded our pursuit. But you watched his escape and even got into a fight with him." Alex paused and let his comments hang in the air. Alex took another sip from his cup, sat back and studied Arbin.

Arbin shifted uneasily. He realized he had been careless. Arbin felt like he had been talking to someone who already had the answers to the questions he was asking. He had to get himself off the hook. "Look, I'm tired, hungry and thirsty. Can you please let me go? I promise I will come back. I am sure my memory will be much better after I eat and get some sleep."

"I am sorry, I cannot do that. The people I report to are not as sympathetic as me." Alex leaned forward, looked at Arbin and said, "Arbin, listen to me!"

Arbin looked up. He could tell that Alex had reached a serious point in his conversation.

"I want you to understand that your very life depends on how you respond. Do you understand what I am saying?"

Arbin glanced at the tent door, then back at Alex. He could see that Alex's expression had not changed. Arbin swallowed a few times, then nodded.

Alex asked slowly and calmly, "What is different about your friend and why could you track him so easily when we could not?"

Arbin froze for a few seconds. His mind spinning as he considered what to say next. He could tell that Alex appeared to be more interested in Jayden than him. *I need to keep their focus on Jayden*, he thought. Arbin took a deep breath and said, "Like I said, Jayden and I have a history. We traveled together for a few years. During that time, I could always detect him when he was using his special talent."

Alex let a slight smile show and asked, "And what is his special talent?"

Arbin paused, then in a low quiet voice said, "He is a Fade."

"I am not sure I heard you right," said Alex, leaning forward. "Please say that again."

"Jayden is a Fade," said Arbin, a little louder than he had expected. He looked around to see who else may have heard him.

Alex sat back for a few minutes, then said, "And you could detect him even when he was acting as a Fade?"

Arbin could see from Alex's face that he knew the answer before Arbin could say anything. Arbin just nodded and looked down, hoping that would be enough.

"Thank you, Arbin. I am sure this information will save your life. It takes an incredibly special Seer to detect and even fight with a Fade."

Arbin looked up surprised and said in a low voice, "Seer?"

Alex was standing and gathering his papers and said, "Yes, but we can talk about that later. First, I need to see about saving your life."

A wave of relief washed over Arbin. *They think I am just a Seer*, he thought. *He cannot tell what I am. If I just keep them focused on Jayden, I might get away from here.* As Alex was getting ready to leave the tent, Arbin asked, "Does that mean you will untie me?"

Alex said, "Not yet. Only Captain Eustace can order that. Oh, I will also see about getting you something to eat and drink."

"How am I going to eat and drink if I am tied up?"

"I'll ask the guards to help you with that," said Alex, and he quickly left the tent.

As Alex left, two guards entered the room and sat at the table Alex was using. These were not the same guards as last night, and they did not look happy about babysitting him. They sat and stared at him, saying nothing. A few minutes passed and Arbin said, "Alex said you would bring me something to eat and drink, I also would not mind taking a walk to the woods to relieve myself. If you untie me, I promise to behave."

"We don't take orders from Seers!" The emotion in the man's voice was clear. His partner nodded and said, "Those guys give me the creeps. Bunch of fakes, if you ask me."

The distrust in the last guard's voice was obvious. Arbin decided he would try to take advantage of it. "I agree with you. That Alex guy is talking all sorts of crazy talk about demons. He has me here because I did not agree with him. Please let me go. I will disappear and you will never see me again."

The first guard let out a laugh that almost frightened Arbin. The other quickly joined him. Arbin stared at the men with a worried look on his face. The guards turned their attention from him, but one continued to let out a light chuckle, as if retelling a good joke. As they got comfortable in their chairs, Arbin could tell the conversation was over. He settled back for what he hoped was not a long wait. The best thing to do, he decided, was to check if there were any other Seers around. It would give him a chance to learn how many he would face if he got the chance to run.

THE GRUMBLING OF ARBIN'S stomach amused one of his guards, who gave him a snicker before returning to finishing a tray of food that had recently arrived. Arbin was sure it was the food Alex had promised but knew asking about it would be useless.

Arbin shifted his position as best he could to help ease the cramping in his legs and arms. He was not sure how long Alex had been gone. His efforts to sense any Seers had been fruitless. *I am really out of practice. I do not remember this making me so tired,* he thought. It startled him when he felt a presence a few seconds before the tent flap opened and the bright light of day entered along with Alex. This time a man wearing a uniform with the same colors of a Shadow Guard accompanied him. The man's uniform was more formal and designed to show authority. His double-breasted jacket had gold buttons and gold trimmed epaulets on his shoulders. A kriegsmesser sword hung on one side, and on the other was a wheellock pistol in a holster attached to a strap that went over one shoulder. His stride and formal bearing left no doubt of his authority. As he followed Alex into the tent, the guards immediately stood and saluted. The bigger of the two said, "Captain." Arbin was a little surprised that a man who looked so young could be a person of such authority. Arbin guessed the Captain was maybe ten or fifteen years his senior. He was stocky but not fat, a little taller than Alex, had a round face with a neatly trimmed light reddish brown, almost copper colored beard that was more of a goatee with a thin section that extended back along the jawline toward his ears. When he stepped into the tent, he removed his helm, showing his hair was cut close, almost to the point of being shaved.

Captain Eustace acknowledged the guards, then stood next to the desk and studied Arbin for a few minutes. Finally, he turned to the guards and asked, "Has he said anything else about what happened?"

"He has been asking for food and water and wants us to release him," the larger of the two guards said. "He promised that if we let him go, he would never return. We were told not to talk to him, so we didn't. But Seer Keller had a conversation with him."

"Yes, Seer Keller has already spoken with me about that. Has he said anything to you about it?" replied Captain Eustace with an annoyed tone to his voice.

"No sir, nothing else," said the big guard. The other guard nodded his head and added, "Nothing, sir."

Captain Eustace turned to Alex and said, "Are you sure about this?"

"He is a Seer, and a very special one," said Alex with a satisfied smile. "I am sure of that, and Seer Lubin will also testify to that. The only thing that I am not sure about is how he could track and do battle with the Fade."

"That is the only thing you are not sure about?" asked Captain Eustace with a look on his face that caused Alex to look down with embarrassment.

The Captain looked back at Arbin and said, "How about the fact that he was friends with the Fade before they had their little falling out, or that he never reported the Fade to anyone as required by law."

Arbin felt uncomfortable sitting there as Captain Eustace stared at him as if he were learning everything about him just from watching. Finally, Captain Eustace asked in a surprisingly friendly voice, "Do you know why you are being held?"

"Because your people could not catch Jayden," said Arbin in an offhand manner.

Arbin could see the Captain's face harden and realized that it might be a good idea not to anger him anymore. "No one will tell me why I am here," he continued, "Other than you were chasing Jayden and you brought me in thinking I was helping him with whatever he did."

Captain Eustace's face softened a little, and he said, "That is correct."

Arbin said, "I already told Alex here, that Jayden and I are not friends. He is the last person I would help with anything."

"That is Seer Keller to you," said Captain Eustace.

"What?" asked Arbin.

"You will refer to him as Seer Keller," replied Captain Eustace calmly and with a surprising level of authority.

Arbin looked over at Alex, who was standing just behind and to the right of the Captain. Arbin noticed that Alex was not smiling.

Captain Eustace continued, "I am Captain Jessup Eustace, Commander of the Shadow Guard. I am also the person who will decide in the next few minutes if you live or die." Captain Eustace paused, then said, "Tell me about your history with Jayden and the events leading up to your capture."

Arbin took a breath and repeated the story he gave Alex, leaving out anything he felt could reveal his Fade talent or the incident with Carl Rupert.

Captain Eustace asked several questions about a rebel group that referred to themselves as supporters of the Adelest Movement. He also asked about any groups Arbin and Jayden may have associated with. It surprised Arbin that the Captain focused more on the rebel group then on Arbin's statement that Jayden was a Fade.

"I never heard of that group," said Arbin. "Jayden, his sister Mia, and I moved around so often we made no close friends."

When Captain Eustace asked about Jayden's ability with a knife, Arbin said, "He used one on his job and was handy with it, but I do not remember him using one in a fight, except when he threatened to kill me eight years ago."

The questioning continued for about an hour and Arbin felt he had answered the same questions over and over. His head hurt, his stomach grumbled, and he had to go pee. Arbin was glad when a person at the tent door, asking to speak with Captain Eustace, interrupted the questioning.

Captain Eustace stepped outside and as soon as the visitor started speaking, Arbin recognized her as Mrs. Sturgeon. She was one of the oldest persons living in the village. She was also the local midwife and self-proclaimed healer. Everyone respected her skill as a midwife, but her healing consisted mostly of herbs, scented candles and a collection of sayings she had for almost every occasion. Arbin was sure his mother knew more about healing than she did. He had made a point of taking care of his own needs in that area.

Arbin could hear them talking, but most of it was in muffled voices. Arbin heard Mrs. Sturgeon say, "He's in awful shape, but he might survive if we can get him some help. He is too weak to move." Arbin heard the Captain speaking but could not understand him. He heard Mrs. Sturgeon respond to the Captain by saying, "He should be here in a day or two." There was a pause and Arbin heard the Captain say, "Do what you can. Also, make it clear no one is to talk about the attack or his conditions, understand?"

The conversation ended, and Captain Eustace came back inside the tent. He called Alex over and said, "I will accept your statements about detecting Seer abilities in this man. However, I am not willing to accept his talk about a Fade without some confirmation from you."

Alex said, "I know there was something strange about the person we chased last night. There have been reports the Adelest supporters are claiming to have recruited a Fade."

"There have been groups making those threats for decades," said Captain Eustace. "This group may be more vocal and active then others in the past, but I am not prepared to accept every threat they make. I think the best thing to do is take this Seer of yours back to the Capital, where we can further evaluate his abilities and loyalties. I put him in your charge. Make sure he is ready to travel with us when we can leave." Captain Eustace took one last look at Arbin and left the tent, the guards snapping to attention as he passed.

As soon as Captain Eustace left, Alex instructed the guards to untie Arbin. It took a few attempts before Arbin could get to his feet. He rubbed his wrists and said, "What now?"

Alex pointed towards the tent opening and said in a pleasant voice, "Now we go, follow me."

Arbin followed Alex out of the tent, struggling to keep up with him because of the cramps in his legs. After a few feet Arbin stopped and called to Alex saying, "Hey, wait a minute. Is someone going to tell me what is going on? You had me tied up for a night, and now you want me to follow you like nothing happened?"

Alex turned to Arbin and said, "Oh that, it was just a simple misunderstanding. Congratulations, you are a lucky person. You are about to start a career in the Shadow Guard as a Seer."

"And what if I do not want to go off to be in your Shadow Guard?" asked Arbin.

"Sure you do. It's that, or we execute you as a criminal and a traitor," replied Alex.

"Criminal and a traitor? What is it you think I have done?" asked Arbin.

"First, you have admitted association with a Fade and did not report it to the local authorities. Second, the Fade you have been associating with, made an attempt on the life of Duke Henry Sumner, son of Chairman Sumner and heir to the Sumner Family Chair on the Governing Council."

Arbin stopped in his tracks and stared at Alex, who looked back at him and said, "You have a choice, return with me and present yourself for examination and induction into the Shadow Guard as a Seer, or be arrested and hauled back to the Capital for interrogation and judgment."

Arbin stood in disbelief. He was not sure he heard Alex correctly. He said in a gloomy voice, "I cannot believe this is happening to me."

Alex gave him a smile and asked, "Are you coming?"

Arbin staggered forward, doing his best to keep up with Alex, who looked back and said, "You can stay at your place until we are ready to leave. We will have to put a guard on you. I am sure you understand."

Arbin nodded, not sure what to say. After a few seconds he said, "I need to take care of something before we head all the way back to my place."

Alex paused and said, "What's that?"

Arbin glanced over at a cluster of bushes and trees just beyond the edge of the camp.

Alex paused, looked in the direction Arbin was suggesting and said, "Oh," then said, "Go ahead, but please do not run away. We are being watched, and as you know, we can find you. I would hate to see all my hard work saving you go to waste."

Chapter 5 - Death in the Family

HANS FABER SAT IN HIS chair whittling on a piece of branch he found nearby. He was a large older man, maybe two or three fists taller than Arbin. He wore a Shadow Guard's uniform, but in the very casual way of someone that had been in uniform for most of their life. Captain Eustace had assigned Hans as Arbin's guard a few days ago. Hans had spent those days parked in front of Arbin's room, only moving when Arbin needed to take a walk to take care of business. In the evening, they replaced Hans with two other Shadow Guards.

During one of Alex's visits, he told Arbin that Hans had been in the Army, but Captain Eustace had him transferred into the Shadow Guard just before they left to escort Duke Henry. Arbin figured that meant there must be something special about Hans. The past few days had not given Arbin any clue to what that could be.

"Have a heart, Hans," said Arbin in as sorrowful a voice as he could manage, hoping to gain the big man's pity.

Hans paused from his work, glanced over at Arbin standing in the doorway. His stare made Arbin nervous. Arbin stepped away from the door and Hans returned to his work.

Arbin made a few tours of his tiny living space. *I got to get out of here*, he thought. Arbin decided to give it another chance and returned to the doorway. "Hans, I just need to visit a couple of people. You can come along, if you want."

"Very funny," replied Hans.

"I have almost nothing. How am I supposed to survive a trip to the Capital? I am not a member of the Army or the Shadow Guard."

"How many people do you need to visit?" asked Hans as he examined his work.

"Like I said, a couple," replied a hopeful Arbin.

"Just so we are clear, how many are a couple," asked Hans.

"Four, maybe five," replied Arbin.

Hans tossed the branch onto the pile that would fuel tonight's fire, slowly stood and said, "Okay, but when I say we're done, we're done."

"Agreed!" said Arbin. *Where to start*, Arbin thought. *I wonder how serious these guys will be in chasing me. No telling how long I will be on the run.* Arbin looked back at Hans and said, "I lost most of my traveling supplies in the woods when you guys...," Arbin paused then said, "Any chance of me getting it back?"

"Don't know about that," said Hans as he stretched. "Anything valuable?"

"Hunting knife, rope, flint and some food," said Arbin. "I was fond of the knife and the bag."

"Well, if you didn't get it back by now, it's gone," said Hans.

Arbin paused again then said, "Any chance we—," but before he could finish Hans answered with a firm, "No!"

"Well, I need to at least replace those items. That should narrow down who—," Hans interrupted Arbin with another firm statement of, "No knife!"

"What do you mean, no knife? It's my right to carry a knife, look around, see any men without a knife?" Arbin said, swinging his arms around for effect.

"No knife!" Hans said again. "In case you've forgotten, I am your guard, not your friend."

"How do you expect me to protect myself?" Arbin asked.

"Do not worry. You will travel in the company of seventeen Shadow Guards and twenty of Duke Sumner's men. We will make sure you are never alone. I am sure others will be waiting to protect you once we reach the Capital."

"I see your point," said Arbin, studying the big man. *Now I know I do not want to make that trip*, thought Arbin. His mind mulling over the ways for him to escape as he walked toward the center of the village.

ARBIN HAD DONE SMALL favors for most of the families in town. It was these favors that made him welcome in the village, and it was these favors he intended to collect on now. Arbin soon discovered he was not as popular as he thought he was. House after house he got cold welcomes. People he had known for the last eight years looked out through partly open doors. It appeared the townsfolk did not view him as harmless anymore. Many appeared suspicious of him. Most glancing nervously between Arbin and his large companion. Even Joseph Mercier, who he had spoken to just the other day, gave him a cold welcome.

"Joseph, you promised," said Arbin through a partly open door. "You told me you would have something for me."

"I got my family to worry about," replied Joseph, glancing from Hans to Arbin. He lowered his voice slightly and said, "You don't know what it's like to have Seers come knocking on your door in the middle of the night demanding information about you. They said you had something to do with the attack on Duke Sumner and they wanted to know how close a friend I was."

"Joseph, you got to believe me. I had nothing to do with that attack. To tell you the truth, I fought with the Fade."

"That's another thing," said Joseph. Arbin could see a strange look in Joseph's eyes as he continued, "There's talk that you're cursed. That you brought that demon to our village." Joseph crossed himself and said, "People are afraid to go out at night."

Arbin replied, "I'm sorry for what this has done to you and your family. I promise, I will be leaving soon, and you will be free of me. Joseph, I helped you when your sister was sick, I wrote letters for you to the Church on her behalf. All I am asking for is some supplies to help me during my travels."

Joseph paused and looked back into the house. Just then Hans spoke up and said, "Pay the man what you owe him so we can be on our way." Joseph stared at the large guard standing behind Arbin. His eyes went to the man's hand resting on the hilt of his sword. Joseph nodded and said, "What do you need?"

"A bag and some food stuff will do," said Arbin.

Joseph disappeared behind a closed door, and Arbin could hear muffled conversation. Joseph returned shortly and said, "Stay here. I will go out back and get some meat from the drying shed," as he handed Arbin a small leather bag.

Arbin looked inside the bag and saw some bread and a small pouch he guessed held flour. Arbin turned to Hans and asked, "What has happened to this town?"

Hans replied, "He wasn't wrong in what he said. You said yourself that the demon followed you here. Leaving will be the best thing you could do for this town."

Arbin shook his head and said, "I thought these people liked me."

Joseph returned shortly and gave Arbin a package wrapped tight in cloth. He turned, and saying nothing more, closed the door. Arbin stood there staring into his bag. This plus a block of cheese he received earlier was the sum of his efforts. As he stared into the bag, he said to himself, "This will not even last me a day on the road."

As he was pondering on where to go next, Hans said, "That will be enough. Time to go home."

Arbin looked up and for the first time noticed how late it had gotten. He looked around, and an idea came to him. Arbin turned to Hans, who was pointing in the direction back to Arbin's little room, and said, "I have one last home to visit." Arbin saw Hans getting ready to object and said, "Widow Weber's house." Hans paused, so he continued, "She does not owe me anything, but she makes a great pie and tea. I am a little hungry. You will like her and it's on the way home."

Hans nodded and waved his hand to let Arbin know to lead the way.

THE WIDOW HAD ALWAYS been helpful to Arbin in the past, plus her home was near the edge of town. It might be a good place to make his escape once it got a little darker.

The smell of fresh-baked bread greeted Arbin before they reached the front door of Widow Weber's home. Both the smell and her greeting were a pleasant welcome. "Arbin, what a nice surprise," said Widow Weber as she opened the door. "I wasn't expecting you. I'm afraid I have no new letters for you to read."

"That's okay," Arbin replied. "I am going away soon, and I wanted to say goodbye." Arbin noticed she did not seem surprised by the news. "I also told my friend Hans," Arbin pointed in Hans' direction, "You make the best pies and baked goods. I was wondering if ...,"

"Of course, come in, but I'm sorry to say that I don't have any pies," she said, stepping back. The smile on her face made Arbin almost feel a little guilty for what he was planning. Widow Webber mistook Arbin's expression as one of disappointment and said, "I have some fresh-baked bread and plenty of jam and cheese, if that will do."

"That would be perfect," said Hans in a soft, pleasant voice that surprised Arbin. "My name is Hans, Hans Faber," he said as he removed his helmet.

"Eila Weber," responded the Widow as she motioned for them to enter the house.

Arbin followed Hans in and saw that the Widow had been busy baking. "Have a seat," Eila said, pointing them to the large table in the center of the room as she cleared a space among the trays of cooling bread. "You're not the only ones wanting to try some of my baking," she said with an air of pride. "I have had several requests from the Duke's people," she continued. "I have also had an order from your Captain," she said to Hans, who had made himself comfortable at the table.

"Captain Eustace has visited you?" asked Arbin.

"Yes, a pleasant man. He ordered some sweet bread for the Duke's son and wife. Are you a friend of the Captain?" Eila asked Hans.

"He is my Commanding Officer." Hans replied. "I knew his father much better."

Arbin looked at Hans and thought, *that explains a lot.*

Hans continued, "I served under his father in the Army before he died. He was a fine commander, but I also considered him a friend. Why do you ask?"

Eila said, "If you see him, please let him know his order is ready." Pointing around she said, "I need the space."

Hans smiled and said, "My pleasure." Hans looked around and asked, "You baked all of this?"

Elia placed a fresh loaf of bread on the table and a board of cheese and said, "I always enjoyed baking but never thought it might bring money into the house."

Hans asked, "Where do you get the flour from?"

Eila smiled and said, "The flour is part of the price," as she set a kettle on the fire. "Someday, when I have enough money, I will join my sister in Sakai. Arbin has been helping me write letters to her."

Hans cut off a piece of bread for Arbin and himself and said, "Nice town."

Elia turned and said with delight, "You've been there?"

Hans replied, "I've been to a lot of places, some not so nice. You will like it in Sakai. Not too big, not too small. You should even be able to continue your baking there."

Arbin watched as Hans and the Widow chatted back and forth. She asked about all the places he had been to and Hans happily snacked on bread and told her his stories.

This could work, Arbin thought. When he was younger, he would use his Fade Talent to slip away from groups of boring people. It required the group to be concentrating on something beside him to work. He remembered once when he was younger and Father Sauer, the traveling priest, came to town. His parents would force him to attend sermons being held in the center of the village. Somewhere in the middle of the endless talk, he noticed that no one was paying attention to him. He found that he could slip into a Fade and simply walk away.

After that, he used his Fade more often. He even tried it on his parents a few times, but that did not work because they always seem to know where his hiding places were. Arbin never worried about using his Talent back then until his mother warned him that people would not understand and might become afraid of him. That is when his father said it was time for him to learn a trade and he started helping his father with his work. They traveled to lots of exciting places and would be away for months at a time. When they traveled, the only reason Arbin had to use his Talents was when he was hunting. It was while he was away with his father that his mother died, and his world changed forever.

Arbin put that old wound behind him and focused on the plan at hand. He saw that Hans and the Widow were deep in the spell of conversation. A Fade now might just work, but Hans might be a problem. Either on purpose or by chance, Hans had positioned himself near the only door. If Hans stayed distracted, there was a good chance of Arbin making it outside. After that, it was into the woods, where the thick cover, the failing light, and a strong Fade could get him far away.

The Seers were the only thing he saw as a possible issue. Alex had always suggested that he was being watched. He was not sure if that was true or if Alex was bluffing. He would not get far if he used his Fade, and a nearby Seer detected him. Hans and Eila were still busy talking, so Arbin took a breath, calmed himself, and concentrated on detecting any presences nearby.

The presence you get from a Seer is more like a scent or a taste. Arbin could identify Mia by her presence without even seeing her. He had learned to recognize Alex, and another Seer named Lubin. Those were the only Seers that had come close enough for him to detect.

The presence you got from a Fade was quite different. The presence of a Fade could cause the hair on the back of your neck and arms to rise. Sometimes it could give you that feeling you get when you hear a noise in the back of that dark room late at night. The feeling that says, "If I just ignore it, everything will be okay." The stronger the Fade, the stronger the urge to just ignore it. Arbin found he could resist that urge. He was not sure if it was because of the time he had spent with Jayden or if it had something to do with his own Talents. Nonetheless, the presence of a Fade, once you learned to detect it, was something you never forgot. It was that presence that he felt now. It was very faint, but it was there. It was a presence that brought him back to full awareness of his surroundings.

Arbin looked around the room quickly. There were only a few windows in the home, but Arbin did not see Jayden through any of them. He looked over at Hans and the Widow, who were still happily talking. Looking down, he noticed someone had placed a cup of tea before him.

What do I do now? He thought as his fingers quickly tapped his knee. *Who are you after Jayden, me or the Duke?* Arbin reached out again, but this time detected nothing. He felt the tension in his shoulders relax. *So it's the Duke. Fine, I will stay here a little longer and leave you to your fate.*

Arbin looked back over at Hans and whispered to himself with a smile, "Getting dark." He lifted the teacup to his lips, took a drink and let out a yelp.

"Be careful," said the Widow. "That's hot."

Hans looked at Arbin, then outside at the growing darkness. Arbin saw his expression change. "We must be going," Hans said to the Widow, and with that Arbin's plan died.

Arbin was worried that Jayden might still be lurking around outside and struggled for something to say, hoping to delay their leaving. In a panic he blurted out, "I'm still drinking my tea." He knew it was stupid the second he said it but continued anyway, "It would be rude to leave. You go ahead without me."

Hans stood, walked over to Arbin, took his cup and finished the tea in a single sip. He turned to the Widow and said, "Thank you Eila, I enjoyed my stay. I will make sure the Captain knows about his order." He grabbed Arbin by the shirtsleeve, pulling him to his feet and said, "Time to go home," as he shoved him toward the door.

ONCE OUTSIDE, THE EARLY evening darkness which he had been counting on for cover now became a thing to fear. As he walked beside Hans, he glanced at every little noise he heard. For the first time, he was glad to have the large guard with him as they walked in silence back toward his room. Arbin did his best to search for any presence of Jayden, hoping that Hans would not notice. He knew that Jayden was out there, and he knew how determined Jayden could be once he put his mind to it.

Arbin racked his brains trying to think of how to make his escape. He decided it would be better to wait until later tonight. The success of a nighttime escape would depend on who relieved Hans. He hoped it would be Lang and Meyer. Normally, he was not fond of their visits.

Lang was a bulk of a man. Hans was large, but Arbin guessed that a lot of that weight was muscle. Lang was, well, just large. He would plop himself down on a stump near the fire and would sit there all night. He would also keep Arbin awake most of the night with his snoring.

Meyer was just a kid. At least six or seven years younger than Arbin. He did whatever Lang told him to do. Which meant he spent most of the night feeding the fire.

Both Lang and Meyer wore full armor while on watch, something Hans never did. Meyer was young and could probably run faster than Arbin, but not in that armor. Arbin was also sure that Meyer would be too afraid to follow him into the dark forest. If it was Lang and Meyer, he would have a chance.

"Hans, who is your relief?" Arbin asked but did not get an answer. A few seconds later he slammed into the back of Hans, who had stopped walking. Arbin looked around. They had stopped near the watering pump and water trough that stood in the center of the village.

"Hey, watch where you're going," Arbin said. When Hans did not answer, he looked at him and discovered Hans was sniffing the air. Arbin did the same thing and smelled smoke. Not an uncommon smell in the town, but this smelled different, stronger.

Hans pointed toward Kroner's barn and Arbin's attached room and said, "Fire!" Those words echoed from the direction of the camp where Arbin could see smoke just starting to rise above a few of the wagons.

Soon people were scrambling out of tents and village homes. The cry of fire becoming louder, and the evening sky filled with flames and smoke. People and buckets quickly surrounded the water trough. Arbin stood there, not sure what to do.

Arbin looked back toward his room and saw that the whole barn was in flames. "No!" He shouted. He wanted to run for his room hoping to save some of his things when someone grabbed him by the arm and pulled him back causing him to fall to the ground.

"Too late," said Hans. "This thing could bring down the entire town if they do not stop it."

Arbin laid there staring at his life going up in flames, including his most prized possession. The little mouse that had sent him on the journey that placed him here. He watched as the only thing that reminded him of his mother went up in smoke. The air filled with the sound of people yelling mixed with the roar of the fire. Arbin could not get himself to move. He just stared at the fire as it reached higher into the surrounding night.

Soon Arbin realized that Hans was shouting at him again. "Get up! We need to get you someplace safe!"

Arbin stared at Hans and said, "What?"

Hans said, "This fire was no accident."

Arbin stared at the chaos around him as he let Hans' last words sink in. "No accident," Arbin repeated. As the meaning of those words became clear, he yelled, "Jayden! you stinking bastard!" Arbin stood, looked at Hans and said, "That stinking bastard Jayden just tried to kill me again! I knew I should have done something when I detected him back at Widow Weber's place." Arbin looked back toward the fire and shouted, "Jayden! I will get you for this!" Arbin turned back toward Hans and said, "We have to get him," but before he could say anything else, he realized that Hans was staring at him.

Hans clinched his jaw for a second then said, "He was here, and you said nothing?"

Arbin realized the mistake he just made. "I am sorry, I was afraid and did not want to deal with him back there. I was hoping I made a mistake because his presence was so faint and disappeared so quickly."

Hans looked around at the chaos and said, "Then this is your fault." Hans grabbed Arbin by the sleeve and walked him to the water trough. He said, "Stay here, fill buckets, do something to help. I will be right back." Hans turned and headed off toward the camp.

"My fault?" Arbin said out loud. "How is it my fault? Jayden is the one that started this fight. He is the one that is taking it to this level. He is the one who attacked Duke Henry." Arbin paused and then said, "Duke Henry! Of course. That is where I will find him."

Kroner had made his guest home available for the Duke and his family during his recovery. Arbin learned this much by eavesdropping on a conversation between Alex and Hans. The guest home was nearby, but he was sure it would be guarded. Arbin looked around at the chaos of townsfolk and guards running everywhere, trying to deal with the fire that was spreading. *In all this confusion, I bet Jayden could walk right up to it,* Arbin thought. *I should be able to do the same. If I find him, I will just point him out to the guards.*

It surprised Arbin how easy it was to approach the guest house. He did not see any guards on the front porch or outside. *Everyone must be out helping with the fire,* he thought. He looked back over his shoulder at the blazing barn. He could feel the heat even from here.

Arbin was familiar with the house. He had cleaned it several times. The downstairs had a living room, a kitchen, and a bedroom. The second floor had two smaller bedrooms and storage. There was an entrance at the front that led to the living room. The back had a door to the kitchen which also had stairs to the second floor. There was also an entrance to a root cellar in the backyard. Arbin figured that the best place to find the Duke would be in the downstairs bedroom. He took a second to check for the presence of Seers or Jayden. When he did not detect anyone, he went into a Fade, made his way along the side of the home toward the bedroom window and peeked in.

The room was lit by only one lamp and the glow of the nearby burning barn. It took Arbin a few seconds to realize what he was looking at. Not because of the lighting, but because of the scene it revealed. On the ground was the body of a man dressed in a Seer's uniform. The red of his torch crest was matched by the red he was laying in. He could just see the feet of another body, in a Shadow Guard uniform, lying just into the living room. Standing amid the grizzly scene were two other men, both in Shadow Guard uniforms. Arbin recognized them as the two men he ran from in the woods.

The smaller of the two was peeking out the bedroom door into the living room. Arbin heard him say in a hushed but forceful voice, "Come on! Get it done already." The other man, the larger and stronger of the two, was standing over a person lying on the bed. Arbin could not see the face of the person in the bed because the large guard had a pillow pressed over it. Arbin watched in disbelief as the large man calmly used his strength to keep the pillow firmly in place despite his victim's weak attempts to fight back. The struggle finally ended, and the killer stood up, tossed the pillow and straightened his uniform. That is when Arbin could see that the man on the bed was Henry Sumner. The smaller guard near the door said, "Finally. We need to get out of here before anyone comes back."

Arbin wanted to run, but his muscles would not obey. He put his hand over his mouth to keep from shouting and let himself slide to the ground. He could still hear the two men talking. The guard by the door said, "I think it's best if we go out the back. We can split up and then meet in the—." His words were cut off and there was a thump.

Arbin fought the urge to run, forced himself up, and peeked back in the window. The body of the small guard had joined the others on the floor. It lay in a pool of blood from the gash across his throat. The larger man was no longer in the room.

"Shadow Guards," Arbin murmured, quickly covering his mouth as soon as he realized he spoke out loud. He looked around, worried that someone may have heard him. He peeked back in the window and saw the scene had not changed. *Who do I tell?* he wondered. He thought about Hans. Arbin liked him but remembered him saying he was his guard and not his friend. Alex had helped him and did not seem fond of Shadow Guards. The one thing he knew was the longer he stayed here, the better chance he would get discovered.

Arbin heard something from the direction of the front of the house and hoped it was the killer leaving that way. From where he was, he could see the road that ran by the door and decided it would be smart to find a less visible spot. He moved around the corner of the house and into the backyard where he hid behind a bush near the entrance to the cellar. That is where he detected the presence of Jayden again and realized he was sitting in his Fade Shadow. An effect caused when a Fade sat in one area too long. A Fade Shadow would only last for a few minutes. That meant that Jayden had recently been here.

I do not understand, thought Arbin. He was sure that Jayden was after the Duke again. Instead, he watched as Shadow Guards killed the Duke. The Fade Shadow convinced Arbin that Jayden must be somewhere in the area. Maybe he was working with the killers. Attacking the Duke and working with these killers did not sound like the Jayden he knew, but a lot of time had passed since he last saw him. That night when Jayden threatened to kill him.

Arbin heard a roar and dropped to the ground. He looked behind him and saw the flames of the barn reaching higher, as parts of it fell.

"There goes everything I own," whispered Arbin. As the flames grew, so did his anger. *Someone will pay for this,* he thought. *I know you are here, Jayden. If not outside, then you must be still inside.* Arbin decided he needed to move now if he would have any chance of confronting Jayden before the guards got back.

As Arbin entered the kitchen, he made sure his Fade was in place. It was dark, but he knew where the stairs were. Three steps up the stairs he heard a sound. Arbin crouched down and focused on his Fade as he tried to see the source of the sound. It was dark, but he caught the movement of a figure. When it passed in front of the window at the top of the stairs, Arbin could see its true size. It was big. Arbin realized that he was looking at the killer and panicked. He jumped the three steps to the bottom of the stairs and ran out the back door, slamming it behind him as he went.

Arbin ducked back behind the bush he had hidden in earlier and held his breath. He knew that even though he had been in a Fade while he was inside, it would not prevent the killer from hearing the sound he made as he ran out of the house. He could only hope that the darkness and his Fade would prevent the killer from getting a good look at him. Being in a Fade did sometimes mess with people's ability to remember details about a person.

The killer was out of the house and in the backyard sooner than Arbin expected. The big man stood with his head tilted to one side, listening for the sound of running feet. Arbin could almost hear the man's breathing. Arbin sat as quietly as he could and hoped his Fade would protect him.

Soon the killer had given up on listening for his prey and glanced around the backyard. Arbin was thinking about making a run for it when he heard someone calling his name. He looked at the killer and saw that he also heard it. The killer looked back at the house like he was trying to decide something, but when someone shouted Arbin's name again, the killer quickly left. Once he was out of sight, Arbin released his Fade.

The next time Arbin heard his name, he recognized the caller as Hans. Arbin made his way onto the road and raised his hand. He watched as Hans headed over toward him at a slow trot. A Seer and three Shadow Guards followed close behind him.

When Hans reached him, he stopped and bent over with his hands on his knees, catching his breath. In between gasps for air he said, "You were told to stay by the water trough!"

Arbin could see that Hans truly seemed concerned about Arbin so he said, "I told you I detected Jayden." Arbin looked back at the guest house and said, "I was afraid he might use the chaos of the fires to try another attack on Duke Henry."

"He was here?" Hans asks as he stood up straight and looked around.

"Is he still here?" asked the Seer who had just arrived. Arbin had never seen this Seer before. He was noticeably young, and his uniform was a little different from the one Alex wore. It had the torch crest but did not appear to have any colorful edging on the tunic.

If I can tell Jayden is not here, this guy should be able to do the same, Arbin thought. Something inside told Arbin to be careful how he answered.

"I am sure he was around here someplace," said Arbin. "When I got here, I detected his presence. I entered the house through the back door and saw a figure at the top of the stairs checking the doors to the rooms up there. I thought it was him. I did not want to face him alone, so I ran out."

The young Seer looked around nervously. One of the Shadow Guards with him said, "Form up!" The others formed a kind of half circle around the Seer and Arbin.

"Whoever I saw followed me out of the home and took off when you showed up," said Arbin, and he could see the relief on the young Seer's face.

Hans turned to the Shadow Guards with the Seer and said, "You need to check on the Duke. I will wait out here with Arbin in case the Fade returns."

"Agreed," said one of the Shadow Guards. "The others should be here soon."

As the group headed to check on Duke Henry, Hans pushed Arbin further down the road and away from the house. There was another loud crash and Arbin jumped back a few steps. He turned to see the rest of the burning barn crash to the ground.

Hans said, "Let me know next time if you detect the Fade. I can't protect you if I don't know he's here."

Arbin looked at Hans and said, "Protect me. I thought you were guarding me."

"Captain Eustace assigned me to you," said Hans. "You said this Fade was after you, right?"

Arbin did not know what to say. He stood there looking at the burning building.

After a few seconds Hans added, "He also ordered me to make sure you didn't escape."

Arbin nodded his head while watching the fire and waiting for what the discovery of the Duke's body would bring. He did not have long to wait. Soon, he saw one of the Shadow Guards leaving the front door at a run. Within minutes, the man returned with several other Shadow Guards who took up stations around the house.

Captain Eustace, Alex, and several others soon joined them. Before entering, Captain Eustace paused and glanced in Arbin's direction. He spoke with two Shadow Guards who saluted and headed over to where Arbin and Hans were standing.

"The Captain wants to make sure no one speaks to this man until he can question him," said one of the Shadow Guards as they approached. Hans nodded as the three of them formed a small group that now circled Arbin, who sat down and waited for the questioning that would soon follow.

Do I tell them who did it? Arbin thought. *They will not believe me. They will ask why I did not do something.* Arbin looked back at the burning barn and whispered, "I know you were here. How are you involved in this?"

"Did you say something?" asked Hans.

The question startled Arbin out of his deep thought. He looked up and said, "No, just thinking about Jayden."

Chapter 6 - Fall from Grace

ARBIN SAT WATCHING the fire from the barn send sparks and embers into the darkening sky. Normally, he would have thought it beautiful except now, as he watched, he knew that each spark, each ember carried with it the treasures of his life.

"It's time to go, Arbin," said Alex.

Arbin looked up from where he was sitting and saw Alex standing there with two Shadow Guards a few feet behind him. Arbin took one last look at the smoldering remains of the barn and shed he had called home, got to his feet and followed Alex and the others back to the last place he wanted to revisit.

A Shadow Guard directed Arbin and Alex to an empty space as soon as they entered the front door. "Don't worry," said Alex. "The others will be here soon." Arbin was not sure what that meant, but it was nice to know that one of them was not worried. From where he ended up standing, Arbin could see Captain Eustace at the far end of the room, speaking with two other Shadow Guards. One was Hans, who Captain Eustace had called for a few minutes before Alex arrived. The other was a big unhappy looking person who Arbin was glad he had not had the chance to meet yet. Both Hans and the other Shadow Guard glanced over at Arbin and Alex as they talked with Captain Eustace.

A few minutes later, Lubin and three other Seers entered the room and Alex motioned for them to fall into a line behind him. He had Arbin stay to his right side while they waited for Captain Eustace to finish his discussion.

Now, surrounded by Seers, Arbin noticed two strange things. First, their uniforms were different. They had the same basic uniform. Light green pants, gray padded jacket and white tunic. Their tunics had the same crest, but Alex and Lubin's tunics were edged in green with an inner line of red embroidered alongside the green edge. Two of the other Seers had only green edging. The young Seer that had been with Arbin outside had no edging on his tunic. The other thing Arbin noticed was that he could only sense the presence of Alex and Lubin.

Arbin looked around the living room of the house. He had been here many times before but had never seen this many people in it. There were two Shadow Guards stationed at the door that led to the bedroom where Arbin had seen the murder. Arbin recognized them as the two that watched over him so fondly that first night in the tent. There were the two guards at the front door and an additional two guards at the door to the kitchen. *A lot of guards just to watch a dead body*, thought Arbin.

The bodies near the bedroom door had been removed, but the bloodstains remained. Arbin noticed the Seers stealing glances at the stains. That was when Arbin remembered that one of the bodies was a Seer.

Captain Eustace finished his meeting and walked toward the group of Seers. As he did, Alex and his Seers snapped to attention. Arbin was not sure what to do, so he stood there holding his hands in front of him. Captain Eustace stopped a few feet in front of them and just studied Alex and his Seers for a few minutes.

Finally, Captain Eustace said. "First, let me say I am sorry for the loss of your comrade. We both lost good men, and I lost a very dear friend. Personal feeling aside, these deaths will demand answers from more than just the Governing Council. Especially if, as you have suggested, a Fade was involved. Do you understand Seer Keller?"

"Yes, sir!" responded Alex.

"I hope so, Seer Keller, because some powerful people will be looking for someone to blame. If it involved a Fade, a clear explanation of your failure to defend against it will be required."

Arbin could almost feel the tension between the two men and did not need to look at Alex to know he had not expected the conversation to go this way.

"My men were properly placed, supported by your men as per procedures," said Alex as he maintained eye contact with the Captain.

"And yet, Duke Henry is dead," said Captain Eustace, still studying Alex. "Tell me Seer Keller, do you still believe a Fade was involved?"

"I do," said Alex. "I also think the Fade is responsible for the fires. I feel it set them as a distraction. An attack by a Fade is the best explanation of how his guards could have been taken by surprise."

"Did any of your men detect this Fade?" asked Captain Eustace.

"No, sir," said Alex, keeping eye contact with the Captain, but the tone of his voice showed he was not happy with his answer.

"Why is that Seer Keller?" asked Captain Eustace. When Alex did not answer the Captain continued, "You insisted that for the first time in over a hundred years a true Fade had appeared and that your men were ready and eager to defend Duke Henry from it. What happened? Where were your people? Why didn't they do their job?"

Alex said, "Sir, we base our training and tactics on everything we have been told about Fades. I was confident in my people's ability to perform as trained. I agree, we should have been able to defend against this Fade." Alex paused than said, "but, after speaking with Arbin, I must admit that our knowledge may be faulty."

"Faulty! Is that what you are calling it?" said Captain Eustace, raising his hand to stop Alex from responding. Arbin did his best to avoid looking at the Captain and could hear the men behind him shifting nervously. After a few more seconds of quiet, the Captain took a deep breath, then shook his head slightly. His gaze focused on Arbin and he said, "Seer Keller, are you aware there was a report of the Fade being in town before the fires and the murders?"

That surprised Alex. He looked at Arbin and then back to Captain Eustace and said, "No, sir."

"I can explain," said Arbin.

"That's right! You will explain," said Captain Eustace. The anger in his voice was unmistakable. "I want to know why you failed to let anyone know, including the guard you were with, that the person you claim wants to kill you and who had attacked Duke Henry once before, was here. I also want to know why we found you lurking outside this house at the time of the murders."

Arbin paused, then looked to Hans, who returned his stare with a surprising lack of emotion. Arbin looked quickly around at Alex and the others in the room, then quietly said, "I thought I detected him, but just for a second. I was not sure it was him," he paused again, then said, "It could have been his shadow, just like what I detected outside this house."

"Shadow, what is he talking about?" Captain Eustace asked Alex.

Alex had not expected the question. He hesitated for a second and glanced over at Lubin, who stared straight ahead. When he looked back at the Captain, he saw an expression of disappointment. Alex cleared his throat and said, "There are stories that a Fade can come and go using shadows."

Arbin could not believe Alex's explanation and gave him a questioning look.

Captain Eustace turned to Arbin and asked, "Can Jayden move in and out of shadows?"

"No. Of course not," said Arbin. "It's not what you think. Shadow is not the best word. It is more like a stain. A kind of presence that remains for a little while after a Fade leaves. It happens if you are under stress and stay in one place while in a Fade."

When Arbin had finished, he noticed that Alex was staring at him with a strange look on his face. "How long does this shadow stay?" he asked.

"I don't know. It depends on the situation. I have used it in the past when hunting Jayden," replied Arbin.

"Hunting him?" asked Captain Eustace. What do you mean hunting him?

"It was a game we played when I was traveling with him," replied Arbin. "Kind of like the children's game of Hide and Seek."

Captain Eustace studied Arbin for a few minutes, then said, "This shadow. You said you found one near this home?"

"Yes, in the backyard near the bushes by the root cellar," said Arbin.

"So, it can happen when someone stays in one place for a while. Like a lookout?" asked Captain Eustace.

Arbin looked at Captain Eustace, shrugged his shoulders and said, "That's possible."

"And I guess you did not see your friend Jayden when you arrived?" said Captain Eustace.

Arbin did not like Captain Eustace's tone and the way he referred to Jayden as his friend. He looked around at all the Shadow Guards and realized for the first time that there was one at every exit. He looked back at the Captain who had been watching him the entire time and said, "I did not see Jayden anywhere. But like I said, I thought I sensed his presence."

"I see," said Captain Eustace. After a few seconds, the Captain smiled slightly and asked, "What did you do next, hunt for him like when you were friends?"

Arbin was getting nervous at the constant references to his friendship with Jayden. He could feel the Captain studying his reactions. He also noticed that some others in the room had picked up on the Captain's questions. Arbin knew he had to get the attention off him, but worried about how to bring up the killers without having to answer questions on how he had avoided discovery by them. Arbin figured the best thing to do was to avoid any mention of the murder.

Arbin was still thinking about what to say when he heard Alex say, "Arbin, the Captain asked you a question."

Arbin nodded, took a breath, let it out slowly, hoping to calm his pounding heart and said, "When I saw the chaos caused by the fire, I guessed that Jayden would use it to try another attack on Duke Henry. Hans was gone, so I went looking for Jayden on my own. When I got here, I thought I detected his presence near the back of the house. While I was there, the barn collapsed. Seeing the barn and my place going up in flame made me so angry. I could not think about anything except getting revenge. I was sure Jayden was near, but I did not see him outside, so I entered the house through the kitchen door."

"And did you find him?" asked Alex.

"No." Arbin paused, then said, "I heard someone at the top of the stairs. As I climbed them, I saw a large figure at the top. I knew it was not Jayden, so I ran outside and hid in the bushes."

"What did this person look like?" asked Captain Eustace, the level of his voice raised as he took a few steps toward Arbin.

Arbin took a step back and said, "I am not sure. It was dark. He was large and could have been in a uniform."

Captain Eustace turned to Alex and the Seers and asked, "Which one of your men discovered Arbin?"

Alex pointed toward the young Seer that had been with Arbin outside and said, "That was First Year Kingsley."

Captain Eustace looked at the young Seer and said, "Kingsley. Is your father Heinrich Kingsley?"

Kingsley answered, "Yes, sir."

"Your father wrote to me about you." Captain Eustace paused, then said, "Several times."

Kingsley looked down, his face was red. After a pause he said, "Yes, sir?"

"Kingsley," said the Captain. "When you arrived, where did you find him?" pointing toward Arbin.

Kingsley replied, "He was just stepping out of a bunch of bushes at the back of the house."

"Did you see anyone else?" asked Captain Eustace.

Kingsley looked at Arbin and then Alex. He was nervous as he said, "No, sir."

"Did you detect a Fade or this shadow Arbin talked about in the area?" asked Captain Eustace.

Kingsley responded more quickly this time and said, "No, sir."

"Then why did you respond as if there was a Fade?" Captain Eustace asked.

Kingsley looked over at Arbin and said, "Because he said so." Kingsley stumbled on his words a bit and then said, "He said the Fade was near and that he was being chased."

Captain Eustace turned to the group of Seers and asked in a raised voice that did not hide his frustration, "Did anyone detect a Fade?"

Arbin raised his hand and Captain Eustace stepped toward him and said, "Are you absolutely sure that Jayden was in the home or even in the area at the time you were there?"

Arbin paused, looked down and said, "No. I was so sure at the time, but not now."

"And are you sure that the person you saw upstairs followed you out of the house?" asked Captain Eustace.

"Someone followed me out of the house," said Arbin. "I was hiding and could not see who it was. Hans and the other guards arrived shortly after that."

Captain Eustace paused then asked, "You are sure the person at the top of the stairs was in a uniform?"

Arbin replied, "I think so."

Captain Eustace stared at Arbin for several minutes. Arbin knew he had been less than honest in his responses. The Captain's stare worried Arbin that he somehow knew.

Finally, the Captain walked back toward the center of the room. Then almost to himself, said, "One thing that has bothered me is how the killings were done." He looked back over at Arbin and the others and continued, "They killed Henry with a pillow. They suffocated him. To kill someone that way takes strength, it takes time and a desire to make someone suffer. That person was sending us a message. He was telling us he can kill who and when he wants. A knife killed the others. Their deaths were quick, almost professional. Captain Eustace paused and stood there, deep in thought, as if he were alone. He looked up after a few minutes and said, "I believe there was more than one killer. Duke Henry's killing would require the callousness brought by years of violence. The other could be almost anyone with some basic training and a knife." Captain Eustace looked at Arbin and asked, "Do you own a knife?"

The question surprised Arbin. He said, "No. I lost my knife in the forest running from two of your Guards." Arbin paused, looking to Alex, hoping he would confirm his story. When Alex nodded, Arbin looked back to Captain Eustace and said, "Even if I had a knife, I would never kill someone."

Arbin became concerned when Captain Eustace did not appear satisfied with his answer. He was thinking of what else to say in his defense when Captain Eustace said, "So you ran unarmed into this house to confront the man that you say attempted to kill you. The man that had already bested you in a fight. What were you planning to do once you found him?"

Arbin paused for a few seconds. It was a question he had been asking himself ever since it happened. Finally, he said, "Like I said, I was angry, and I was not thinking that far ahead. I am not sure; tell someone I guess."

Captain Eustace looked at Arbin and then said, "My reports tell me you are a self-centered loner. You help only when there is something in it for you. I believe you when you say you did not kill anyone. I do not think you have the courage to kill someone. I also believe it is possible that you would do nothing to prevent a murder if it worked to your advantage. In my opinion, you are a wasted life, and I am sure your death would go unnoticed."

The Captain's statement shocked Arbin. He whispered in a questioning voice, "My death?"

Captain Eustace watched Arbin, studying his reactions. The longer the silence, the more Arbin felt like just making a run for it. He needed to get the focus off him but did not know what to say. To his relief, Alex broke the silence.

"Sir, I know that it looks as if a group did the murders, but I still believe Jayden is a Fade and was involved in some way."

Captain Eustace pointed at Arbin and said, "So far it appears as if he is the only one that has detected a Fade. To tell you the truth, Seer Keller, I am questioning the existence of this Fade."

"Our people chased him after the first attack on Duke Henry," said Alex. "I can assure you there was something strange about him."

"As you have said many times," said Captain Eustace. "I agree that they chased after someone but are any of your men willing to go on record saying they detected a Fade."

The Seers looked at each other but remained silent. Arbin said, "Captain, Jayden is a Fade."

Captain Eustace gave Arbin a stern look, and he understood that the Captain was not interested in his opinion.

"Seer Keller," said Captain Eustace, turning his attention from Arbin to Alex. "I am asking if you can prove we are dealing with a Fade and not some skilled assassins."

When Alex did not answer Captain Eustace said, "Seer Keller, once again, for the record, did you or any of your Seers detect a Fade?"

Alex looked at Arbin, then back to the Captain and said, "No, sir."

Captain Eustace said, "I am sorry, but until you can convince me that this is a threat that requires your services and that your people are capable of addressing, I will take the action needed to defend against a small group of highly skilled assassins. As of now, I will assign you and your men to support duties."

"Please Captain," said Alex. "You must let us continue to do our duty."

Captain Eustace studied Alex and the Seers for a few minutes. "I can see that you genuinely believe that Arbin's friend is the true threat here, but I need to respond to the facts. Duke Henry's killing was done by professionals. Your Fade may have been involved. Based on his first attack, he is dangerous but not a professional."

"Sir, the Fade is pure evil," said Alex. "You cannot let it go unchecked. Fighting this evil is the reason they created the Shadow Guards."

"I want to make sure you understand what is at stake here, Seer Keller!" said Captain Eustace. "This group, the supporters of the Adelist movement, has shown us what they are capable of. Do you think they will stop now? They have stated many times it is their goal to take down the entire Council and return us to rule by nobility. If they continue their attacks, it will be civil war all over again. That is the threat I will not let go unchecked! I understand your loyalty to the Order and your beliefs. I am not stopping you from considering changes to your methods, but you must understand, I must free up fighting men to address what I see as the larger threat."

"And what of Arbin?" asked Alex.

"Since you insist that he is a Seer, I leave him in your charge until we reach the Capital," said Captain Eustace. "But I am warning you, his connection to the Fade worries me. Unless you can convince me he is not a danger and can offer something of value, his Seer's gift will not be enough to protect him. As it stands now, I will have nothing good to say about him or you at my next meeting with Chairman Sumner and Bishop Sorren. Now, if you will excuse me, I would like a moment with the Duke before I have to arrange for the transportation of his body back to his hometown for burial."

"That would mean splitting our forces," said Alex. "Wouldn't it be safer if we traveled together to the Capital. Duke Henry could receive the honors he deserves there."

"I had a lengthy discussion with Lady Casandra, and she agrees with this decision," replied Captain Eustace. "I believe the Adelist, embolden by their success, will quickly take additional action. If their goal is to destabilize the Governing Council, that means Dylan, as the new Heir to the Sumner Family Chair, is the most logical target. I do not believe they have the forces to attack both groups. It will be safer for Lady Casandra if we separate, and she returns home with any of the less necessary wagons and support staff."

"Then at least allow one of my people to travel with her and offer some protection," said Alex.

Captain Eustace looked at the group of Seers and said, "Kingsley, can you drive a team of horses?"

"Yes, sir!" responded Kingsley, glad to have something positive to say.

"Then your father will be happy to hear that I am giving you the honor of driving the wagon that carries Duke Henry's body. Do your best to guard him," said Captain Eustace.

"Yes, sir," replied Kingsley, looking back at Alex.

Alex said, "Captain—," but before he could finish Captain Eustace said, "That will be all, Seer Keller. We will hold a small service for both Duke Sumner and our fallen comrades before we leave." Captain Eustace paused, looked in Arbin's direction and said, "I want him kept out of sight until we leave. Now if you will excuse me. I would like to pay respects to my dear friend." Captain Eustace turned and walked toward the door to the bedroom where the body of the Duke still rested.

Chapter 7 - Better Safe Than Sorry

ARBIN FOLLOWED THE little group of Seers outside, happy to be back in the open and away from the crowded living room, which felt like it was getting smaller and smaller with every angry glance from both Seers and Shadow Guards. The Captain's remarks hung over Arbin like a dark cloud. *'A worthless life,'* he thought. *'The cause of everyone's problems.'* That last part came from his father on the day he disowned him. Standing in front of Captain Eustace was much like standing in front of his father that day. Both casually threw out words that cut him deeply.

"You dropped this," said Hans as he tossed a bag at Arbin's feet.

Arbin reached down and picked up the bag containing the items he had collected from the townsfolk earlier in the day. It seemed like it happened a lifetime ago. "What do I do now, Hans," Arbin asked as he looked inside the bag.

"It's time to decide which side you're on before it is finally, and I mean finally, decided for you," said Hans as he turned and walked away.

"Hans, wait," said Arbin "You can't just leave me here. Where am I supposed to stay?"

Hans pointed in a general sweeping movement toward Alex and the other Seers and said, "You're one of them now," and continued to walk away.

"One of them?" Arbin muttered to himself as he looked at the group of Seers. Alex and Lubin were standing to one side, having what looked like a serious conversation. The rest of the Seers were gathered in a grassy spot and doing their best to ignore him.

"Hey, Alex," shouted Arbin. "What now? I need a place to stay and would like to get something to eat."

His shout got the attention of Alex and received some dirty looks from the others. "That's what we are discussing," said Alex. He appeared to say a few final things to Lubin then turned back to Arbin and said, "Lubin will take the others back to their tents and you and I will have a small talk."

"Let's go!" said Lubin as he waved to the small group of Seers and headed off toward the direction of the camp.

Arbin looked at Alex and said, "Look, I am sorry about—" Alex stopped him by putting up his hand.

"This place is too crowded for me," said Alex, looking back toward the house they had just left. He walked off, leaving Arbin standing there. A few seconds later Alex looked back and said, "You coming?"

Arbin did a quick trot and caught up with Alex. They walked together in silence for a few minutes until Alex stopped. He looked around, then looked at Arbin and asked, "What did your parents say when it was discovered you were Blessed?"

That was not a question that Arbin had expected. He looked at Alex and said, "What?"

"My parents said it was the greatest day of their life," said Alex. "They said it brought great joy to them and the entire town where I lived. I was told to be able to answer God's call to defend the country from evil was the greatest honor a man could have."

"My Talents never brought me anything but trouble," said Arbin as he looked back at the smoldering remains of the barn and his little shack. "That's why I want nothing to do with this Seer business."

"Talents?" asked Alex.

Still looking in the barn's direction, Arbin said, "What you call gifts, my mother called Talents," He pictured his mother's smile, and it brought a brief smile to his face. Looking back at Alex, he let that smile slip away and said, "Both my parents would say I was special but did not really understand what I could do. Heck, I did not understand it until I met up with Jayden and his twin sister. Why do you ask?"

"Both Lubin and I agree you have the gift," said Alex. "You are the real thing,"

"I know that!" said Arbin.

Alex said, "What you don't know is how rare and special this gift is. It is a gift that comes with great responsibilities and great burdens."

Arbin let out a soft chuckle and said, "I have heard that talk before. I can agree with the burdens part. Pain and burdens." Arbin was tired and hungry and did not like where this conversation was going. "Look, I am glad you found something that made your parents proud, but I really want to know what I am going to do now that they have burned my place to the ground?"

Alex studied Arbin for a few minutes then said, "When I first met you, I was excited to find another True Seer." Alex paused and then said, "But it also terrified me."

That last comment worried Arbin. He studied Alex for a few seconds, trying to decide if he needed to run. When Alex gave him a slight smile, Arbin relaxed and asked, "Why would you be terrified of me?"

"Not of you personally, but of the fact for the first time in over a hundred years a Seer and a Fade have done battle," replied Alex. "I am also worried because the only person who can defeat this Fade rejects his gifts and responsibility. I fear for the future of our country."

"Jayden is only one person," said Arbin. "You cannot believe he will bring down the nation. Besides, you have the Shadow Guard, Seers and all."

"Just as there is more than one Seer, I believe there must be more than one Fade," said Alex. "But what you do not understand is how fragile our system is. The people believe that in times of danger, the Shadow Guards will protect them from attacks by Fades. I am sure you know by now that none of the True Seers has the training needed to fight this Fade. Captain Eustace was right about one thing. The Adelist supporters are a genuine threat. Now that they have recruited a True Fade to fight on their behalf, I fear there will be a civil crisis. One which could lead to the fall of the current government."

"You keep saying True Seers. What are you talking about?" asks Arbin.

Alex said, "There are a limited number of people who truly have the gift we share. I'm sure you have noticed that already."

Arbin nodded and said, "I've noticed."

"What you may not know is that number keeps getting smaller," said Alex.

Before Arbin had his run in with Alex and his Seers, Mia was the only other Seer he had ever met. He had heard stories of Seers and assumed there were lots of them out there, busy hunting down Fades. *Just how many people are there like me?* He wondered.

He was still thinking about that when Alex said, "You may also have noticed we are not always treated with the respect our Order and mission should deserve."

Arbin had noticed the tension between the Shadow Guards and their Seers. He was not sure where Alex was going with this, so he just nodded.

"The Captain and his men routinely deal with threats against the government. Their value, though currently different from the reason they found the Shadow Guard, is routinely demonstrated to the public. We, on the other hand, are fast becoming a ceremonial unit. Many see us as just another way into the church. One not as demanding as other methods. Some families see it as a way to deal with the problem of feuding siblings or prevent the loss of property and wealth that results through the current inheritance system. We are not the Order we started out as, or who we should be. Fewer and fewer people believe in the true power of the Seers or in their true mission. There is no need for a group to defend against a threat that does not exist."

"Well, now you have one, so, problem solved," said Arbin.

"Not really," said Alex, looking off into the distance. After a short pause, as if deciding if he should continue, Alex looked at Arbin, smiled and said, "The process for deciding who has the gift and who does not, has changed over the years from a system of proof to a system of faith. As a result, not everyone who claims the gift has the gift."

"So, the guards were right," said Arbin. "You are a bunch of fakes. No wonder you could not find Jayden." Arbin could see that his comment angered Alex. He put his hand in front of him and said, "I am sorry. That did not come out right."

"Sometimes the truth is painful, but that does not make it any less true," said Alex in a surprisingly calm voice. "I would prefer the term 'Faithful Hopefuls' for those where God's calling is different from the Truly Gifted. Most people in the Seer Core are committed to our mission of fighting evil. It's just that for some, that evil does not reveal itself in the same way."

"What do you expect me to do? Pick out the True Seers for you?" asked Arbin.

"No, we True Seers are very much aware of who is who," said Alex. "The recent events have shown we are not properly prepared to deal with the threat of a True Fade," said Alex. "Time has weakened our understanding of the lessons learned by our founders. You know things about Jayden we can use to defend against him. Teach us. In turn, we will do our best to keep you safe. However, we need positive results now, before we get to the Capital, where you will find people less willing to take the time to separate your past from the recent events."

If I teach them how to hunt Fades, how do I protect myself? thought Arbin.

"Arbin, do not be fooled into thinking you can just run away from your responsibilities," said Alex. "Just because you are assigned to me does not mean they will not be watching you. One more mistake and you will make the trip in chains. If you managed to escape, they know who you are. They will decide you are working with Jayden, charge you as a traitor. They will put a bounty on your head. One that will have half the world looking for you. You have been able to escape attention while living here only because you are currently of no value to anyone."

Arbin realized what Alex was saying was true. *I got no choice right now,* he thought. *Better safe than sorry, but I got to be really careful what I share.* Arbin turned to Alex and said, "All right, but how can I show you how to track a Fade without one to track."

Alex smiled and said, "Tell us what you know. What are we doing wrong?"

Arbin said, "Well, there are a few things I can tell you."

Alex smiled and said, "Great. I want Lubin to hear this too. Now that you have decided to help us, I will see about finding you someplace to stay and something to eat."

Arbin followed Alex as he headed toward camp and thought about that last statement by Alex. *What was he going to do if I had not agreed to help him?*

ARBIN HAD NOT BEEN back in the caravan camp since they had released him. He had spent time looking at the camp from afar. Now, as he walked through the camp, he realized this was a living place. It was a collection of tents and wagons, each gathered around campfires. Most of the tents were much larger than Arbin remembered. Many were decorated, some with banners, others with clothing. Now that the events of the night were over, those campfires had people gathered around them. Some dressed in colorful clothes, others in uniforms. Very few even stopped their conversations to notice Arbin and Alex as they walked past.

"This is it," said Alex, pointing to one of three tents and a wagon clustered around an unlit fire pit. "Father Schafer uses one and we use the others. The wagon holds his supplies." Alex pulled back the tent flap and said, "I share this with Lubin. Go in."

Arbin entered and looked around. The tent was almost like the ones he had been in earlier. There were two cots, a small folding table and two small folding chairs. It was lit by a small lantern hanging off one of the poles supporting the tent. Lubin, who was lying on one of the cots, sat up and pointed to a chair. Arbin tossed his bag on the floor next to it and had a seat.

Alex, who was still standing at the tent entrances, said to Lubin, "Arbin agreed to help us." He turned to Arbin and said, "I will see about getting you someplace to stay. When I get back, you can tell us how to deal with Jayden."

The tent flap closed, and Arbin and Lubin sat in silence. Arbin looked around the tent, not sure what to say. He spotted small buckler shields and strange looking skinny clubs leaning against small chests at the foot of each cot. A simple half dome helmet sat on each chest.

"What's with the stick?" asked Arbin.

Lubin looked over toward the club and said, "They do not allow Seers to carry weapons. That is supposed to represent a torch, as he pointed to the crest on his tunic hanging on the back of the other chair."

"Captain Eustace lets us carry these when we are on guard duty. Sometimes we do have to carry real torches. We have a real fancy one we use for ceremonies."

"I guess that makes sense," said Arbin. "Looks kind of heavy."

"You get used to it," said Lubin. "The thing I really hate is this helmet." Lubin held up one of the half dome helmets. Arbin could see it was designed to be held on with a strap. "It's this bit of cloth that hangs down in the back that bothers me. Plus, the stupid thing keeps sliding off to one side. The Shadow Guards get to wear proper helms. This one looks like they made it for a girl." He gave the helmet a toss, and it landed with a soft thump on top of the chest.

An uncomfortable silence returned. Arbin could feel Lubin's eyes on him. He knew that the Seers did not trust him and probably blamed him for their being demoted to support duties. Arbin looked around for something else to talk about and saw Lubin's tunic. It reminded him of the difference in Seer uniforms he noticed before. He was glad to be able to ask a question that really interested him. Arbin pointed to the tunic and asked, "What's with the colors on the edges of the tunics?"

Lubin looked over at his tunic and said, "That is how you tell our ranks. When someone joins the Seer Core, we consider them pledged, a First Year we call them. If you make it past a year, you become a Third Rank, get green trim and can start using the title of Seer. Second Ranks get to add red trim. If you get promoted to First Rank, you get to add gold trim. After that, it's the big man. The High Seer."

Arbin remembered Alex had only green and red trim and said, "I would have thought Alex was a First Rank since he appears to be in charge."

"It's hard to make First Rank," Lubin looked around, smiled then said, "You have to know someone important or someone has to die before you can get it." Lubin laid back on his cot with his hands behind his head and said, "I am happy where I am. Last thing I want is all the headaches that come with being in charge. Just look at Alex. This whole Fade thing has got him stressed out. I told him we would get blamed for anything that goes wrong no matter what we do. They have done it before, and they are doing it again."

Alex entered the tent and looked at Lubin and Arbin. "You two getting along okay?" he asked as he made his way to the empty cot. He took off his tunic, folded it and placed it on the chest at the foot of the cot and sat down.

Lubin said, "We were just talking about how we are getting blamed for everything again."

"That will change soon," said Alex, looking at Arbin. "Now that Arbin has agreed to help us fight this Fade."

Lubin sat up and said, "Okay, tell us how we fight your old buddy."

"Be nice Lubin and listen up," said Alex. He turned back to Arbin and said, "Let's start with some basic stuff. Something that will help us right away."

Arbin shifted in his chair. He was not sure what would be safe to share, but he would have to give something. He looked at the two Seers waiting there. After a few seconds he said, "Okay, first you got to understand how the Fade Talent works. They do not step into and out of shadows, or anything like that. It is simple, really. A Fade just convinces you not to see them."

"Are you saying they can become invisible?" asked Lubin.

"No, nothing like that," said Arbin. "When they are in the Fade you will choose not to look in their direction or pay attention to them in a crowd. A better way of saying it is you ignore them."

"That's it?" asked Alex. "What about all that talk about shadows or stains?"

Arbin laughed and said, "It's like I told you. If you stay in a Fade too long, the power used to Fade becomes associated with a place. Mostly to living objects such as trees, plants and such."

"Could that have happened outside the house where the Duke was killed?" asked Lubin. "Maybe that could explain how the other killers got into the house."

"The effect does not last very long and lots of things can prevent them from being used that way," said Arbin.

"So, what can we do to overcome the effects of the Fade?" asked Alex. "If he can force us to ignore him, how do we fight him?"

"By understanding the weakness of the Fade," said Arbin. "The biggest problem a Fade has is blending in. If the Fade is acting in a threatening manner, or in a way not normal for the surrounding, he will stand out more. That is why Fades don't wear armor or carry swords or other large weapons. They do their best to blend in."

"That's a little helpful," said Lubin. "I guess that is how he got so close. He looked like everyone else."

"The other weakness is the longer you are around a Fade the harder it is for him to be ignored," said Arbin. "You will notice a person you already know."

"So, what you are saying is your ability to detect Jayden is better than ours because you spent so much time with him," said Alex.

Arbin smiled. *Could not have come up with a better lie myself,* he thought. Arbin yawned and said, "I think that's a good place to stop for now."

"This has been helpful, Arbin," said Alex. "I agree we should stop for now. Lubin and I have a lot to think about."

"I have one more question," said Lubin.

"Okay, what is it?" asked Arbin.

"How could you be friends with such an evil person?" asked Lubin.

The question made Arbin uncomfortable. He hated talking about his past. Alex saw Arbin's hesitation and said, "You do not need to answer that if you do not want to."

"No, it's okay." Arbin took a deep breath and said, "I was involved with his sister. Jayden and his sister took me in when I was going through a bad time. We traveled together, almost like a family." He paused for a few seconds more and then said, "Plus, we did not really know we were supposed to hate each other. In fact, we learned from each other. There were lots of times we disagreed, but I never considered him as an evil person."

"Not evil!" said Lubin. "Look what he's done. He even tried to kill you."

"That is true," said Arbin. "If you asked him, he might even say I deserved it. Jayden would always give a justification for the crazy things he did. I do not know how he would ever justify attacking the Duke."

"Evil does Evil. Fades are destined to act according to their nature," said Alex. He looked at Arbin and saw his last comment bothered him and said, "That's enough for now. Father Schafer said he will give you some blankets and rations. The food will be cold, but it will do for now. You should be able to make a spot near his wagon. We will do our best to find a better spot later."

"Outside?" said Arbin. "You want me to sleep outside, under a wagon?"

"The weather is good, and that is the best we can do for now," said Alex. "Oh, and there will not be a guard on you now since you have agreed to help us."

No guards, thought Arbin. *Do I stay or go?*

"Remember what I told you," said Alex. "I am not the only one interested in you. Run and you will make someone an extraordinarily rich person."

"Point taken," said Arbin, as he followed Alex out of the tent.

Chapter 8 - Homeward Bound

THE JOURNEY SO FAR had been slow, hot and involved a lot of walking. They had assigned Arbin to a wagon filled with furniture and pulled by oxen. There was no room to ride on it, so he had to walk alongside. The wagon was almost at the rear of the caravan which meant that he had to deal with the dust and droppings from the ones ahead of him. The wagon came with its own guards. Two of Duke Henry's men. Arbin was actually glad to be stuck with them instead of Shadow Guards. Word had gotten out that he was in the area when Duke Henry was killed. He had not seen the Duke's killer in the caravan, but that did not mean the killer was not looking for Arbin.

The caravan had finally made a rest stop and Arbin was trying to get in a nap while he could. He had found a shady spot and was on the edge of drifting off to sleep when he heard the boy speak.

"Did it burn when you touched the demon?"

Arbin opened one eye and saw a young boy about eight years old staring at him. At first, he was not sure if it was a dream or if the boy was even talking to him. He closed his eye, took a deep breath, and opened it again. The boy was still there, standing about ten feet from him. He was well dressed and stood in a way that showed he was comfortable talking to adults.

"Did it hurt when you fought the demon?" the boy asked again.

Arbin had both eyes open now. He had heard the question, but the meaning seemed to elude him. After a few seconds, Arbin realized that his mouth was open. He closed it, sat up straight, stretched and said, "What are you talking about, kid?"

The boy took a few steps closer, studying Arbin. In a softer voice he said, "They told me you are the one that fought with the demon that killed my Father."

This young child could only be Dylan, son of Henry Sumner. Arbin had heard people talk about him but had never seen him. The wagon Dylan traveled in was somewhere further ahead. Arbin stared at Dylan, not sure what to say.

Dylan walked a little closer to Arbin and after a few seconds said in a serious and mature voice, "I was told a Fade killed my Father. A demon disguised as a man. A creature able to evade discovery by our best Seers. I was also told that you are the only person to fight him and live. I plan to hunt down and kill this demon. What I want to know from you is, did it burn when you touched it?"

"I am sorry about your father," Arbin said. "Losing a parent is very painful. I know. I lost my mother when I was about your age." When Arbin saw that his words had no effect on Dylan, he said, "I do not know who you have been talking to, but you need to believe me when I say, the man I fought was not a demon. He was an ordinary man, just like me."

Dylan said, "My Uncle Jessup said my father was a skilled fighter. My uncle trained him personally in close combat. There is no way an ordinary man killed my father." Dylan looked at Arbin, then at the guard sitting close to him and said in a disappointed voice, "You are right, I do not believe you fought the demon that killed my father."

Before Arbin could reply he felt a sharp pain in the back of his neck followed by a wave of nausea. Arbin steadied himself with one arm as his horizon shifted slowly to the left. He closed his eyes and tried to fight the dizziness. Arbin heard a woman's voice calling for Dylan. He opened his eyes and saw an attractive young woman, about his age, nicely dressed, with auburn shoulder length hair and bright blue eyes, walking up to Dylan. She scolded Dylan for leaving the area of his wagon.

As she talked, Arbin's dizziness increased. She sent Dylan away, then turned to say something to Arbin. The urge to throw up made it hard to focus on her. From her expression, he guessed she was telling him to stay away from Dylan. Arbin stood up, fighting the dizziness and the urge to get sick. He raised his hand to acknowledge her and walked away. He only got about ten feet before he threw up.

The young woman turned away from Arbin in disgust and looked at the guards still sitting on the ground. One of them just shrugged.

Arbin continued to stagger away from the woman and the guards, looking for a better place to be sick. When he got to the next wagon, he felt much better. He looked back towards his wagon and was glad to find the young woman gone. He found a small wooden bucket hanging on the side of the wagon with some rainwater still in it, so he splashed it on his face. The water was colder than he expected and felt good. Arbin stood up straight, took a deep breath and was relieved that the dizziness was gone. "It must be the heat. I need to make sure I'm drinking enough water," he said, mostly to reassure himself.

During his journey, Arbin spent most of his time looking down. Now that he was on a break and did not have to worry about where he stepped, he took the time to look at his surroundings. This was the second day with the caravan. They had been traveling for the past few hours through a light forest that was now thickening. He had never been this way before, and the area was not familiar. The sun told him they were heading north, which meant the river was to his left, somewhere beyond the forest. How far he did not know. From what he had been told, it would take them another two full days to reach the Capital. He guessed the forest ahead offered his best chance of slipping away. He looked back at the guards sitting by the wagon he was with and thought, *I wonder how fast a man in armor can run? Even if I could outrun them, there are the bowmen and guards on horseback to deal with.* Arbin looked back out at the woods, and Alex's warning about a price on his head made them look less appealing. *I am sure there will be a better time to make an escape. I only hope there is still some time for a nap before we start out again.* As Arbin thought about how to make that last idea happen, he felt an old familiar sensation. His body stiffened, and he said, "Jayden!" quietly to himself.

Arbin forced himself to look in the direction that gave him the most resistance and saw Jayden standing beside a set of bushes that Arbin had been looking at a few minutes ago. Arbin and Jayden stood there looking at each other. Neither making a move to attack or run.

This was the first time Arbin had seen Jayden in the daylight in eight years. It was the same Jayden, but a little taller and a little thinner. He still had the same dark black hair and brown eyes as his sister, but Jayden's eyes were never as wide open as Mia's. His eyes had always seemed to be on the edge of a scowl. Except today they looked softer and there was a trace of a smile on his face, more like a snicker.

Arbin did not see a knife in Jayden's hand, but he shifted his weight so he could dodge if Arbin tried to attack. Arbin could normally tell when Jayden would charge or attack. The last face off they had, back on the docks, Jayden caught him off guard. Arbin would not make that same mistake. He studied Jayden for any suggestion he would attack but did not see any.

What is he waiting for? thought Arbin. Just when it looked like Jayden would say something, someone behind him yelled, "Hey you, where do you think you are going?" Arbin turned and saw one of his wagon guards heading his way. "You're not supposed to leave off on your own. You know that. Back with you" said the guard, pointing toward the wagon.

Arbin looked back in Jayden's direction expecting to see him charging at him but was surprised to see he had gone.

"I guess you are good for something," said Arbin as he walked past the guard toward their wagon. *Jayden, you can really carry a grudge.* he thought. *Who are you after now? Must be me.* Arbin did not want to face Jayden and any of his new friends alone. The Captain had assigned Alex and the other Seers to wagons just like him. *They are probably scattered throughout the caravan,* he thought. Arbin imagined that most of the Shadow Guard would be around Dylan's wagon, which he believed would be closer to the front of the caravan, so that is the direction he headed. He continued to walk past his wagon and its other guard, who was comfortably leaning against a wagon wheel.

"Hey" said the guard a few times before getting to his feet. Arbin ignored him and kept walking. The guard who had been following Arbin stopped at the wagon, and the two guards looked at each other.

Arbin was not running but was walking at a quick pace. It surprised him how quickly both guards caught up with him. One of them stopped Arbin by grabbing his arm and asked, "Where are you going?"

Arbin pulled his arm loose from the guard's grip and said, "The Fade is in the forest over there. I'm going somewhere safer."

The two guards looked around as Arbin walked off, heading in the direction he hoped would take him to Dylan's wagon. One of the guards shouted after him, "Hey, come back here. We're supposed to stay here and guard this wagon."

Arbin looked back and said, "Good luck with that," and continued walking. As he walked, he did a quick check and could no longer feel the effects of Jayden's Fade behind him. Arbin knew that Jayden was not one to give up easily, so he kept walking.

EVERY YEAR ARBIN WATCHED as small groups traveled passed by Noor Point on the way to the Capital to enjoy the Annual Unification Celebration. This year was the Sesquicentennial Celebration, and the numbers of people on the road surprised Arbin. Each little country road that joined the Capital road brought more travelers, many mixing in with the caravan as it traveled. The forest along the roadway at this point was still sparse, and there was a grassy area on both sides. Now that the caravan was taking a break, many of the travelers joined them. The caravan had split up into small clusters, with wagons finding places on either side of the roadway. Arbin felt strange as he and a few diehard travelers wandered along the trail through the collection of resting wagons. It reminded Arbin of walking through the campsite back in Noor Point.

As he made his way towards where he hoped Dylan was, he passed two Seers who just watched as he walked by. He thought about stopping but remembered that only Alex and Lubin had Talents.

It did not take long before he reached a cluster of wagons with one large gold trimmed carriage. The collection of Shadow Guards standing around and several people busily doing things nearby made it clear he had found Dylan. Arbin scanned the group, looking for someone he might know. Someone he could talk to about Jayden. Sitting near the back of the gold trimmed carriage was the pretty young woman who had come for Dylan. He was relieved to see Alex standing nearby, talking to a couple of Shadow

Guards. Arbin could tell Alex was having a serious discussion with the man that he now knew was Sergeant Gruber. This was the same unpleasant person he has seen with Hans, speaking to Captain Eustace during their meeting in the guest house.

Arbin called to Alex, who signaled for Arbin to join him. As Arbin got closer to the carriage, he felt a slight dizziness again. Alex noticed and asked, "You okay?"

Arbin nodded and said, "A little tired."

Sergeant Gruber asked, "What are you doing here?" At first Arbin thought he was talking to him, but soon realized he was talking to his wagon guards who he now saw had followed him.

"He said the Fade is here, Sergeant," said one of the guards, pointing to Arbin.

"Where?" asked Alex as he looked around. "Is he still here?"

Sergeant Gruber made an expression of surprise followed quickly by anger and said to Alex, "You're asking him if the Fade is still here? You just finished telling me how important it was for me to station your people with Dylan, and now you're asking this fool if the enemy is near!"

Arbin ignored the Sergeant and said to Alex, "He was back by my wagon. I lost him shortly after I left the area, but I am sure he is still out there."

"How do you know?" asked Alex, also doing his best to ignore the Sergeant's comments.

"Because I know him. He has no problem with waiting and watching," replied Arbin.

"Seer Keller!" said the Sergeant. "I need you to do your job and tell me if there is actually any danger here!"

Alex closed his eyes and took a deep breath. Arbin stared at Alex and thought, *what is he doing?*

"I do not detect the Fade right now," said Alex after a few minutes of silence. "However, this man has detailed knowledge of him. I suggest you take this report seriously, even if it came from him."

Arbin continued to stare at Alex, surprised to see him trying to detect Jayden the same way you would detect a Seer. It was then that he understood how little these Seers knew about hunting Fades. *This will make things a lot easier*, he thought.

Sergeant Gruber studied Arbin for a few seconds, then said to the other guard, "Sound the alarm. Make sure we protect Dylan." Turning to Arbin's guards, he said, "You two return to your post! Sound off if you hear or see anything but stay at your post! Is that clear?"

"Yes, Sergeant," said the guards as they turned and headed back the way they came. They moved at a slower and more cautious pace.

Sergeant Gruber was not happy with the response from his man and shouted, "Form Up! Move it, Move it!" When that did not get him the results he wanted, he shouted again, "What is this your first day? Move it! We have a Fade to fight!"

One of the men asked, "How do we form up without a Seer to form around?"

"Pretend you have one, just like we will pretend like you didn't ask that question," said Sergeant Gruber, shaking his head.

The Shadow Guards quickly formed into four small groups of three. One man in each group was equipped with a bow and sword. The others with round shields and swords. They positioned themselves as best they could around Dylan's wagon.

Alex turned to Sergeant Gruber and said, "You need to let my men join the fight. You have no need for them as drivers now."

Sergeant Gruber said, "Until the Captain returns from scouting ahead, I have strict instructions that all wagons are to be manned and ready to move out if needed. That means you two need to be on your way."

Alex said, "This is stupid! You do not understand what you are up against."

Sergeant Gruber said, "Orders are orders," as he turned and walked away.

Alex walked in the direction Arbin had come from. As he passed Arbin he said, "Let's go!"

Arbin watched him walk past but did not follow. He really did not feel well and was finding it hard to concentrate. He felt like he would get sick again. He looked around and saw the young woman from before staring at him. *Great, I am sure she is thinking pleasant things about me.* Arbin heard

Alex calling him. He looked up and gave Alex a nod and started walking toward him.

"Something wrong?" Alex asked as Arbin joined him. "We got things to do."

Arbin said, "I don't know. I might be getting sick. I threw up earlier, just before I detected Jayden."

After walking far enough to be out of the view of Sergeant Gruber, Alex stopped. He turned to Arbin and said, "It's time for you to continue your training. First, we need to get Lubin."

"You want to go after Jayden?" Arbin asked. "Where is your shield and that stupid stick? How are you going to fight him?"

"Padded jackets will have to do for now," said Alex. "Besides, I do not want to fight him as much as I want to scare him off. It's our chance to show we can defend against a Fade."

"What, only the three of us?" asked Arbin. "Without weapons, what is to stop him from coming after us?"

"You're still convinced that he is after you?" asked Alex.

"Duke Henry is dead, and I detected him near me. Who else could he be after? I'm the one he has a grudge with," said Arbin.

"Okay, we use that to our advantage," said Alex. "If he sees you protected by a couple of Seers, he will not be so eager to attack. If I can talk some wagon guards into helping, we should be able to discourage him enough that maybe he will leave."

"Look, I do not want to be mean, but Jayden is smart enough to see what I have seen. You and the others are having trouble stopping him," said Arbin.

"What's with you?" Alex said angrily to Arbin. "I am disobeying an order to do this. That could get me discharged from the Seer Core. You do nothing to help us or yourself. Have you forgotten what he did to you? He burned down your home and now he's hunting you."

"I gave the alert about Jayden," Arbin said, a little embarrassed at making it sound like something brave.

"Yes, you let the dogs loose," said Alex. "Do you think that will be enough to protect you? Face it, your friend has joined the Adelist Movement. Do you think we can fight both Jayden and the Adelist? It's my guess Jayden is here scouting, like back at the village. If we do not show that we can defend against him, we will not make the Capital without being attacked."

Arbin realized what Alex was saying made sense. He had seen how determined Jayden could be in the past. He knew little about the Adelist, but if the Duke's killer was working for them, he understood how ruthless they could be. "I can teach them a few things, but these Seers will never detect him as well as I can," Arbin whispered to himself.

"I agree!" said Alex. "You made the right choice. Let's go get Lubin and a few guards. You can decide on how best to prepare us."

Arbin looked up, startled by Alex's response. *That is a habit I must break before it gets me in big trouble*, he thought. It was too late to take back his words. He nodded and reluctantly said, "Let's go."

THEY FOUND LUBIN SLEEPING on a cot under the shade of the forest. Lubin had been assigned to the wagon belonging to Father Schafer. The wagon did not have a guard because they believed no one would attack a wagon that belonged to the Church.

Lubin sat on the edge of his cot, listening as Alex explained what was happening. They were soon joined by Father Schafer, who insisted on being a part of whatever they decided to do. Alex rejected Lubin's suggestion that they should follow the Sergeant's instructions or at least wait for Captain Eustace to get back. Alex said, "We need to do something now, while we have the chance to do it our way." Lubin finally agreed and Alex turned to Arbin and said, "Okay, time for you to tell us how we will deal with Jayden."

Arbin looked at the group, waiting for him to give some great words of wisdom. He was angry with Jayden, but deep down knew he did not want to see him killed. Arbin knew he had to do something and working with this group looked like his best choice. Arbin looked around at the woods they were standing in and said, "I dislike talking in the woods where someone could be hiding." He walked over to the nearby wagon and was followed by the others. He looked around to make sure no one was near and said, "First, understand that you will never detect him like you do another Seer."

"Are you saying we cannot detect him?" asked Lubin.

"No, I am just saying you need to remember that he is a Fade and not a Seer," said Arbin.

"Okay," said Lubin. "I cannot believe I am saying this, but how do we detect a Fade?"

"We focus on detecting the affects of the Fade," said Arbin. "Also, a Fade has a limited range and requires a lot of concentration to maintain. Those are the two key points to consider when you are dealing with a Fade."

"I still do not understand how we will detect him if he is forcing us to ignore him," said Lubin.

"We will play something like the game I used to play with Jayden. The purpose of a Fade is to discourage you from paying attention to a person. Think of it as an urge not to look in a certain direction. What you need to do is learn to detect the urge. It is difficult but can be done. You can even learn to resist the urge. If we spread out while searching, we should be able to point toward the area that gives the most resistance. Once we have a direction, we send someone to beat the bushes. When Jayden knows we have discovered him, it will break his concentration. He will either attack or run."

"Let's hope he runs," said Lubin. "That still means we need someone to beat the bushes."

"I can do that," said Father Schafer.

"No Father," said Alex. "I would appreciate it if you could convince others to assist us. If we cannot get soldiers, maybe we can convince some travelers on the road to assist us."

"I will do my best," replied Father Schafer.

"And Father," said Alex. "Please do not say what Jayden is. We can say we are searching for someone that may be a threat to young Dylan."

Father Schafer told the group to wait while he dug around in his wagon and pulled out two large candlesticks. He gave one to Alex and one to Lubin saying, "I do not have any swords, but this would be a decent replacement for your clubs." He opened a large box and unwrapped a cross on a short pole. He said, "It's time for that Fade to face our true defender!"

By the time the small group had reached Arbin's wagon, they had collected three men armed with knives. The guards at Arbin's wagon were quite surprised to see the small group approaching. Arbin had to admit it must have been an impressive site to see the determined group walking with Father Schafer and his cross leading the way.

Arbin asked the guards to join them, but they refused. "We are to guard the area and call out if we saw the Fade," they said. Just when Arbin had given up, Father Schafer said, "We understand. That is valuable cargo you are guarding, and I applaud your decision to protect it from the Fade alone." A few minutes later the small group, including the two guards, were ready to search for Jayden.

"What next?" asked Alex.

Lubin said, "I would suggest we place a group on each side of the caravan and do a sweep of both sides. If one group finds something, they call for the other."

"It would be better if we stayed in a line," said Arbin. "Lubin takes up a position at the front of the line, Alex to the rear, and I stay in the middle with Father Schafer and the others. If we have distance between us, we can get a better idea on the direction to send the men to beat the bushes."

"Agreed," said Alex. "We start at the end of the caravan and walk to the front. If we find nothing, we head to the rear again. How much space should we have between us?"

"If I remember, the most Jayden could project a Fade was about twenty-five feet," said Arbin.

Alex said, "That's all, well I guess we should keep about fifteen feet between us. Arbin, since you are the best at detection, if anyone detects him, we keep moving until he is closest to you. Then Lubin and I will close in on you until the three of us are pointing at the same location."

Lubin turned to Father Schafer and said, "Father, please try to recruit more people."

Father Schafer said, "God will provide."

The small group walked toward the last wagon where they spread out as planned. Alex, Arbin and Lubin stood, with eyes closed, concentrating on detecting Jayden's Fade. Next, they moved until Alex was at the spot where Lubin last stood. Then they would stop and repeat their search.

It must have given the impression to passers-by that the group was part of a religious procession, possibly a blessing of the caravan. As they continued walking toward the front of the caravan, the group picked up a few additional people. The party was about three wagons away from the area of Dylan's wagon and its Shadow Guards, when Arbin raised his hand and pointed out into the nearby brush. Just as planned, Lubin and Alex moved toward Arbin until all three were pointing toward the same area.

Father Schafer turned to the group and said that someone who wanted to hurt young Dylan was hiding some place in the bushes. He asked the group to take arms and find him. A group of seven armed men walked in the direction that the Seers were pointing.

"There, over there, get him!" came a shout from the small group searching the area.

Arbin watched as the group searched through the bushes with the two guards swinging their swords. "I think we need to call the crowd back before Jayden gets around us," Arbin said, "Remember, they do not know how to resist the Fade. I am sure he has moved by now."

Father Schafer called the crowd back, congratulating them on scaring off the threat. There was some cheering, and curses were directed at the coward in the bushes by the group of men. None of them knew they were chasing a Fade.

Alex said, "I think it would be best if we disband this group and set up a defense closer to Dylan."

Lubin agreed and said, "Now that we know it works, we can use the Shadow Guards."

Arbin thanked the two guards and sent them back to their post. "I do not want you to get in more trouble," he said. They looked at each other and headed back toward their wagon, looking out at the brush and woods to their right as if expecting to see the person they just chased.

Arbin watched them leave and wondered where Jayden had gone. *That was too easy,* he thought. Just as Arbin was going to speak with Alex, he heard sounds of horses coming from the front of the caravan. Arbin turned and saw Captain Eustace and three Shadow Guard on horses heading in their direction. They had just returned from scouting and were attracted to the noise from the crowd.

Captain Eustace looked around at the group and said, "What's going on here?"

There was some nervous chatter until Captain Eustace shouted, "Quiet!" He looked at the group, then to Alex, and said to him, "Explain!"

Father Schafer turned to Captain Eustace and said, "We have just chased off a demon Fade with the help of these good people and the direction of these gifted Seers." As Father Schafer finished his statement, there were expressions of surprise and fear from the men gathered there. Father Schafer turned to the crowd and said, "Have no fear, you have done the work of God today and you were under his protection."

Captain Eustace looked at Alex and said, "How long ago?"

Father Schafer pointed to the area where the group had just searched and said, "Just now, but these brave people chased it away."

"Father, please," said the Captain. He looked at Alex and said, "Well, report!"

"Arbin detected the Fade and reported it," Alex answered. "The Shadow Guards took up defensive positions around Dylan while Seer Lubin, Arbin and I deployed a tactic developed by Arbin to detect and attack the Fade. We detected him in the brush just over there. We were just successful in driving him off and were heading toward Dylan's carriage to prepare for a possible attack there."

Captain Eustace turned to one of the shadow guards with him and pointed to the brushes. The guard removed his short bow and sent a few arrows into the bushes and the surrounding area beyond. After a few shots, the Captain turned to Father Schafer and said, "Return to your wagon and send these people on their way." He turned back to Alex and said, "I will see you three at Dylan's carriage." He turned to his guards and said, "Stay here, watch this flank," then turned and rode away.

Alex and Lubin returned the candlesticks to Father Schafer, thanked him for his help. As they headed off for their meeting with Captain Eustace, Arbin could see that they were in a good mood, excited over what had just happened.

I should have known something would go wrong, thought Arbin as he fell in behind them. *Every time I try to do the right thing, I get in trouble. This* was not my fault. They forced me into this. I will keep quiet and let them take the blame.

AS ARBIN, ALEX AND Lubin approached the area of Dylan's carriage, they could see Captain Eustace and Sergeant Gruber standing next to it. The Sergeant was standing straight as a board and doing most of the speaking while Captain Eustace stood casually listening. The Captain saw the group approaching and signaled for them to stay where they were. Arbin looked at Alex and said, "I do not think this will go well."

Alex said, "Captain Eustace can be hard but is fair. I think he will see the value of what we have done. The Sergeant is the one you need to worry about. I have known the Captain to leave discipline to him. The Seers do not technically report to the Sergeant, so I think we are safe from that."

Sergeant Gruber looked over at Arbin before saluting the Captain and walking away. Captain Eustace signaled for the group to join him. As Arbin approached, he felt strange again.

Alex noticed that Arbin was looking uncomfortable and said, "Whatever you do, please do not throw up on the Captain."

Arbin smiled but quickly regretted it as he heard Captain Eustace say, "You think what you did was funny?"

Not knowing what to say, Arbin just looked down.

Captain Eustace turned to Alex and said, "Sergeant Gruber tells me that after the Fade was reported he instructed you both to return to your wagons, is that true."

"I wanted to have my men assist with protecting Dylan from the Fade," said Alex. "Sergeant Gruber would not allow that."

"Sergeant Gruber was following my orders, which is something I expect you to do as well!" said Captain Eustace.

"Captain, you told me to continue to work on ways to defend against the Fade," said Alex. "Well, we just did that. It's like I said, Arbin was the key to helping us understand what we were doing wrong. This new method of fighting the Fade works!"

"I did not tell you to disobey orders, or apply any alternate methods without permission," said Captain Eustace. "I understand that you want to help, but there is a reason why we do things. Your actions could have gotten you and your small group killed. It could have even caused a bigger problem if it caused us to weaken the defense on Dylan to save you."

"Sorry Captain, I did not think about that," said Alex. "But you have to agree that we were able to scare off the Fade."

"So you say, Seer Keller," said Captain Eustace. "Did anyone ever see the Fade, or are we relying only on the word of Arbin again?"

"I felt him this time, Captain. So did Lubin. Plus, the group chased someone in the bushes," said Alex. "Everything was just like Arbin said it would be. There is no doubt in my mind that this Fade is real."

"You misunderstood me, Seer Keller," said Captain Eustace. "I believe that Fades existed. I was also ready to accept that a Fade was involved in the Attack on Duke Henry. I just believed that there was a greater threat."

Arbin saw a slight look of satisfaction on Alex's face.

"It may surprise you, but I have given a lot of thought to how I would use a Fade," said Captain Eustace. "It appears the rebels, and I were thinking in the same way."

Arbin had done his best to look uninterested in the conversation but could not help but react with surprise at hearing the Captain of the Shadow Guards talking about how he would use a Fade.

Captain Eustace saw Arbin's expression and said, "Know your enemy!" Next, he turned to Alex and asked, "Where is this Fade now?"

"We lost him, but if you give me a few men, we can start looking for him."

"For now, it's best if you return to your wagons," said Captain Eustace. "I am sure your Fade is not working alone. He is probably on his way to report what he has learned about us. If we are going to keep Dylan safe, I think it's time we got moving again."

"You said it was our job to find the Fades so you could fight them, well now we can," said Alex. "This Fade knows we can detect him now. The best way to keep Dylan safe is for him to see us protecting him."

Captain Eustace could see that Alex would not let this go until he said his piece. He walked over and sat on a nearby crate and said, "You will explain this new method to me, and I will decide if and when we use it."

Alex turned to Arbin and said, "I want you to tell the Captain what you told us about Fades and about how we detected him."

Arbin did his best to explain things, but Captain Eustace's rapid questioning made him nervous. He was still having difficulty concentrating on the conversation. After several minutes of questioning, Captain Eustace stood up, straightened his uniform, then said, "Where you located this Fade confirms to me that Dylan is their next target." Captain Eustace looked out to the wooded area beyond the roadway and said, "If I understand you correctly, only you three have been trained in this new method."

"That's right," said Arbin. "Unfortunately, training additional Seers in this method would require the cooperation of a Fade. While the concepts are easy to understand, they are difficult to learn without real exposure to a Fade."

"I think with the threat against Dylan confirmed, it would be best if we took actions to get him to safety as soon as possible," said Captain Eustace. "The Capital is about a half day's hard ride. I will split up the caravan. Seer Keller, your men and Duke Henry's men will stay with the caravan. The Shadow Guard will escort Dylan to the city. You three will come with us. Go get your gear and report back here to Sergeant Gruber."

"Yes, sir," responded Alex and signaled with his hand for Arbin and Lubin to follow him as he turned to leave.

"Seer Keller," said Captain Eustace, pausing to make sure he had Alex's attention. "None of this, excuses your disobedience. I still intend to report you to Bishop Sorren when I see him."

ALEX, ARBIN AND LUBIN walked away from the area of Dylan's carriage in silence. After a few minutes Alex said to Lubin, "Get your gear and meet us back here. I want to speak to Arbin." Lubin nodded and headed off toward his wagon.

Now would be the perfect time to just slip away, thought Arbin as he hoped Alex would not follow him all the way back to his wagon. Alex appeared to be in deep thought as he walked beside Arbin. After several minutes of silence Arbin said, "Hey look, I am sorry you got in trouble."

Alex said, "Don't worry. What you do not understand is you have given the Seer Core what it needs to regain its proper place."

"So, you will not be in trouble?" asked Arbin.

"Oh, I am sure I will get yelled at. They may even demote me, but they cannot deny the value of what we have done. Do not worry about it. Since Lubin, you and I are the only ones that can use this new method, I think all their yelling will amount to nothing."

"That's good," replied Arbin. "But I still do not want to join your Seers Core. I'm not really a joiner and I dislike not being in control of my life."

"That's funny," said Alex. "The Seer Core is probably the one place where you would have the most control over your life based on who you are."

Arbin stopped, looked at Alex and asked, "What do you mean?"

Alex smiled and when he saw he had Arbin's attention said, "Back when we first met, you talked about you and Jayden. You said you watched Jayden running from us."

"Yeah, what about it?" asked Arbin.

"I watched you today. Did you see him today as well?" asked Alex.

Arbin started walking again, and Alex followed beside him. After a few seconds Arbin said, "Jayden has never been successful in using his Fade talent on me. I can quickly overcome it if needed."

"I suspected as much," said Alex, his smile growing. "That means you were really the one that found Jayden today. We were just along for show."

Arbin stopped, looked at Alex for a few seconds, then turned and continued to walk toward his wagon.

"Don't get me wrong. I did feel something and believe your method has value. We just need to figure out how to get better at it. In the meantime, I am happy to keep what happened between us."

Arbin stopped and said, "That still does not explain how being a Seer will give me control over my life."

"How much do you know about the history of the Fades and Seers during the civil war?"

Arbin shrugged and said, "Just your basic stuff. Fades killed lots of people until the Seers stopped them."

"Maybe you do not know this, but the Fades were stopped by three Seers with gifts greater than the other Seers," said Alex. "Those Seers where later referred to as High Seers and were the three original holders of the Family Chairs on the Governing Council."

"High Seers, Lubin mentioned them, First Rank Seer or something like that." said Arbin.

"That is a little different. We give the title of High Seer to the highest-ranking member of the Seer Core," said Alex. "The position is more ceremonial and administrative than anything. He is technically equal in rank to Captain Eustace, but in the field the Captain is in charge."

"That's nice, but what does it have to do with me?"

"I can tell you in private that the current High Seer is not even a Seer," said Alex.

"So, he is one of the people you talked about earlier, a faithful fake," said Arbin.

"Faithful Hopefuls," Alex said with a smile. "That's not what's important. It's what you have in common with the High Seers from history that should matter to you. I have done a lot of reading, and one of the main things I found is that they appeared immune to the powers of the Fades of that time."

"What do you want me to do? Walk in and take this guy's place? Be the new boss?"

"Nothing like that," said Alex, waving his hands slightly in front of him. "Nothing that dramatic. It's just over time people have forgotten about the true history of Seers and the evil they defeated. We have too long been a force without a foe. Now, with the return of a Fade, it's time to remind people that only true Seers can save them from the true evil. What I need you to do is help me make the Seer Core valuable again. Get back its honor."

"And how am I going to do that?" asked Arbin.

"I am not sure," said Alex as he started walking. "but you just need to trust me. After what we did today, you will have no problems getting through the approval process for the Seer Core. After that, no one will give you a hard time, and we can work together on regaining the lost knowledge of the True High Seers."

Arbin stood there looking at Alex as he walked ahead. It was the approval process that he was worried about. While he had Alex and Lubin fooled about his Talents, he was sure there would be something in that approval process that would expose who he was. "About that, what kinds of things should I expect?" asked Arbin.

Alex stopped and looked back at Arbin, chuckled a bit and said, "Don't worry, I will coach you what to say and do. The Application Committee for the Seer Core is a lot easier than the review board that my sister and I were questioned by when we were first brought to the Capital. We were both scared out of our minds," said Alex.

"You and your sister, why would your sister go before a review board? Is she a Seer too?" asked Arbin.

"No, thank goodness. We are twins and all twins must be examined to ensure they are not contaminated by the devil," said Alex. "They confirmed I was the only one with any gifts. That is a good thing because the Church says only men can receive the gifts. They say if a woman has a power, it comes from the devil, and both twins are to be put to death before the other twin can become corrupted as well."

Arbin had heard stories about twins being killed but did not fully understand the reason behind it. He thought about Mia. Her gifts were the same as Alex, and she was definitely not an evil person. In fact, she was the only thing keeping Jayden in line. *These people are really wrong about a lot of things,* he thought.

"That's enough for now," said Alex. "Go get your gear and meet me back at Dylan's carriage. We'll talk more later, but for now, keep this conversation to yourself."

Arbin stood there watching Alex walk away. He looked out into the forest and did a quick check for Jayden. He thought about his choices. He could not go back to Noor Point. It was clear he was not welcome there anymore. He did not have the supplies or the willpower to go back on the road. He had been able to fool these folks. Based on what he had learned about them, he might be able to do the same in the Capital. If things got scary, he would just leave.

Arbin quickly collected his bag and a few items of food off the wagon guards, who said they were grateful for his promise to forget about their involvement. As he approached Dylan's carriage, he found he was in a good mood. He spotted Alex talking to the woman he had met earlier today with Dylan. Alex gave her a hug before she turned and walked away.

"Girlfriend?" asked Arbin as he reached the group.

Alex looked a little confused then said, "Ah, no that is my sister, Elizabeth. She was traveling back to the Capital along with Lady Casandra. She had been working on something for her, and they became friends. Lady Casandra asked her to keep an eye on Dylan. But now that we are splitting up, she is staying with the original caravan to make room on Dylan's carriage for you."

"Me?" asked Arbin.

"Captain Eustace wants you to ride as escort on Dylan's carriage," said Alex. "Lubin and I will ride alongside on horses. That way we can spread out as needed if you detect Jayden. That is, if you're feeling up to it."

"I feel great and I will be more than happy not to be walking. Tell your sister thanks," said Arbin as he jumped into the space next to the driver's seat.

"You can tell her yourself," said Alex. "Since you do not have a place to stay, I got her to agree to let you stay at our place."

"Thanks, I really appreciate that." said Arbin.

"No problem," replied Alex. "When I told her, I would charge the Council for your room and board, she finally agreed, but she said you need to take a bath and get into some clean clothes before she arrives."

Chapter 9 - Unwelcome Blessing

"I'M SORRY, CAPTAIN, but you know that the Chairman doesn't allow weapons inside the house. If you please," said Jacob, pointing to an ornate chest just beside the door.

Captain Eustace looked at the elderly man standing in the doorway of Chairman Sumner's home. It was a face he was very familiar with. "Sorry, Jacob. I guess I was in a hurry to get young Dylan here and forgot," said Captain Eustace as he took off his sword and pistol and handed them to Jacob, who locked them in the chest. Captain Eustace straightened his uniform and said, "Thank you for sending word that Chairman Sumner had moved back into his home."

"He made the move shortly after you left," said Jacob. "We were expecting you and Master Dylan tomorrow. The Chairman is in a meeting with the other Family Chairs. If you give me your jacket and boots, I will freshen them up a bit before I announce you." While Jacob waited for the Captain to remove his jacket and shoes, he looked at young Dylan standing just beside the seated Captain and said, "We have a room already prepared for you, Master Dylan. Would you like something to eat before I show you to it?"

Dylan grabbed the sleeve of Captain Eustace's uniform and said, "Uncle Jessup, I want to stay with you."

"Remember what we talked about," said Captain Eustace as he put his hand on Dylan's. "You need to stop calling me uncle now. It does not mean I do not care about you, but once you become Heir to a Family Chair, it might confuse people."

"Yes, sir," Dylan said. He continued holding on to the sleeve until the Captain tapped his hand, stood and handed his jacket and shoes to Jacob.

Captain Eustace looked around at a place he had known since childhood, then said to Dylan, "You will like it here, I promise." He smiled and continued, "I used to enjoy visiting this house. I spent hours playing with your father in the large field out back. Besides, I will be busy trying to get the people that killed your father."

"That's what I want to do," said Dylan. "That should be my job as the Heir. Give me a weapon and I will hunt them too."

"I am sure you would be good at it, but I will really need your help to protect your mother once she arrives," said Captain Eustace. "I tell you what, I will start training you in using a weapon for self-defense. I might even let you learn how to use a pistol." Captain Eustace rubbed Dylan on the top of his head and said, "I am counting on you to show a strong face. Off to the kitchen with you."

Dylan nodded, gave the Captain a hug, and followed Jacob down the long hallway toward the kitchen.

As he watched him go, Captain Eustace thought about those days here with Henry. It was a simpler time when two young boys with wooden swords could solve the world's problems. This was also the place where he first met Casandra, who was promised to Henry at a young age.

Eustace was separated from his memories by the voice of Bishop Sorren calling to him, "Jessup, my son, good to see you. Where is young Dylan?"

"You just missed him," said Captain Eustace. "He is in the kitchen getting something to eat."

"How is he handling things?" asked Bishop Sorren.

"Better than I expected. He is a little too focused on revenge. He has interrogated several of my men and the Seers on the attack and is becoming somewhat of an expert on Fades. I am hoping he will find a different outlet for his grief when his mother gets here."

"He has been in my prayers," said Bishop Sorren.

Captain Eustace thanked the Bishop, then said, "I was a little surprised to hear Chairman Sumner was meeting so soon with the Family Chairs."

"He called the group together to inform them about Henry's death and to give them what information we have on the attackers," said Bishop Sorren. "The other Councilmen are worried for their own safety. Based on your reports, the Family Chairs are obviously the focus of the attacks."

"I agree," said Captain Eustace. "That is why I am surprised everyone is meeting here. The Chairman's office in the Government Building is much safer."

"Chairman Sumner does not want word of this meeting to get out," said Bishop Sorren. "He wants the time to speak with the others in a more casual environment. He is sure that Councilman Darr will use this attack as a reason for the Council to move toward joining the Alliance, to get their military support. He wants to see privately where the other Family Chairs stand."

Jacob returned with the Captain's boots and jacket. Captain Eustace sat on a chair near the door, and as Jacob helped him put on his boots, he looked up at Bishop Sorren and said, "I did not think the member states of the Alliance employed Shadow Guards or Seers."

"They don't," replied Bishop Sorren. "That is a point the Chairman wants to make. This is a threat that we are experienced in handling. We need no help on this."

Captain Eustace stood, rocked back and forth in his shoes a few times then said, "In that case it may be better if I discuss my finding in a less public setting because I am not sure if it would strengthen the Chairman's position,"

"What do you mean?" asked Bishop Sorren.

Captain Eustace said, "I did not include in my reports, the full extent of how unprepared and unsuccessful your Seers were in defending Henry from multiple attacks by the Adelist rebels or their Fade."

"Explain," said Bishop Sorren.

Jacob cleared his throat to get the attention of Captain Eustace and the Bishop.

Understanding the meaning of Jacob's interruption, Captain Eustace said, "That would take some time and I believe the Chairman and his guests are waiting, I will do my best to limit my responses in that area."

"Agreed," said Bishop Sorren. He paused, put his hand on Captain Eustace's shoulder briefly and said, "One word of warning. Otis is also attending the meeting."

"I guess that means food is being served," said Captain Eustace with a look of disgust.

"Step lightly, Jessup. He is my duly appointed High Seer. As such, I need you to show more respect for his office."

"I respect the work you do and understand the purpose of the office he holds," said Captain Eustace. "I just have difficulty understanding why he holds it. He has turned your Seers into parade fodder. Why would the Family Chairs want to consult with him?"

"The man is an authority on the events of the civil war, including the conflicts between Seers and Fades," said Bishop Sorren. "He has compiled most of the material we have on Fades. We often referred to his commentary during the development of our procedures."

"I will be the first to admit that I have more experience dealing with thugs, rebels and heretics than Fades," said Captain Eustace. "However, I just got a firsthand glimpse into that world and would be very interested in hearing how the High Seer's expertise compares to what I just experienced."

"I am sure the others are thinking along the same lines, but I am cautioning you again, keep it professional, not personal or I will be forced to defend my people," said Bishop Sorren in a somewhat serious tone.

"I am sorry, forgive me. I will take your advice to heart and I will do my best to act accordingly," said Captain Eustace in a sincere tone as he put on his jacket. He reached to position his missing pistol out of habit, forced a smile and said, "Let's go."

CAPTAIN EUSTACE ALWAYS liked the sunroom. It was a large space that ran almost the full width of the back of the house and was divided into three sections. A wide center section which led to a patio outside, and two small sections on either side, each with a small table and chairs. The whole sunroom was overflowing with plants of all sizes. As children, Captain Eustace and Henry had spent hours pretending to be hunting as they crawled through the jungle of potted plants. The sunroom was also the first place he ever kissed a girl.

As they quietly entered, Captain Eustace could see Chairman Sumner and the two other Family Chairs, Councilman Martin Kauffman and Councilman Herman Werner, sitting at a small table in one of the side sections. High Seer Otis Kindermann was standing nearby, picking at the food put out for the meeting. The Bishop pointed to a spot in the other side section where they could listen to the meeting without interfering.

"This is not like the last time," Kauffman said. "If the reports are true, we may need to take more serious action."

"I agree," said Werner. "Councilman Darr may be right, we may need more help in putting down this group."

"The only thing Councilman Darr wants to put down is this Council," replied Chairman Sumner. "Councilman Darr and these supporters of the Adelist Movement are both arguing for the return to aristocratic governance. The only true difference between them is who they want for the ruler."

"We are under the rule of Emperor Charles," said Kauffman. "I cannot see how what Councilman Darr wants will change that?"

"To this point, Charles has let the nations within the Empire manage themselves as long as we send him tribute and make public pledges of support. If we join the Alliance as Darr wants, it will reduce us to handing local issues while the Alliance's Council of Nobles decides how best to manage our military and financial resources. They would also be the ones voting for the next Emperor if needed. This Alliance was not Charles' idea, but one being forced on him by his advisers as a counter to never ending threats by his kin. Follow Darr and we lose everything," said Chairman Sumner, rapping his fist on the table with each of those last few words.

"I think you are exaggerating things, Chairman," said Kauffman. "I agree with Councilman Darr that the likelihood of a war between the houses is growing. Joining the Alliance may soon be our best option."

"Gentlemen, we have a battle at our doorstep in case you have forgotten," said Chairman Sumner. "One that threatens your very lives. There is always a likelihood of war between the houses. I need to make sure we agree on how we are to address this current problem before we look for more trouble."

"That brings us back to my original point," said Kauffman. "This is not like the last time we dealt with rebels. The report said they were successful in recruiting a Fade. It has been centuries since we had to face the evil of Fades. Have you forgotten the chaos and death of that time?"

"Once again, I agree," said Werner. "I think we need to discuss this at a full meeting of the Council."

"Herman, we are the Council," said Chairman Sumner, doing his best to keep the frustration from his voice. "As long as we are on the same page, the Family Chairs cannot be outvoted."

"Your Honors," said High Seer Otis Kindermann.

The group, surprised at his interruption, turned to look at him. "You have something to add, High Seer?" asked Chairman Sumner, glad for the break in the direction the conversation was going.

"Thank you, Chairman," replied Kindermann. "It is just that I would like to bring up the obvious fact that each of you sitting here are holders of Council Chairs established to honor the three brave individuals who put down the original threat by Fades. A threat that almost cost us our nation during the great civil war. Those men entered the battle late and had almost no understanding of their enemy. Two serious handicaps which you do not possess."

Councilmen Kauffman and Werner sat in silence as they thought about what Kindermann had just said.

Chairman Sumner smiled. Hoping to prevent the moment from slipping away, he said, "Martin, Herman, he is right. We are a strong established nation. One with resources lusted after by others. The rebels we face now are a small group hanging their hopes on a single Fade. We have dealt with worse in the past. Now is the time to act and show both the nation and our hungry neighbors that we can defend our nation from threats both foreign and domestic."

Councilman Werner nodded while Councilman Kauffman appeared to be in deep thought.

"Gentleman, I see that Bishop Sorren and Captain Eustace have joined us," said Chairman Sumner. He waved for them to join the meeting. "Now would be the perfect opportunity to speak with the Captain about the report we just read."

Both Councilmen Keller and Werner stood and greeted Captain Eustace with a handshake. Kindermann did not present his hand, and Captain Eustace was not expecting it. Chairman Sumner did not get up but extended his hand while saying. "You made good time, Captain. I was not expecting you until morning."

"The rest of the caravan should arrive in the morning," said Captain Eustace as he found a place where he could stand at a respectful distance but still speak without having to raise his voice. It also put some distance between him and Kindermann. "I found it necessary to ride ahead, at a faster pace, with your grandson," he continued. "We just arrived an hour ago."

Chairman Sumner leaned slightly forward and asked, "Did something happen to Dylan?"

"Your grandson is fine." When he saw the Chairman relax, the Captain smiled and continued, "Dylan is in the kitchen having something to eat."

"Why the change in plans?" asked Kauffman.

"We stopped for a break a little over a day's ride out," said Captain Eustace, looking at the Councilman. "We detected the Fade in the area. We scared him off, but I felt it would be best to hurry Dylan's arrival."

"Then it's true about the Fade. Did it follow you here?" asked Werner, looking nervously toward the windows of the sunroom.

"The Seers chased him off," said Captain Eustace, glancing toward the Bishop. "I do not think he followed us at the pace we traveled."

"Do you think he was after young Dylan?" asked Werner.

"That would be my guess," replied Captain Eustace. "However, an individual traveling with us, who is familiar with the Fade, insists it was after him and not Dylan."

"That would be the person in your report named Arbin," said Bishop Sorren. "Were you ever able to get his last name or where he came from?"

"I am suspect of the information he gave us on himself," said Captain Eustace. "He provided information on the Fade which he calls Jayden. Seer Keller feels that information is believable."

"Where is this Arbin now?" asked Chairman Sumner.

"He is with Seer Keller," said Captain Eustace. "It's my understanding that Arbin wishes to join the Seers. I have assigned someone to monitor him until you are comfortable with him moving freely around town."

Chairman Sumner and Bishop Sorren looked at each other for a few seconds, then Bishop Sorren said, "A wise decision, Captain. I am glad to hear that my Seers were successful in protecting young Dylan. I would like to talk to you more about this Arbin after the meeting."

Captain Eustace said, "Of course Bishop, but before I forget," He reached into his pocket and pulled out a letter and held it out toward Chairman Sumner. "I have a letter from Lady Casandra to you, sir. Would you like it now or later?"

Chairman Sumner took the letter, placed it on the table in front of him and asked, "Has Casandra spoken with you about the contents?"

"No," said Captain Eustace. He hesitated for a second and then continued, "We had little time to speak before she left for home with your son's body."

Chairman Sumner said nothing but drummed his fingers lightly on top of the envelope.

"Lady Casandra is planning to return to the Capital to be present for her son's confirmation," said Captain Eustace. "I would like your permission to escort her back."

"I am sorry, but I cannot allow that," said Chairman Sumner. "Your report and this recent news have made an excellent case that the Council and young Dylan are most at risk. I will need you to make sure we take all necessary precautions for their protection."

Kindermann spoke up and said, "They will have the protection of my Seers. Now that we will be at full force again, I can guarantee that you will have nothing to fear."

Chairman Sumner forced a thin-lipped smile, turned to the High Seer and said, "Thank you, High Seer Kindermann. I am sure the other Family Chairs feel as relieved as I do."

"Captain Eustace, did my nephew, Jonathan Kingsley, return with you?" asked Werner. "He is my brother-in-law's boy and I know my wife will be concerned about him."

"Your nephew was with the group that found Duke Henry's body," said Captain Eustace. "He handled himself well in that situation, so as a reward I gave him the honor of being an escort for Duke Henry's body to his hometown for burial."

"That was kind of you, Captain. I am sure it will comfort my wife to know that he is safe," said Werner.

"I have a question for you, Captain," said Kauffman. "You said that you scared off the Fade from the caravan, but you could not prevent him from attacking Henry Sumner. Why is that?"

Captain Eustace looked at the Chairman who said, "Answer the Councilman's question."

Captain Eustace looked around the room then said, "First, I do not believe the Fade killed Henry Sumner." Captain Eustace saw Councilman Kauffman's expression and before the Councilman could object, Captain Eustace raised his hand and said, "Let me continue."

When Kauffman nodded, Captain Eustace said, "I believe that the Fade was responsible for the first attack and that this Fade may have been in the area during the last attack. However, I believe that the Fade created the distraction needed for a small group of highly trained assassins to kill Henry Sumner, and three of my men."

"So, you are saying the Fade is not that big of a threat?" asked Kauffman.

"The Fade is dangerous but appears to be inexperienced. It was, however, necessary to make adjustments in the tactics used to deal with him," replied Captain Eustace.

Kauffman said, "Just to be clear, you are saying that the Fade could make the first attack on Duke Henry because you were not ready to deal with him, but you can deal with him now?"

Kindermann spoke up and said, "The tactics used by our Seers are the same used by the original Seers. If supported properly, there should have been no problems defending against this Fade."

"Otis, you were not there!" said Captain Eustace angrily. "Your men were useless until Seer Keller developed a new tactic that was successful in chasing the Fade away from the caravan. I would suggest you investigate the performance of your Seers when faced with an actual threat before you suggest my men caused the problem."

"Captain, that will be enough," interrupted Bishop Sorren. "I will meet with both of you to discuss the matter in more detail. I will also remind you that all changes to procedures require the approval of the High Seer or myself."

"I think that is enough discussion for now," said Chairman Sumner. "We are all tired and stressed. I would very much like to reunite with my grandson. Martin, Herman, do you have questions that cannot wait?"

Both Councilmen Kauffman and Werner agreed that they would like to meet again after they have had time to think over the information discussed.

Chairman Sumner stood slowly and put out his hands toward the Councilmen and said, "Thank you for meeting with me." He turned and said, "Bishop Sorren, would you, Captain Eustace and High Seer Kindermann remain please."

As the two Councilman left, Chairman Sumner returned to his chair. Bishop Sorren joined him at the table. High Seer Kindermann found a chair nearby while Captain Eustace remained standing.

Chairman Sumner turned to Captain Eustace and said, "You and your people did a fine job in safely seeing Dylan here. The loss of his father is hard for both of us. I am sure I will find it to be a little easier with him here."

"That is kind of you, sir," said Captain Eustace. "I am a little surprised and concerned that you would stay here instead of the island. Your residence there is much safer considering the current situation."

"I understand your concerns, Captain, but I find this place better for my spirit. My Sophie poured her heart into it and I find that in troubled times I need to be here. Besides, I am sure that between you and the High Seer this will become just as safe as anywhere else."

"I will do my best, Chairman," said Kindermann.

"And that is precisely why I asked you to stay," said Chairman Sumner. "I will need the both of you to do your best for me and the nation, together, as a team."

Captain Eustace started to apologize, but Chairman Sumner put his hand up, stopping him.

"Captain, you said some things at the meeting that concern me," said Chairman Sumner. "For one, I am concerned about your suggestion that the rebels are more of a threat than the Fade. It sounded like you suggested the Fade was nothing more than a distraction so that the rebels could carry out what you describe as a bold and ruthless attack. If they have such highly skilled people, why recruit a Fade?"

Captain Eustace said, "The evidence suggests the attack that killed your son was conducted by someone with a history of violence and someone who is not afraid to take risks."

"Are you suggesting mercenaries?" asked Chairman Sumner.

"It has been done before," said Captain Eustace. "If so, it might make them easier to deal with if we can get an idea of who they are. There cannot be too many people out there with those skills. I would like to work on coming up with a list of candidates."

"I think it would be better if you took a lesson from the past," said Bishop Sorren. "Search for their hiding places. Look for weak links by offering substantial rewards for information. Use the tools that God has given you to fight this evil. Let the gifts of the Seers and the greed of man be the path to ending this."

"I agree with the Bishop," said Chairman Sumner. "I want you to work on increasing security around the Council and increasing citizen morale by making yourself more visible."

"Yes sir," replied Captain Eustace. Seeing Otis smile at the Bishop's mention of his Seers made it almost impossible for him to hide his disappointment. He could not understand why both the Chairman and the Bishop were so focused on the Fade. They refused to see the genuine threat.

"I agree with your assessment that the Fade may be inexperienced," said Chairman Sumner. "However, in all your encounters with the Fade, the best you could do is chase him away. I worry that he may become bolder in his attacks now that he must know you are having problems dealing with him. Your reports were very carefully worded. I want to know more about your dealings with this Fade and what changes you made."

Captain Eustace said, "During the first attack we set up in standard units of one Seer and three Shadow Guards. We had a unit stationed at key locations around the camp as per standard procedures. None of these units detected the Fade. He was discovered when he bumped into someone as he ran out of the tent where Henry was staying. That person saw a man with a knife and yelled. We started the hunt for an intruder that led us to the Fade and Arbin fighting in the woods."

"That can't be right," said Kindermann. "My men should have found him before he made his attack. Are you sure this person was really a Fade?"

"I had my doubts at first," said Captain Eustace. "I interviewed the Seers afterward. None of them would go on record as saying they detected the Fade. They said there was a strange feeling in the area. They were only able to track the person they were chasing because he left a trail for them through the forest. It was the incident at the rest stop that changed my mind. It was there that Seer Keller claimed he and another Seer could detect the Fade using a method taught to them by Arbin. It appears that Arbin was able to detect the Fade with ease and is the only person to lay a hand on him."

"And you allowed the use of this method?" asked Kindermann.

"Seer Keller put it into action without authorization," said Captain Eustace. "It appeared to be effective, so we used it to protect Dylan on the trip here."

"And what is this unauthorized method?" asked Bishop Sorren.

"It would be better if you let Seer Keller give you the details," said Captain Eustace. "My concern was keeping Dylan safe and as long as it appeared to work, I left it to him to apply it."

Chairman Sumner said, "High Seer, this method needs further investigation. I will leave that to you. Captain, figure out how to best use the findings of the High Seer."

Both Captain Eustace and High Seer Kindermann nodded.

"I think that will be all for tonight," said Chairman Sumner. "Bishop Sorren, could you remain please? I have some personal issues I would like to speak to you about."

Both Chairman Sumner and Bishop Sorren remained seated as Captain Eustace and High Seer Kindermann left the room. Chairman Sumner picked up Casandra's letter and studied it as Bishop Sorren poured some tea.

"Where do Martin and Herman stand?" asked Bishop Sorren.

Chairman Sumner looked up from the letter and said, "It's clear that Darr has been working on them. I think if we waited any longer, we would have lost them. As it is, we have a good chance. Martin is the key. Convince him and Herman will follow."

Bishop Sorren nodded in agreement, and Chairman Sumner returned to reading Casandra's letter. After a few minutes, Bishop Sorren asked, "What does she want?"

Chairman Sumner handed the letter to Bishop Sorren and said, "She wants Captain Eustace appointed as Dylan's guardian. I must admit, I did not see that one coming."

Bishop Sorren took the letter and looked it over and said, "I will admit the boy is fond of Captain Eustace." The Bishop paused for a few seconds then said, "We could always play to the Captain's weakness of pride and honor. We could remind him that his strengths are in providing security and not in the muddy waters of politics. In his current position he has the ability, authority and responsibility to act against the people who killed Henry and threatened Dylan."

"I don't think that will work," said Chairman Sumner as he crossed his arms and brought the fingers of one of his fists to his lips. After a few seconds of thought he uncrossed his arms and took a sip of tea then said, "Her letter makes it clear she will not drop this even if Captain Eustace refuses. We will need to be more successful in our attempts to prevent her interference."

"Hasn't there been enough violence?" asked Bishop Sorren.

"I am open to suggestions," said Chairman Sumner as he put down the teacup. "But we do not have a lot of time to act."

Bishop Sorren said nothing but continued to look at the letter.

"We also need to do something about our Fade," said Chairman Sumner. "Thanks to the Captain's little speech, the Councilman fear Mr. Bergman's men more than our Fade. We need to change that fast. Darr's arguments for joining the Alliance falls flat in the face of the nightmare of Fades."

"What do you suggest?" asked Bishop Sorren.

"I do not know," said Chairman Sumner with a slight wave of his hand. "You deal with managing public opinion all the time. Spread some rumors, do whatever it is you do. We need to remind people why they need to be afraid of this Fade, and why we need you and your Seers."

"That hurts a little," said Bishop Sorren. "I will figure something out. However, while we are on the topic, Captain Eustace said that Arbin was thinking of joining the Seer Core. What do you want to do about him?"

"To tell you the truth," said Chairman Sumner. "I hoped that once he went missing, we would never see him again. Now we know where the last of our special children was hiding. I should have listened to you back at the Nursery."

"You made the right choice," said Bishop Sorren. "We needed to know what was so special about them and why they set up the Nursery."

"Yes, and now we know," said Chairman Sumner. "That Nursery was part of an attempt to breed Fades. I bet they never guessed they would end up with Seers."

"Based on some things Captain Eustace has said, Arbin may be a High Seer," said Bishop Sorren. "That may be an unexpected blessing."

"More like an unwelcome one," said Chairman Sumner.

"I am sure we could turn the battle between a Cursed one and a Blessed one in our favor," said Bishop Sorren. "It would give people hope. And it would remind the Council of the reason the Family Chairs exist."

"Do not let that idea get hatched," said Chairman Sumner. "Another contender for the Family Chairs could destroy our entire plan. Last thing I want is for Arbin to take Dylan's place."

"Keeping Arbin's abilities a secret will be a problem if he becomes a Seer," said the Bishop. "Otis is no fool. He will discover what Arbin is as soon as he talks to him. I am positive we can deal with Otis because he will see Arbin as a threat to his position. But there is Alex and the other Seers that encountered Arbin."

"I think the best thing to do is have Otis interview him for knowledge and then discredit him," said Chairman Sumner. "We need to prevent him from being accepted into the Seers or being of any political value to anyone. After that, no one will care what happens to him."

"I agree, what will you say at the next Council meeting? They will want a full report and I am sure someone will bring up the subject of Arbin. We will also need to present our choice for Dylan's guardian soon."

Chairman Sumner agreed but said, "I think it best if I do not attend the next meeting. I do not want to show up sick and appear to be weak." He handed the Bishop another letter.

"This will give you the authority to speak on my behalf," said Chairman Sumner. "I want you to present our candidate. That will give the Council a chance to comment without challenging me directly. I want to find out who needs our attention. If they ask about me, you can explain that I am taking time to mourn the loss of my son. As for Arbin, I think we should form the Application Committee as soon as possible."

Bishop Sorren agreed. He started to return Casandra's letter to the Chairman, but he refused it. "You hold on to it for now," said Chairman Sumner. Bishop Sorren agreed, stood up, put his hand on his old friend's shoulder, and said a quick prayer asking for improvement of his health.

Chairman Sumner thanked him, slowly stood, and walked the Bishop out of the sunroom. "Now if you will excuse me, old friend, I need to find my grandson."

Chapter 10 - Matter of Character

ARBIN DID NOT LIKE Ackerman the instant he met him and in the three days he had been staying in the staff quarters his feelings about him only got worse.

"Pack your stuff, it's time to go," said Ackerman, an unpleasant, thin, elderly man, who was the Head Steward for the service staff of the Government Compound.

"Why do I need to pack my stuff?" asked Arbin.

"Because you are not coming back here," said Ackerman.

"What do you mean?"

"You have been ordered to appear at the Application Committee. If you pass the application process, your new home will be the barracks with the other Seers," replied Ackerman.

"And, if I fail?"

"That's your problem, but you won't be coming back here," Ackerman said with a smile. "The quarters are for working staff, not someone like you."

Arbin had learned that the Government Compound, or the Island as some people referred to it, was in fact an island. It was huge, surrounded by a wall and located in the middle of the river that divided the Capital city of Leaboro in half.

The island had once been the home of the former Royal Family. The grounds and Palace became the center for the Governing Council which was formed shortly after the civil war. It was during the civil war that Fades killed the Royal Family and many other nobles and military leaders.

Even though he had spent three days on the island, they had not allowed him to explore it. He had seen even less of the Capital city. Within hours of his arrival at Alex's home, a group of Shadow Guards had collected Arbin and moved him to the Government Compound staff quarters. Arbin learned later that the instructions came from Bishop Sorren, the head of the Shadow Guard Order.

Ackerman made it clear at the time of Arbin's arrival he was none too happy about being saddled with a guest who was not expected to work for his stay. He was also not happy they were required to feed and clean up after a person of low stature, as Arbin obviously was. When it was learned that Arbin was here to spend several days visiting with the distinguished High Seer, Otis Kindermann, his status improved in Ackerman's eyes. After returning from his first visit with the High Seer, Arbin found his little room clean, and was served an enjoyable meal.

Things quickly changed by the end of his second day of visits when High Seer Kindermann left instructions that Arbin could not speak with anyone without the permission of the High Seer. On the morning of the third day, Arbin received nothing to eat, and no one came to empty his bed pot. Arbin just wanted to leave, but that would not be easy because High Seer Kindermann would send for Arbin several times each day, and each time Shadow Guards escorted him.

At first, Arbin met with High Seer Kindermann in his office. Their conversations consisted mostly of a retelling of the events of Noor Point. Their meetings soon moved to a nearby chapel once their discussions focused on Jayden and Arbin's understanding of Fades. High Seer Kindermann clarified that their conversations were touching on sensitive issues that required the protection of Holy Ground.

Each time Arbin used Jayden's name, High Seer Kindermann cringed. "You must not say his name," the High Seer would say as he looked around the room. "Calling on the name of a demon gives it power. Are you trying to summon it here? How can you claim to be blessed by God and not understand these things?"

Arbin soon confirmed Alex's statement that the High Seer had no Seer ability. He also learned that the High Seer had no firsthand knowledge of Fades and was probably the source of most of the bad information others had on Fades. Their meetings always followed a similar pattern. The High Seer announced the topic for discussion, Arbin shared something, and the

High Seer would then correct Arbin, saying he did not have the experience needed to see things correctly. Next, the High Seer would waste Arbin's time talking about himself and his extensive studies of Fades. The subjects that upset the High Seer the most were any discussion of the true nature of a Fade and Arbin's claim that even non-Seers could defend against them.

The meeting this morning had ended with an argument and the High Seer storming out. Shortly after, Arbin found himself standing in front of the staff quarters, with his bag and a summons unceremoniously shoved into his hands, ordering him to appear before the Application Committee in the Grand Council Meeting Room. The meeting time was in about an hour.

Arbin stood looking around at the unfamiliar landscape of the island. Several things came to mind, but it surprised him to realize that one thing he was not thinking about was running away.

The sound of Ackerman clearing his throat behind him brought Arbin's focus back to the issue at hand. He looked back at Ackerman, still standing near the entrance to the staff quarters, and asked, "Worried I might want to sneak back in?" Ackerman's expression did not change. "Well, can you at least tell me which way is the Grand Council Meeting Room?"

Ackerman pointed south and said, "You can't miss it."

After a few yards Arbin asked what appeared to be a friendlier face, who gave him a strange stare and pointed south and assured him he could not miss it.

After a few more requests for directions, Arbin figured out that where he wanted to go was the enormous building, at what he guessed was the southern end of the island. Arbin had never seen a Palace, but it was easy for him to decide that this was one. Not one of those fairytale ones, but a huge four-story building fit for a king, or a prince at least. He could easily see the top part of the Palace above the buildings in front of him.

Arbin soon learned the island was divided in half with a wall between each section. At one end of the island was the small chapel, and at the other was the Palace. The northern section, including the chapel and surrounding buildings, supported the Shadow Guard, the Seers, and the support staff. The southern section, including the Palace, was used mostly for government and housing of key officials. Both sections had squares with a single exit and bridge leading to different sides of the city. The exit in the northern square led to the east side of the city, and the exit in the southern square led to the west side.

With each step toward the Palace, more and more of its beauty was revealed. Up close, it was larger than any building Arbin had ever seen. Its four stories seemed almost as high as the building was wide. The building, with its light pinkish stonework, dark green tiled roof, white trimmed windows and doors almost sparkled in the sunlight. Stained glass accented several of the windows, and most of the second floor had balconies. Seeing the Palace framed by the bright blue cloudless sky almost took his breath away.

A small courtyard, landscaped with flowering plants, shaped shrub, statues and a few bright white benches welcomed visitors to the entrance marked by a large double door with a canape, under which stood two Shadow Guards. An almost steady stream of people came and went. The guards spoke with each person who entered, sometimes having them check their weapons.

Arbin approached the two Shadow Guards, and guided by what he saw others do, presented his summons to one of them. The man studied it for such a long time that Arbin doubted if he could read it.

The guard stuck his head inside the door and shouted, "Page!" A few seconds later, a boy of about ten appeared, dressed in a green and white uniform. The guard handed him the summons and said, "Council Business."

The young boy nodded, smiled at Arbin, then headed inside the building. The guard who had called the Page looked at Arbin and with a movement of his head toward the door communicated that Arbin was to follow the boy.

Arbin found it difficult to keep his attention on his guide because of the grandeur of the building. This was the most beautiful place that he had ever seen. The high ceiling and windows, the colors, the tapestries, not to mention the people in brightly colored clothes. With all the stairs and corridors, it soon became clear to Arbin that he would need help to find his way out after the meeting.

The young boy soon turned down a long corridor that ended in a large stained-glass window. To one side was a large double door guarded by two Shadow Guards. Printed on a plaque above the door was 'Grand Council Meeting Room' in large golden letters. Across from the door along the opposite wall were four sets of benches. Each bench looked like they could seat five or six people.

The Page handed Arbin's papers to one of the Shadow Guards who gave it a quick glance, opened the door, and the Page quickly entered. The guard looked at Arbin and signaled with a nod for him to take a seat. *Doesn't anyone talk around here?* Arbin thought. He had a seat on the bench and made himself as comfortable as possible. After several minutes of waiting, he grumbled, "Everything takes so long in this town. Go here and wait, go there and wait. All this waiting is tiring me out." Arbin stretched out on the bench, using his bag as a pillow. *They can wake me when they need me,* he thought, and despite the stern looks he got from the guards, soon fell asleep.

ARBIN HAD THAT NIGHTMARE about being trapped in a burning building again. He woke with a start, not sure where he was for a few seconds. He sat up, took a deep breath and rested his head in his hands. *Why the dream again?* he wondered. The last time he had that dream was in the forest, just before he struggled with Jayden. He was thinking about that night when he heard his name being called. He was not sure if he had really heard it until he saw one of the guards looking his way. When the guard saw that he had Arbin's attention, he stood up straight, took a deep breath and said in a clear loud voice, "Arbin Adean, present yourself for consideration."

It shocked Arbin. It had been years since he heard his last name used. Mia and Jayden were the only people he had told his real last name to since he had left home. Now he was being called by it loud enough for the dead to hear.

Arbin was halfway between standing and sitting, still trying to come to terms with hearing his name, when he heard the guard that called his name clear his throat and nodded toward the open doorway. They placed a piece of paper in Arbin's hands as he stepped through the doors, which closed seconds later, leaving him staring at the crowded Grand Council Meeting room and not knowing what to do next.

The room was in fact grand, but it surprised Arbin to see he had entered the room from the side of it instead of from one of the ends as he expected.

On the right side of the room was a bank of huge stained-glass windows, much like the one in the corridor. In front of these was a long table with nine high-back chairs. Three men, dressed in black robes, were seated at the table. Arbin recognized one man as High Seer Otis Kindermann.

There was a space of about ten feet in front of the table where the three men sat. A waist high banister separated the space and the robed men from the rest of the room.

Around the walls were three rows of benches, each stacked a little higher than the one in front of it. These benches were surprisingly full. Another waist high banister also separated these benches from the collection of chairs in the center of the room. These were full of people dressed in wonderfully colored clothes. Those chairs were also full.

At first glance Arbin did not recognize anyone in the audience, but finally saw Alex, dressed in his uniform, sitting in the center area. His sister Elizabeth, sitting next to him. *Wow, she looks a lot better today than she did the last time I saw her,* he thought. Arbin blushed when she caught him looking at her. He looked away and pretended to be looking at the crowd.

The number of people in the room frightened and confused him. *Why would anyone come to see me go through this thing?* he wondered.

The clerk, a young man dressed also in black, stepped up to Arbin from somewhere and asked for his notice. He pointed to a small platform a few feet in front of Arbin. The platform had a railing around most of it, and on it was a single chair. "Please stand by the chair until I announce you," said the clerk. The clerk then walked up to the robed men and presented Arbin's summons to them.

They looked at it, handed it back to the clerk who turned, took two steps toward the center of the room and said in a clear, loud voice. "Let it be known to all present here that Arbin Adean, a citizen of legal age, wishes to apply for acceptance into the Holy Order of the Seers of Leaboro. This

Application Committee is being chaired by his Excellency, the Bishop of Leaboro, Phillip Sorren. He is being assisted by the honorable Councilman Martin Kauffman and the High Seer of the Holy Order of the Seer of Leaboro, Otis Kindermann. The Committee would also like to recognize the presence of Council Chairman Morgan Sumner, Councilman Herman Werner, and Councilman Thomas Darr."

There was a small round of polite applause.

"Now, to the business at hand," the clerk continued. "Is there someone here that would second the request of Arbin Adean, and act as a sponsor for his application?"

"I will stand as sponsor" said Alex as he stood.

The clerk said, "Come forward."

Alex made his way toward another platform located directly in front of the three men in black. That platform was also partly surrounded by a railing but did not have a chair. Alex made a point of walking past Arbin on his way to the platform. As he passed, Alex placed his hand on Arbin's shoulder and said, "Just sit here, speak only when spoken to, and try to look important."

"Okay?" Arbin nodded, not sure how he would do that last thing.

The clerk spoke to Alex as he stepped on to the platform, waited until Alex indicated he was ready, then said, "Seer Keller, please make your case for acceptance of the Candidate."

Alex nodded, paused for a few seconds while he looked at each of the men before him and said, "Your Honors. Before I begin, I would like to point out one item of procedure. Any nomination requires the testimony of two witnesses. I had made a request that Seer Lubin Bauer be allowed to be present to act as that second witness. I learned this morning he had been dispatched on assignment and would not be available to stand before this Committee."

Bishop Sorren, seated in the center chair, said, "High Seer Kindermann advised the Committee in advance of this issue and has presented the Committee a signed statement from Seer Bauer."

Alex asked, "Your honors, would it be possible for me to review his statement prior to my presentation?"

"That would not be necessary or prudent since Seer Bauer is not present," said Bishop Sorren. "The Committee has reviewed it and accepted it as his position on the application. Please continue with your presentation."

Alex looked over at Arbin and then back to the Committee. "Your honors. First allow me to introduce myself, and my qualifications."

Bishop Sorren looked at the other two members of the Committee. Councilman Kauffman nodded, and High Seer Kindermann waved his hand affirmatively. Bishop Sorren said to Alex, "We all know who you are, Seer Keller, but continue if you feel this is necessary."

"Thank you, your Excellency," said Alex as he bowed his head slightly to Bishop Sorren. He looked slowly around the room at the people gathered there and then said, "My name is Alexander Keller. I am a second level Seer and have been a member of the Holy Order of Leaboro Seers since I was twelve. If you remember, Bishop Sorren, you sponsored my application." The Bishop nodded his acknowledgment.

"I have been on six campaigns to root out evil in the lands to the east," said Alex as he looked around. "I see several individuals sitting in this room who rode with us," continued Alex. "In addition, I am the most senior individual of my rank and command a full squad of Seers."

High Seer Kindermann leaned over and whispered something to Bishop Sorren, who nodded and said, "Seer Keller, the court will gladly recognize your long and honorable career as a Seer. However, I must remind you that you are here to speak about this individual," pointing toward Arbin. There was a slight amount of laughter from the audience.

Alex waited for the laughter to die down, then looked at Arbin and back to the Committee and said, "I thank the Committee for that recognition. I would also like to have the Committee recognize that to reach a status as a Seer of my level takes years of hard work, training, dedication and sacrifices."

Bishop Sorren looked at the other Committee members. When both showed no objections, Bishop Sorren turned back to Alex and said, "You have our agreement with your last statement, but I still do not understand why it's necessary."

Alex said, "Your honors, I believe it necessary to establish my credibility before I make my statements on the abilities of Arbin Adean."

Bishop Sorren asked, "Are you saying this is necessary because of a lack of evidence that he possesses any abilities?"

"Not exactly, your Excellency," said Alex. "I would like to remind the members of this Committee that prior to this meeting, in association with your position outside of this Committee, I presented each of you with a report of the events associated with the assassination of Duke Henry Sumner."

There was a low murmur from the people gathered in the room. Bishop Sorren tapped his gavel lightly a few times, and the noise disappeared.

"I must warn you, Seer Keller, much of that information is still under review and is not for public release," said Bishop Sorren. "Because your reports have not been fully reviewed, they are not eligible for submission to this Committee."

"I understand your Excellency. That is why I need you to recognize my credibility as a witness," said Alex. "I do not intend to discuss in detail, the events in those reports. However, my knowledge and understanding of the applicant's abilities are tied to those events. Because of the sensitivity of this case, it may be necessary for you to accept what I say, simply because I said it."

The three Committee members huddled together in hushed discussion. After a few minutes Bishop Sorren said, "Your point is well taken. We concede that your credibility will be the major evidence for evaluation by this Committee. High Seer Kindermann has also pointed out that while your time with that applicant is limited to the events described, he has just finished up three days of intensive interviews with the applicant. The Committee will use the information he collected during those interviews to balance your comments."

Arbin chuckled softly to the idea of intensive interviews. *More like bragging sessions,* he thought. His little chuckle got him more attention than he had expected. Alex's stern look made him shift in his chair. *Sit still, be quiet,* he thought as he looked down.

Alex took a few seconds to recover his focus and said, "Thank you for that consideration. In that case, my presentation will be short and, as I have said, based on my personal experiences with the applicant and supported by my authority as a credible witness."

"Get on with it then," said Bishop Sorren.

Alex took a deep breath and then said, "Your honors, Arbin Adean is a Seer. I have witnessed his use of his Seer gifts in several situations which leave no doubt as to God's blessing on him. He is untrained but has demonstrated that he can use his gift in ways that no other Seers can match. The fact that he can use his gift at the level he does, with none of the training needed by others in the Order, suggests he has the potential to become one of our greatest Seers."

"One of our greatest Seers," said Bishop Sorren. "That is high praise indeed. Are you sure about your assessment?"

"I am your Excellency. In fact, I believe his gift is greater than mine," said Alex.

That last comment caught both Arbin's attention and many in the audience, including Alex's sister. It also resulted in another low murmur that went through the room that was only silenced after several sharp raps of the Bishop's gavel.

Councilman Kauffman said, "I appreciate your limitations in presenting evidence, but I would caution against any exaggerating, no matter how well intended, for the benefit of this applicant."

Alex paused as if he was not sure he wanted to continue. He looked back at his sister, then at Arbin. He took a deep breath and said, "I am not exaggerating, Councilman Kauffman. In fact, based on what I saw and experienced during my time with him, I believe that Arbin Adean may have the gifts of a True High Seer."

Arbin was amazed at the uproar Alex's comment created. The only thing Arbin knew about the original High Seers came from Alex. He had been told they were good at finding Fades. His recent experiences made it clear his ability to find Jayden was better than any Seer he had met so far, including Mia. *Who knows,* he thought. *Maybe there was something in what Alex had said.*

Bishop Sorren banged his gavel several times, attempting to quiet the room. He waved at the clerk who shouted, "Order, there will be order." Just as the room finally quieted down, High Seer Kindermann pointed his finger at Alex and in a raised voice said, "Be careful what you are saying! I am the only rightful High Seer of the Order." Waving his arm toward Arbin, he continued, "Are you suggesting I be replaced by this person?"

There was another round of noise from the audience. Bishop Sorren motioned for the High Seer to control himself, then warned the audience that if they did not maintain the proper decorum, he would have no choice but to clear the room.

Arbin looked at Alex, who stood calmly watching High Seer Kindermann. Arbin smiled and thought, *so that is what you had planned all along. This was really your way of calling out the High Seer.*

When both the audience and High Seer Kindermann calmed down, Councilman Kauffman said, "Explain yourself, Seer Keller!"

"Your Honors," said Alex calmly. "I am not talking about the ceremonial position held by High Seer Kindermann. I am suggesting he is blessed with the same gift that allowed the Seers of old to battle the Fades of their time."

"Are you suggesting that this individual is equal to, or a descendant of, the founding members of the Family Chairs?" asked Councilman Kauffman.

This time the Bishop's gavel, and the clerk's warnings, were not enough to calm the room, so Bishop Sorren signaled for all spectators to be removed. A few minutes later, only the Committee Members, Chairman Sumner, Councilman Werner, Councilman Darr, Alex and Arbin remained.

Councilman Kauffman could not control his anger as he said, "Your Excellency, I will not sit by and allow the suggestion that this nobody is equal to, or a descendant of the blessed three. Our greatest heroes. The men that saved our nation from the greatest evil it has ever faced. What's next? Are we to give up our seats on the Council to him?" Turning to Alex, Kauffman said, "Careful of your words. One might almost think you serve those that would see an overthrow of this Council."

Bishop Sorren said, "Calm yourself, Councilman! I believe that Seer Keller spoke out of an affection for the Core and not as one working against us. I have firsthand knowledge of Arbin's past and can assure everyone here that Arbin is not related to any of the Family Chairs. He is not a threat to your Chair or the stability of the Council."

The Bishop's comment on his past surprised Arbin. He looked up, stirred in his chair as if he wanted to say something, but held his place after receiving another stern look from Alex.

Councilman Kauffman looked at Bishop Sorren and said, "Then on what grounds does he make his assertion that Arbin is a True High Seer?"

"Councilman, please," said Alex. "If you will give me a moment. I feel you have misunderstood my statement. Please allow me to explain."

Councilman Kauffman looked at Alex and then said, "Explain, but make your words clear if you do not want charges brought against you."

Alex stood up straighter and said, "Your Honors, since everyone here is on the Council or a privileged individual, I will say that my comments were meant only to highlight Arbin's ability to detect and battle the Fade that attacked the Chairman's son and later threaten his grandson. It is his ability to do what the Seers of old did that suggest there is something special about his gift. One that we should study further. A valuable and timely gift the Seer Core needs now that the evil of a Fade has returned."

"Your report claims that you also detected the Fade, does that make you a High Seer as well?" said Councilman Kauffman.

"Of course not, Councilman," said Alex. "We only followed Arbin's direction using a method he instructed us in. In truth, we only detected the Fade after he did. Arbin's ability to detect the presence of the Fade greatly surpasses anyone else. In fact, he has confided in me that he can actually see the Fade when others cannot. I would remind you he is the only one to have physically engaged the Fade."

"What you and Arbin detected was the taint of evil put off by the Fade." said High Seer Kindermann.

Everyone in the room, including Arbin, turned and looked at High Seer Kindermann. "Explain what you mean," said Bishop Sorren.

High Seer Kindermann continued, "I have determined, based on my interviews with Arbin, that his proximity to the Fade allowed him to become sensitive to the taint. It was this sensitivity that you misunderstood to be some special gift."

"In your opinion, High Seer, does Arbin have any Seer abilities?" asked Bishop Sorren.

High Seer Kindermann let out a slight laugh and said, "Minor, at best. Certainly not the level needed to be considered the great Seer that our noble Seer Keller suggests."

"You said Arbin was exposed to the taint of the Fade. Is there any danger that he may in fact become a Fade as well?" asked Councilman Werner.

The Councilman's question surprised the group and Bishop Sorren said, "Councilman, I must respectfully remind you we are still in committee. However, High Seer Kindermann, I think it would be prudent for you to address the Councilman's question."

High Seer Kindermann smiled and said, "In my three days with Arbin, I discovered that his understanding of the true nature of the Fade is distorted. It was obvious to me that the Fade took advantage of their supposed friendship to corrupt Arbin's understanding of who the Fade was and how his powers operate. It's possible that what little of God's blessing he has is what is protecting him from complete corruption. I do not currently view him as a danger, but I would remind you that he spent a long time under the influence of the Fade."

"I am glad the High Seer agrees that Arbin has God's blessing," said Alex. "I would suggest that his acceptance into the Core would give us the opportunity to train him properly."

High Seer Kindermann snapped back at Alex saying, "I said any abilities he has are minor! I also have concerns about whether he has the moral character to be a Seer."

"My abilities are greater than yours, High Seer," said Arbin. "Everyone is so busy talking about me, like I am not even here. When are you going to ask me something!"

Alex said, "Arbin, please be quiet."

"Why," asked Arbin "It's clear these people do not want me in their club. They do not care about, or even want to understand, what I can do. Have they even thanked you for what you did back at the caravan?"

"Are you saying that you are a True High Seer?" asked Chairman Sumner.

The group turned to look at the Chairman and then waited for an answer from Arbin.

Arbin said, "I don't know what this True High Seer is. I know what I am and what I can do, just as I know what Jayden is and what he can do." Arbin saw the High Seer cringe at the mention of Jayden's name. "I also know that if Jayden wanted to get in this place, the only persons in your Seer Core that could stop him are Alex and Lubin."

High Seer Kindermann said, "I told you not to call that demon by name! I fear your time with that Fade has weakened you to a point that you do not fear its evil nature. This is why I do not believe he has the moral character to become a Seer."

"You of all people should not talk. You do not understand what a Fade is or what I can do," said Arbin. "I thought this was supposed to be some kind of test of my Talents."

"That is enough," said Chairman Sumner, slamming his fist down on the arm of his chair. Everyone turned to look at him. "Bishop Sorren, this is getting out of hand. High Seer Kindermann and Seer Keller are both suggesting Mr. Adean has some abilities. It appears the only way forward now is to take Mr. Adean up on his suggestion of testing."

"Chairman Sumner, that kind of testing has not been done for a long time," said High Seer Kindermann.

"Bishop Sorren, do you feel the Committee can reach an unbiased decision at this point without testing?" asked Chairman Sumner.

"It would be difficult," said Bishop Sorren. "However, I must remind you that testing would require the acceptance of both the person being tested and the sponsors."

"Arbin, are you willing to have your abilities tested?" asked Chairman Sumner.

"If it will put an end to all of this, yes," said Arbin.

Chairman Sumner turned to Alex, "Do you agree as well?"

Bishop Sorren said, "Remember Seer Keller, we have not needed those methods of testing for years. You understand that if Arbin fails the test, he will be rejected, and we will call your abilities into question."

"If testing is the only way for you to believe he is gifted, yes," said Alex.

The Bishop looked at the other two members of the Committee. When he saw there were no objections, Bishop Sorren said, "It will take us two days to set up for the testing. We will let you know the time and location once it has been determined. In the meantime, Mr. Adean, we will not allow you any contact with individuals from this Committee or any members of the Seer Core. Do you understand?"

Arbin nodded his head. The Bishop slammed his gavel and before he knew it Arbin found himself outside the meeting room, alone and with nowhere to go.

ARBIN WANDERED THE hallways in a daze. When he finally found an exit, it led to the southern front of the Government Building. He thought the Palace was the southernmost part of the island, but now in front of him, he found a park and a bridge that joined both sides of the city.

The bridge was slightly raised, and the two sides were joined in the middle by a large structure with a roof held up by columns. There were wide curved stairs that led up to the bridge section that ran through the structure. There was another set of wide stairs on the far side that led down into a multi-tiered park and gardens that filled out the rest of the island and ended at the water's edge. Engraved on a section of the structure roofing was 'The Bridge of Sorrows'. Arbin learned from a passerby that this was a memorial to Prince Carl and Princess Hanna. The former inhabitants of the Palace. The park on the other side was a wedding gift from Prince Carl to his princess. It was also the place where they both had been murdered by a Fade. A murder that started the great civil war almost one hundred fifty years ago.

Arbin wandered around the park and found a set of benches where he could sit and overlook the park and the river beyond it. Just to his left was a nice little rose garden and in front of the garden was a bench that had a statue of two people, obviously in love, sitting and enjoying the view.

Arbin watched the river and the few barges that moved with it. He knew the river would take them past his old home of Noor Point. It was so close, but so far away. Just another place where he could never return. The park gave him a view of the city on both sides of the river. The size of the place made him feel small and out of control, much like how he felt in the Committee meeting. There, they had forced him to just sit and watch as the meeting drifted by him without being able to control where it was going. When he had done something, it felt like he had lost even more control. The more he thought about it, the more depressed he got. Arbin closed his eyes and did his best to relax, hoping to let the sound of the river chase the sad thoughts from his head. After a few minutes, he felt a discomfort and the once soothing sounds of the river irritated him. As the discomfort increased, it reminded him of the feeling he had back in the caravan. Arbin looked around for another place to sit and saw Elizabeth standing about fifteen feet behind him.

Arbin looked back out at the river and said, "Did Alex send you?"

Elizabeth said, "So you know who I am."

"Of course, I know who you are. Alex told me all about you."

"Yes," said Elizabeth. "He sent me. He is worried about you and wanted me to tell you about what will happen."

"Well, to tell you the truth, I was just sitting here deciding if I should go through with this testing thing. After all, it was not my idea to be here."

Elizabeth took a few steps forward and said, "You cannot honestly be thinking about running away!" Arbin could hear the anger growing in her voice. "My brother has done a lot for you. If not for him, you would probably be dead right now. I cannot believe you would just run off now. He trusts you and needs your help."

Arbin felt a little light-headed as she approached. He closed his eyes and put one of his hands on the bench to steady himself.

Elizabeth stepped closer, "Are you all right?"

The discomfort continued and Arbin took a few deep breaths and said a little too loud, "I'm fine. I just feel a little tired."

The loudness of Arbin's response surprised Elizabeth, and she took a few steps back. As she did, she could see Arbin relax slightly.

Arbin took a deep breath, "I will be alright."

Elizabeth acted like she had not heard him and said, "I have seen men react to me the way you are now. But none as strongly as you are. When

I was younger, my mother would always say that it was because I was so pretty."

Arbin looked at her for a few seconds and then said, "You are pretty, but I have been feeling funny ever since I got dragged to this place. Please do not blame yourself."

Elizabeth took a few steps forward and watched as Arbin closed his eyes and put his hand back on the bench to steady himself. "You need to stay and see this testing through," said Elizabeth. "Both yours and my brother's future depend on this."

"What trouble could your brother be in?" asked Arbin. "He is the one that chased away the big bad Fade."

"Are you really as ignorant and self-centered as my brother said?" Elisabeth asked, shaking her head.

"Thank you?" said Arbin, not sure how to take her last remark.

"You are only free to sit here and feel sorry for yourself because my brother has vouched for you. I do not understand what makes you so important to him, but he has decided that he will place his career and possibly his life on getting you into the Seers."

"His life? What are you talking about?" asked a surprised Arbin.

"You heard what High Seer Kindermann was saying about the taint of evil and misunderstanding the truth. That's just another way of saying heresy, and you know what they do with heretics around here. They burn them at the stake!"

Elizabeth realized that she was speaking loudly and in anger at Arbin. She glanced around, took a deep breath, stepped forward, and pulled Arbin up by his arm. "Let's walk!"

Arbin staggered to his feet and tried weakly to pull his arm away, but she only held on to him tighter and said, "We need to move someplace else."

Arbin held on to Elizabeth's arm for balance as they walked to a set of stairs leading to a lower-level garden and walkway along the river. Elizabeth helped Arbin down the stairs and headed toward a bench near a hedge under an arch for the bridge. Elizabeth guided Arbin as he sat down, then fixed her dress. She looked around to make sure no one was watching them, stepped a few feet away from Arbin and asked, "Is this okay?"

Arbin looked up, still kind of in a daze, and said, "What?"

Elizabeth looked at him and said, "Are you feeling better?"

Arbin saw the concern in her eyes, "Yes, a little."

"See, all you needed was a little walk." Elizabeth smiled, then looked around. "Besides, there were too many people around back there."

Arbin took a deep breath and found he did feel better. "Look, I do not want your brother to get into any trouble, but like I told him, I do not want to join the Seers. I especially do not want to have anything to do with that pompous High Seer. Plus, that Bishop worries me."

"You need to trust my brother," said Elizabeth. "I remember they scared me when I first met them, but my brother told me it would be okay, and it was."

"That's right, Alex said something about you being tested because you are twins," said Arbin.

"Yes, fraternal twins," said Elizabeth.

Arbin thought about Jayden and Mia. He studied Elizabeth for a few seconds. "Alex said you do not have any Talents like him."

"That's right," said Elizabeth. "Bishop Sorren and High Seer Kindermann tested me and said so. It's a good thing because nothing good happens to girls with abilities."

"How did they test you?" Arbin asked. "The same way the Committee wants me tested?"

"No, they both interviewed me and then decided that I did not have the Seer's gift or the Fade's curse," said Elizabeth.

"Ha, those two could not find poop in a manure pile," said Arbin. "No one in that room today has any Talents except your brother. What gives them the right to test anyone?"

"That's the way it's been for a long time," said Elizabeth. "Besides, it's the boys that get the Blessings."

"That's not true. Jayden, the Fade everyone is talking about, has a twin sister named Mia. She has a Talent."

"Well, that would make sense. She must have been cursed by her brother who is evil," said Elizabeth.

"Mia is not evil!" said Arbin a bit too loud before looking around. "She is the most honest person I have met. Her brother has done some bad things, but in my time with them he did nothing truly evil."

"He attacked Duke Henry," said Elizabeth. "I hope you agree that was an evil act."

"Yes," said Arbin. "That was evil, and not something I would have expected from the Jayden I knew."

"My brother says the Fade wants to kill you as well," said Elizabeth.

Arbin looked down at his feet, not saying anything right away. He finally nodded and without looking up said, "There is that."

Elizabeth stared at Arbin for a few seconds then asked, "How well did you know Mia and her brother?"

Still looking down, Arbin said, "Three years. At one point, I thought I was in love with Mia and we had plans to get married."

"And what happened?" asked Elizabeth.

Arbin studied her, trying to decide how much of his past he wanted to share. He was feeling a little dizzy and really did not want to put the effort into coming up with a carefully crafted lie, so he said, "Her brother and I had a fight, he tried to kill me and now I am here."

"What did you fight about?" asked Elizabeth.

"Jayden is very protective of his sister. When Mia and I separated, he said I was unfair to her. That led to our disagreement."

Arbin could see that Elizabeth was waiting for him to continue his story. His discomfort and being forced to think about his past had put him in a bad mood. He said with a little too much anger, "That's all you need to know. It's none of yours or anyone else's business." Arbin could feel his discomfort growing again, and when he looked back up at Elizabeth, he could see a bit of anger in her eyes. After a few minutes, Arbin asked, "Why are you here again?"

Elizabeth stiffened up, smoothed her dress and said, "Alex said he thinks you will fail the test."

"What?" Arbin looked at Elizabeth, not sure he understood her. "I thought you came by to cheer me on. What makes him say that?"

"Alex is worried about the fairness of the testing process," said Elizabeth. "He said if the test is run honestly, you would pass. He will do his best to make sure that happens. Alex also said you must stop talking back to everyone you meet. Every word out of your mouth can hurt you."

"Hurt me, No one said anything about this testing hurting," said Arbin.

"No, it won't hurt. You really are a big baby," said Elizabeth as she ignored Arbin's look. "He did not say it would hurt you. He meant people would use what you said to get you in trouble."

"Sorry," said Arbin. "I am still a little light-headed. Makes it hard for me to concentrate. Do you know what the test will be like?"

Elizabeth took a step back and said, "They set up three curtains. A person stands behind each curtain, and you must pick which curtain has a Seer behind it. You do that three times. If you are right two out of three times you pass. My brother said you have more Seer ability than anyone he has ever met. That means this test, if done fairly, should be easy for you."

"Yeah, except one thing and your brother knows it," said Arbin.

"What's that?" asked Elizabeth.

"So far I have only met the Seers from the caravan and out of all those, only your brother and Lubin have any Talent," said Arbin.

"You have met no one else from the Seer Core?" asked Elizabeth.

"Only the High Seer and he is no Seer," said Arbin. "They have been keeping me away from everyone since I got here. Today was the first time I saw your brother in three days."

"Well, I trust my brother. You should take his advice and not talk about your gift or the test to anyone," said Elizabeth.

"That should not be hard," said Arbin. "I got no one to talk to."

"Do you have someplace to stay tonight?" asked Elizabeth.

"That is a good question. I am not sure if they will let me back in where I was staying," said Arbin as he looked around for his bag. "I think I left my bag back up near that statue of the couple sitting near the little rose garden."

"Princess Hanna and Prince Carl," said Elizabeth. "They dedicated this place to them." She looked around and smiled. "The Bridge of Sorrows. It's hard to believe that such a beautiful place could be the scene of such a hateful act."

"Yeah, I guess it's kind of pretty here," said Arbin.

Elizabeth studied Arbin as he looked out at the park. After a few minutes of silence, she shook her head, looked up at the sky and said, "I think he might still be there." She looked back at Arbin and said, "I would like you to go to the National Library. Ask for a man named Masimo Vinetti. He should be doing research there. If he is there, tell him I sent you, and that you need a place for the night. I am sure he will be happy to help. One word of warning. He is a talker. He will probably have you up all night answering questions."

Arbin nodded and said, "Thanks. You are the first pleasant thing that has happened to me since I got here."

Elizabeth smiled and Arbin could tell she was a little embarrassed by his comment. She turned and started walking away. After a few feet she turned back and said, "I hope you feel better soon," then continued on her way.

Arbin watched her as she walked away thinking to himself, *your mother is right, you are very pretty.*

"Excuse me, are you Arbin Adean?" said a man to Arbin's right.

Arbin had not seen the man approach and was so startled that he almost tripped as he quickly stood and turned to see who was speaking.

"What?" replied Arbin as he stared at the stranger that used his name, then said, "Sorry I did not see you there."

The stranger smiled and politely asked again, "Are you Arbin Adean?"

Arbin looked around, not sure what to say, then nodded.

The man smiled again and handed Arbin a letter and said, "I am employed by Councilman Thomas Darr. He has asked me to deliver this letter to you and extend his invitation to dinner tomorrow."

"Councilman Darr," said Arbin. "I do not know him."

"The Councilman was present at your application today. He was most impressed and would like to have the opportunity to speak with you," replied the stranger.

"But I do not know where he lives," said Arbin.

"Everything you need is in the letter," said the stranger. "I would also suggest that you change for the meeting and not be late."

Arbin looked down at his clothes and said, "Change, how?"

The stranger said, "It's all in the letter, good day, Mr. Adean," as he turned and walked away.

Arbin stared at the letter for several minutes. When he looked back up for the stranger, he could not see him anywhere.

The envelope was heavy in his hand. Arbin looked around before opening it and was surprised to see it contained two pages of writing paper wrapped around what he guessed was money. He had heard about banknotes but had never seen one. Arbin quickly closed the envelope and looked around again.

When he was sure no one was watching, he opened it and carefully removed the papers. The two pages were written in different handwriting. The first contained a brief note instructing him to visit a tailor and a barber. It gave an address for both. It also said that he was to meet Chairman Darr at a party he was giving and that he was to arrive early. The second paper was wrapped around the banknotes and simply said, "For past and future services."

Arbin sat back down on the bench with the envelope held tightly in his hand and said to himself, "You are right Elizabeth, this is a beautiful place."

Chapter 11 - Something New

ARBIN HAD BEEN TO A few big cities when he traveled with his father, but none as big as Leaboro, the Capital city. The last time he had been in a large city was a little over eight years ago when he worked for Mr. Hahn in his warehouse. His time in Noor Point had erased most of the memories of city life. He had gotten use to everything being within shouting distance. Here, if he shouted, he was not sure if anyone would even notice. Each time he left the park in search of the people listed in the letter, he felt like he was stepping into a river of people that threatened to drag him along with the current. So far, he had made it about an hour in each direction from the safety of the little park. Besides the constant movement of people, the other thing that surprised him was the smell of the place. Noor Point had its smell, mostly that of dirt and animal droppings, but the smells of the city of Leaboro ranged from the wonderful smells of new and interesting foods to the sickening smell of rotting trash and waste that ran off into the river near the docks.

His first success was in finding the bank named on the banknotes. It was on the east side of the river. However, his request to trade in the banknotes for coins cost him over an hour of his quickly vanishing day. They shuffled Arbin from one bank official to another. It took showing the letters from Councilman Darr and opening an account before he got what he wanted.

The visit to the bank also presented him with a problem he never thought he would have. How would he carry the money he was getting? At the recommendation of the bank, he took his money in gold coins. The bank official said, "Sometimes less is best and gold speaks the loudest."

Of the seven bank notes he had received, he cashed in two and deposited three in his new bank account. He kept the last two and his coins in a small pouch he hung from his neck. The official also gave Arbin a quick lesson in the value of the various coins he might run into around town. Arbin found he really missed the barter system back in Noor Point.

After a lot of asking, Arbin learned that the tailor was on the west side of the island, about a fifteen-minute walk from the bridge.

One thing he soon learned was the west side had more shops, and the people were more eager to talk, but when it came to directions, what he got were things like "It's a little past Jaeger's place," or "Just keep going for a few blocks and someone will help you."

When Arbin finally found the tailor shop, he was not sure he was in the right place at first because the sign on the storefront just read 'Schneider & Sons'. Arbin's dress got him some strange looks as he entered the shop. He could tell from the items on display this was not a place he would ever visit on his own. The tailor, Mr. Schneider, became almost excited once he learned that Councilman Darr had sent Arbin. He talked nonstop as he guided Arbin to the little platform where he took measurements. Arbin soon learned more about Schneider than he wanted to know, including that he was the 'Son' in the store name. Schneider asked Arbin several times to thank Councilman Darr for selecting his shop for such a great honor.

Arbin learned that Councilman Darr's party was to be a masquerade and considered the biggest event of the season. Schneider talked on and on about how his design would be so much more original and exciting than the past costumes. He also learned that Councilman Darr always picked a celebrity, someone of importance, for the position that Arbin would fill. A position Schneider called the Master of the Torch.

The best Arbin could understand was that he would keep the torches at the party lit. It did not sound like something that a celebrity would be doing. In fact, it sounded like the work he did in Noor Point. Arbin said nothing about his concerns and did his best to follow Schneider's constant talking.

Schneider made several tactful attempts to determine what made Arbin so special, and Arbin did his best to avoid any direct answers to the tailor's questions. Frustrated at the probing, Arbin finally said that he was a visitor to the city. He had traveled here from the south and had spoken before members of the Council. He said that Councilman Darr was a big supporter of his work and had asked him to assist him with the party. Arbin's exaggeration of the truth seemed to satisfy the tailor's curiosity for a while.

Schneider continued with the measurements, pausing every few minutes to study Arbin as if he were trying to decide who Arbin really was. Once the tailor finished Arbin asked "What now?"

"Councilman Darr has taken care of everything. You will find the costume waiting for you at his home tomorrow," said Schneider. "Now, what about you, sir? I am sure that you will want to change back into something more comfortable for the rest of your stay. I have items in both the northern and the new southern styles."

Arbin was a little surprised at the question. He looked down at his clothes and said, "Something new would be nice. I would like something better for traveling, and some daily wear would be nice. I would also like something better for carrying around money."

Schneider excitedly left the room saying, "I think I have just what you're looking for."

Arbin took several minutes studying the clothes the tailor placed before him. Schneider took Arbin's expressions for one of disappointment. "I have others in the back if these are not to your liking."

Arbin quickly said that he was just surprised at the quality of the material and the work. That seemed to put the tailor at ease.

The materials were in fact wonderfully light and had a clean feel and smell to them. He had seen a few people in the Grand Council meeting room wearing similar clothes. Arbin had never imagined himself wearing anything as fancy and impractical as these clothes. He was not even sure how you wore some items. He was intrigued by where the money pouches were hidden.

Arbin selected three outfits. Schneider said they would be ready for pickup late tomorrow morning. When Arbin paid Schneider in gold coins, it only added to the tailor's suspicions that he was someone of great importance traveling in disguise. Schneider promised he would tell no one that Arbin had been in his shop until after the party.

Arbin's next task was to find the barber listed in his note. He was disappointed when Schneider told him that the barber's place was not far, but that he was sure the man would have gone home by now. Schneider also said that the person he asked about was a fine barber but had lost a few patients lately. Arbin was a little surprised at Schneider's response. He soon learned that there were only two barbers in town. Both were also surgeons, and both were currently feuding. Arbin put the tailor at ease by saying he was just looking for a haircut.

As Arbin left the tailor shop, the air felt a little colder and the lateness of the day reminded him of the problem of where he would spend the night. It was obviously too late to meet up with Elizabeth's friend in the library. He was sure that with his newfound wealth, finding a place in town would not be a problem. Unfortunately, he did not know where to look. He found himself asking people on the street if they knew where he could stay for a few days. The few suggestions on places proved useless. Each place he visited said he should have been here a few days ago, before the crowds for the celebration arrived. The last person he asked looked at him, laughed and was soon lost from view in the crowded street.

That last response just made the futility of his situation clear, and the laughter just left him angry. *What good is it to have all this money if I cannot find some place to stay*, he thought. Maybe I can find Alex and see if he would let me stay there. The problem was, he did not know where Alex lived. If he asked about him, it might get back to the Application Committee. He could always try to bribe old Ackerman to let him stay in the service quarters again. The image of Ackerman smiling as he sent Arbin packing was still fresh in his mind. Arbin did not want to waste his newfound wealth on that grumpy old man. He could always just camp out for the night. That park he was in earlier had a spot under one of the bridge overpasses that he could use.

Arbin leaned back against the wall of the building behind him as he thought over his options. Soon he noticed a smell of cooked food, chicken stew if he was right, coming from inside the building. He looked up and was startled by the image of a large bear on the sign above his head. He stared at it for a while, trying to decide if the bear was laughing or growling. Arbin looked inside and his stomach reminded him loudly that he had eaten nothing today. "I might as well do my thinking on a full stomach," he whispered to himself.

The room was crowded, but he found a spot just inside the doorway. It was a small stool at a window which had an oversize ledge. The stains on the window ledge suggested they had used it as a table several times. The pleasant looking girl, who asked for his order, was not sure how to respond when he asked if he could pay for his meal with a gold coin. She left without answering him.

She returned shortly, accompanied by the tavern owner, who introduced himself as Godfrey Kruger. He had short blond hair with a beard to match. He was shorter than Arbin and many pounds heavier. Most of the weight hidden under an apron. Arbin had noticed him much earlier because of his laughter and booming voice. Godfrey appeared to be able to carry on conversations with people no matter where they were in the room.

"Welcome to the Laughing Bear," said Godfrey. "I apologize for not having a table available when you entered. Luckily, one has just come available if you will follow me." Godfrey led Arbin towards a table near the fireplace where he saw two muscular men convincing the present occupants to move. On the way there Godfrey said in a much quieter voice, "There might be a slight delay in getting change for your coins. Unless you wanted to order something of finer quality to eat."

Arbin said, "That would be wonderful, and you can keep the change if you can tell me where I can find a place to stay for a few days."

Godfrey laughed and said, "I might know a place, but it's expensive."

"That will not be a problem," said Arbin. He used the same exaggeration he had used on the tailor. "I'm an out-of-town guest of Councilman Darr. In fact, I will be the guest of honor at his party tomorrow night."

Godfrey smiled and said, "Then you're in luck. We do have a room for you, and it just so happens the current guest will be leaving shortly. Please enjoy yourself while we get your room and food ready."

Godfrey walked to the back of the room and spoke with the two men Arbin had seen clearing his table earlier. The men listened to Godfrey quietly, then nodded and headed upstairs. After several minutes, Arbin saw one of the two men return, leading a man and a woman, both carrying a bundle of clothes, out the back of the Inn. A few minutes later the other man returned and signaled to Godfrey, who walked over to Arbin and said, "Your room is ready when you are. I will have food and drink more fitting for a person of your character brought out."

Arbin knew what was going on here. *That banker was right. Gold speaks loudly,* he thought. As for the couple that checked out earlier, he assured himself that he was not responsible. After all, it was not his job to tell the innkeeper how to run his business. He was tired and needed a place to stay for a few days. He was not sure if he wanted to join the Seers, but he was sure of two things. First, he did not want to sleep in the park tonight. Second, he did not like how that fraudulent High Seer talked about him.

Soon a large plate with a whole roasted chicken and vegetables arrived, followed by a large mug of ale. The fire was warm, and the pleasant barmaid made sure his mug was full. For the first time since arriving in this city, he felt at ease. No, what he really felt was important. Arbin let himself relax and enjoyed the food and drink before him.

Chapter 12 - A New Man

A LOUD NOISE, LIKE the banging on a door, brought Arbin out of his sleep. He looked around and tried to focus on the source of the noise. The effects of his drinking last night made it hard to focus on anything. It took him several minutes before he could remember where he was.

Arbin was never any good at drinking, mostly because he got little practice at it. His life back in Noor Point did not provide the income needed, and his desire to avoid questions about his past meant he lived a somewhat solitary life. Invitations to join others for drink were rare and mostly resulted from him agreeing to clean up after events.

He slowly raised himself upright, sat on the edge of the bed, and rocked slowly back and forth with his face in his hands. He took a couple deep breaths through his cupped hands, then stretched a bit and looked around at his surroundings.

It was a small room, but larger than where he had called home back in Noor Point. It contained a bed, a dresser, a chair, a few stacked boxes and had a large window which, from where he sat, gave a delightful view of the wall of a building across the street.

Arbin took in another deep breath, and while looking at the window, wondered what time it was. As the fog in his head cleared, he discovered he was partly dressed. His shirt was on the floor along with one of his shoes. He had one leg out of his pants and the other pant leg was caught up in a ball just above his other shoe. In his drunken state last night, he must have been unable to get his pants fully off and just fell into bed.

That is when he remembered the loud sound that woke him. He was sure the sound came from the door to his room but did not know if it was caused by the door slamming or someone striking it. He vaguely remembered buying drinks for people in the tavern. There were a few women among them, and he did some flirting with the barmaid, but he did not remember going upstairs for the night.

The brightness of the morning sun reflecting off the white walls of the building outside and the increasing sounds of people in the street below reminded him he had things to do. The mysteries of last night could wait.

Arbin got up, struggled back into his clothes, then made a halfhearted attempt to straighten up the bed. He paused at the door before opening it and did a quick check of his money. He still had his bank notes in the little hidden purse, and he had considerably fewer gold coins than before, but that might be explained by last night.

He was not sure how much a trip to the barber would cost. He hoped that he would not need to go to the bank because that meant walking all the way to the east side of the river. Maybe he would feel a little more energetic after breakfast.

Arbin made his way down the stairs and quietly out the back door. He found a small green area with a garden on one side and a coop for chickens on the other.

He saw a rain bucket nearby. He took off his shirt and used the water to wash off his face and wet his hair. Next, he grabbed a handful of grass, got it wet and scrubbed the taste of last night's drinking from his mouth.

Standing up, he felt better. He used his fingers to squeeze the water out of his light brown hair and then combed it back into what would have been a two-fisted ponytail if he had something to fasten it.

Arbin put his shirt back on and as he turned around to head back into the tavern, he noticed the barmaid from last night standing in the doorway giving him an unpleasant look. He was not sure what to say, but before he could think of anything, she turned and went back into the tavern.

Arbin tried to remember her name, but it did not come to him.

He headed back inside, but the girl was nowhere to be seen. He did see Godfrey, who was doing some cleaning in the area behind the bar. Godfrey looked up as Arbin entered and smiled. "Will you be wanting the room for another night, my friend?"

Arbin nodded and said, "I have a few stops to make today." He handed Godfrey a gold coin and said, "I will pay the balance for the room tonight."

Godfrey pocketed the coin and said, "Did you want something to eat before you headed out? It would take a few minutes to make something fancy, but we have porridge and bread if you are in a hurry."

Arbin nodded and said, "Porridge would be fine, thanks."

"Have a seat," said Godfrey as he signaled to someone. "I will have it out to you right away."

As if on cue, the barmaid arrived with his food, dropped the plate in front of him and stormed away.

What did I do to upset her? Arbin thought. He looked at Godfrey, who had a large smile on his face and seemed to find the barmaid's behavior amusing. "Will there be anything else?" Godfrey asked.

"There is one other thing," said Arbin. He got out Councilman Darr's letter and said, "I need to visit the person listed here, do you know where I can find him?"

Arbin saw Godfrey blink a bit as he looked at the paper and then said, "Sorry, sir, but I can't do script. If you tell me the name, maybe I could help you." Arbin read the barber's name off the paper and Godfrey's face soured.

"He would not be my first choice, but if that is where you want to go, I will have a boy take you after your breakfast," said Godfrey.

Arbin devoured his breakfast. It was simple and cold, but he felt a lot better with something in his stomach. He signaled to Godfrey who soon joined him accompanied by a small boy about eight years old. "This is Carl, he will get you where you're going," said Godfrey. "Just send him back when you're done."

THE STREETS WERE ALREADY full of people, and Arbin worried that Carl would get lost in the swirling maze of bodies. After a few minutes, he decided that he better worry about himself. Arbin's first visit would be the tailor. Carl looked confused when Arbin gave him the tailor's address. When Arbin said the name of the tailor, the boy's face brightened up and he started off, stopping every few seconds to make sure Arbin was following him.

With Carl's help, Arbin quickly found the tailor shop and picked up the clothes he purchased. Next it was off to the barber. It surprised Arbin to find that the barber's place was only about twelve buildings away from the tailor. He must have passed it a few times in his journey.

A small sign hanging from an iron bracket out front said 'Stefano Viaro, Barber & Surgeon'.

The front of the store had several large shudders propped open to show a beautiful room decorated with a few statues, several chairs, and a colorful settee. On one wall was the painting of a countryside. Across from it, on the other wall, was a painting of a city. In the back of the room, in one chair, sat a small, modestly dressed man. Arbin could not guess his age, but figured he had to be over fifty.

Arbin could tell that Carl did not want to enter, so he gave him a few of the lesser coins in his purse and sent him on his way.

As Arbin entered the building, the small man stood up and approached him, smiling the entire time. He said nothing but directed Arbin to a chair and quickly left the room through a door hidden behind curtains. Arbin was not sure what to do, so he just sat there and looked around.

A few minutes later, a tall man in his late thirties entered the room through the draped doorway. His hair was short, and his smile was large. He was dressed in a smock which Arbin noticed had some dark stains on the side, as if someone had wiped something on it. He walked toward Arbin with both his hands stretched out in front of him in a very welcoming way. Arbin stood as he approached and found himself reaching to take the outstretched hands.

"Dear friend, welcome," said the man as he took Arbin's outstretched hand in both of his and shook it. "My name is Stefano Viaro. Welcome to my place. I am so glad you came in to see me today." Arbin was waiting for the man to release his hands and was getting a little worried. The man smiled, released his grip and motioned for Arbin to sit down while he took the chair next to him. "Is there something special I can do for you?"

Arbin was getting ready to answer Stefano's question when he was interrupted by the sounds of the older man returning with a tray that contained two glasses and a decanter.

Stefano smiled at Arbin as he waited for the older man to place the tray on the table next to him. Stefano pointed to the decanter, and as he poured himself a glass, asked, "Something to drink?" Arbin shook his head no. Stefano took a sip, then thanked the older man, who promptly left the room. Stefano turned back to Arbin, smiled and said, "Continue, please."

"I am here at the request of Councilman Darr."

Stefano's smile widened even more. "So, you're the young man that Thomas told me about. Stand up, stand up, let's have a look at you."

Arbin stood up as instructed and Stefano took him by one arm and led him to the center of the room where he walked from one side of Arbin to the other saying, "Yes, yes, I think I can do something here. Tell me, are these the only clothes you have?"

Arbin indicated the bundle he had just picked up from the tailor.

Stefano asked, "May I," pointing to the bundle and had the three outfits laid out on the settee almost before Arbin could even answer.

Stefano carefully examined the items then said, "Nice work. It would be my guess that these are from Tailor Schneider." When Arbin nodded, he continued, "Interesting choice. I see you favor the southern style." Stefano studied Arbin for a while and said, "I have decided. First, we must clean you up and then the genuine work can start." Stefano clapped his hands twice and the older man returned. Stefano turned to Arbin and said, "Follow my assistant. I am sure he has everything ready for you."

Following the older man through another set of curtains, Arbin entered an outdoor space setup with a tub and several benches. The assistant directed Arbin to a bench which had a bucket of water and some towels and motioned for Arbin to wash his hair in the bucket.

Arbin now understood that the older man did not speak. Nodding, Arbin took off his shirt, which the older man took from him, folded, then set it on the bench. As he poured the water over his head, Arbin noticed it had the smell of flowers. Once he finished, the old man presented him with a robe. Arbin followed him to another outside area, but this one was beautifully landscaped with a small fountain, statues and seating areas.

Stefano was already in the small courtyard, fiddling with three boxes on a small table. He directed Arbin to a bench and said, "Time spent in peaceful environments allows one to focus more clearly. It's essential for the mind to be at rest before starting any artistic endeavors."

Arbin watched as Stefano took various shiny instruments out of the two boxes. He also took glass bottles and clay bowls with cloth coverings from the third. Arbin asked quietly, "Artistic endeavors?"

"Some people work with stone or paint; my work is much more demanding because my canvas is ever changing. I must capture the essence of my subject in a way that will survive those changes," said Stefano.

"What are you going to do with those?" asked Arbin.

"I will bring out the true you," replied Stefano. "Relax and trust me. Would you like some wine or treats while I work?"

Arbin shook his head and said, "No drink for now, thanks."

Stefano worked surprisingly fast. He would pause from time to time, take a sip from his glass or sample some dried fruit, smile, then continue his work. Arbin was grateful that he was not as talkative as the tailor.

Arbin was a little resistant when Stefano lathered him up for a shave.

"Trust me," Stefano said again. "I am the artist; you are my canvas. The clothes you selected and your frame conflict with your facial hair. Conflict is the enemy of grace and sophistication."

Arbin was not sure what that meant, but it sounded good, so he did as Stefano said and trusted him.

Before he knew it, Stefano announced, "Perfetto!" He stood looking at Arbin with a smile. Stefano clapped his hands again, and his assistant appeared.

"I took the liberty of selecting the outfit that best goes with our fresh new look. Now if you follow my assistant, he will take you back to the bath area. The water is ready, and we have added fragrances to complement the new you. Please call on my assistant if you need anything."

Arbin was not too keen on taking a bath in strange places, but he agreed that it would be best considering the price he paid for his new clothes. He did his best to figure out how to wear the outfit Stefano selected for him. Soon, with a little help, Arbin was dressed and looking at himself in a small hand-held mirror.

The change was amazing. He could hardly recognize himself. His long stringy hair was now much shorter with clean straight ends. His clean-shaven face made him look younger, and he felt much lighter. His new clothes made him feel taller and maybe a little smarter. The longer Arbin looked in the mirror, the better he felt. He was looking at a 'new man'. He was no longer that old man who spent his time hiding. No longer a simple street cleaner. He was now a man whose appearance demanded respect. He was a man with style, and the money to go with it.

Arbin handed the small mirror back to Stefano's assistant, who directed Arbin back into the room at the entrance. The old man pointed for Arbin to have a seat, then disappeared back into the bathing area. He soon returned with Arbin's original clothes wrapped in paper.

Stefano entered the room shortly after that with another paper wrapped bundle that contained the rest of the new clothes Arbin had just picked up. Stefano handed him the bundle and Arbin saw a piece of paper held to the bundle by the wrapping string. Stefano said, "I have also made a note for you on what items you should select the next time you visit our friend, Tailor Schneider."

He thanked Stefano and said he would tell everyone who asked who his barber was.

Stefano smiled and said, "Everyone who is anyone already knows." He took one last look and said, "If you will excuse me, I have other less pleasant business to tend to," and left Arbin standing with his assistant who presented Arbin with a written bill.

Arbin was a little surprised at the amount of the bill. The barber would cost him more than he spent on everything else so far. He did his best to smile as he handed over his money. He did a quick check and decided he had enough money for tonight but would need to visit the bank again tomorrow.

ARBIN MADE HIS WAY back toward the Laughing Bear tavern. As he walked through the streets, it surprised him how he was treated. His haircut and new clothes really made a difference. He did not have to weave in and out of people, but his path opened in front of him. He also noticed that no one looked directly at him. "This is almost like being ignored without having to use my Talents," he whispered to himself with a smile.

When Arbin entered the Laughing Bear, he received a much different reaction. Everyone looked at him, some with murmurs of suspicion. It was clear he was not viewed as belonging like before.

Godfrey came over to welcome him, and it took a few seconds before the look of recognition could be seen. He greeted him exclaiming, "My friend! I'm glad you found your way back; your regular table is ready." With that, most of the people in the room returned to the business of enjoying themselves.

As Arbin followed Godfrey through the crowded room, he had to struggle with the urge to turn around and leave. He had enjoyed the effects of his new persona outside, but in here the attention was uncomfortable.

Arbin reached out and tapped Godfrey on his shoulder to stop him. "Can we go someplace to talk?"

Godfrey nodded and headed towards the back door. Once outside Godfrey said, "I take it you will not want dinner."

Arbin nodded and looking back inside said, "I can see that business has picked up and I appreciate you making space for me, but I have someplace I need to be tonight. I just wanted to pay the balance for my room and drop off some things before heading to Councilman Darr's home."

"Now about your room," said Godfrey. "As you say, business is picking up. The closer we get to the Unification Day celebrations, the more demand there will be for rooms."

Arbin looked at Godfrey and said, "I hope you have not rented it to someone. I gave you a deposit this morning."

Godfrey said, "I would never do that to my best customer. However, with the increased demand, I will need to charge you more. It's only good business. I am sure a man of your sophistication would understand."

"A man of sophistication," said Arbin almost to himself. The words put a finishing touch on what he saw in the mirror at the barber's shop. He smiled just thinking about it. "Yes, that is a good way to describe it," whispered Arbin as he stood a little taller.

Godfrey saw the change come over Arbin and in a worried voice said, "I said it would be expensive." When Arbin did not answer, Godfrey said,

"I should charge you double what I am. I gave you a great price because you are a close associate of Councilman Darr."

"Yes, Councilman Darr," said Arbin. "When I attend his party tonight, I will be sure to mention your hospitality."

Godfrey laughed and slapped Arbin on the shoulder. "My friend, you are too kind. I hope you understand the demands on me. I think we can agree that a small increase is not unreasonable."

Arbin was a little impressed that his new look and the drop of a name could have such an effect on Godfrey. He really was a new man. Arbin smiled and then said. "I understand the demands you are under. I will take back the deposit and leave tonight. After all, I am not a man to stand in the way of business."

Godfrey, for the first time, was silent. After a few seconds, Arbin reached into his purse and brought out two gold coins. He held them up for Godfrey to see and then said, "Here is the balance of what I owe for tonight and another coin just as my way of saying thank you. Now I really need to be going. I have to get to Councilman Darr's party."

Godfrey took the coins and said, "Are you planning on walking all the way to Councilman Darr's home? If you are, it will take you a few hours to get there."

"Do you have a better plan?" asked Arbin.

"I have a friend with a cart. I will send for him. That way you can be there within the hour," said Godfrey.

"And what will that cost me?" asked Arbin.

Godfrey smiled and said, "No charge, consider it a thank you, from me to our favorite guest. I am sure Councilman Darr would appreciate me getting you to his party on time. You can wait in your room. I will let you know when the cart arrives."

Chapter 13 - Party of One

"HEY, YOU, GET OUT OF the way. Can't you see we're trying to get by," shouted the cart driver. This same scene repeated itself several times as the cart that Godfrey had arranged for him made its way through the crowded streets toward Councilman Darr's home. The trip by cart was a little uncomfortable, but Arbin had to admit it was much better than walking. It would have been impossible to arrive on time if he had made the trip through the crowded streets on foot.

The travel got a little easier once he got past the business district on the east side, which clustered mostly along the river road, between the Bridge of Sorrows and the Eastern Gate of the Government Compound. Unlike the west side, this business district was only a few buildings wide.

The buildings on the east side of the city differed from the west side where they were a collection of businesses and living spaces, some on top of others. The buildings on the east side were more spread out and there appeared to be more homes than businesses. Arbin guessed this was because the west side was bordered by some low foothills and the east side, which was mostly flat, extended out until it joined a forest.

Arbin soon found himself in a section of town that was a combination of different size homes with varying architecture. Some larger homes, built more recently, must have involved knocking down some surrounding homes. Councilman Darr's home was one of these.

He felt a little strange about arriving this way. The small cart appeared even smaller as it made its way through the gate, past the small garden and looking pond at the front of the home. Arbin was a little upset when the cart driver took him past the front door and to the side entrance where he could see staff preparing for the party. "Why did you take me here?" he asked. "I am a guest, not the hired help."

"I'm sorry, sir," the driver responded. "I guess I just did it out of habit."

Before Arbin could say anything else, a woman came over to the cart and asked if he needed any help. Arbin had seen her directing some workers as he approached. Arbin did his best to get out of the cart with as much grace as he could manage. He stood up straight and said, "My name is Arbin Adean. I am here at the request of Councilman Darr. I will be the Master of Torches for tonight's party."

The woman, who he learned was named Agnes, did not appear to be as impressed by Arbin and his new title as he expected. She was obviously in charge of setting up for the party and was more interested in that than in Arbin. She led him through a large kitchen, pausing to bark out instructions or criticisms every few seconds. "Your clothes arrived earlier," said Agnes. "I have instructions to see you're fed before you change."

When Arbin asked if Councilman Darr was in, Agnes said, "Councilman Darr has a habit of always arriving late for his own parties. That was why it was so important for you to arrive early, sir."

"I do not understand what my arrival time has to do with anything," said Arbin.

Agnes stopped and looked at him for a few seconds. She shook her head and said, "Simon will go over your duties with you. As you can see, I am terribly busy. You can eat here." Agnes pointed to the room they had stopped at, where Arbin saw a dining table setup and two serving staff standing by. Agnes walked off, shouting more instructions to the workers as she disappeared back into the kitchen.

As soon as Arbin sat down, people brought food. They placed several platters of meats, bread, vegetables, fruits and cheeses in front of him. He just pointed and was served. "This is great. Councilman Darr really knows how to live," he said.

As Arbin was enjoying his food, he was startled by a voice behind saying, "I am glad you accepted Councilman Darr's invitation, Mr. Adean." Arbin turned and recognized the man that had delivered the envelope to him the other day. "My name is Simon. I am Councilman Darr's assistant.

When you have finished eating, I will show you to a room where you may change for the party."

Simon stood quietly a few feet behind Arbin. Even though he could not see him, Arbin knew he was there watching him. Arbin looked around at the extensive amount of food before him, many items he wanted to try, but the thought of Simon's watchful eyes discouraged him. Arbin gave up, said he was finished eating and followed Simon up a grand set of stairs to a room where Arbin found his costume. Simon asked if Arbin needed his help to get ready. Arbin thanked him politely and directed him to the door.

"Very well," said Simon. "I will be back to get you when it's time to perform your duties."

During his visit to the tailor, Arbin had never seen the clothes he was being measured for. Now, as he looked at it laid out on the bed in front of him, he said, "You got to be kidding me."

It was a collection of colors. The main outfit was in several loose-fitting sections and appeared to be in various shades of white with gold stitching. There were also what looked like layers of lace in red, orange, yellow and blue violet attached to several sections. He also found several arms and leg bands with long colored ribbons connected to them. The costume also came with a cap and shoes that look more like slippers than regular shoes. The best Arbin could figure was that he was supposed to look like something on fire, or maybe some big ugly bird. It would be a lot easier to wear this thing if they allowed him to wear a mask.

There was a knock at the door. Simon entered, looked at the costume still on the bed and said, "You need to get dressed now, sir. The first set of guests have almost finished with their dinner and the other guests will arrive soon."

"First set of guests?" asked Arbin.

Simon said, "Councilman Darr always has his guests arrive in two groups. The more favored guests arrive first. That allows them first rights at the buffet tables. Being in the first group is an enormous honor."

Simon looked at the costume and back at Arbin and said, "You need to be ready to greet the guests in less than twenty minutes. Are you sure you don't need any help to get ready?"

Arbin reluctantly accepted Simon's offer and about halfway through getting dressed was glad of it. The costume was the most complicated and uncomfortable thing he had ever worn. While he got dressed, Simon briefed him on his duties. He was to thank the host and guests, announce the rules of the party and light the first torch. *How am I going to light a torch in this outfit without lighting myself on fire?* Arbin thought as he looked down at the ribbons and lace hanging off his sleeves. As Arbin fidgeted with the arm straps, something that Simon said now returned to him. "Wait, rules, you said something about rules." It was bad enough he had to stand up in front of everyone in this thing, but now he had to memorize a bunch of party rules. "No one told me about the rules."

"The rules are very simple," said Simon. "No one is to call a person by their name as long as they have their mask on. Masks are to stay on until you announce for masks to be removed. If people want to remain at the party after that, they must remove their masks."

"That sounds easy enough," Arbin said as he relaxed and looked at himself in the mirror. "I still do not understand this costume," he muttered as he turned from side to side, allowing him to get the full effect of the ribbons and lace hanging off his outstretched arms.

There was a knock on the door and Simon said, "It's time to go, sir. Once you're down the stairs, stand on the small platform. I will announce you, then you give the welcoming address." Simon looked at Arbin struggling with the waistline of the costume and said, "Keep it short and simple, sir. They are here for the party."

As Arbin came down the stairs, the number of people surprised him. *This is the first group? How big is this party going to get?* he thought. They had removed most of the furniture in the rooms on the first floor and the collection of people spread through the house and outside into a beautifully decorated patio that stretched out into a walking garden backed by a row of trees and a very high fence.

There were color streamers everywhere, many matching the colors of his outfit. The guests were all dressed in amazing costumes, many of which made him look plain. Looking around, he said, "I can do this."

"I am sure you can, sir. Just remember to keep it short," said Simon, who was standing next to him and pointing towards the small platform.

As Arbin stepped on to the platform Simon said in a loud and clear voice "Ladies and gentlemen, honored guests, I present to you our Master of the Torch, the hero of Noor Point, the only man alive to have battled a demon Fade hand to hand and survived." With that, Simon pointed to Arbin and started clapping. Soon every guest had followed Simon's lead.

Arbin was speechless for a few seconds. He had done his best to be unnoticed for the last eight years. The sudden attention was overwhelming.

Fortunately, Simon came to his aid and exclaimed, "Now for the welcoming announcements," Simon looked up to Arbin to make sure he was listening, then said "and the rules for tonight's party."

The next few minutes went by almost without him realizing it. He did his best to keep it short. He thanked Councilman Darr and his wife, pausing for the short round of applause. He gave the rules and then did his best to get off the stage without falling.

A man, dressed in black and white, approached Arbin holding a lantern. He handed Arbin the lantern and pointed towards the patio. Arbin made his way through the party guests to an area where a group of tall torches were standing. The torches must have been at least four feet tall. Another man, also dressed in black and white, took the lantern from Arbin and used it to light the torches. Once the torches were burning, Arbin turned to the gathered guests, and as instructed, announced "Let the merriment begin!"

There was a cheer and music began from a small group of musicians which Arbin had not noticed before.

Arbin made his way back to Simon, who was still standing near the little platform. When he asked what he was supposed to do now, Simon said, "Enjoy yourself. When we need you, someone will find you." With that, Simon quickly disappeared back into the house.

The number of people at the party made Arbin uncomfortable. 'New Man' or not, he was not sure what to say or do. He thought the masks would make it easier, but it did not help. Arbin noticed that several of the guests were stealing glances his way. Maybe he should just wait in the room where he got dressed until he was needed again. Arbin was a little disappointed that he had not gotten to speak to Councilman Darr. He was a little curious about that comment on past and future services. It was while

Arbin was thinking about what to do, someone asked if he had his drink yet.

It was a woman in a very colorful dress that had a long trailing veil attached to a headpiece that reminded Arbin of a bird. She was bubbly, a little chubby and wearing a dress that revealed way too much cleavage. A thin man whose outfit resembled a crow, including a mask with a long beak, accompanied her.

The woman put a glass in Arbin's hand and said, "You must let us hear all about your battle." She took Arbin by the arm and led him toward another group of people who looked eager to meet him. The woman did most of the talking, telling the others with a giggle, "Look what I have. Please good sir, you must tell us all about fighting demons. I only hope I will be able to sleep tonight," she said as she squeezed his arm and giggled again.

The man with the crow face said, "I was told these demons can spit fire. Tell me," he said looking at Arbin, "is that what started the fire?" Before Arbin could answer, another person in the group said, "I heard nothing about fire, but I was told by a reliable source they can walk in your shadow."

Arbin listened to the group exchanging bits of information while asking him to confirm it. As Arbin listened, he took a drink from his glass and was pleasantly surprised. It did not have the bitter earthy taste of the ale he had at the tavern. "This is good," he said. "What is it?"

The woman on his arm said, "It's champagne, a bubbly wine. The first time we've served it here. I think it's wonderful, and it's delightfully expensive."

Arbin agreed and finished his glass. The crow waved his hand, and more glasses arrived, which Arbin gladly accepted.

At the group's urging, Arbin told the story of the events of Noor Point and the caravan's journey to the city. It surprised Arbin how much these people already knew about the events.

Arbin soon found himself shuffled from group to group. In each, one woman would take his arm and after a while would hand him off to a woman in another, all the time laughing to each other about what a special treat it was to meet such a brave and famous person. Somehow the masks made it much easier for him to accept the flirting from the women and the handshake and pats on the back from the men.

As the number of glasses climbed, so did the intensity in his retelling of his adventure. His description of the burning anger in the eyes of the Fade and the heat of the fires caused women to gasp. He would receive a "Well Done" from the men as he described the majestic sight of the small group from the caravan as they searched the woods in defense of the helpless Dylan.

Soon the questions focused on fears about the possibility of more Fade attacks. "Are we safe?" they asked. Arbin was also asked more than once about rumors he was training the Seers in a modern way to battle the Fade. There were expressions of concern when he replied that he had trained two Seers but was unable to train others.

One man in the group said, "I am sure the High Seer is prepared to defend us. A man of his skills could probably defeat the Fade single handedly."

Arbin laughed so hard that his drink came out his nose. "Him?" said Arbin with a slight laugh as he wiped the drink from his face. "He is the last person I would depend on." His comments only brought more expressions of concern. "Don't worry," he said. "You need not be a Seer to detect Fades. It's something that most people could learn. It's just that Seers will be better at it than non-Seers."

"That's amazing," said one man in the group. He was dressed in what Arbin had first thought was a turkey outfit until the man clarified it was an eagle. The man had a heavy accent and Arbin could hear a bit of anger as he said, "If that is true, then we need not depend on these Seers for our safety. Will you be training others? I must ask Councilman Darr about this tomorrow."

The woman next to the man laughed and said, "I can see you now commanding that Fade to leave, my hero."

The man was wearing a mask, but under it Arbin was sure he was blushing.

The entire group laughed, and the conversation changed to one of discussing the various costumes in the room and trying to guess who was under the masks.

Arbin took this chance to slip away from the group. He made his way to the food table and was enjoying some cake when Simon found him again. When Arbin saw him he asked, "Party over already? I was just starting to enjoy myself."

"No, it's nothing like that," said Simon. "Councilman Darr has asked to see you."

"Great," said Arbin, looking around at the guests. "Point him out for me, please."

Simon smiled and said, "The Councilman is in his den. If you would follow me please, sir."

Arbin nodded, grabbed another small cake and followed Simon, stopping along the way to receive handshakes and thanks. Arbin did his best to acknowledge the greetings while finishing his cake. He almost bumped into Simon as he stopped before a closed door. "Wait here please," said Simon, as he knocked on the door which opened just a crack. Simon spoke briefly to the person on the other side. The door opened further, and Simon pointed for Arbin to enter.

THE ROOM WAS LIT BY three standing candle holders. The moonlight, entering through a single window, was filtered through a light veil of smoke. Scattered around the room were twelve men, all wearing costumes. Some leaned against the wall, some stood, while others sat in the few chairs. In the middle of the group was the tall, thin crow Arbin had met earlier. As Arbin looked around the room, he found it difficult to suppress a giggle. It was like something out of a children's story.

The crow stepped forward removing his mask revealing the face of a man in his mid-forties wearing a large welcoming smile. Arbin found it difficult to not smile in return as he accepted the outstretched hand. "Welcome, I am so glad you accepted my invitation. Your presence has been most enlightening. Did you get enough to eat?" asked Councilman Darr.

Arbin nodded, but before he could get a word out the Councilman continued, "Good, as you must have guessed I am your host, and these are a few of my closest friends and associates." As Councilman Darr pointed to the people gathered in the room with a sweeping gesture, many nodded their greeting. "I think you had the pleasure of meeting some of them already."

Arbin looked at the group and saw some costumes he recognized from earlier, including the man he had mistaken as a turkey.

"I hope you do not mind if my friends keep their masks on. It makes for a friendlier setting if we all feel we can speak freely," said Councilman Darr.

Arbin nodded his agreement, though he was sure he would not know who these people were even without the masks.

"Now down to business," said Councilman Darr, sitting on the edge of his desk. "First, we want to say thank you for your heroics in defending young Dylan Sumner from an attempted attack by the Fade you call Jayden. A hard decision, I am sure. Acting against someone you once called a friend, to protect someone who represented a group that gives you little to no respect at all."

Arbin was a little surprised at that comment and was happy to find someone who thought he had been getting the wrong end of the stick. He nodded his agreement, but once again before he could say anything Councilman Darr continued, "Good, I see you are a man of few words. That will make it easier for us to get to the point of this meeting."

Councilman Darr signaled Arbin to sit down in a chair one of the other men had just vacated.

"My position on the Governing Council grants me access to a lot of information. This includes the reports on the events at Noor Point. I am not sure if you remember, but I was also present during the Committee meeting on your acceptance into the Seers."

Arbin remembered seeing him there, so he just nodded.

"We enjoyed your recounting of the events of Noor Point and find that we are in agreement with many of your concerns about both the capabilities and leadership of the Seer Core. We also worry about the fairness of the upcoming testing," said Councilman Darr. Several of the men in the room nodded and murmured their agreement.

Both the drink and a room full of outlandish costumes made it a little difficult for Arbin to follow that last statement from the Councilman, so he simply said, "Okay,"

He could see that this seemed to encourage several of the men including Councilman Darr who looked around at the others then said, "We believe what was said about you having greater than usual ability to detect Fades and Seers. My chief concern with tomorrow's test is that it would be difficult to detect a Seer if, as you have said, one is not present. Wouldn't you agree?"

Arbin had been thinking much the same thing himself, so he nodded and said, "I was worried about that very thing."

"Good," said Councilman Darr. "Then we are in agreement," as he looked around the room, receiving nods from the other men in the room. Arbin was not sure what he had agreed to but nodded as well.

"We have already decided on how to best deal with tomorrow's test. You leave that to us. We want you to show up and do your best. We will do our best to make sure the test is properly conducted."

It relieved Arbin that someone else shared his concerns and said, "Thank you," as he started to stand. Councilman Darr raised his hand, signaling Arbin to stay seated, and said, "No thanks needed. We are all after the same thing."

Arbin sat back down and nodded again.

"Good, that's one concern out of the way," said Councilman Darr. "Now I understand that you feel the information that the Seers are working with to defend the country is not necessarily accurate."

Arbin was wondering how so many people had heard these things he was supposed to have said. He sat quietly looking back at the Councilman, not sure how to answer that last question.

Councilman Darr, realizing that Arbin was having difficulty responding, said, "Is it true that you know more about fighting Fades than the Seers you have met so far?"

Arbin smiled and said, "Yes. I would say that almost everything they have told me about Fades is wrong."

This last comment got a stir from the group of men and Councilman Darr who stood, looked around the room, then sat back on the edge of his desk. He studied Arbin for a few seconds before he asked, "Do you think it's this lack of understanding that allowed the Fade to attack Henry Sumner?"

Arbin said, "None of the Seers I met could detect a Fade until I taught them. I am sure they would have never learned how to defend against Fades based on what they believed about them."

The room went quiet. Arbin looked around and realized he may have said something serious. "I will say that the Seers I met were honest in their desire to defend against an attack. It was Alex and Lubin that came to me asking for help. Both learned quickly."

"Have no fear," said Councilman Darr. "It's not our aim to bring harm to your two new friends. We are just trying to understand what needs to happen next to defend us all from attack." Arbin relaxed a bit, and Councilman Darr continued. "Now, maybe you can explain to us some misunderstanding the Seers had about Fades."

Arbin explained some misunderstanding based on myths such as being able to burn someone or disappearing into shadows. Next, he explained how the Fade Talent worked and how he had trained Alex and Lubin to detect it.

During his explanation he was interrupted several times, and he could see that the group of men were fascinated by what he was saying. One of them asked if anyone could be taught to detect a Fade. Arbin nodded and said, "Yes, to a degree. It depends somewhat on the person. The more committed and aware they are, the better the chances."

The man Arbin had met earlier, dressed in what looked like a turkey outfit, asked, "Then, what value is the Seer Core, if we can do it?"

The question surprised Arbin and a few of the others in the room. "Well," said Arbin. "While it's possible for some Non-Seers to learn how to detect a Fade, Seers can be more proactive and deal with Fades in a way that Non-Seers cannot."

"And what does that mean?" asked Councilman Darr.

Arbin took a second to decide how to best answer that question. Finally, he said, "At a very close distance it's possible for a Seer to determine if a person has a Talent, even if they are not using it."

"Can you determine if the person is a Fade or a Seer?" asked Councilman Darr.

"No," responded Arbin. "I only know they have a Talent. However, once I have learned their presence, I can use that to know the person behind a Talent."

The group looked at him for a few minutes and he said, "Think of it like this. Each person has a smell. When they use their Talent, they smell the same as when they are not using it."

He saw the nods of understanding this time and one of them said, "Like during the Purge. That would explain how the Seers could search out the evil ones."

One of the others said, "But you're saying you can only determine that they are a Fade if you have detected them using their Talent as you say."

Arbin nodded and said, "That is basically right."

The man then said, "Who knows who was killed during the Purge. If the persons killed never used their powers, it would be almost impossible to know if they were Fades or Seers."

Arbin looked around at the men in deep thought. He knew about the Purge, but that was ancient history to him. Like others his age, he had learned little about the civil war or the period after its end except for the Purge. Everyone knew about the Purge.

Councilman Darr stood up and looked around. Several of the men nodded. He turned to Arbin and said, "Thank you very much. I do not want to keep you any longer from the party and your final duties." Arbin stood, and Councilman Darr put his hand on Arbin's shoulder and escorted him to the door. A quick rap on the door and Simon opened it. Councilman Darr nodded to Simon, who signaled for Arbin to follow him back to the main party.

ARBIN WAS NOT SURE of how long he had been in Councilman Darr's den, but the party had noticeably fewer people. The cakes he had enjoyed earlier were gone. Replaced by small plates of pudding, which he found unpleasant. He found several glasses of champagne set out on the tables. He did not know if they belonged to anyone, but he decided not to let them go to waste. He was not looking for a repeat of the morning after headache the ale gave him and felt that he could drink more of this stuff without getting drunk.

Arbin tried to think about the meeting with Councilman Darr, but he was feeling a little dizzy and had difficulty concentrating. The music and chatter of the nearby guests was also becoming annoying. Arbin decided he needed to get as far away from the main group of party guests as possible. The garden and the cluster of trees nearby the back wall of the property looked like a good place to wait until he had to make his big announcement.

Separated from the crowds, he found it easier to concentrate. Arbin made himself as comfortable as he could on one of the stone benches. The first thing he noticed once he sat down was how tired he was. He also had to admit he had maybe a little too much to drink. *Time to head back to the tavern for a good night's sleep*, he thought. *I only hope that my cart is still waiting.*

It was while Arbin was worrying about how to get home that he first felt it. The tensing of his shoulders and the feeling of being watched. It only lasted for a few seconds, but he knew Jayden had found him again.

Instead of looking around, Arbin stood up and walked back toward the house. He figured the best thing to do now was let Councilman Darr know that a Fade was watching his party. He found the door to the Councilman's den locked, and no one answered his knocks. He stood there wondering what to do next.

It is possible that Jayden was just passing by, thought Arbin. There is no way he could have known I am here since he cannot detect me. I wonder who he is after now. I think the best thing to do is wait here for a while to make sure he has gone, then head back to the tavern. The only problem is that before I can leave, I must stand on that stupid platform and shout loud enough for everyone, including Jayden, to hear me.

Arbin found Simon cleaning up near the food table and decided he would just ask Simon to make the announcement for him.

"Look, Simon," said Arbin. "I think the champagne did not agree with me. If I do not go home now, I am sure I will get sick."

Simon said, "Don't worry, this happens a lot. I will make the announcement."

Arbin thanked him and asked which way was the exit. Simon pointed and was starting to say something when Arbin said, "Sorry, no time. Got to go."

Arbin made his way through the kitchen and found the back door. There were no lights outside, and it took him a few minutes for his eyes to adjust to the darkness. He spotted a group of people near what looked like wagons. *That is probably the best place to look for my cart,* he thought.

The alcohol and the darkness caused him some difficulty, and he tripped several times, almost falling. When he got to the group of men, he discovered the cart was not with them. The men stopped their talking when he approached. He asked if any of them had seen a cart driver. The men only laugh between themselves as if they were sharing a private joke.

Arbin looked down at his outfit and figured they were laughing at that. *It will be a long walk home, I guess.* As Arbin walked away, he tripped again, falling to his knees. As he was getting up, he saw that the band with ribbons that should have been around his knees had slid down and the ribbons were dragging on the ground.

Arbin was trying to adjust the band when he heard something behind him. Seconds later something hit him on the back of the head, and he fell forward onto his stomach. Next, someone kicked him in the side, and he realized that he was being attacked by the group of men from the wagons.

One man held Arbin down while the others punched and kicked him. He felt someone searching through his clothes. When one attacker complained that Arbin had nothing on him, another one said, "It must be in his other clothes or back in his room." This only seemed to anger them. They continued to kick and punch Arbin until one of them yelled out in pain. That was when Arbin realized someone had come to his defense. It was also obvious that the attacker surprised the men.

The sounds of the fight continued behind him. Arbin tried to use his Fade, but the pain and alcohol prevented him from succeeding. He finally got to his feet and stumbled toward Councilman Darr's house. His head hurt, and he was having trouble standing up. He kept stumbling forward toward the light coming through the now open kitchen door.

Arbin heard someone ahead of him shouting and before he could stop, he ran into a man wearing a masquerade costume. Both Arbin and the man he ran into fell to the ground. The costumed man got up and extended a hand to help Arbin. The alcohol, the beating and the spinning in his head, overwhelmed him. Arbin laid on the ground holding his head.

A woman's voice asked, "Who is it, Masimo?"

Masimo replied, "I think it's your hero."

"Is he okay?" asked the woman.

"Looks like he got attacked," said Masimo. "He took a blow to the head. There is some blood, but I think it's not too bad."

"Who did it?" asked the woman.

"I'm not sure," said Masimo. "I saw a group of men running off in that direction as we exited. I do not see them around now. Help me get him back into the house."

Arbin tried to focus on who was talking, but his head was spinning, and he was struggling to stay awake. As he looked up, he saw Elizabeth standing over him in a silver and golden dress decorated with feathers and a beaded cape wrapped around her shoulders.

"An Angel," said Arbin, and then passed out.

Chapter 14 - New and Old Faces

"WHERE AM I?" ASKED Arbin in a quiet voice as he touched the cloth wrapped around his head.

"In the realm of mortals, I'm afraid. A far fall from your time with the gods last night," said a man's voice from somewhere out of Arbin's view.

A young man, somewhere in his early thirties, walked into Arbin's view and sat down in a chair near the foot of the couch Arbin was lying on. He had short dark curly hair, a thin, neatly groomed goatee, a slightly dark complexion, pleasant smile and bright green eyes. The man mimicked a slight bow, using his arms while remaining seated. "I am your host, Masimo Vinetti. We met during that unfortunate situation at Councilman Darr's party."

Arbin tried to move but was quickly stopped by a sudden pain in his right side, which caused him to take a quick breath. "Ow," he said almost to himself. He lifted the blanket that was covering him and studied a couple of large bruises on his side. He also found smaller but more numerous bruises on his left side and arm. He looked up at Masimo and said, "Thank you for your help. I was not sure if anyone heard me calling for help."

"I'm sad to say we did not. By luck, we were just leaving when we met. I hate to think of the outcome of your struggle if your Guardian Angel had not insisted that we check on you," said Masimo.

"Guardian Angel?" asked Arbin.

Masimo noticed the confused expression on Arbin's face and said, "Ah," nodded his head and said, "Pardon me, I was just making light of your comment last night." Arbin continued to stare at Masimo, trying to understand the meaning of his last words.

"I had the pleasure of attending the Darr family party as the guest of the charming Miss Keller," said Masimo. "She saw you leave the party and said we needed to follow. I was a little disappointed because I was having a fascinating conversation with a person on the social and economic benefits that resulted from the great plague. Miss Keller claimed woman's intuition, and I had no choice but to agree to her request. That is how we met. Both of us on the ground and Miss Keller standing over you, every bit the angel you claimed."

Arbin relaxed, put his hand back on his head and looked at the ceiling, trying to remember. Slowly, it came back to him and he remembered someone in a beautiful outfit standing over him. This memory brought a flood of others and the feeling that there was something important about last night that he needed to remember. After more thought, he looked back at Masimo and asked, "Did anyone else get hurt?"

Masimo put his hand to his mouth to politely hide a smile and said, "I'm sorry friend but from what I could see the struggle was a little one sided. It was obvious you put up a valiant defense, but the assailants fled once help arrived."

"No, not me. Did anyone else get hurt?" Arbin asked again. Now it was Masimo's turn to look confused. Masimo opened his mouth like he would say something but closed it again. "Not that I know of," he said. "Why, do you think you hurt someone?"

"No, Jayden. Did Jayden hurt anyone?" asked Arbin.

"Jayden!" said a familiar voice. "Did you say Jayden?"

Arbin recognized the voice and without getting up said, "Alex, what are you doing here?"

"They sent me to check on your condition, but never mind that. Are you saying you saw Jayden again?"

Arbin attempted to turn on his side so he could see Alex, who was sitting in a chair at a table just inside the next room. "I'm not sure if it was him. That is why I was asking," said Arbin.

"What do you mean you are not sure?" asked Alex as he got to his feet and headed towards Arbin carrying the chair he had been sitting on. He put it down a few feet from Arbin and as he sat down, he said again, but slower and with more urgency, "Did you see Jayden?"

Arbin rolled onto his side and slid back to give him a little distance from Alex who was staring at him waiting for his answer.

"I'm not sure, I think I did. I was—," started Arbin, but before he could finish Alex said, "What do you mean you think you did? You either did or did not! Which is it? If he is in town, I need to take steps immediately to deal with him!"

"I did not actually see him," Arbin said, looking down. "I thought I might have felt him in the area. Now that I think of it, I could have been wrong. I was a little drunk and was not feeling right."

"Did you say anything to anyone about it?" asked Alex as he sat back a little in his chair.

"I looked for Councilman Darr," said Arbin. "When I could not find him, I left. That is when I got jumped."

Alex stood up, looked at Arbin for a few minutes, shook his head, then said to no one in particular, "I think it's time that I leave. I need to report this possible sighting." Alex looked at Arbin and said, "If Jayden was there, were you going to leave the people at the party to his mercy?" When Arbin did not reply Alex said, "You really need to think about the responsibilities that come with your gift."

"I did not want these Talents! They have always brought me nothing but trouble. I'm not like you. They do not define who I am." Arbin paused, then looking down said, "I wish I had just let Jayden run by me in the woods. If I did, this whole thing could have passed me by."

"Sometimes our lives are moved by forces beyond our understanding," said Masimo.

Alex and Arbin looked at Masimo who had been sitting quietly nearby listening to their discussion. He put the cup he was drinking from down and said, "If you are really a force of good than you are destined to confront evil, no matter how hard you try to avoid it. Just as your friend, Jayden, cannot help but be put in situations where he must do the unthinkable. This is the theme of fables and great tales handed down through history. One word of warning. In some of these stories, the hero sometimes dies in a selfless sacrifice to defeat evil."

"Well, that is a cheery thought," said Arbin. "If that is the case, I might as well lay here all day and forget about going to that stupid test."

"That is the other reason I came by," said Alex as he gripped the top part of the chair he was now standing behind. "There will be no test today thanks to your little meeting with Councilman Darr."

Arbin put his hands on his face and rubbed his eyes, trying to get the sleep out of them. With a sigh said, "You heard about that?"

Masimo laughed and when Arbin looked at him he said with a smile, "Pardon me."

"Everyone has heard about it," said Alex. "Most of the elected Council members and several influential members of the business community attended Councilman Darr's little private meeting with you."

"How was I to know that?" asked Arbin. "They were all wearing masks. I doubt I would have known anyone in the room, even if they were not wearing masks. Still, I do not understand how that is a problem."

"Councilman Darr and a few other Councilman had an informal meeting with Bishop Sorren on your behalf this morning," said Alex.

"My behalf?" said a surprised Arbin. "Why would they do that?"

"It appears you asked them to," replied Alex.

"What," said Arbin, sitting up straight on the edge of the couch. His actions caused him to take a deep breath because of the pain in his side. He let out his breath slowly then said, "I do not remember asking for them to do that." Arbin rubbed his head a few times, paused, then looked up at Alex and said, "Oh."

"Oh, what?" asked Alex, leaning forward against the back of his chair. "Did you, or did you not, ask them to act on your behalf?"

"There were a lot of questions at the meeting. I did my best to answer them and when I was leaving, they said not to worry, that they would do their best to make sure the test was conducted properly," replied Arbin.

Alex did not respond but stared out the window. Arbin felt a little nervous at Alex's silence and said, "I do not know why you agreed to that stupid test. How am I supposed to pick Seers from a group if there aren't any Seers in the group to pick from?"

It surprised Arbin to see genuine anger in Alex's eyes. Alex looked at Masimo who raised his hands in front of him as to say he heard nothing, and then he turned back to Arbin and said, in a tone that caused Arbin to realize he might have gone too far, "You need to choose your words more carefully. Statements like that in the wrong company could get you and others in serious, and I mean deadly serious trouble."

Arbin tried to apologize, but Alex interrupted him saying, "I did what I thought was the best for the Seer Core and not just you. If you remember, it was your outburst that resulted in the Committee deciding to use the test instead of my reputation. I had no choice but to agree. Until now, I felt I might still be able to arrange for the outcome needed."

Arbin looked at Alex, then to Masimo, who smiled and said, "He was going to cheat."

Alex gave Masimo a quick glance, but before he could say anything Arbin asked, "How has my meeting with Councilman Darr changed things?"

"Councilman Darr demanded the Committee change their testing process," replied Alex. "He is claiming that since the safety of the Council members and their families are in the hands of the Shadow Guard and the Seers, it's only natural that the Council have more oversight on the selection process. He has called for a meeting of the full Governing Council a week from now to consider his demands."

"I do not really understand the politics of this. If Councilman Darr is on our side, what is the issue?" asked Arbin.

Alex laughed and said, "Councilman Darr is not on our side. He and Chairman Sumner have been feuding for some time now, and both sides have used the Shadow Guard and the Seer Core to support their arguments. The Councilman would be just as happy seeing the Order discredited, dissolved, or put fully under the control of the Governing Council."

"So, because of that they now allow you to talk to me?" asked Arbin.

"Councilman Darr demanded that Lubin and me take the test with you since we were the ones sponsoring you. Thanks to you, he questioned our ability to vouch for you, saying he needed proof that we are actually gifted. Bishop Sorren agreed, and now, as a participant of the test, I can no longer meet with any of the Seers or Committee members."

"What does the High Seer say?" asked Arbin.

"He would be happy to see the whole thing go away. He has strongly suggested the Committee reject your application, and you be asked to leave town," said Alex.

"That is a great idea. We call this whole thing off and I go somewhere far away. That way everyone is happy," said Arbin as he looked around. "Where are my clothes?"

"You really do not understand, do you?" said Alex as he slowly shook his head. "The testing will continue with or without you. The very credibility of the Seer Core is at stake. Plus, you have made yourself the focal point for three powerful and ruthless groups."

"Three groups?" asked Arbin.

"Have you forgotten your true nemesis, demon hunter?" asked Masimo. "The supporters of the Adelist Movement are a genuine threat, and you have publicly claimed to be the only person who can defeat their new weapon. If the Seers fall, it will be you standing alone between them and their revolution." Masimo turned to Alex and said, "Excuse my interruption."

"You stated the situation quite clearly," said Alex. He looked back at Arbin and said, "You can run, but you cannot hide forever. Your chances are greater if you are not alone." Alex took a deep breath and stepped back from his chair and said, "I have to go. I hope you make the smart decision." Alex turned to Masimo and said, "If you see my sister, tell her I might be home a little late tonight."

Masimo nodded and Alex left, saying nothing else.

Arbin watched Alex leave and after a few minutes of silence he turned to Masimo and said, "That went well."

Masimo let out a loud laugh that startled Arbin. His laugh ended with a large smile as he slapped his knees and stood. Masimo walked towards the door to another room but paused at the doorway and said, "Miss Keller was right about you. She also got you some clothes since that clown suit you were wearing got damaged. I will be right back."

Arbin wrapped himself in the blanket since he was only partly dressed and looked around the room. He saw that he was on the ground floor of a small home. The room he was in was cluttered with books and crates, as if someone had started to move in, but decided it was too much work to put everything away. There were two adjoining rooms and stairs leading to a second floor. To his right was an eating area with kitchen. That had the table where Alex must have been sitting. To his left was the room Masimo had disappeared into. Arbin guessed it must be a bedroom.

He took a deep breath, braced for the pain, and took a few steps. It was not as bad as he expected. Dragging the blanket behind him, he walked over to peek at the books and papers stacked on Masimo's desk.

Arbin had always loved books. He loved the feel and smell of books. When his father was still working, he would travel and bring back books for Arbin. Mostly children stories in small four or six page pamphlets that were folded and stitched in the center. When he was old enough to travel with his father, he would visit printers and watch how the books were made. He always felt that just owning books made you a smarter person. It brought a smile to his face, seeing so many books. He was a little disappointed to see them so casually tossed around. Some on the floor, some in boxes and some left open with other books on top of them.

Arbin looked around a little more and noticed a few paintings and drawings. Some were rolled up and others in frames leaning up against the wall. He noticed that there was a drawing laid out on another small table off to the side. There were a few items placed on it to keep it from curling.

Next to the table was a frame attached to a stand. It held a large work of needlepoint. The artist appeared to be making a copy of the illustration on the table.

Arbin studied the drawing. In the background was the front of a large fancy building that was familiar to him, but he could not really place it. In the foreground were a group of people engaged in battle. Even though the drawing had no color, Arbin could still pick out the familiar uniforms of the Shadow Guards. There was a man standing in front of the guards who must be the main subject of the drawing. He was standing with one arm raised as if pointing to the heavens and another pointing at a group of what looked like demons on the ground before him in what appeared to be agony. There was a caption on the drawing that read 'The Blessed Leaboro at the foot of the Bridge of Sorrows.' There was also another line that read 'Evil's power vanquished by his presence.'

"Miss Keller was not sure of your size, so she brought a few items," said Masimo as he entered the room carrying an armful of clothes which he tossed on the couch.

"Thanks," said Arbin as he stepped away from the drawing. As he walked toward the couch, he said, "What's with all of this. I have only seen this many books and items in the home of a former and very rich employer."

Masimo smiled and said, "It's for my work. My cousin Casandra lent them to me."

"You mean Casandra as in Lady Casandra?"

"Yes," said Masimo. "She purchased me this small home as well. Things were not going so well where I was, so she invited me to come stay here for a while."

"So, you're an artist?" said Arbin as he pointed toward the needlepoint he was just examining.

Masimo laughed and said, "No, no, I'm a scholar. I conduct research and write on a new area of philosophy. I like to refer to myself as a 'Culturist'. However, some of my more backward peers have seen fit to call me something else. Hence, my new home."

Masimo could tell by the confused look on Arbin's face that he had not made himself clear.

"I study the culture of different people. Specifically, the things that act on the culture either natural or man-made, that move it in a particular direction."

He saw Arbin nod in understanding and then said, "What really fascinates me are the things people will tell themselves that keep a group behaving in a certain way. I am especially interested in how moral stories and myths are used to keep people in check, to protect them from outside influences."

Arbin said, "You mean like children stories and such?"

Masimo smiled and said, "Kind of, yes. I ask myself how two groups of people, living next to each other, have different moral beliefs about the world."

Arbin pointed to the needlepoint and said, "I thought that was your work."

"No," said Masimo with a smile. "That belongs to Miss Keller. Casandra commissioned her to do some work for the upcoming Unification Celebration. Miss Keller was not happy with the work she had done and was looking for something grander."

"Why this drawing?" asked Arbin.

"Casandra gave me a bunch of her father's and grandfather's items to help me with my work. Her grandfather was a Council Member. Her father fought alongside Chairman Sumner against a group of rebels, much like the ones you are facing today. When Miss Keller found out about the material, she hoped she would find the right subject for her work. I helped her look through the material and read some of it for her. When she found that drawing, she said it was perfect and has been working on it almost every day."

Arbin rooted through the clothes on the couch. They were nice clothes. Not like the ones he had purchased, but much better than his Noor Point clothes. He found some items that fit and was soon dressed in pants, a shirt and a vest. He would have rather had a nice pair of boots than the shoes he found, but he was happy to be dressed again. "Elizabeth did a good job of finding me clothes. I hope she did not spend too much on these."

"To tell you the truth, I think she swiped some from her brother and his friends. The shoes are mine. I hope they fit," said Masimo.

"Yes, they are great and much appreciated. I will return them when I get the chance," said Arbin.

"Please, keep them," said Masimo. "I had to buy some new clothes once I got here. I was just going to toss them out."

Arbin walked around the room getting used to the new shoes and outfit. He stopped at the drawing on the table that Elizabeth was using and studied it intently. "The caption talks about a battle at the Bridge of Sorrows between Evil and a Blessed one," he said after a few minutes. "I never followed civil war history, but I heard that the war started and ended there. I guess that would be a perfect subject for her project. It has an interesting sub-caption, but I cannot believe it happened as they show it in the drawing, based on what I know about Seers and Fades."

"I'm impressed," said Masimo. "I had heard you could read, but to translate that caption is impressive. Even I struggled with it a bit. I was never any good with northern and eastern dialects."

"My father traveled a lot," said Arbin. "He was a surveyor tasked by the government to chart boundaries and assist with map making. He also did surveys to help with taxes. He taught me to read and write, and I would often help him with his work. When I got old enough, I would travel with him. I picked up on the languages quickly. My father said it was one of my better talents."

"I have been looking through the material that Casandra gave me and have become interested in the powerful effect the Seer and Fade stories have on this country," said Masimo. "There are a lot of countries that have stories of good and evil, but none has ingrained itself into its society as deeply. It has become a part of both the government and the Church here. I would be most appreciative if I could get your help with my research."

"I do not mind sharing. However, every time I do, I seem to get in trouble," said Arbin. "Plus, I am not sure how much longer I will stay around."

"I understand," said Masimo. "I would be careful not to name you as a source. I would love to have your perspective on things. Maybe you can confirm or deny what I find."

"I guess I could drop by a few times depending on how things go," said Arbin. "I am not sure how far you live from the Inn where I am staying," Arbin paused for a second and added, "At least where I think I am staying if the innkeeper has not rented my room, or the price has not gotten too high. What time is it? I need to get to the bank. I would also like to go back to Councilman Darr's home and try to get my clothes back."

"Miss Keller said she would collect your clothes from Councilman Darr's house," said Masimo. "As to your lodgings, I would be more than happy to have you stay here. I have a spare room and we could say that your help with my research would offset your room and board."

It is only for a few days, he thought. *It would save me a lot of money I could need later. Besides, how much more trouble could I get into by talking to him.* Arbin put out his hand and said, "You got a deal."

Masimo shook Arbin's hand and with a smile said, "I look forward to hearing your stories. When can we start?"

Arbin said, "I just need to step out and collect the things I left at the Inn where I was staying. I should be back before nightfall."

MASIMO'S HOUSE WAS on the eastern side of the city, on a narrow street that led directly to the small business district just outside the Eastern Gate of the Government compound. From there, the Bridge of Sorrows would normally be a five or ten minute walk south. Today the trip would take twice as long because of the crowds. The Unification Celebration was still about two weeks away, and the crowds got bigger each day. *I will have to skip the bank if I want to get to the Laughing Bear and back by nightfall,* thought Arbin as he made his way through the crowd toward the Bridge of Sorrows.

The trip was taking its toll on Arbin. The walking and occasional bumping from his fellow travelers was causing his sides to hurt. He was tired and wished he had one of those little carts he had used the other day. It seemed like every building had a small stand outside with goods for sale, making the streets narrower and more crowded than before. It also made it harder for him to pick out the landmarks he used before, and he got turned around a few times. He was thinking about turning back when he saw the familiar sign of the Laughing Bear a few buildings ahead.

He did not want to deal with Godfrey right now. He remembered there was a gate that would allow access to the small yard behind the Inn. From there, if he was lucky, it was up the stairs to the second floor. He would have to use his Fade. It was a good thing he was not dressed in the clothes he purchased because they would make it much harder to be ignored.

Arbin took a deep breath, relaxed his mind, and concentrated on being nothing. He soon felt the familiar sensation as the Fade took effect.

As Arbin passed the front door of the Inn, he saw that it was busy. *Good,* he thought. *That will make it much easier to blend in.* He found his way to the back of the Inn and through the small gate. He was a little worried about the chickens sounding an alarm, but they ignored him, as if he were not there. He had used his Fade to help him when hunting but had never had the chance to use it this close to livestock.

Arbin paused for a few minutes in the shadows of a tree to check out the back door. It was open, which was helpful, and he did not see anyone standing near it. He made his way to the door and paused again.

He looked for Godfrey and soon found him by following the sound of his laughing. He was clear across the room, speaking with a group at a table. The barmaid who had so cheerfully served him breakfast was there as well, laughing and flirting with the men at the table. She was not acting like the girl he imagined her to be. For some reason, it upset him a little to watch her acting in this way. It was then that he had the feeling that two of the men at the table looked familiar. He felt a quick wave of anger when he realized that they were part of the group that attacked him at the party.

He tried his best to calm down. Getting upset would make it difficult for him to keep his Fade going. He stepped inside and climbed the stairs.

Stopping outside the door to his room, Arbin listened for the sound on the other side. Satisfied that the room was empty, he tried the door and was thankful that it was unlocked. He stepped in, closed the door and looked around for his clothes. It did not take him long to learn his things were not here. *Darn, looks like I will have to talk to Godfrey,* he thought.

Arbin headed back down the stairs and stopped a few steps from the bottom and looked for Godfrey. He spotted him several tables away from where he had been, but the barmaid was still laughing and flirting with that group of thugs. *What is wrong with her? Doesn't she know what type of men they are?* he thought. *Forget about it. I need to get my things and get out of here without them seeing me.*

Arbin waited, and waited some more, as Godfrey worked the room. It seemed like he was making a point of speaking to every single person in the pack room. *Come on already,* he thought. He knew he needed to get his mind off the wait. He tried to listen in on some nearby talk. Occasionally, he would hear the barmaid's laughter, and it was irritating him. Arbin decided he had waited enough. He needed to go speak with Godfrey. Arbin was getting ready to get up when someone he had not expected to see walked by him. Arbin's heart almost stopped. It was a large man dressed in dirty clothes, like he had been traveling. He had a face and manner that

Arbin would never forget. The last time Arbin had seen this man he was wearing a uniform and had a pillow over the face of Henry Sumner.

Fear edging on panic was what Arbin now felt. He sat down on the steps, clinging to the stair banister. He closed his eyes and focused on pulling his Fade tightly around him like a blanket. He had found that imagining a blanket covering him helped him be more successful in using his Fade. When his breathing had calmed down, he opened his eyes and looked for the killer. He saw him just as he exited the Inn and turned east toward the river.

Arbin stood and made his way toward the door as quickly as possible. He knew this would weaken the effect of his Fade and was not surprised to hear Godfrey's voice calling to him from across the room. He ignored him and kept going. He glanced over at the table of thugs just before he reached the door and saw a look of surprise on their faces. Arbin put that out of his mind and did his best to locate the killer on the busy street.

Once he found him, Arbin relaxed and focused on his Fade.

The killer was in no hurry. He crossed from one side of the street to the other several times, stopping to study the shop windows. It was then that Arbin realized the killer was using these window shopping stops to look around discreetly.

Watching the killer, Arbin started to worry. He knew from experience that the effects of his Fade would only reach about twenty-five feet, and that was under the best of conditions. Beyond the range of his Fade, he had no protection. Plus, a vigilant person who was expecting to be followed might resist his Fade. The killer appeared to be working his way toward the Bridge of Sorrows. Worried about being spotted, Arbin took a chance and headed for the Bridge using a different route, hoping he would get there before the killer.

It was getting darker and Arbin used that, and the landscaping around the bridge entrance to find a place where he could watch for the killer without being noticed. He feared he had lost the killer until he recognized him moving through the flow of people and wagons heading for the bridge.

Arbin got a chill just watching him. The man had a hard face, one that could stop an argument with only a glare. *What am I doing?* he thought. *This guy is a killer. Just look at him.* Despite his mental warning, Arbin found himself slipping into the crowd of travelers and following the killer. Arbin tried using a small cart as cover but had to abandon it because the killer stopped too often.

Suddenly the killer's behavior changed. He picked up his pace, his attention was focused on something further up the bridge.

Arbin followed the killer's gaze until it led to a man standing in one of the little balconies made into the bridge where the arch supports meet the water. Arbin had seen people fishing off these balconies on his past visits to the bridge.

As Arbin got closer, he saw that the man standing there was no fisherman. The killer's gaze was still fixed on the man, as his pace picked up. *Is he going to attack him?* Arbin wondered. *It would be crazy to kill him here in public, on a crowded bridge.*

Arbin was relieved when the two men shook hands. The weakening light prevented Arbin from getting a good look at the person the killer was meeting with, but there was something familiar about him. Arbin could not see his face, but his thin frame and the ponytail reminded him of the person the killer had been meeting with back in the camp in the woods of Noor Point. The one that had yelled, "Kill him."

Arbin wished he could hear what they were saying but did not see a place where he could get close enough. There was the little balcony across from the one they were in, but he doubted he would learn anything from that distance. Plus, he was not sure he could depend on a steady flow of bridge traffic and his Fade to keep him unnoticed.

He could not just hang out in the area. He figured the best thing to do was to go past the two and get a good view of them. He would also try to find a place closer to the center of the bridge where he could watch them. *I did not see ponytail guy enter the bridge. Maybe he came from the east side, I can always wait for him there and then follow him,* Arbin thought. *It is worth a try.*

As Arbin walked by the two men, he saw that the killer was doing most of the talking. The ponytail man was doing a great job of keeping his back to the bridge traffic, stopping the killer occasionally, with just the raise of his hand. It almost looked like the killer was apologizing for something. *What kind of person could have that killer afraid of him?* Arbin wondered.

Arbin got another chill when the killer looked in his direction. There was no sign that the killer noticed him, but Arbin focused on his Fade and kept moving. Using what he had learned from the killer, Arbin changed sides every few feet, glancing back to make sure the two men were still where he last saw them. It was during one of these maneuvers that Arbin bumped into a horse pulling a wagon coming the other direction. The startled animal reared up and whinnied loudly. Arbin had forgotten that not only was he being ignored by the killer, but he was also being ignored by the bridge traffic. The driver of the wagon, the horse and Arbin were all just as surprised at the accident. It was also clear from the looks and angry comments from others nearby that he was no longer in a Fade.

He was sure that the fuss had gotten the attention of others. He took a quick glance back to the place where he last saw the killer and found the little balcony empty. He glanced around, expecting the killer to be making his way through the crowd toward him, but he did not see him.

The wagon driver was still yelling at Arbin as he turned and hurried, almost at a run, toward the center of the bridge. He knew he would find cover there, and it would give him a chance to regain his Fade.

Once he reached the monument structure, he ducked behind a column and took a few deep breaths, trying to relax. He let himself fall back into a Fade. When he felt he had control again, he moved back out to the edge of the bridge and looked down the way he had just come. He scanned the crowd for the killer or the ponytail man but saw neither.

After about fifteen minutes, he relaxed and decided that they must have gone to the west. "What was I thinking? That was a stupid thing to do!" He whispered to himself. "Time to go home. I need to figure out what to do next."

As he walked back onto the bridge, he looked to his left and noticed people gathered in small groups in front of the Government Center. He could see they were talking among themselves and appeared to be upset. He also noticed that someone had plastered some fliers to the walls of the building. He watched as a man tore one of them down and tossed it on the ground while others cheered.

"What now?" he asked himself. "This entire place seems to be one dramatic event after another. I miss the simple life of Noor Point."

As he stood there watching the group, he realized there was something familiar about this scene. "The drawing," he said to himself. "That's the building in the drawing, I am sure of it. This is where it happened. At the foot of the Bridge of Sorrows. They must have meant the foot of the stairs. I want to take another look at it when I get back to Masimo's place."

A grumble in his stomach reminded him he had not eaten in a while. *Masimo said room and board*, he thought. *I wonder if Masimo cooks or has someone do it for him. Maybe even Elizabeth. He said she is there almost every day working on her project. I wonder what the relationship is between those two*. He thought about that for a few seconds and then said, "Enough of that. I'm hungry."

He took one last look behind him and headed in the direction that would take him back to Masimo's place.

Chapter 15 - Painful Truth

ARBIN AWOKE TO THE sound of someone banging on the front door. The light in the room told him it was well before noon. "Again? Doesn't anyone sleep in around here?"

Arbin turned on his side, winced at the pain, then rolled over to the other side. As he did, he heard something heavy hit the floor. Arbin rolled back over and, using his good elbow as support, peeked over the edge of the couch. On the floor was a large book. *Oh, I forgot about that,* he thought. When he got home, he was so upset about seeing the killer that he could not relax. He decided the best way to relax was to do some reading and found the diary of Casandra's father and grandfather. He did not remember how far he had gotten, but it did the trick of getting him to sleep.

The door banged again. This time with a little more urgency. "Masimo!" Arbin shouted. "There is someone at the door for you." This was not his home, so it only made sense that it was for Masimo.

The third knock was more of a pounding followed by a voice saying, "Masimo Vinetti, open the door! We have an urgent message from Captain Eustace."

See, Arbin thought. *It is for Masimo.* He rolled back over on the couch and thought about sleeping, but there was something familiar about that voice. Arbin gave one last shout for Masimo as he sat up and made his way slowly to the door. He opened it and found Hans and two other Shadow Guards standing there.

"Hans!" said Arbin with a smile, "You miss me?"

"Funny," said Hans. "Get Masimo. It's important. Tell him we are waiting outside for him."

Arbin nodded and closed the door. *That felt kind of good,* he thought, and walked back toward the couch just as Masimo was coming down the stairs. He was wearing a dark blue robe and slippers. "It's for you," said Arbin. "It's Hans. He said it's important."

"Who?" asked Masimo through a yawn.

"Shadow Guard with an important message from Captain Eustace," said Arbin.

"This early?" asked Masimo.

"My thoughts exactly," said Arbin as he flopped back down on the couch.

Arbin heard Masimo and Hans talking, but did not put any effort into listening to what they said. As Masimo made his way back toward his room, Arbin glanced his way and was a little taken back by Masimo's expression. He looked white as a ghost. Arbin propped himself up and asked, "Everything okay?"

Masimo did not pause but said, "Don't know. I need to go. I might be gone for a while."

Arbin said, "Okay," and laid back down, but the expression on Masimo's face bothered him.

Masimo returned a few minutes later, but he was not his smartly dressed, cheerful self. He walked past Arbin and out the door, saying nothing else.

Hum, that was weird, Arbin thought as he rolled over on the side that was not hurting him as much and pulled the blanket back up round himself. He remembered the book lying on the floor and thought, *I will get it later.* Before long, he had drifted back off to sleep.

The knocking on the door this time was different, but still just as irritating. *Well, Masimo is out, so there is no need to answer it this time,* thought Arbin.

There was no second knock. Instead, the door opened, and a woman's voice called for Masimo. He thought he might be dreaming until the voice called his name.

Arbin rolled back onto his back and looked up into the pretty blue eyes of Elizabeth. He could not help but smile, even though her nearness was having a slight effect on him. When she saw that he was awake she smiled, picked up the book and placed it on Masimo's desk in the same place he had found it last night. She turned back to Arbin and asked, "Where's Masimo?"

Arbin looked around and pointed to a robe on a chair nearby. "Can you hand it to me, please?" he asked as he sat up. As Elizabeth handed him the robe, Arbin said, "You just missed him. Hans came by and took him to Captain Eustace."

Elizabeth nodded and said, "I wanted to be here when he got the news."

"What happened?" asked Arbin as he found a pair of nearby slippers. "When he left here, he looked like death warmed over."

"It's serious," said Elizabeth. "Lady Casandra and her escorts were returning to the Capital to be here for Dylan's confirmation. They were attacked. Lady Casandra was wounded but escaped. They killed most of her escorts, including one of my brother's people."

"You mean the kid, what was his name... Kingsley?" said Arbin. "Who would do a thing like that?"

"There are posters around town that say a Fade working for the Adelist is responsible," said Elizabeth, as she sat in the chair near her needlepoint.

"So that's what had everyone so upset last night," said Arbin almost to himself. "Jayden, what is wrong with you?" He looked back at Elizabeth, who was watching him talk to himself. He gave a brief smile and asked, "When did this happen?"

"Three days ago," said Elizabeth. "Alex said the messenger just arrived this morning."

"Three days? Jayden was here three days ago, outside the party," said Arbin.

"That's what I was told," said Elizabeth. "Anyway, I was sure that Captain Eustace would go to visit Lady Casandra and would probably want to give Masimo a chance to go with him. I just wanted to see him before he left."

"Are you going?" asks Arbin.

"No," said Elizabeth sadly. "I can't go without Bishop Sorren's or my brother's permission, and Alex has already said no. There is nothing stopping Masimo, so I wanted to ask him to take a letter to Lady Casandra for me."

"What do you mean you can't go?" asked Arbin. "That's silly. You are a grown woman. Just get Masimo to take you with him. You are his girlfriend after all."

Elizabeth stood and fiddled with the drawing on the table near her needle point. She turned, sighed and said, "You really understand nothing. First, Masimo and I are not a couple. Second, I am the sister of a Blessed one. The Church and my family determine who I court and who I marry. As the saying goes, Blessed from the Blessed."

"I thought I was the one being held prisoner," said Arbin.

"You have more freedom than I will ever have. It upsets me to see someone waste the opportunities you have been given. At the same time, I envy your freedom to do as you wish, even if you are making stupid choices," said Elizabeth.

"Thank you, I think?" said Arbin. "I just assumed you were with Masimo based on the way he talked about you."

"I am sure Lady Casandra would be happy if it ended up that way. My brother is pushing for his friend Lubin. Bishop Sorren will give the final decision, only he is taking a very long time in making that decision. I hope I do not get stuck with someone like the High Seer or some other older member of the Seers. At first, when you showed up, I was a little worried they might pick you based on how important Alex said you were, but now I am not sure how the Bishop feels about you."

"I'm pretty sure how Bishop Sorren feels about me," said Arbin with a quick laugh. "My vote would be on Masimo. He is the least involved in the drama that is going on around here, and he has been the nicest to me."

"Masimo has his faults too," said Elizabeth. "It really upsets me that I have to accept whoever they say and try to make the best of it. Sometimes I feel like running away. I worry about what would happen to my brother if I did, and I guess I am too accustomed to the comforts of my current life."

"Well, from one who has spent a lot of time on the run and sleeping on dirt floors, comfort is a powerful motivator," said Arbin. "I still think the idea of sitting around waiting for them to decide for you is horrible."

"Thank you," said Elizabeth. "I take small pleasures where I find them, plus my brother is kind of helpless without me. There is also the work I am doing," She said, pointing to the needlepoint. "I am becoming recognized for my skills with the needle. I have also learned a lot about the history of the country thanks to all the research I did getting ready for this current project. I would like to be able to do my own research, but most of the information has been beyond my abilities. Masimo has been extremely helpful but spending so much time with him has started people talking."

"Then learn," said Arbin. "My parents taught me the basics. I studied and improved on my own. It just takes time, patience, and the desire to learn. You strike me as a smart person and heaven knows it takes a lot of patience to do the work you do."

"Time is another one of those freedoms you enjoy. Plus, I am sure you were not under the watchful eyes of those that view such things as unnecessary."

"Well, you can add that to the list of things I dislike about this place," said Arbin.

There was a knock on the door and Arbin said, "That's probably your brother coming to yell at me about something again."

Elizabeth sat back down and said, "Believe it or not, my brother likes you. Just like me, he is confused by your refusal to consider the bigger picture."

Arbin stood and walked towards the door. On the way, he said, "I like your brother, but like you, I enjoy having a choice in how I will live my life."

Arbin opened the door and was stunned to discover Jayden standing on the other side. He froze in place, not sure what to do. He tried to close the door, but Jayden had his foot in the way. He attempted to close the door a few more times, gave up, and put his hands up to prepare for the attack he was sure was coming, but Jayden shouted, "Mia is in danger. Please Arbin, help me or they'll kill her."

That was the last thing Arbin had expected from Jayden. He stood there staring, not sure he understood him. Jayden put his hands out in front of him as if he were begging for something and said, "Please, Arbin, let me in. I do not want to fight you. We really need your help."

Arbin stepped back from the door, still trying to come to grips with what Jayden had said. He raised his hand, ready to defend himself as Jayden stepped in and started to close the door. Arbin had learned earlier that

Masimo's home did not have a back door. He was not about to let Jayden block the only hope he had for escaping. "Leave it open!" he said.

"I would prefer a little more privacy," said Jayden. "I'm not sure when your roommate will be back."

Arbin heard a stirring from behind him. In the few seconds after seeing Jayden, he had forgotten Elizabeth was in the room. His only thought had been to escape. "It stays open or you can leave," said Arbin, stepping between Jayden and Elizabeth and pointing toward a chair in the kitchen.

Jayden nodded and stood by the chair.

"Arbin, what is going on?" asked Elizabeth.

Jayden looked over at Elizabeth who is still sitting near her needlepoint and said, "Would you please stay seated, Miss Keller."

"You know me?" asked Elizabeth. "I don't think we have been introduced."

"Aren't you going to introduce us, little brother?" said Jayden with a sly smile on his face.

"I told you not to call me that anymore!" said Arbin.

"Arbin, who is this?" said Elizabeth. Arbin both heard and felt her anger start to rise.

Still looking at Jayden, Arbin said, "Elizabeth, this is Jayden."

Elizabeth let out a gasp as she stood. The sounds of her chair sliding caught the attention of Jayden who looked in her direction and said, "Please stay seated or I'll call forth my demon." A strange smile grew on his face.

"Okay, enough of that Jayden!" Arbin glanced in Elizabeth's direction and said, "He cannot call up a demon Elizabeth." Arbin turned back to Jayden and said, "Behave yourself or get out now!"

Jayden let out a little laugh and said, "Just having some fun little brother." Next Jayden opened his coat enough to show the hilt of a knife and said, "I've something important to talk to Arbin about Miss Keller and things will go much faster if you just stay where you are."

"Is this man really your brother?" asked Elizabeth.

Arbin had always hated that nickname. He stood there looking at Jayden who just dropped back into his life acting like the past had never happened. Here was the person who had tried to kill him once. The person who had caused him to be yanked from his life of hiding, standing there acting like the Jayden from years ago. Back then, it was Arbin who was always getting Jayden out of the messes he made. He was not sure who was the oldest. but Jayden always claimed he and Mia were a few months older. However, most of the time Arbin felt like he was the big brother. Maybe that is why Jayden always used that nickname. It was Jayden's way of teasing him.

Jayden laughed and said, "I like her. Pretty, but not so smart."

Arbin did not have to see Elizabeth to know her anger was rising. He kept his eyes on Jayden and said, "I do not want her involved with this."

Jayden looked at her and said, "Your new little girlfriend stays. Less chance of violence if she's here."

Arbin heard the chair move as Elizabeth sat back down. He gave her a quick glance and was surprised at how calm she appeared. She gave Arbin a slight nod, and he turned his attention back to Jayden.

"Okay, get on with it," said Arbin

"Like I said, Mia and her kids are in danger. I need your help to save them."

"Children?" said Arbin, a little surprised.

"Twins," said Jayden.

The idea that Mia was married with children left him speechless. His mind wandered back to the last time he had seen her eight years ago. He remembered her crying as he left her. She had always said she loved him and could not live without him. Even though he had said he was leaving forever. She had told Jayden she would wait for him. It took him a few seconds to return to the present. "Who wants to kill them?" he asked.

"People working for the Adelist Movement have them. They left a letter for me saying their lives depended on me killing Henry Sumner before he arrived in the Capital. They even sent one of her fingers with the instructions to prove they had her."

Jayden appeared almost in tears and looked like a man that was finally getting a great weight off his shoulders. Arbin had almost forgotten how Jayden could change moods so quickly. As he looked at him, Arbin saw a little of the man he had called friend so long ago.

"I tried my best but failed," said Jayden as he sat down in the chair.

"That explains why you were in Noor Point," said Arbin.

Jayden just nodded.

"It does not explain why you attacked me in the woods and set the fire that destroyed my home plus everything I owned." said Arbin angrily.

"I didn't attack you in the woods," said Jayden. "You jumped me as I was trying to escape from the guards, and I had nothing to do with that fire. In fact, I had returned to finish the job when the fire broke out. I had to leave my hiding place because of all the activity. I only found out later that someone had killed Henry Sumner."

"Why did you try to attack us while we were heading to the Capital?" asked Arbin.

"I didn't. I was trying to get close enough to talk to you, but that little stunt you pulled almost got me killed. After that, I decided to see if Mia had been released since Duke Sumner was dead. I found out they still have them."

"Are you sure she is still alive?" asked Arbin.

"I don't know," said Jayden, looking down, shaking his head slowly. He paused for a few seconds and when he looked up, he said, "When I went back to her home, I found a new letter telling me I was to go to the Capital and wait for instructions which would be delivered to one of six sites scattered around the city. It also said I was to make sure I did not harm Duke Henry's son, Dylan."

"Dylan!" said Elizabeth. Both men turned to look at her. "You stay away from him, you demon."

Jayden smiled and said, "Like I said, pretty, but stupid."

"That's enough!" said Arbin, louder than he expected. There were a few minutes of quiet while both men looked at each other, then Arbin said, "What do you expect me to do?"

Jayden stood and ran his hand through his hair. He looked at Arbin, shrugged and said, "I don't know, think of something. You were always good at that kind of thing."

"This is a lot different from the things we did," said Arbin. "It sounds like you do not even know who has her. Do you have any idea where she is? Was there anything in the instructions that can help?"

Jayden shook his head and said, "No." He held a piece of paper out for Arbin.

Arbin waved it off and said, "I guess no one witnessed who dropped off the letter."

Jayden shook his head again and said, "Maybe we could split up watching the places where they are leaving the messages."

"That will not work," said Arbin. "It will take too long. Plus, we would need to get a lot more people involved to do it right."

Jayden took a deep breath and let it slowly out. The room was silent until Elizabeth said, "That was you at the party, the one who chased off the men attacking Arbin."

Jayden smiled, let out a quick soft chuckle and said, "Arbin never was good in a fight."

"How did you know Arbin was there?" asked Elizabeth.

"The same way I knew he was staying here," said Jayden. "I followed the men that were following him."

"What?" said Arbin as he walked to the open door and looked out. "What did he look like?"

"Don't worry, you're not being followed now," said Jayden. "They stopped following you after the party for some reason. That's what gave me a chance to speak to you."

"I still want to know who it was," said Arbin.

"It wasn't just one person, and they would come and go from the Government Building."

"I still do not understand why someone would follow me," said Arbin. "If I am being followed, it will make finding Mia harder."

"We've dealt with tails before," said Jayden. "We won't have a problem with these guys."

"It's not losing them that is the problem," said Arbin. "We need to know who we can trust if we need help. To do that, we need to find out who was having me followed and why."

"Are you really going to help him?" asked Elizabeth.

Arbin looked at Elizabeth sitting in her chair. Her fists were clenched, and he could see the anger in her eyes. The entire time he had been talking to Jayden he had felt a discomfort growing much like the times in the past when he had been around her. He realized that somehow, she was causing this, and it seemed to grow with her anger. "Elizabeth, please calm down. I have to help. You heard what he said about Mia and her children."

"He's evil!" said Elizabeth. "How do you know anything he says is true?"

"Sorry, I buried Mia's finger!" said Jayden as he glared at Elizabeth.

"Shut up!" replied Elizabeth as she stood, returning Jayden's glare.

Arbin felt her words more than heard them. He glanced at Jayden and saw him wince as well.

"You're responsible for the death of Duke Henry, the husband of a very dear friend of mine," continued Elizabeth. "Plus, the death of two Shadow Guards and two of my brother's men."

"I didn't kill anyone!" said Jayden loudly.

"I don't believe you!" replied Elizabeth just as loud.

"I believe him," said Arbin almost to himself.

Both Jayden and Elizabeth stopped and looked at Arbin, who was just as surprised to hear himself saying it.

"You believe him?" asked Elizabeth. "You are the one that has been telling everyone that he wants to kill you."

"I do want to kill him," said Jayden with a slight smile.

Both Elizabeth and Arbin turned to look at Jayden. Arbin took a step back.

"I tried in the past and I may try again, but now I need him to help save my sister," said Jayden, his hand on the hilt of his knife.

Elizabeth, pointing toward Jayden, said, "See, he's an evil person who only wants to kill people. He admitted it!"

"He did not kill Henry, the guards, or your brother's people," said Arbin, still watching Jayden.

"How do you know that?" asked Elizabeth, staring at Arbin.

"Yeah, I'd like to know that myself," said Jayden. Elizabeth met his question with an angry glare.

"Because I saw who killed them," said Arbin.

There was a minute of silence as Elizabeth and Jayden stared at Arbin. Finally, Elizabeth asked, "You saw it?" She put her hand to her mouth for a few seconds, then continued in a quiet voice, "Saw what? The killer, the murder, what?"

Arbin turned toward Elizabeth and in almost an apologetic manner said, "I saw two men in Shadow Guard uniforms standing over the bodies of Henry's guards." It surprised Arbin he was saying this, but once it started coming out, he could not stop. "I watched as one of them killed Henry with a pillow, and then he killed the person who was helping him. The killer almost caught me. Hans and the other guards showing up was the only thing that saved me."

Arbin watched Elizabeth as she opened her mouth to say something, but she stopped, shook her head and sat back down in her chair, looking at him in disbelief.

"I believed you!" said Elizabeth finally. She shook her head again, still staring at Arbin. "I was even starting to feel sorry for you."

"I'm sorry, Elizabeth," said Arbin.

"How could you do that? You knew, and you did not tell anyone. Why?" asked Elizabeth.

Arbin suddenly felt small and ashamed and mumbled, "I wanted to but couldn't."

"Couldn't!" said Elizabeth, staring back at Arbin.

Arbin took a step toward Elizabeth and said, "It's complicated." Arbin realizing how stupid that sounded as soon as he said it. "There are things you do not know that make it difficult, even dangerous for me if I said anything."

Elizabeth put up her hand, making it clear she did not want him to come any closer. He could feel the anger growing in her again as she said, "I don't understand. All you had to do was say you saw who did it. They might even have caught the killer if you had done that much. You are eager to run off with your demon buddy and save your old girlfriend but wouldn't even take a second to stop the person who killed Henry and the others."

Arbin stared at Elizabeth, not knowing what to say next. He watched as she looked down and covered her eyes with one of her hands. When Elizabeth finally looked up, she said, "You said you saw the murder. Could you have stopped it?"

"It was over before I could do anything," said Arbin. "I was so surprised by what I saw that I froze. I was not sure what to do next."

"You tell someone!" shouted Elizabeth. "That's what you do. That's what anyone would do."

"I couldn't," said Arbin sadly.

"Why?" asked Elizabeth, almost crying.

"I told you, the killers wore Shadow Guard uniforms," said Arbin. "Ever since Jayden attacked Henry, they have been acting like it was my fault. Like I was working with Jayden. I did not know who to trust. I was trying to think of ways to tell your brother, but Jayden got in the way. By the time I got to town, I figured it was too late and we would never see the killer again. That was until I saw him again yesterday."

Arbin could see the surprised look on Elizabeth's face. He could not tell what she was thinking but decided it was too late to stop now so he continued, "Plus, if I told them how I could stay hidden while I watch the murder it would probably mean my death."

The puzzled look on Elizabeth's face told Arbin she did not understand. He was about to explain more when they both were startled by Jayden laughing from the kitchen. Arbin had almost forgotten he was there.

Arbin turned around and stared at Jayden, who was leaning against the door frame with a disturbing smile on his face. Arbin continued to stare at Jayden for a few seconds and then asked, "What's so funny?"

Jayden looked from Arbin to Elizabeth and back and laughed again.

"Stop it," shouted Elizabeth.

"I am sorry," said Jayden. "I guess your boyfriend forgot to tell you a few things."

"Enough, Jayden!" shouted Arbin. "I was just getting ready to tell her when you interrupted."

"Tell me what?" said Elizabeth, looking back and forth between Arbin and Jayden.

"Jayden, if you want my help you let me do it," said Arbin. It was clear from his stance and tone that he was ready to attack Jayden if he continued.

"Tell me what?" said Elizabeth again, standing back up.

Arbin turned back to Elizabeth and said, "I will tell you everything as soon as he leaves."

"Leaving sounds like a wonderful idea," said Jayden. "Before I go, give me a description of this killer and where you saw him. He might be a good place for me to start."

Arbin looked at Elizabeth, who was still standing, but said nothing else. He turned back to Jayden and said, "He is a big man, about five inches taller than me and well built. He is in his late forties, early fifties, blond or grayish short hair that comes to a peak at the bangs. He has a close-cut beard, deep eyes, and a long flat nose that looks like it could have been broken. He also has large hands."

"You got all that from just a peek?" asked Jayden.

"I followed him for most of yesterday evening, hoping to find out where he was staying so I could report him," said Arbin, turning to Elizabeth. "Honest."

She just continued to glare at him.

"Did you find out where he was staying?" asked Jayden.

"No, he met up with another person on the Bridge of Sorrows. I could see that the killer was nervous around him."

"What did this other person look like?" asked Jayden.

"I did not get a good look at him. However, I am sure he was the same person I saw the killer and his partner talking to back in Noor Point."

"Do you have any kind of description?" asked Jayden.

"I could see that he was your height and thin. He had a long blond ponytail. I'm sure he was much younger than the killer. I noticed both times he was a nice dresser. His clothes looked new, clean. They were simple, not upper class like what I bought, but expensive."

"Well, that gives me someplace to start," said Jayden. "I think you will have your hands full here. I'm not sure how much help you're going to be for a while." He took a few steps toward the door, then paused and said, "I had an idea while you and your girlfriend were fighting."

Arbin looked back at Elizabeth, who had taken a few steps back to put more distance between her and Jayden. "What's that?" he asked, hoping that Jayden would make it quick. He was not sure if it would be better for him to stay and talk to Elizabeth or follow Jayden out the door and make a run for it.

"The thing that has been bothering me about those instructions was the warning to leave Dylan alone," said Jayden, almost talking to himself. "Why would they want me to kill his father but protect him? Strange, right?"

Arbin was looking back at Elizabeth when Jayden said that, and he saw her eyes focus on Jayden.

"Well, I guess it makes sense if the Adelist Movement has people in the Government and the Shadow Guard like you say," said Jayden. "You know, if he is that important to the Adelist may be the best thing to do would be to kidnap him and use him to force Mia's release. What do you think of that idea?"

Arbin turned back to Jayden, but before he could answer he felt Elizabeth's anger seconds before he saw a book go past his head toward Jayden with surprising speed. He saw Jayden raise his hands as it bounced off his chest. Jayden's next move was for his knife.

As Arbin turned around, he saw Elizabeth heading toward Jayden yelling, "You stay away from him, you demon or I will kill you!"

He could feel Elizabeth as she got closer. He reached out and grabbed her as she was passing and pushed her toward the couch.

The closeness of Elizabeth in this angry state caused his head to spin. He looked back toward Jayden and prepared for his attack but was surprised to see him on his hands and knees struggling to crawl toward the door.

Elizabeth was yelling again and attempting to get up when Arbin pushed her back onto the couch.

Arbin turned back toward Jayden, who was still struggling to get back to his feet but had made it several feet beyond the door. Arbin made his way to the door, slammed it shut and locked it. He then slid down to a seated position with his back against the door.

He looked back over to Elizabeth and saw her begin to cry as she got up again. He put up his hands and said, "Stop, stop, he's gone. Calm down. He will not hurt Dylan. We will make sure of it."

Elizabeth walked over and pushed and kicked Arbin, trying to move him from the door. When she realized that was not working, she stepped back and yelled, "You let him get away! How could you? You're on his side!" She then turned and went over to Masimo's desk, gathered up a few books and started throwing them at Arbin, saying, "Get out of my way! I need to tell my brother and the guards. They need to do something to protect Dylan. They also need to do something about you!"

Arbin had his arms crossed, trying to protect himself. He shouted, "Stop, did you hear what I said? The killer and the person following me are working for the Shadow Guards. I agree, tell your brother, but you are all we need to keep Jayden from attacking Dylan."

Quickly Arbin found himself surrounded by most of the items off Masimo's desk, including several books, a paperweight, a book end and a box of quills. Thankfully, Elizabeth had not thrown the inkwell. Something had caused a slight cut on his forehead, which he just noticed now that items had stopped coming his way.

He was not sure if Elizabeth had heard what he had said to her, so before she could find something else to throw, he shouted, "You have the power to stop Jayden from attacking Dylan! Can't you see that?"

Arbin could feel her anger starting to build again, and when she could find nothing handy to throw, she shouted, "Shut up! Get out of my way or I will hurt you!"

"Look at your drawing!" shouted Arbin, hoping to get through to her. "Don't you understand? Look at the Seer and the Fades. That happened just now with you and Jayden. You have the power to stop Jayden. You are a High Seer, just like the one in the picture. That is your Talent!"

This time, Elizabeth heard him. She stood still for a few seconds. She glanced over at the drawing that she had spent so many days studying. After a few seconds, she put her hand to her mouth and walked over to her little desk. She had her back to him, but it almost appeared as if she was crying. It surprised Arbin when she took a swipe at her needlepoint, knocking it to the ground. She sat down hard in her chair and cried again.

Arbin stared at her. He was not sure what just happened. After a few minutes she stopped crying, reached over and picked up the drawing and put it on her lap, smoothing out the curls. She studied it for a while and then let out a small sigh that sounded more like a laugh. "Figures," she said. "Just another thing to worry about. I have been looking for some way of helping Dylan and Casandra, and when I find it, I cannot use it. This makes things complicated."

"Tell me about it," said Arbin, more to himself than to Elizabeth.

She looked up at Arbin and shook her head as she let out a strained little laugh that sounded like an expression of disgust, then looked back down at the drawing.

Arbin stood up and said, "Look, I am sorry. Please give me a chance to leave town before you talk to your brother. Once he learns what you can do, they will not need me around anymore to deal with Jayden."

"I told you before, only men can be blessed with gifts," said Elizabeth as she continued to stare at the drawing. She looked up at Arbin and he could see that she looked scared. "Do you understand how dangerous this is? They will kill me. This can't be true."

"I think you have known there was something special about you for a while. You even said so in the park. I'm sure your brother will not let anything happen to you," said Arbin.

Elizabeth sat looking away from Arbin for several minutes, then said, "My brother is driven by his desire to defeat the evil of the Fades. If I have this power and he found out, he will insist that it is our duty to use it to defeat Jayden, even if it cost both of us our lives."

Arbin looked at Elizabeth. She had stopped yelling at him, but he was sure she was still furious with him. He felt it. He was not sure what to do next, so he said, "I'm sorry. I did not want to get you involved in this. My talents have been a curse to me and anyone I get close to. I promise I will tell no one about your secret. I will find Jayden and do my best to convince him to leave Dylan alone. If he will not listen to me, I promise, I will do whatever is needed to keep him from harming Dylan."

As he stood and turned to leave, the door opened again and Masimo entered. Arbin could see there were two Shadow Guards just outside.

Masimo stopped a few feet inside the door and looked around at the mess. Before he could say anything, Arbin said, "We'll clean it up." It surprised Arbin when Masimo just nodded and walked by him and headed up the stairs that led to his room.

Arbin could tell that he was very troubled, and he guessed it was because of the news about Casandra. Arbin looked back at Elizabeth, who watched Masimo walk by in a daze. She looked back at Arbin. They stared at each other for a few seconds, Arbin fully expected her to call the guards in to have him arrested. Finally, she looked away.

Arbin decided it was time for him to disappear while he had the chance. He walked out the door and headed south, mostly out of habit. As soon as he was a few minutes away from Masimo's house, he slipped into a Fade and kept walking.

Chapter 16 - One Fade too Many

"WELL, AT LEAST IT FINALLY stopped raining," said Arbin, as he looked out from the little resting place he had found under an overturned rowboat. The boat was in the northernmost section of the docks on the western side of the city. It sat on blocks along with several others and looked long past the need for simple repairs.

After leaving Elizabeth, Arbin had wandered around, not sure what to do next. He was poorly dressed, had no food, no money and was afraid to go to the bank for fear guards would be waiting for him.

He had never seen Elizabeth that angry before. He did not know what she would do but had to accept the possibility that she would bring down the wrath of her brother and the Shadow Guards upon him. *I saved her from a knife attack by Jayden. I hope she knows that.* At least he thought he was doing that at the time. Remembering Jayden crawling out the door on all fours made him wonder who saved who.

Arbin gave serious thought to just leaving town. However, he believed that Mia was in danger. He was not sure what he could do about it, but he knew he had to help her. Once again, he found himself in trouble and thinking about running away. This time, if he ran, it would mean her death. "My past always seems to find me no matter where I hide," he murmured as he looked out from under the rowboat.

His little hiding spot had given him some shelter from the rain, which started a few hours after he reached the docks and lasted through the night. Both the rain and his Fade had kept him hidden overnight, but now the morning light and the improving weather would make it much harder for him to go unnoticed if the area got busy. He needed to get moving again and look for a better hiding spot. That would be a problem since he had seen so little of the city. He sat there in the cold, doing his best to think of where he could go to be warmer. He also needed to get some food.

He was thankful for the robe and slippers he had put on during Elizabeth's visit. He knew that he could not go unnoticed wearing them, so using his Fade to steal food or a change of clothes was out for now. He could always dump the robe, but the damp, cool morning convinced him to hold on to it a little longer. *Where to now?* Arbin thought. *Maybe Godfrey, but with all these visitors, I doubt the room will be available. Plus, I do not know how I would pay for it. I really need to get my hands on some money.*

As the morning sun got higher in the sky, it's warmth on his face made him feel a little better. He still needed to decide what to do next. *How do I help Mia? Jayden has been working on this for a few weeks and he does not know where she is. The only thing I got to go on is the killer and his boss. They must be linked to the group that took Mia. Maybe Jayden's idea of watching the message drop points was not that bad. It is that or sit on the Bridge of Sorrows and watch the traffic, hoping the killer or his boss walk by. Either way, I cannot do this alone. I guess I need to team up with Jayden, but I will not help kidnap Dylan. I made a promise to Elizabeth, and I will keep it no matter what happens.*

Arbin stood up and stretched. His robe was still damp from the night air. *I need to do something about this,* he thought as he opened the robe, hoping to let in a little of the sun's warmth. *I think my best option is to head back to Masimo's house. With any luck, both Elizabeth and Masimo will be gone. I just hope no one is watching the place.*

Standing at the entrance to the Bridge of Sorrows, Arbin watched the morning traffic. *I wish there were another way to get over to the east side. Dressed like this, I cannot Fade. I am not looking forward to walking in front of the Government Building in the daylight.* Arbin pulled the robe tight around him, put his head down and joined the bridge traffic. The number of wagons on the bridge that morning surprised him. As he approached the Monument section of the bridge, he could see several wagons unloading timber. It was being taken to what looked like a stage and seating areas being built near the entrance of the Government Building. Arbin also noticed that they had replaced the Shadow Guards that normally guarded the Government Building, with soldiers from the Army. *I guess that makes sense*, he thought. *Masimo left yesterday. I am sure he traveled with a sizable group of Shadow Guards. They probably sent them to deal with the group that attacked Casandra.* Arbin relaxed for the first time since starting for Masimo's house. *This will make things a lot easier. The Army does not know who I am.*

After watching the work for a while, Arbin asked another spectator near him, "What is with all the construction?"

"It's for the upcoming celebration," the man said. He gave Arbin and his robe a few strange looks, then continued, "They had a smaller stage last year. I guess we're in for a lot more speeches this year."

Arbin smiled and said, "Why is the Army guarding the Government Building?"

"Not sure," said the man. "Saw a bunch of Shadow Guards ride out yesterday. Must be something big. The Army normally helps during the celebrations, but this is the first time I have seen them guarding the palace."

That might explain why I have not seen any Shadow Guard this morning, thought Arbin. *Hope that means I will not see any near Masimo's home.*

The little hiding spot he spent the night in had been helpful in staying unnoticed, but it did not keep his clothes from getting damp. Now that he had been walking for a while, he was feeling the effect of the dampness in the form of a chill which convinced him to keep moving. Arbin thanked the man and continued across the bridge and headed north to the business district near the Eastern Gate of the Government Compound.

Arbin was happy to see the Army was also guarding that gate. He saw a few Shadow Guards inside the compound area but did not slow down to investigate. The foot traffic in the area made it easier for him to keep out of the line of site from anyone in the compound. A feeling of relief came over him as he made the turn onto Masimo's street.

The buildings near the business district were close together, some had small alleyways and common courtyards. A few were set behind small walls, all of which offered more chances for Arbin to take cover if needed. The buildings near Masimo's home were much different. They were more often two stories and looked as if they were shared by more than one family. They were flush to the street with no real gaps between them. There were no fences or hedges to provide cover. It was simple and pretty, but very exposed. The only good thing was anyone watching Masimo's home would find it difficult to go unnoticed.

Arbin could see Masimo's home long before he reached it. It looked peaceful, with no evidence of any kind of activity. It was midday, but a few of the homes showed small amounts of smoke, either from cooking fires or maybe just for warmth. There were a few people walking in the street and he could hear some chatter from women in the doorways of two of the nearby homes.

Arbin was sure that Masimo would be on his way to see Casandra by now. It was Elizabeth he had to worry about now. She had been working on her project here. He was not sure if she would visit Masimo's home without him. *I do not know which would cause more talk, spending time there with or without him,* he thought.

A little shiver from the chill and his damp clothes gave him the courage to get out of the cold. He was just a little concerned when he found the front door of Masimo's house unlocked.

The house was quiet. Noticeably quiet and very neat.

Masimo was a pleasant person to share a place with, but he was anything but neat and quiet. Elizabeth was right when she called Masimo a talker, and he was passionate about his work. He could carry on a conversation about almost anything. Arbin often heard humming as he moved around the house. Masimo also enjoyed his teas. He almost always seemed to be boiling water and was eager to explain the story and benefits of each of the various blends he would brew throughout the day. Arbin would often find an empty cup or two scattered around. Often near or on one of the books Masimo was reading. Arbin could never understand how someone could be so casual with books. Some of them were old and probably valuable. Masimo also had a fondness for robes, which he would change often to match his mood or activities.

This is not the place I left, he thought. The mess of his disagreement with Elizabeth had been cleaned up and someone had removed the evidence of his stay on the little couch. Arbin stopped in place and listened to make sure the house was empty. After a few minutes, he felt comfortable enough to move around.

I need to get busy before someone shows up, he thought as he looked around the room. *Money, clothes and food. Then I can decide what to do next.* Arbin went into the room that Masimo had offered him. It was just off the little room he was in now. He had not really settled into it yet.

Over the past days, Arbin had rooted through most of the clothes Elizabeth brought for him and left them in a few piles based on likes and dislikes. Those piles were gone. The clothes were now neatly folded and stacked in new piles on his bed.

Nothing was how it was when he left it. He looked around in a bit of a panic and soon relaxed when he found his money pouch where he cleverly left it under a pillow of a chair in the corner. A quick check showed that his banknotes and the few coins were still there.

Arbin grabbed his small travel bag he had stashed under the bed. He stared at the new piles of clothes. He did not have time to sort them again, so he just grabbed a pile and shoved it in his bag.

He looked down at his dirty robe and slippers and decided it would be better if he cleaned up a bit before he changed. Arbin used some water he warmed in a pot to freshen up. Next, he looked over the food in the pantry, deciding what he would take. *Cannot just let it go bad,* he thought.

An hour later he was clean, fed, packed and felt much better.

Arbin wished he could take more food and clothes with him, but he wanted to move around without calling a lot of attention to himself. He noticed how many of the visitors to the town dressed and decided the best thing to do was try to pass as a visitor.

Before leaving, Arbin stood in the living room looking around one last time to see if there was anything else he wanted. It was then that he saw that Elizabeth's needlepoint was still there, but it was turned to face the wall. However, the drawing she was using was gone. The diary of Casandra's father and grandfather was also missing. *That is strange,* he thought. *Why would she take those? I thought she could not read. Too bad I was starting to enjoy reading it.*

Arbin peeked out the window to make sure no one was lurking there. It was now mid-afternoon, and he had to decide if he would take a chance leaving now or wait for it to get darker. There were a few people walking outside, and he was sure it would be quieter as the evening approached. He had been lucky so far and did not want to chance someone might show up to check the home.

He looked around, picked up his bag and stepped outside. He paused to lock up the house. "No reason to invite trouble," he said. "Beside I kind of owe it to Masimo."

ARBIN MADE HIS WAY back toward the business district. While cleaning up and eating, he had given his next actions some thought. He wanted to keep his promises to both Jayden and Elizabeth but had no idea how to do either. Arbin was not sure if Jayden was serious about his threat to kidnap Dylan. If he was, then finding Dylan was his best chance of both finding Jayden and keeping his promise to Elizabeth.

Based on what he had learned while traveling in the caravan, he felt that Dylan would be with his grandfather, Chairman Sumner. He was not sure where the Chairman lived, but he was sure that most people in town would. If he asked nicely, he was sure they would point him in the right direction. He figured the western side of town would be the best place to ask about the Chairman since people there had proved to me more eager to provide information. Now that he had some money, he might take a chance and check out the Laughing Bear again. That might also solve the problem of where to stay for a few days. The trip back to the western side would be easier now that he was dressed appropriately, and the Army was guarding things.

Arbin had just reached the end of Masimo's street and was getting ready to head south to the Bridge of Sorrows when he spotted a small cluster of men standing across the street from the compound's Eastern Gate. They appeared to be checking out something inside the compound. His curiosity got the better of him and he walked over to discover what the group was so interested in. As Arbin approached the small group, he heard a loud bang plus a faint echo. He looked at the overcast sky and said, "Great, more rain."

One man in the group he had just joined looked back, shook his head and said, "Rains done for now."

Arbin heard another boom and looked toward the compound. He saw a puff of smoke rising near two Shadow Guards in full armor and a young child. Arbin recognized Captain Eustace in his green and gold plate armor. He also realized that the child was Dylan. "What's he doing here?" said Arbin.

"Looks like they're teaching the child to fire that weapon. Been at it for about an hour," said one of his fellow spectators.

Arbin looked back into the compound and thought, *I was sure Captain Eustace would have been leading the group that went to root out Casandra's attackers.* Arbin watched as Captain Eustace instructed Dylan in using the pistol. After each shot, Captain Eustace would hand the pistol to the other uniformed man who quickly reloaded the pistol with Dylan listening intently.

That was easy, Arbin thought. *Now that I found Dylan, what do I do? I wonder if Jayden is here somewhere.* Arbin took a quick look around but did not see him. *I do not think he would be foolish enough to Fade this close to Seers. If he is here, I can only hope he will want to talk to me again. Best thing to do is just find a good place to watch for him.*

The sound of another shot brought Arbin's attention back to the compound. He watched Captain Eustace and Dylan walk to the targets and examine the results. Captain Eustace pointed out different things on the target and explained something about the pistol. Arbin knew nothing about guns, but it was obvious Dylan was excited about his results.

As Captain Eustace and Dylan walked back to the other Shadow Guards, they talked. Arbin felt like he was looking at father and son instead of teacher and student. It reminded him of the times he had spent with his father so long ago. After a little more talking, it was clear the lesson was over.

Captain Eustace signaled to someone just out of sight. It was Elizabeth. She walked over to Dylan and stood behind him with her hands on his shoulder and listened as Captain Eustace appeared to be giving some instructions. While they were talking, a Shadow Guard brought over a box which Captain Eustace took and handed to Elizabeth. Even though Arbin could not hear what was being said, he could tell that the conversation had become serious. When Captain Eustace finished, he turned and mounted a nearby horse. Elizabeth and Dylan stepped back as Captain Eustace and several Shadow Guards rode out of the compound.

Arbin turned his back to the departing Shadow Guards. He had not seen Captain Eustace or any of his people since he had gotten his new haircut but did not want to take a chance that they would recognize him. When he turned back, he could see the small group riding south and could just make out the uniforms of three Seers at the rear of the group. Based on what Alex had told him about formations, he guessed there must have been around nine Shadow Guards. They did not have a supply wagon like they did when he was traveling with them. Instead, they were followed by two riderless horses with packs on them. Once they were well down the road, Arbin looked back into the compound, but could no longer see Elizabeth and Dylan.

Great, I lost them, he thought. *They must still be in the compound. I need to find a better spot to look for them.* Just as Arbin was getting ready to leave his little group, he heard a carriage departing the compound. Inside were Elizabeth, Dylan and two Shadow Guards. After exiting the compound, the small carriage headed north.

Arbin did his best to keep track of them without breaking into a full run, but he soon lost sight of them behind buildings as the north road bent to the right as it followed the river. "North," said Arbin. He stopped to catch his breath and looked around. He had never been this way before. *Where are you going, Elizabeth?* he thought. *I do not know where you and Alex live, but I know it is south of the Bridge of Sorrows.* Arbin thought for a while, trying to decide where she might be going. *The Captain just left town, so that rules him out. Maybe Lady Casandra has a place here. She bought one for Masimo. No, I remember back in Noor Point they said she would stay with Henry's father. That means I was right all along. You are heading for Chairman's Sumner's house. Now, where does he live?*

It took fewer questions than he expected for Arbin to learn that Chairman Sumner had a large estate on the northernmost part of the west side of the city. It was near the edge of the foothills where he had a vineyard and orchard. Arbin also learned that there was another bridge across the river about five miles north. Once across, the road led almost directly to Chairman Sumner's estate. During normal times it would be faster to go through the western side of the city to reach the Sumner estate. Now, with the streets crowded with people coming for the Unification Celebration, the north route was the fastest way. It gave Arbin a chuckle when he realized that Chairman Sumner's estate was only a few miles from the dock area where he had started the day.

Arbin decided it would be smart to take the north route because there was less chance of meeting someone that might be looking for him. He guessed it would take almost two hours to reach Chairman Sumner's estate. It would still be light out when he got there, but it would give him some time to check the area around the home before sneaking inside and locating Elizabeth and Dylan. He did not know if Jayden would be there, but it was the best option for now.

ARBIN DID NOT HAVE any problems finding Chairman Sumner's estate. It was bigger than any home he had ever seen. It was at the end of the road that crossed the northern bridge, just where the foothills started. It was a two-story house, set about thirty feet from the road and surrounded with a shoulder high fence. The gated entrance was too far for him to see any guards, but he was sure they would be there. The vineyard was on the far side of the home and stretched up into the nearby foothills. To the south of the home was a small apple orchard that filled the space between the Chairman's home and a few homes clustered around the bridge. A thick forest ran from the northern edge of the vineyard, behind the back of the home, down along the northern side of the orchard and almost to the river.

The fence around the Estate was a good sturdy fence that had sections of metal in a fancy floral design that allowed someone to see out as much as in. Arbin had to assume that the fence ran all the way around the home. The height of the fence suggested it was more for appearance than security. Getting over it would not be a problem if he could find an unguarded section.

Arbin figured his best bet would be to approach the home from the forest side since it offered more cover. His two options for getting to the forest were through the vineyard or the orchard. The vineyard appeared to have people working in it, so that way was out. Plus, he would have to walk past the gate to get there. The trees in the orchard were organized in nice rows with lots of space between them. There did not appear to be anyone working in it, but he worried that he might be easily spotted if he walked through it. Even in a Fade he could be visible at a distance. Arbin was sure it would be someone's job to watch for anyone foolish enough to wander through it.

Looking back at the bridge and the small cluster of homes near it, Arbin thought, *I guess the best thing to do is just follow the riverbank and then head for the forest once I passed the orchard.*

Walking along the river's edge was pleasant but slow going. Arbin had to stay close to the river's edge because of the tall grass which got higher and thicker the further he walked from the cluster of homes. He soon realized at this pace, it would be dark before he got where he wanted to be. While darkness would give him some cover, he did not want to be stumbling through a dark forest. He had no choice but to cut through the orchard.

Arbin stopped in the high grass at the edge of the orchard and studied the Estate. It was early evening. There was some candlelight coming from a few of the windows, but he did not see any workers or guards. Arbin let himself slip into a Fade and made his way through the orchard along the edge of the forest. While the orchard, with its well-kept, nicely spaced trees, offered little cover, the forest was thankfully wild and overgrown. Arbin was glad when he was close enough to the home to step into it.

Arbin made his way through the forest to the back of the Sumner home and was surprised to discover that the fence line did not go completely around the house. Instead, it extended along the back of the home about fifteen feet and met up with a small building. He guessed the fence did something similar on the far side. *This will be easier than I thought.*

Arbin guessed the gardener probably used the small building. He knew there must be one because the backyard, what he could see of it, was beautiful. Even as a gardener's shack, it was nicer and bigger than what he had spent the last eight years living in back at Noor Point. It was about twelve feet high, had a window in back and a roof, the color of which matched the main house. The walls were pale white, and Ivy covered. There were several chest high bushes planted around it and the branches from a nearby tree extended over the roof.

Arbin quickly scanned the rest of the backyard which was obviously designed more with beauty and enjoyment in mind than security. There were several small clusters of trees and hedges, some surrounded with smaller colorful plants. There were a few benches scattered around, plus a small and a large gazebo. He was not sure because of the low light, but he thought there might be a small fishpond on the far side of the yard. The other thing that he noticed was the absence of guards.

The jewel of the backyard was the sunroom. While someone could enjoy the backyard from inside that room, the sunroom itself was beautiful to look at from the outside. The candle lights coming from inside almost sparkled as it shone through the collection of glass windows. The total effect was dazzling. The sunroom extended out from the back of the home about twenty feet, and on top of the sunroom was a balcony for a second story room which had two large windows set around what looked like a glass door. White drapes covered these windows, but the light from the room behind those windows showed the shadow of people inside. Arbin guessed it was either a bedroom or an office. The balcony would give someone a splendid view of the backyard. He would need to be careful that someone looking out from there would not spot him.

Arbin waited on the edge of the forest, watching for patrolling guards. He waited a good thirty minutes for the patrols but saw nothing. *Something is not right here,* he thought. *There should be at least two guards at the gate and two more for their relief. There were two guards in the carriage with Elizabeth. I did not see any Seers, but I am sure they are here.* Arbin was not sure if he was close enough to the house to detect anyone but tried it. *Nothing,* he thought after a few minutes of searching. *I need to find a better hiding spot closer to the house.*

Looking around, he felt the small gardener's building offered the best cover because of the high foliage and the few trees surrounding both the building and the wall that led up to it. *I might even be able to get on top of it,* he thought. Arbin was sure that any patrols worth their salt would check the bushes. They might not check the roof if he was in a Fade, but someone looking out the second-floor balcony might see him. The more he thought about it, the more the roof of the gardener's building sounded like the best choice.

The bag of belongings he had been carrying was going to be a problem. One he had not thought about earlier. He looked around and found an area in the forest where he felt he could stash it. He only hoped that it would still be there when he came back for it. All that food would surely be a temptation for whatever lived in the forest.

Now for the gardener's building. Since he had not detected a Seer nearby, he let himself Fade. He slowly made his way from cover to cover until he reached the fence. He followed it the few yards to the gardener's building, made sure no one was around, hopped onto the fence and then climbed up onto the roof. He quickly laid down flat and waited, hoping no one noticed him.

When he felt that it was safe, he moved until he found a place where he could see into the sunroom. A few branches from one of the nearby trees extended out in front of the building and blocked some of his vision to his left. He had not realized the branches might be a problem until he was on the roof. The other thing he had not realized was just how close the little building was to the back of the house. It gave him a much better look into the second-floor room, where there were still shadows of people in that room. It also gave him a view deep inside the sunroom, past all the large potted plants, to a couple sitting at a table.

Elizabeth and Dylan sat with a book on the table open before them. Elizabeth was drinking from a cup as Dylan appeared to be reading. *Ah*, he thought. *She is having Dylan read it to her. Now that is smart.*

Arbin settled in and let himself slip deeper into a Fade. He was not sure if Jayden would show up and kind of hoped he would not because he was enjoying watching Elizabeth and Dylan but kept a worried eye on the balcony. It was getting much darker and a little cooler. Arbin made a mental note to find some warmer clothes if he did this again tomorrow.

The longer he watched, the less sure he was on who was reading to whom. *I thought she could not read. I am sure that is what she told me.*

He watched quietly as Elizabeth and Dylan appeared to discuss things. Occasionally, Elizabeth would smile or even let out a little laugh. Each time she did, Arbin could not help but smile too. Dylan even looked like a normal kid now. Not that brat that he had met back in the caravan. *I am sure she can take credit for that,* he thought.

Arbin was enjoying the scene when four people entered the room from a door in the back. Two of them were wearing Shadow Guard uniforms. They stopped just inside of the room. Another wearing a Seer uniform and someone looking more like a servant walked over to where Elizabeth and Dylan were sitting. The sight of a Seer caused Arbin to panic a bit, and he let his Fade slip. Keeping up the Fade was making him tired. He was not worried about being detected by the Seer, but he was still worried about patrols, so he relaxed and slipped back into a Fade.

The servant said something, and Elizabeth closed the book they had been reading. After a few seconds, Dylan got up, hugged Elizabeth and left the room with the servant. The two Shadow Guards followed them out the door. *Must be bedtime,* he thought. *Well, that is probably it for tonight.*

Arbin was thinking about what to do next when he saw the Seer and Elizabeth sit back down at the table. Arbin now had a better view of the Seer and knew it was Lubin. *Why that little..., what does he think he is doing, he is supposed to be guarding them.* It was then that Arbin remembered Elizabeth saying that Alex was trying to set her up with Lubin. He felt a little embarrassed intruding on Elizabeth but found he could not stop watching.

The cool of the evening and the strain of maintaining the Fade was making him uncomfortable. It was getting late and Jayden had not shown. *Maybe I was wrong about waiting for him here,* he thought. Arbin had just decided to call it a night when he heard a branch snap near him. He took a deep breath and focused on his Fade.

He slowly looked to his left and thought he could make out some movement along the fence. His staring into the lit sunroom had weakened his night vision a little. He closed his eyes and listened. There was another snap. This time when he opened his eyes, he looked just to the side of the sound and focused on catching some movement in the corner of his eyes.

A few minutes later, Arbin was rewarded with seeing something move. He could not make out enough to tell if it was a person or an animal. Arbin focused through the branches at the movement and soon made out the shape of a man wearing dark clothes and hood. *Jayden,* he thought. The shadow was about the right size, but Arbin did not detect a Fade. *He must know there are Seers nearby.*

It was possible that the shadow had seen what had just happened inside the sunroom because he changed the direction of his movements and started slowly toward the bushes at the far-left end of the sunroom. *I wonder if there is some way up to the second story from there,* Arbin thought. Soon the shadow reached the edge of what Arbin considered safe hiding, but instead of stopping, the figure took another step. *Idiot, he must not know there are people in that upper room.*

Once the shadow reached the wall of the sunroom, Arbin knew he had to do something. He focused on his Fade, wrapping himself in it tightly, and slowly slipped off the roof, back onto the wall and then down. The shadow was so intent on listening to the talking inside that Arbin got within arm's reach before the shadow turned around.

Arbin put his finger to his lips to let Jayden know to be quiet. As the shadow turned around, Arbin found himself looking into the face of a stranger who was just as startled to see Arbin looking at him.

"Who are you?" Arbin said, and seconds later he heard a whistle coming from somewhere in the sunroom. Both Arbin and the stranger looked toward the sound of the whistle. It was then that Arbin realized he had not dropped his Fade.

The stranger pushed Arbin as he tried to run past, but Arbin grabbed his clothes, causing the stranger to stumble and fall to the ground face down. Arbin scrambled to get on top of the stranger, and that is when he saw the knife. It was a big knife too. The stranger was wearing it on his belt across the small of his back. Arbin saw the stranger reach for the knife, but Arbin got to it first.

Arbin had never learned how to use a knife in a fight, so he pulled it out of the sheath, and just tossed it as far to the side as he could. If he could keep the stranger away from the knife, he would have a better chance of surviving until help arrived. It surprised Arbin when the stranger quickly rolled in the knife's direction, easily breaking free of Arbin's grip.

The stranger was crawling quickly toward the knife as Arbin made it to his feet. He did not know what to do, so he jumped forward and landed on one of the stranger's legs. The stranger yelled, turned over and kicked at Arbin's legs, knocking him down. Both men got back up at the same time, but this time the stranger had the knife in his hand. He was limping badly, but Arbin was sure that was not enough to stop the stranger from reaching him. Arbin readied himself for the attack, hopeful that the stranger's injured leg would make it easier to dodge.

The stranger lunged at Arbin instead of swiping as he had expected. The stranger's injured leg caused him to stop short of his target and Arbin stepped forward quickly grabbing the extended arm and spun around pulling the stranger's elbow tightly against his side.

The stranger continued struggling to get his arm free as Arbin tried to keep pressure on the elbow. The stranger stepped on Arbin's ankle, causing him to stumble. Arbin knew he could no longer keep his hold on the knife arm and decided the best thing to do was to get as much distance between him and the stranger, hoping he could run away. He turned toward his attacker and prepared to push him away as hard as he could. Before he could, he heard a loud sound like the crack of thunder. He heard it echo in the surrounding woods and then felt a burning in his left arm just as he lost grip on the attacker. He heard his attacker gasp and double forward. Arbin knew he had to get away from his attacker and pushed hard, causing his attacker to stagger backward. Arbin heard another crack and he saw his attacker drop to the ground.

Arbin stared at the stranger, not sure what had happened. Soon the pain in his arm was the only thing he could think of. He dropped to one knee and was surprised when he felt someone grab him from behind and push him to the ground. He felt the weight of someone on top of him. The pain in his arm was almost more than Arbin could bear as the person on top of him pulled it behind him while using his weight to hold him down. He tried to yell out, but the pain took away his breath. He heard someone shout, "He's dead. I think we just killed the Fade!" Arbin looked in the voice's direction and saw a Shadow Guard holding a pistol give a few kicks to the body of the stranger.

The person sitting on Arbin was joined by another who grabbed Arbin by the hair and turned his head enough for Arbin to make out the uniform pants of a Seer. He heard Lubin's voice ask, "Arbin, what the hell are you doing here?" The pain in his arm was getting stronger and Arbin felt dizzy.

Just before he passed out, he heard, "Someone get a kit. I think he has been shot."

Chapter 17 - We Agree at Last

THERE WAS A DEFINITE cheeriness to the Grand Council meeting room. The recent defeat of the Fade had brought a great feeling of relief with it.

"Gentlemen, please, I would like to begin this meeting," said Councilman Kauffman, as he rapped a few times politely with the gavel. The sound of talking gave way to the sound of the movement of chairs as Councilmen and guests each found their proper seats.

Kauffman stayed standing until everyone had found their seats, then said, "As some of you know, Chairman Sumner will not be attending today's meeting. He is not feeling well, plus the attacks on his family, including the recent attempt at his home, have taken a toll on him. He sends his apologies."

Kauffman gave the guests and Councilmen a chance to finish expressing their condolences and wishes for a quick recovery.

"As per our traditions, the two Family Chairs drew lots, and I have won the honor of acting as the Chairman for this meeting. Are there any objections?"

Kauffman looked at each member of the Council and when no objections were raised, he rapped the gavel and continued, "Chairman Sumner has also sent a letter to the Council asking Bishop Sorren to vote on his behalf. Bishop Sorren will not have the authority to vote on ties, since that authority remains with the acting Chairman. Once again, as per our traditions, I have accepted Chairman Sumner's request. Are there any objections?"

There were a few side comments but after a minute of silence Kauffman rapped the gavel and said, "Bishop Sorren, if you would take a chair with the Council. You can sit in mine for today."

Bishop Sorren stood up from the guest gallery where he had been sitting with High Seer Kindermann, Elizabeth and Dylan and made his way to his council chair, stopping a few times to greet the other Council members. Once Bishop Sorren was seated, Kauffman said, "With that business finished, I call this meeting open," and rapped the gavel once, then sat down.

Kauffman straightened up some papers in front of him then said, "Besides the opening prayer, Bishop Sorren has asked to say a few words at the start of the meeting. Understanding the nature of his comments and seeing that it addresses some items we have scheduled for today; I have decided to allow it. Bishop Sorren, if you please."

Bishop Sorren stood and nodded his acknowledgment to the other members of the Council. Then, looking out at the gallery and in a well-practiced manner said, "I would like to begin with a quick word of thanks to the Lord."

The members of the Council and gallery looked downward and Bishop Sorren said, "Lord, we give thanks that Your hand of protection and guidance has been on this country since its foundation. It was during that time that we suffered death and chaos brought by the appearance of agents of Evil. It was only through Your blessing on the founding members of this Council we could defeat this Evil. Once again, as Evil threatened to return, You showed Your favor by bringing forth leaders and men with the courage and faith needed to continue this battle. Now, as Your chosen leaders come together to decide how to best care for Your people, in accordance with Your will, we ask for Your continued guidance and support. This we pray in the name of the Father, the Son and the Holy Spirit."

There was a scuffing of chairs and papers as people prepared for what many worried would be a long meeting. After a few minutes of silence Bishop Sorren, who was still standing continued, "I would like to publicly acknowledge the brave work of High Seer Kindermann and his Seers, as well as Captain Eustace and his Shadow Guards in defeating the Fade that threaten to destroy this Council and this Country."

There was a round of healthy applause that High Seer Kindermann felt obligated to acknowledge by briefly standing.

"I am sure that Captain Eustace would have liked to be here today," said Bishop Sorren. "But he is still on patrol, leading the effort to root out the members of the misguided group that brought the evil of the Fade back to our country. I know we all wish him great success in his effort."

After the applause died down, Kauffman tapped the gavel a few times to bring the room back to order. "Those were words well said Bishop. I am sure the other members of the Council agree wholeheartedly with you. I believe you have something else to say?"

The Bishop, who was still standing, turned to Councilman Darr and said, "I am honored to sit with these esteemed leaders today. I feel that I must clear up any issues that would prevent us from attending to the important business at hand. So, in the spirit of unification so honored by our upcoming celebration, I would like to offer my apologies to any of the members of this council who I may have offended during our struggle with how best to address the return of a Fade to our nation."

Councilman Darr, who was looking straight ahead during Bishop Sorren's speech, now turned toward the Bishop and gave a small nod of his head.

Bishop Sorren continued, "After an encouraging discussion with High Seer Kindermann and the Family Chairs, and if given the opportunity today, I would like to present a compromise to the process for selecting and promoting Seers."

When he finished talking, Bishop Sorren sat down. Kauffman looked around the room and then said, "We have several important items to discuss today. I agree with Bishop Sorren that resolving this issue now will prevent any delay in addressing the issues on our agenda. If no one has any objections, I would like to make this our first order of business." When no one objected, Kauffman rapped his gavel and said, "Bishop Sorren, please continue."

This time Bishop Sorren remained seated and said, "The first thing I want to do is make sure there is an agreement on what the main issues are. I think we can all agree that the role of the Seers in both discovering and fighting Fades is essential, as shown by recent events," Bishop Sorren paused and saw heads nodding in agreement.

"I think we can also agree that a Seer's gift is a divine mystery. Something detectable only to those that have been called," said Bishop Sorren. Nods of agreement again met the Bishop's comments. "Then, the issue is not the value of the Seer Core, but a fear that the current selection process may not be adequate in verifying a candidate's claim of God's calling on him." Bishop Sorren paused, then said, "Have I expressed the issue correctly?"

Darr said, "If by God's calling you are referring to their ability to detect and fight Fades, then we are in agreement."

The Bishop smiled and said, "I will leave it to God to determine how His Calling is to be manifest, but for sake of discussion let us say we are talking about a person's gift to detect and stand against a Fade."

Darr took a few seconds to think about Bishop Sorren's comments, then said, "Continue, please."

Bishop Sorren said, "I also want to confirm that you feel the old testing method is more desirable because it allows an observer to see, through demonstration, that at the time of testing the Seer or candidate possesses this divine gift."

"At the time of testing?" asked Darr. "What do you mean by that?"

"I mean that a divine gift is God's to give and take away, as is his right in all gifts he gives," said Bishop Sorren.

"So, what you are saying is that a person who passed the test could lose his gift, at any time, based on the will of God," said Darr.

"Correct," said Bishop Sorren. "However, I would like to return to the question of whether the old testing process would satisfy your need to know if someone was gifted or not."

"Yes, I feel the old testing process would provide a reasonable demonstration that someone has this gift if properly conducted." said Darr. "However, your comments about a person losing their gift concerns me and I wonder just how that issue is being monitored without ongoing testing."

"Then you properly see the dilemma we faced and why we relied on the word of honorable men who had the gift to verify and stand up for candidates," said Bishop Sorren. "I agree after reviewing our process, that we had no way to verify that our honorable men still have the gift, so we have come up with what we feel is a reasonable solution. But first, I need you to agree that the continual testing of all Seers is unreasonable because of the time and money it would waste."

"I don't see the time for testing being an issue," said Darr.

"The testing takes many hours to set up and conduct. The judging panel, which includes members in this room, must be scheduled so as not to interfere with other equally important business," said the Bishop. "We also would lose the ability of the Seers to train and patrol with the Shadow Guard until their gifts were re-confirmed."

"I guess I see your point," said Darr. "What is your suggestion?"

Bishop Sorren took a slight breath of victory and continued. "First, we would like the addition of an elected Councilman to the Application Committee. This need not be a permanent position. We can change who holds the position to meet schedules. Do you agree to this?"

Darr nodded his head and said, "I see nothing wrong with that."

"Next," said Bishop Sorren, "We suggest that only Senior Seers, that have passed an annual test, and are in good standing, be allowed to nominate new members."

"So, you are saying we would not test new candidates but would still need to rely on the word of someone? How does that give me confidence in the candidate?" asked Darr.

"As you know, our new candidates must spend a year in apprenticeship before being approved as a Seer. We find that new candidates rarely have the proper training or confidence needed to pass the old test. It sometimes takes time to properly develop their gifts. Some may never be as good as others, but we cannot reject them if they have evidence of God's hand on them and they show the proper moral character. We also feel that the apprenticeship period would give us the time needed to evaluate if the person is gifted."

"You said Senior Seers would do the nomination," said Darr. "Can we at least agree that before anyone is advanced, they go through this annual testing."

"Advancement is a complicated thing. We would like to keep that process under the authority of the office of the High Seer and myself," said

Bishop Sorren. "We plan, going forward, conducting annual testing on all 'First Rank' members. As you know, we select our High Seer position from First Ranks."

"And what rank was the Seer that was recommending Arbin for admittance into the Seers," asked Darr.

"Seer Keller is a Second Rank. However, he is being considered for promotion. It was our intent that if he passed the test, we would promote him to First Rank," said Bishop Sorren.

"Where does that leave Arbin?", asked Darr.

"Once Seer Keller completes the testing process using the old method, he will be advanced to First Rank," said Bishop Sorren. "After that, if he still wants to nominate Arbin, then we will convene an Appointment Committee and hear the facts supporting his nomination just as before. If approved, he will become a First Year Candidate and start his training."

"An Elected Councilman will be on the Appointment Committee that monitors the testing for Seer Keller?" asked Darr.

"Correct," said the Bishop as he sat back in his chair.

Councilman Darr looked to the other elected members of the Council and saw them nodding in agreement. He turned back to Bishop Sorren and said, "We have an agreement."

"Fine," said Kauffman. "Are there any objections from any members of the Council?" After a few seconds he tapped his gavel and said, "Now we can move on the other items on our agenda."

Kauffman looked at the papers in front of him and said, "Next, we have some budget issues to discuss." There were sounds of scuffing feet and the moving of chairs as the members of the gallery prepared for what was always the most boring part of the meeting. Kauffman looked up but did not reach for the gavel. Instead, he studied the papers in front of him and then said, "The first item is a proper memorial for Henry Sumner. We need to approve the study for the proper placement and design. The one restraint we have agreed on is that we will not make it a part of the Bridge of Sorrows Park or Memorial. Any objection to starting the process?" When there were no objections, Kauffman turned to Councilman Blazys and asked if he could oversee the project since he had the most construction background. Councilman Blazys agreed.

"Next is a request from Captain Eustace to be reimbursed for the purchase of firearms made with his own funds," said Kauffman. "He is also asking the Council to approve the purchase of additional firearms, supplies, and uniform modifications required to support the incorporation of eight armed men into the Shadow Guard formations. I can tell you that based on the success of firearms against the Fade, I see no problem with this request." Kauffman looked at the other Councilman and said, "Any objections?"

Councilman Roth raised his hand. "I have no problem reimbursing him for his current purchases. I would like to have more time to investigate the type and suppliers of these firearms. I have heard that the type of firearm he has selected has a limited supplier and there is talk that the wheellock firing mechanism may be banned in a few countries because of its extremely successful use by a few rebel groups."

"What are you suggesting?" asked Kauffman.

"Give me a few months to speak with my contacts and make sure we have reliable suppliers before we commit to a particular weapon," said Roth.

"Do you doubt Captain Eustace's judgment on weapons?" asked Bishop Sorren.

"I am a businessman, and a successful one at that," said Roth. "Captain Eustace is not. I doubt he understands the politics or economics entanglements that come from what might first appear a simple purchase. If we will take the time to form a committee to discuss the design of a monument, then I think it's only prudent to spend a little time studying the effects of forming trading alliances before we commit ourselves to a particular weapon."

"How much time do you think you would need for this review?" asked Kauffman.

"I think three months would be sufficient for me to bring an initial report before the Council," said Roth.

Kauffman nodded and said, "Councilman Roth is requesting a delay of three months on the decision to change the Shadow Guard budget to support the permanent addition of firearms. He is also requesting that he be allowed to collect information on alternatives in weapon type and supplier. Are there any objections?"

Bishop Sorren and Councilman Werner raised their hands. "Bishop Sorren's two votes and Councilman Werner's two votes puts it at four against. I vote in favor of Councilman Roth. That puts the vote at four against and two in favor. Any objections from the elected members of the Council?" After a few seconds of silence, Kauffman tapped his gavel and said, "The final vote is four against, and eight in favor. Councilman Roth's request has been approved."

"Our next point of business is the start of the confirmation process for Dylan Summer as the legal and rightful Heir to the Sumner Family Chair. In addition, because Dylan is a minor, we must appoint a male guardian to act on his behalf in matters of state and the management of his family estate until he reaches the age of sixteen," said Kauffman. "While Chairman Sumner is the patriarch of the Summer Family, we cannot consider him as Dylan's legal guardian because we are discussing a plan of succession for the Sumner Chair."

Kauffman rapped his gavel to quiet some discussion that started in the gallery.

"It has been some time since we have done this," said Kauffman. "I remind everyone, we are following a well-established process based on years of tradition. There may be some points that are confusing or that you do not agree with, but I ask that you keep a proper decorum. With that being said, the first thing that must be done is the verification of Dylan Sumner's lineage. Bishop Sorren, I believe you have something to say on this point."

Bishop Sorren held up a collection of documents and said, "The Church is prepared to state for the record that Dylan Sumner is the only living male child of Henry and Casandra Sumner, who were married by the Church. We also state that Dylan Sumner was born as a result of the marriage and was properly baptized."

When he finished, Bishop Sorren passed the collection of papers to Kauffman who said, "The Council has accepted the information provided by Bishop Sorren and now sets a one-week period where any challenges to these facts can be offered in writing. At our next meeting, any reasonable claims disputing the confirmation of Dylan Sumner as Heir to the Sumner Chair will be heard."

Kauffman rapped his gavel and the feeling in the room changed to one of excitement, as many knew what was to follow.

"Now for the nominations of candidates for Guardian," said Councilman Kauffman. "The Council will have the final approval of the Guardian, and if the Council finds that none of the candidates are appropriate, it can make its own appointment. Nominations must be presented in writing and have the endorsement of more than one signature. I want to take time to remind everyone that if the Heir cannot take his place as chair holder and no other qualified male relatives can be found, the Guardian will assume the duties, as well as all rights and titles of the Sumner Family Chair. I now open the floor for nominations from the public."

After a few minutes had passed, it was clear that no one in the gallery would make a nomination. Kauffman rapped his gavel and said, "Since there are no nominations from the gallery, I now ask for nominations from the Council Members."

Both Bishop Sorren and Councilman Darr raised their hands. Kauffman said, "Bishop Sorren, since you are speaking on behalf of Chairman Sumner, you may present first."

Bishop Sorren placed two documents in front of him and studied them for a few seconds, as if making some last-minute decision. He finally said, "My fellow members of the Council and gathered guests I have two nominations to present. The first is from Chairman Morgan Sumner and the second is from Lady Casandra Sumner."

"Mr. Chairman point of order," said Councilman Darr.

Bishop Sorren had paused after making his announcement, knowing the interruption would occur. He was not happy about it, but he had committed to the action. He looked over to Darr, who again said, "Point of order, Mr. Chairman."

Kauffman looked over to Darr and said, "Go ahead, Councilman."

"As a point of order, the nominations from the public have closed," said Darr. "Since Lady Casandra is not a Council Member. I would suggest that she missed her opportunity to put forward a candidate."

"I am sorry, Mr. Chairman," said Bishop Sorren. "I guess I misunderstood. Because I was acting as a Councilman, I did not realize that I had to present the two nominations at separate times."

"An understandable error, Bishop Sorren," said Kauffman. "May I see the nomination letter from Lady Casandra please?"

Kauffman took the letter and after a few minutes of reading, he frowned, looked back toward the Bishop and said, "This letter was written by Lady Casandra the day after Henry Sumner's death. She asks that Captain Eustace be nominated as Guardian. I would have no problem overlooking the point of order, but unfortunately this letter only has the endorsement of Lady Casandra. For it to be considered, she would need at least two endorsements. Has this letter been in your possession since its arrival?"

"No, it was presented to Chairman Sumner upon Captain Eustace's return and was just given to me by the Chairman along with his nomination letter," said the Bishop.

"I am surprised that Chairman Sumner would miss that detail," said Kauffman. "I am afraid I cannot accept this letter unless we get a second endorsement. At this late point in the process that endorsement would need to come from a Council Member," Kauffman looked at the other members of the Council and said, "Unfortunately, I have given my endorsement to someone else already. Are any of the other members willing to give their endorsement?"

The other Councilmen, in turn, shook their heads no. Kauffman turned to the Bishop and said, "I am sorry, Bishop Sorren, but we need to refuse Lady Casandra's nomination."

Bishop Sorren said, "I understand. Then I will continue with Chairman Sumner's nomination." He handed Kauffman a letter as he said, "Chairman Morgan Sumner nominates High Seer Otis Kindermann as Guardian. The nomination has the endorsement of all the Family Chairs as well as myself."

There was some conversation in the gallery as the High Seer received congratulations from his neighbors.

Kauffman took a few seconds to review the letter and then said, "The nomination meets the requirements and has been accepted. Councilman Darr, please present your nomination."

Darr held up a long document with a large red seal attached. He handed it to Kauffman and said, "Mr. Chairman, I present a nomination letter that has been endorsed by all the Elected Council Members and twenty of our most influential citizens. We nominate a man who recently put his life on the line protecting Dylan Sumner and is now the only man living that has twice battled a Fade in hand-to-hand combat and survived. We nominate Arbin Adean as Guardian."

The announcement brought a flurry of comments, much to the delight of Councilman Darr. It was obvious he had expected as much.

Kauffman rapped on the gavel several times until the room quieted down.

"Mr. Chairman, I object to this nomination," said Councilman Werner.

"I agree with the good Councilman," said Bishop Sorren. "Surely there must be something in the rules about the character or even the experience of the candidate. I fail to see how Councilman Darr could put this young nobody, a person of questionable loyalty and character, in the same company as the High Seer or even Captain Eustace."

"Arbin is a man who has shown both strong character and loyalty," said Darr. "He stood up against a flawed and unfair evaluation system. He single-handedly hunted down the Fade and put his life on the line protecting both Chairman Sumner and Dylan Sumner."

There was the sound of acknowledgment from several Council members as well as people attending.

"Even your man, Seer Keller, put Arbin on a level with the original founding members of this Council," said Darr.

"You do not understand who this man is," said Bishop Sumner. "I know his background and I know what he may be capable of. He is not a person with the character or loyalty of the original three Blessed Seers. No matter what anyone might say."

"Gentlemen, please. This is not the place for this discussion," said Kauffman with a few raps of the gavel. "The nomination letter for Arbin Adean meets the requirements, and we are accepting it. The Council will take any objections in writing and will interview the candidates before it takes the final vote. Now, with all the nominations made, we are at the end of our scheduled agenda. I am making one last call for any further issues that need to come before this Council."

Kauffman waited for a few seconds, then rapped the gavel and said, "Meeting adjourned."

Bishop Sorren gathered his things and joined Elizabeth, Dylan and High Seer Kindermann on the gallery floor. Both Dylan and Kindermann were receiving congratulations from the people gathered there while Elizabeth stood to the side watching.

As Bishop Sorren joined her, she said, "I did not realize my brother was up for promotion."

"There is a very real chance that Alex may become the next High Seer thanks to all the attention he has received," said Bishop Sorren.

"Next High Seer? What about the current one?" she asked, as she watched Kindermann chatting away with Councilman Kauffman.

"Once he is appointed Guardian, Otis will need to step down from that position," said Bishop Sorren.

"The nomination of Arbin honestly surprised me," said Elizabeth. She paused a few minutes as if deciding on what to say next. Elizabeth looked at High Seer Kindermann who was standing next to Dylan, but clearly showed no affection for the boy. "Is there a chance of him being appointed Guardian?"

Bishop Sorren saw Elizabeth looking in the High Seer's direction and misunderstood who she was talking about. He said, "Don't worry. Otis will be Dylan's Guardian. I can guarantee that."

Elizabeth looked back at Bishop Sorren and said, "Guarantee it? What about Arbin? The number of endorsements is impressive."

"That was Councilman Darr's little way of sparring with Chairman Sumner," said the Bishop. "The vote is tied right now, with the Family Chairs having two votes each to the Elected Chairs one each. Everyone knows how Chairman Sumner will cast his tie-breaking vote. Give it a week and the resolve of some Elected Chairs may slip. Especially once they start bargaining."

"You don't think Arbin has a chance of being selected?" asked Elizabeth, looking back at Dylan.

"Not unless something major happens," said the Bishop. He looked at her and said, "You sound a little disappointed. Do you think they should select him?"

"He fascinates Dylan," said Elizabeth.

"Dylan is a child. You, on the other hand," said Bishop Sorren. He paused before continuing, then said, "I hear you have been spending time with him. It would interest me to hear your opinion of him?"

"I have not spent that much time with him. Most of that was at the request of others and was not always pleasant," said Elizabeth.

"So, would you agree that Arbin is not the type of person we want around Dylan or even making decisions about running this country?" asked Bishop Sorren.

Elizabeth looked back at Dylan and said, "He did risk his life to keep Dylan safe. Arbin can be a very frustrating person to deal with at times. I don't understand why he does the things he does. He is capable of great things, like battling with the Fade, but at the same time he does not seem to understand the opportunities that are before him. I am not sure if he really knows what he wants to do with his life."

Bishop Sorren studied Elizabeth for a few minutes and said, "I know many important men who did not know what they wanted until the right person came along and gave them the guidance and motivation needed."

Elizabeth looked back at the Bishop, not sure what to make of his last comment.

"Speaking of Dylan," said Bishop Sorren, deciding to change the subject. "How is Dylan handling the Fade incident?"

"He found the whole thing exciting," said Elizabeth. "He can't wait to tell Captain Eustace about his part in the death of the Fade that killed his Father. He is a little upset that his shot hit Arbin at the same time. He has made me promise to apologize to him the next time I see him."

"And when will that be?" asked Bishop Sorren.

"I am not sure," said Elizabeth. "We did not part on good terms the last time I saw him. I think it would be best if I waited for Masimo to return before I visit him."

"Yes, Masimo," said Bishop Sorren. "Lady Casandra has mentioned him to me a few times. She has also mentioned you, as well. She is curious about the status of your future plans. I have also had inquiries about you from several families of good standing."

"I am aware of Lady Casandra's interests in my future," said Elizabeth with a slight blush. "Just as I know that my brother has made suggestions to you as well."

"We all only want what's best for you, my dear," said Bishop Sorren with a smile.

"I am happy with my life as it is," said Elizabeth. "I am too busy with my crafts and the duties Lady Casandra has given me to worry about suitors."

"Young Dylan will need guidance and emotional support, especially now, since it may take some time before his mother can join him here," said Bishop Sorren. "That is why it's so important that we select the right person for Guardian. Besides all the financial and social benefits that come with the position, The Guardian will be greatly involved in the development of young Dylan. Perhaps even more so than his mother."

Elizabeth looked at Kindermann and said, "The High Seer doesn't really strike me as the fatherly type. He has never had a conversation with Dylan, and I am sure Dylan would never think of him in that way. The only two people he talks about are Captain Eustace, who he truly loves, and Arbin, who he views as a hero and a mystery."

"A very insightful and thought-provoking observation," said Bishop Sorren. "I am starting to believe that the Guardian, no matter who it ends up being, would benefit from the keen insight and guidance that someone like you could provide. Dylan's fondness for you is also an exceptional asset. I think it's about time we started giving your future some serious thought."

Elizabeth was a little startled by what the Bishop had just suggested. She could see by the far off look on his face that the Bishop was deep in thought and was not expecting an answer to his last comment. She looked over at where Dylan was standing. The High Seer was nowhere to be seen, and Dylan had been joined by one of the Shadow Guards. She could see on Dylan's face that he wanted to leave, so she turned to the Bishop and said, "If you will excuse me, I think it's time that Dylan and I left."

Elisabeth walked over to Dylan and said to the Shadow Guard with him, "Is Captain Eustace back yet?"

"Not yet," he replied. "We expect him within the hour."

Elizabeth turned to Dylan and said, "Time to go if we are going to be there when your uncle arrives."

Dylan said, "I thought we would visit Arbin."

"We will, but not today," said Elizabeth. "You don't want to be late for your uncle's arrival, do you?"

"I wanted to give Arbin my gift," said Dylan.

"I will make sure he gets it and your apology," said Elizabeth.

"Promise?" asked Dylan.

"I promise," said Elizabeth. "Now, let's go before we get stuck talking to someone else that we don't like."

Chapter 18 - Really Nice Knife

"I HEARD A RUMOR THAT one of us died. I knew it wasn't me, so I came by to see if it was you."

Arbin stood staring out the front door of Masimo's home at Jayden. It had been two days since Arbin had been shot, and he had spent most of that on the couch in the living room. He had wondered how he would find Jayden, and now here he was standing at his door. "My arm is really hurting, so if you are here to finish me off, can we do it another time?" he asked as he stepped back to let Jayden in the room.

"Don't worry, I still need you," said Jayden, as he peeked into the room. "Is your little girlfriend here with you?"

"I am alone," said Arbin. "I have not seen her since your last visit, and I would not call her my girlfriend."

Jayden stepped in and found a chair in the kitchen as Arbin looked out the door. He was still worried about Jayden's revelation that he was being followed. He closed the door and leaned back against it. His arm hurt and just getting up for the door took more effort than he thought it would.

"I don't know what she did, but I have never felt that bad before," said Jayden.

"I had much the same experience the first time I met her," said Arbin with a chuckle. "I am not sure, but I think she has a Talent much like the one used during the civil war against Fades. The one everyone had been trying to accuse me of having. I was starting to believe them until I saw what she did to you."

"You thought you were special, please. Now your girlfriend, she is special in more ways than one," said Jayden with a smile, as he got up and grabbed a small biscuit out of a basket sitting on the table in the kitchen, then sat back down.

Arbin ignored Jayden's comments and said, "Sure, go ahead, help yourself." He wrapped the robe he was wearing back around himself and headed back to the couch. "I have been getting baskets of stuff from people I never heard of. Everyone thanking me for my involvement with killing the Fade. I'm not complaining because the place was getting low on food without Masimo around to buy stuff."

"You're lucky the kid didn't kill you along with that other idiot," said Jayden.

"Thanks," said Arbin. "I watched Dylan shoot a pistol earlier, but never expected he would have one in his room. I was glad they shot the guy when they did. He was good with a knife. Much better than you."

"So, who did they kill?" asked Jayden as he reached for another small biscuit.

"I have no idea," said Arbin. "It really surprised him when I tapped him on his shoulder. I am not sure if he was there to attack someone or just spying."

"They really think he was me?" said Jayden with a big smile.

"I was in a Fade while I was hiding," said Arbin. "One of the Seers I trained sounded the alarm. He knew there was a Fade outside, but he did not know it was me he detected."

"How many of these people did you train?" asked Jayden.

"Only two," said Arbin. "You saw them back at the caravan, but do not worry. They cannot train any more without a Fade to learn from."

"What are you going to do when they figure out it wasn't me they killed?" asked Jayden.

"It will be difficult to identify him since they burned the body. What with him being evil and all," said Arbin. "I am hoping we can find Mia and be out of here before anyone figures out the truth."

"So, you will still help me look for Mia?" asked Jayden. "Any ideas on where to start?"

"Pass me that rolled up paper on the desk," said Arbin.

Jayden grabbed the roll of paper but stopped when he noticed a long ornate box next to it on the desk. "What's in the box?" he asked.

"My attacker's knife," said Arbin. "Elizabeth had both items delivered today. Plus, a note from Dylan saying he was sorry for shooting me. He said he would be more careful next time."

Jayden opened the box and took out the knife. "Nice blade," he said. "Looks like your attacker had a little money." he put the knife back in the box but did not close the top.

"So why do you have it?" asked Jayden.

"I guess it's a kind of trophy," said Arbin "The person who delivered it acted like it was cursed."

Jayden drugged a chair over by Arbin and said, "And this paper?"

"Elizabeth used the description of the killer I gave you and tried to draw a picture of him," said Arbin.

"Really," said Jayden as he sat down unrolling the paper. "And this is who you saw killing Henry Sumner?" ask Jayden as he held up the paper for Arbin to see.

"Yeah, it's a little rough, but it surprised me how close she came to getting it right," said Arbin.

"I agree," said Jayden. "This is a very good likeness."

"You know him?" asked Arbin.

"His name is Arron Schilling," said Jayden. "I was asking around about him after you gave me his description. I was told he was a real bad guy. Someone I didn't want to get involved with."

"That's great," said Arbin. "Now we have someplace to start. We find him and we find Mia."

"Yeah, about that," said Jayden as he rolled up the paper and tossed it over his shoulder toward the desk. The roll bounced off the desk and ended up on the floor. "The only problem is he's dead."

"Dead, what do you mean dead?" asked Arbin.

"Like I said, I was asking around about him. I even saw him once," said Jayden. "They found him dead, stabbed in the back, a day ago near the river. You said his boss didn't look happy with him," said Jayden.

"I cannot believe this," said Arbin as he slowly shook his head. "First good break we get and now we are back to nothing again."

"I wouldn't say that. I made it known that I wanted to meet him because I was looking for work. It's possible that someone who knew him may get in touch with me."

Arbin stood up, and holding on to his arm, headed toward the kitchen.

"Where are you going?"

"I was going to make some tea," said Arbin.

"Sit down, I'll do it," said Jayden, pointing toward the couch. "You would just make a mess with that bad arm."

There was a knock at the door just as Jayden reached the kitchen. Jayden looked over to Arbin and asked, "Should I get it?"

"I am not expecting anyone," said Arbin. He could not see out the window from where he was sitting. A second knock quickly followed and Arbin said, "Go ahead. Might be more food."

Jayden opened the door and the person on the other side said, "Good afternoon. I am Councilman Darr. Is Arbin Adean here?"

Jayden stepped back and nodded toward the couch, "Come in, sir. He's over there. I was just going to put on some water for tea. Would you like a cup?"

"No thank you," said Councilman Darr as he looked around the room. "I need to be somewhere else soon. I just wanted to stop by and update Arbin on the significant progress we made today at the Council meeting."

Arbin started to stand, but the Councilman said, "No, please sit. I am sure your arm is hurting. I can send my doctor to see you if needed. You remember Stefano."

"Thank you, sir," said Arbin, directing the Councilman to the chair near him. "I think I am healing quite well."

"Good, I'm glad to hear that because we have big plans for you," said Darr.

"Really," said Jayden.

Darr turned and glanced toward Jayden and said, "Have we met?"

Before Arbin could say anything, Jayden said, "I am Hugo Winters. I am an old acquaintance of Arbin. We used to work for the same employer several years ago."

Arbin gave Jayden a worried look but got one of his mischievous smiles back. "Hugo Winters," he said to himself with a slight laugh.

Darr looked back at Arbin, who realized that he had said that out loud. Jayden smiled, enjoying the worry on Arbin's face, then quickly said, "I reunited with him a few days ago and discovered we share a common enemy. I came to town looking for information on followers of the Adelist Movement."

"Adelist," said Darr. "Were you looking to join them or fight them?"

"They harmed someone very dear to me," said Jayden. "I am looking for revenge. Arbin told me he saw one of them at the village where Duke Sumner was killed. He also said he saw the same person here. Using the description he gave me, I have been searching the city for him."

Darr turned back to Arbin and asked, "You saw one of the people involved in the attack on Duke Henry here?"

Arbin nodded, not sure what to say.

"And this was not the person you fought with the other day?" asked Darr. He paused a second, then almost quietly said, "The Fade."

"That's correct," said Arbin. The Councilman's hesitation when saying the word Fade surprised him. He had heard that Councilman Darr did not believe in Fades.

"Arbin and I are working to track this killer down," said Jayden.

"Have you involved anyone else in this effort?" asked Darr.

"No," said Jayden. "We were not sure who to trust, so we kept this to ourselves."

"Well, you will have my support from now on. I would agree with keeping it between ourselves," said Darr.

Arbin agreed then said, "You had something to tell me, sir."

Darr clasped his hands together and said, "Great News! First, Bishop Sorren conceded to my requests for changes in the appointment process for Seers."

"That's good, I guess," said Arbin. "What was the change?"

"The basic change is that if you still want to join the Seers, you will not need to take the test," said Darr.

"That is great, but I am not sure that I want to join the Seers now," said Arbin.

"I believe that might be a wise choice," said Darr.

"Good, because I was not looking forward to spending the rest of my life working for that High Seer," said Arbin.

"That's funny," said Darr. "Because the second bit of news I have is that they nominated two people to be Dylan Sumner's Guardian. They were the High Seer and you,"

Arbin sat in silence for a few seconds, not sure that he had heard that correctly. "What?" he finally said just as Jayden broke into a loud laugh.

"That's perfect," said Jayden.

"I don't understand," said Arbin. "Why would I get nominated for that?"

"You have more friends in this town than you think Arbin," said Darr. "Your stand against the Appointment Committee and your battle with the Fade outside of Chairman Sumner's estate has many believing that you are the best choice to defend young Dylan. You have done things because you thought it was the right thing to do. A true champion of the people."

"I would have guessed they would have given it to someone like Captain Eustace or even Masimo who is a relative."

"We all know that the High Seer is just in it for personal gain," said Councilman Darr. "Masimo is a distance relative but is not a citizen, and that disqualifies him. That is something that could be overcome, but the fact that Lady Casandra did not nominate him says something."

"Councilman," said Jayden from the kitchen. "What authority does the Guardian have?"

Darr smiled and said, "Dylan is a minor, so until he comes of age, the Guardian will assist with the management of Duke Henry Sumner's estate. If Chairman Sumner dies before Dylan is of age, the Guardian sits in his Family Chair at the Council meetings. If something happens to Dylan before he comes of age, the Guardian becomes the Chair Holder."

"But what if I do not want to be the Guardian?" asked Arbin. "I do not understand how to manage an estate or how to be a Chair Holder."

"Do not worry," said Darr. "We will help you. Besides, as long as Chairman Sumner is alive, you will not really need to do anything. Plus, there is a chance that you will not get selected because the Council vote is tied, and Chairman Sumner can cast the tie-breaking vote. The important thing is to stand up to the current stagnant leadership. Your voice is fresh and will carry a lot of weight in the future."

"Councilman, excuse me," said Jayden again from the kitchen, this time holding a turkey leg that Arbin had planned on enjoying later. "When does this vote take place?"

Darr looked back at Jayden and quickly said, "In about two weeks," then turned back to finish his conversation with Arbin.

"And the only thing stopping Arbin from becoming this Guardian is the Chairman's vote, right?" said Jayden.

"Correct," said Darr, a little irritated. "Any other questions?" he asked.

"No, thank you very much," said Jayden with a slight bow.

Darr stood, looked at Jayden as if he was expecting another interruption, then said, "I really must be going. I will send someone by to collect you later this week. We have a lot of work to do before you appear before the Council." He took an envelope from his jacket and handed it to Arbin. "Read these papers. It will give you some background before we meet. There is also a little something in there to help with your expenses." He turned and as he started to leave, he noticed the knife on the nearby desk. He picked it up, examined it and said, "Nice knife, where did you get it?"

"It's a trophy," said Jayden from the kitchen.

"A trophy? For what?" asked Councilman Darr.

Arbin could see that Jayden was enjoying this. Arbin looked back to the Councilman who was examining the knife and said, "It was a gift from Dylan Sumner. It belonged to the attacker they killed the other day."

Darr dropped the knife and looking at his hands said, "A Fade's knife! Why in the world would he send it to you?"

"I guess he thought I would want it," said Arbin.

"Children!" said Darr. "Now you can see why he needs the guidance of an adult."

Arbin did not know what to say, so he just smiled.

"Well, I need to go," said Darr. He nodded towards Jayden in the kitchen and said, "It was nice to meet you, Mr. Winters."

Arbin started to get up but Darr said, "No, please stay seated. You need to rest. We have big things to do together. Look for my man in a few days."

The Councilman left the room, leaving the door open for Jayden to close behind him. Arbin heard the Councilman, and his companions ride away.

Arbin looked over to Jayden, who had returned to working on the turkey leg. "Okay," asked Arbin. "What's with the name?"

Jayden paused from his meal and said, "Hugo is my father's name. I needed a fake name for a while. One I could remember."

"Winters?" asked Arbin.

"My father is a very cold-hearted man." said Jayden. "But what about you? Duke Arbin. Has an interesting ring to it, don't you think?"

"I told him I am not interested in becoming the Guardian," said Arbin. "And I am not sure being one makes me a Duke."

"Well, maybe you should be interested," said Jayden, tossing what was left of the turkey leg on to the table. "Or weren't you listening?" he said as he wiped his hands on his pants.

"Okay, tell me, why do you think I should be interested?" asked Arbin.

"Soldiers, Money and Power," said Jayden. "You said it yourself, we don't have enough people to properly look for Mia. Well, now you will."

"Does this mean you have given up on kidnapping the person who I would be the Guardian of?" asked Arbin.

"Well, let just say that it's not my first choice," said Jayden. "Especially with your girlfriend hanging around him all the time."

"Have you been following them?" asked Arbin.

"I did, you know she is quite pretty," said Jayden, heading back into the kitchen.

That last comment did not sit right with Arbin. "Well, you can stop following her now," he said. "Arron Schilling's employer is still out there, or have you forgotten?"

"I haven't forgotten," said Jayden. "I'm just not sure where to look for him. Besides, I think my time would be better spent working on how we make sure you become this Guardian."

"I think we can leave the Guardian part to Councilman Darr," said Arbin. "I have a guess he wants me to have it as much as you do," said Arbin. "What we really need to worry about are the people that kidnapped Mia, and what they will do now that everyone thinks you are dead."

"Why? What do you mean?" asked Jayden, coming out of the kitchen, his full attention on Arbin.

"They kidnapped Mia and her children, so they would have some control over you," said Arbin. "They have even shown that they will hurt her to get you to do what they want. If you are not around anymore, why do they need Mia and the children. Look what they did to one of their hired killers. In truth, that's what you are to them, a hired killer. Only they are paying you with Mia's safety."

Jayden thought for a few minutes then said, "Then, I guess I will just need to let them know that I am still alive."

"If you do that, it will cook my goose," said Arbin.

"Why?" asked Jayden.

"Everyone thinks the person they killed was a Fade because a Seer detected one," said Arbin. "I was forced to agree with them. If you show up again, they will know I was lying and will probably figure out what I am. If that happens then it's no Soldiers, Money and Power. It would probably mean my death."

"Don't take this wrong, but Mia and her kids are more important to me than you are," said Jayden, pointing his finger and taking a few steps toward Arbin.

"You have gotten nowhere by yourself," said Arbin, a little surprised at Jayden's sudden change in attitude. "Give me some time to figure this out. I have come through in the past, haven't I?"

Jayden stood staring at Arbin. There was a silence that lasted a little longer than Arbin was comfortable with. *I wish that knife was over here instead of on his side of the room,* he thought.

Just as Arbin was thinking about getting up to make his way to the side of the room with the knife, there was a knock on the door.

Arbin looked out the window and could just make out the figures of two Shadow Guards and four horses.

"Guards!" said Arbin in a hushed voice. "And possibly a Seer."

"Back door?" asked Jayden, looking around quickly.

"No," said Arbin. "Go upstairs and be quiet."

As Jayden started for the stairs, Arbin said, "Do not Fade, they will know you are here."

There was a second knock on the door. Arbin stood and wrapped himself in the robe as best he could. He looked back at the stairs and as soon as he saw Jayden disappear out of sight, he shouted, "Coming. Just give me a second, please."

Arbin opened the door to see Captain Eustace standing on the other side. Behind him on horseback were two guards with firearms he did not recognize and Lubin. "Captain Eustace, I am surprised to see you. I thought you were out on patrol."

"I just got back a few hours ago. May I come in Mr. Adean?"

"Yes. Of course, Sir," said Arbin as he stepped back. The 'Mr.' comment was not lost on him. He guessed that this would be a formal visit. *What did I do wrong now?* he thought.

"Do you want something to drink or eat?" asked Arbin.

"No, thank you." Captain Eustace stepped in and took off his hat. "Please have a seat if you need to. I will understand. A wound can take a lot of strength from you. Believe me, I know."

Arbin returned to the couch as the Captain stood looking around the room. "Masimo is quite the scholar." He picked up a nearby book, looked at a few pages and put it back. "Lady Casandra has told me a little about him. How are you two getting on?"

Arbin was getting a little nervous. This was not the Captain he had met in the field. The one that talked about how selfish Arbin was. About how his life was a wasted life. About how his death would go unnoticed. He took a breath and did his best to focus. "He is a good sort. I have not had to spend much time with him yet because of ..." Arbin paused. Seeing the way Captain Eustace stiffened, he knew he had stumbled onto a sensitive subject. "I was sorry to hear about Lady Casandra. I'm glad that Masimo could travel to see her."

"I had wanted to join him, but duty required me to be somewhere else," said Captain Eustace as he continued to look around the room. The Captain's voice was steady, but Arbin thought he could detect a bit of anger in his response.

"Is there something that I can help you with, Captain Eustace?" asked Arbin, not sure what to say next.

"Actually, that is the reason I am here. I heard about what you did and wanted to make sure you are being properly taken care of."

"I am getting on all right," said Arbin, forcing a slight smile as he placed his hand on his wounded arm.

"Good," said Captain Eustace as he continued glancing and poking at items. "I would like to have my surgeon stop by a few times to check on your wounds."

"Thank you, Captain Eustace," said Arbin, hoping his stay would end sooner if he agreed.

"I see you finally got your knife," said Captain Eustace.

"What?" said Arbin. He could see that the Captain was now standing in front of the desk that had the knife Dylan gave him on it.

"Dylan told me he sent this to you as a gift," said Captain Eustace.

"Yes, it was a nice gift," said Arbin. "I've been without a knife for a long time."

"Yes, I remember," said Captain Eustace. "Dylan was impressed that you fought that Fade with your bare hands. He wanted to make sure you would have a knife for your next battle."

"I was kind of hoping that was my last one," said Arbin.

Captain Eustace smiled and said, "Dylan is at that age where boys adopt role models. They act out the adventures of their heroes. Lately he has been playing the part of the demon hunter, stalking the evil Fade through the dark forest of the plants in the sunroom of Chairman Sumner's home."

"The truth is," said Arbin. "I would be dead right now if he had not fired that gun hitting the attacker and giving your guards enough time to kill him."

"I agree. But a boy needs his heroes." The Captain held the attacker's knife in his hand. He gripped it and turned his hand back and forth a few times as if to check the balance. He put the knife back down and said, "That leads me to the main reason I am here." Captain Eustace turned and looked at Arbin and said, "I have learned that both you and Otis Kindermann have been nominated as a candidate for Dylan's Guardian."

"I just learned the same thing from Councilman Darr minutes ago," said Arbin.

"Councilman Darr informed you of the appointment himself. That is interesting," said Captain Eustace. "What else did he say?"

"Basically, that he did not really expect me to win, but he would work with me to make sure we put on a good effort," said Arbin.

"You need to be careful," said Captain Eustace. "The battles between Councilman Darr and Chairman Sumner can get ugly with lots of political casualties and believe me political wounds can hurt just as much as physical ones."

"Do not worry, sir," said Arbin. "I have no intentions of accepting the nomination. It should have been someone like you that got nominated."

"I am upset that my name was not accepted," said Captain Eustace. "I rarely side with Councilman Darr, but this time, if the choice is between Otis and you, I see you as the better choice."

"You want me to try for Guardian?" asked Arbin.

"I will do whatever I can to prevent Otis from getting his hands on Henry's estate and the Sumner Chair," said Captain Eustace as he stared at the wall in front of him. The anger in his voice was obvious. Captain Eustace took a breath and turned to face Arbin. "That is the main reason I am here, Mr. Adean. I will announce my support for your nomination, and I am asking you to accept the position of Guardian if they offer it to you."

Arbin could see that the decision Captain Eustace had made was a difficult one. His decision would not sit well with Chairman Sumner or Bishop Sorren. Arbin could also see that it was difficult for the Captain to even ask him for this favor. "I will do what you ask, but I will need guidance," said Arbin.

"I am giving you my support and I will even call in a few favors," said Captain Eustace. "With that and Councilman Darr's supporters, there is a good chance you will get appointed." Captain Eustace paused for a moment then said, "A word of warning, I will not leave Lady Casandra and Dylan unprotected." The look on Captain Eustace's face let Arbin know that he was deadly serious. "I do not trust Councilman Darr and will not let him get access to the estate as well. I will cut your strings if I believe you have become a puppet. Do you understand?"

Arbin got the Captain's meaning and nodded. He could see Captain Eustace's posture relax, and a slight smile formed on his lips.

"Thank you for your time, Mr. Adean," said Captain Eustace. He turned and walked toward the door but stopped when his foot kicked a roll of paper laying on the floor.

As Captain Eustace bent to pick up the roll of paper, Arbin said, "That's for you, sir. I had planned to take it to you when I was feeling better."

Captain Eustace unrolled the drawing and laid it out on the desk. "What is it?" he asked.

"That is Arron Schilling," said Arbin. "The person I think killed Duke Henry Sumner."

Captain Eustace looked at the picture and said, "What makes you say that?"

"I saw that guy a few days ago and recognized him as the person who chased me out of the house back in Noor Point," said Arbin.

Captain Eustace held up the picture and said, "You are sure this is that person?"

"Yes," said Arbin. "I described him to Elizabeth, and she made that picture."

"You saw him a few days ago? Where?" asked Captain Eustace.

"He was coming out of a tavern," said Arbin. "I followed him, and he met with another person on the Bridge of Sorrows. I think it was his employer. I lost track of them and was afraid of being spotted, so I did not go looking for them again."

"Another person?" asked Captain Eustace. "Do you have a picture of the other person?"

"No," said Arbin. I did not get a good look at him, but I am sure he was one of the people I told you about at the camp in the woods near Noor Point.

"Do you have any description?" asked Captain Eustace.

"Thin, middle age, long blond hair in a ponytail and neatly dressed." said Arbin. "That's the best I can do."

"You really should have gotten this to me sooner," said Captain Eustace. "I am surprised that Elizabeth didn't give it to me herself."

"That's my fault," said Arbin. "I was going to tell you about him, but things just got in the way. Elizabeth only just got the description the other day."

Captain Eustace rolled up the picture and said, "I will use this to search for Arron Schilling. Let me know—,"

Before the Captain could finish the sentence, Arbin said, "He's dead."

"What!" said Captain Eustace.

"Arron Schilling is dead," said Arbin.

"How do you know that?" asked Captain Eustace.

"I have a friend that has been helping me look for him," said Arbin. "He told me a little while ago that Arron Schilling was discovered murdered a day ago."

"There was a body found recently," said Captain Eustace. "I will take this picture and look into it. In the meantime, if your memory improves, let me know right away. If you see this other man, I do not want you or your friend to follow him. Let me know. Understand?"

Arbin said, "Yes sir."

Captain Eustace walked to the door and before leaving he said, "I will check on you from time to time," and left, closing the door behind him.

"Well, that was exciting," said Jayden as he came down the stairs. "I wonder who will visit us next."

"I think very soon I will have more visitors than I really want," said Arbin.

"The busy life of a politician," said Jayden.

"A life I would very much like to avoid," said Arbin. "We both have reason to lead a more solitary life."

"Then we stick to the plan," said Jayden. "Take advantage of things to help us find Mia and the kids and then bail. Still, it might be fun playing nobles. Who knows, we might even be able to get away with it."

Arbin looked at Jayden and said, "We? I am the one they will want to burn at the stake if things go wrong. You are dead. You can slip away anytime."

"The old Jayden is dead, but Mr. Winters is very much alive. I have established a rather good cover so far. No one knows who I am except you and your girlfriend."

"I wish there was some way to keep her out of this," said Arbin. "I do not want her to get hurt."

"I don't think that is possible," said Jayden. "Where the kid goes, she goes. Besides, how can she get hurt by this."

"If anyone finds out about her Talent, they will kill her," said Arbin.

"How could anyone find out?" asked Jayden. "You and I are the only ones that she has an effect on right, and I will not say anything."

"I guess so," said Arbin. "I really dislike lying to her about things."

"Look, the important thing is finding Mia, right," said Jayden. "Who cares if you have to lie to her. You have lied to people you cared about before. She is nobody to us. She'll get over it."

Arbin stared at Jayden for a few seconds, thinking about what he had just said. He stood up and wrapped the robe around him and said, "I think it's time for you to go."

Jayden was a little surprised at Arbin's sudden change in attitude but said, "Yeah, you're right," and headed to the door. Before he left, he said, "We need to stay in touch. This place will become too busy soon. I will send a message to you every few days with instruction for a meeting."

"Sounds good," said Arbin kind of halfheartedly.

"Oh, I almost forgot." Jayden turned and walked over to the desk and said, "Can't leave without my knife."

"Your knife," said Arbin. "That was a gift to me."

"It's a Fade's knife, and you have given up on being a Fade, so now it's mine. Besides, call it the price for me staying away from Dylan and your girlfriend."

Arbin stood staring at Jayden. He guessed that part of why Jayden wanted the knife was to upset him. To take away something special of his. He also knew if he gave him his little victory, Jayden would keep his promise. He would leave Elizabeth and Dylan alone. *I am not sure what I will tell Dylan or Elizabeth, but I really have no choice.* Arbin just waved his hand and said, "It's yours."

Jayden smiled and headed to the door. Just before leaving he said, "It really is a nice knife."

Chapter 19 - The Nursery

"MY NAME IS ARBIN ADEAN. I was told that Chairman Sumner wanted to see me."

"Please wait, I will let Chairman Sumner know that you are here," said Jacob as he looked Arbin over. Before he closed the door, Jacob said, "Would you be so kind as to clean the dirt off of your shoes before you enter."

Arbin was a little surprised at the welcome. He looked down at his shoes, looking at one sole, then the other. They did not look that bad to him. He could understand the request if he had walked all the way like last time. This time he had traveled by carriage. It was the first time he had entered using the main gate. It had been guarded last time. However, now he could not see a guard anywhere.

Jacob soon reopened the door. He handed Arbin a small brush and something that looked like a pointed stick. He looked back down at Arbin's shoes, then closed the door again.

Arbin walked over to the porch railing. Leaning against it, he did his best to clean his shoes. He walked back over to the door, waiting to be let in. After a few minutes, he returned to his spot at the railing and continued to work on his shoes until he heard Jacob open the door.

Arbin looked up from his work, smiled at Jacob, pointed to his shoes and said, "Well?"

Jacob put his hands out for the brush and stick and said, "Please come inside." Jacob took the brush and stick from Arbin and pointed to a spot just inside the door near a coat rack. Returning the brush and stick to a box next to the door, Jacob instructed Arbin to wait while he announced him.

Arbin was left standing in a breathtaking foyer. The inside of the home was grand. Almost on the level of what he had seen in the Palace. There was color everywhere. It took several minutes to take it all in. In front of him was a long hallway that passed under a beautiful double staircase that was the primary focus of the entrance. The huge double stairway was the widest he had ever seen. The steps were covered in a deep red carpet held in place by little gold colored bars on each step. Where the steps were not covered, he could see a bright white stone. It had a dark black ornate metal banister and the whole staircase appeared to be held up with large columns. At the top of the stairs, Arbin could see two rooms and a hallway leading to the back of the home. Hanging down between the staircases was a dazzling chandelier. Light flowed into the home from several large windows. The main floor had two rooms off each side of the main entrance. From what he could see, each room had a fireplace, paintings and mirrors. The floor was a bright white colored stone matching the stone of the stairs. During his time outside, he never imagined that all of this was inside. Arbin was still enjoying the view when he heard Jacob clear his throat.

Jacob led Arbin down the long hallway that went between the two stairways. They walked past several closed doors and past an opening that led to what must be the kitchen area. At the end of the long hallway, there was a double glass door. "Wait here, please," said Jacob just before he entered the room beyond the glass doors.

Arbin knew that the room on the other side was the sunroom. He had only seen it from the outside, but the glass walls and the forest of potted plants could not be mistaken.

Jacob opened the door and said, "Chairman Sumner will see you now."

Arbin stepped through the door and heard it close quietly behind him.

"Over here, Arbin," said Chairman Sumner, pointing to the only other chair at the table. "I hope you do not mind me calling you by your first name?"

"If you do not mind me calling you Mr. Chairman," said Arbin in return.

Chairman Sumner let out a slight laugh. "I would prefer if you called me by my name. Titles can get in the way of a friendly talk."

It surprised Arbin at how frail Chairman Sumner looked. Arbin had imagined him to be some giant of a man based on the way everyone talked about him. Instead, he was standing before an old man wrapped in a shawl sipping tea. His movements were slow as he again pointed toward a nearby chair. As Arbin took a seat, he glanced outside and could see the place where he fought with his attacker.

Chairman Sumner caught Arbin looking at the backyard and said, "This was always my favorite view. It will take me awhile to fight the thought another Fade might lurk just outside the windows."

Arbin rubbed his arm where he had been shot and said, "I am afraid I will always think of it as the place where I almost died,"

"I am thankful that you came along when you did," said Chairman Sumner. "But I am a little curious why you were out there."

"It was more of a spur-of-the-moment thing," said Arbin, hoping to change the subject, but he could see that the Chairman was expecting him to continue.

"I was out walking, clearing my mind when I saw Dylan practicing his shooting. When he finished, I saw him leave in a carriage with Elizabeth, eh Miss Keller. They looked so vulnerable. I could not help but follow them. When I saw the Estate, it surprised me how open and poorly guarded it was. I became worried that someone could get to them, so I stuck around for a while. I would be dead now if Dylan had not saved me with a pistol shot."

"A simple and somewhat believable answer," said Chairman Sumner. "You are not what I expected based on what everyone else has said about you."

"I can say the same about you, sir," said Arbin.

Chairman Sumner laughed, then took a few seconds to study Arbin as if trying to decide what to say next. Finally, he said, "In fact, you remind me a lot of your father."

The words stunned Arbin. He looked at Chairman Sumner, not sure he had heard him correctly. After a few seconds he heard himself asked, "You knew my father?"

"Oh yes," said Chairman Sumner, taking another sip. "He was a good man. We met quite a few times. I was sorry to hear about his death."

Arbin was quiet. He had not spoken to his father since he left home after fighting with him almost thirteen years ago. He was not aware that he had died.

"Ah, I am sorry," said Chairman Sumner. "I thought you knew. It has been a few years now. I can have Bishop Sorren give you the details if you wish."

Arbin looked off to the side, trying to hold back a sting of emotion he felt coming. He and his father had left on bad terms. His father had not handled his mother's death well and turned to drink to deal with it. Soon it became hard for Arbin to be around him. It hurt him to see what his father was becoming, and he was tired of being blamed for every hardship they suffered. The day his father rejected him was the hardest day of his life. Harder even then the death of his mother. He loved his father, but he could not forgive him for his rejection. He was sorry to hear about his death but was not really surprised by it.

Arbin took a deep breath and said, "No, thank you. I do not think I am ready to know that right now. I am just a little surprised that you of all people would know him."

"I knew your father and your mother both," said Chairman Sumner. "Your father did a lot of work for the government, as I am sure you know. In fact, I even met you once when you were small. Now look at you. A grown man, and apparently a powerful Seer at that. How did Dylan put it? Oh yes, a Demon Hunter."

"You went to our house?" asked Arbin, almost in a whisper.

"No. I met you in the midst of battle," said Chairman Sumner. "There is no reason that you would know anything about it, but you could say that I saved your life."

Arbin sat staring at Chairman Sumner, not sure what to say. This was the last thing he expected to be dealing with when he sat down.

"I can understand your confusion," said Chairman Sumner. "I think it's time that I told you the story of your life, at least the part I was involved with."

Arbin sat with his mouth open for a few seconds, trying to think of what to say. He finally managed a simple "Okay."

"I am sure you have heard of the rebel group that calls themselves supporters of the Adelist Movement," said Chairman Sumner.

Arbin said, "Yes, the ones behind the attacks on your son and Lady Casandra."

"That's right," said Chairman Sumner.

Arbin thought Chairman Sumner would show more emotion when talking about his son and Casandra. He remembered seeing Captain Eustace struggle when talking about it.

"Well, about twenty-seven years ago there was a group associated with Adelist that called themselves the Second Wave," continued Chairman Morgan. "What a stupid name," he said with a slight smile.

"I have heard nothing about them before," said Arbin.

"They were a group founded in the beliefs of the original group, the Adelist, that started the civil war," said Chairman Sumner.

"They were against a Governing Council and wished to return to rule by Nobility. "They were a small group. However, they soon got a following. They also threaten they would bring about the fall of the Council through the return of Fades. There were fears of another civil war.

"We searched and searched for their headquarters, and it was actually your father who stumbled upon it during one of his surveys. Back then, Jonathan Lehmann was the Council Chairman. He led a force to attack them. I was part of that group. Bishop Sorren was also there, but back then, he was just a priest."

"The rebels put up a very ferocious resistance, and we lost a lot of good people, including Chairman Lehmann. Besides the headquarters, we discovered a nursery full of what we assumed where children of the rebels."

Chairman Sumner shifted in his chair. He poured himself another cup of tea and took a few slow breaths before continuing.

"A fire started in the nursery and despite our best efforts, we could only save five of the children."

Chairman Sumner stopped again and looked off into space for a few seconds. Arbin could see the distress on his face. That was the look he had expected when Arbin had mentioned Henry.

"So many children died that day. I do not even think I know how many. I can still hear their crying sometimes," said Chairman Sumner, taking another drink.

Arbin saw a calm come over the Chairman's face. "We saved five of them!" said the Chairman with a sound of pride.

Arbin was confused. *What does this have to do with me*, he wondered. He worried that the Chairman was having some sort of episode. He was wondering if he should call for Jacob, who he could see standing beyond the glass door.

Chairman Sumner looked at Arbin and smiled. He took another sip of tea and then said, "We discovered that the children were part of some strange project. The 'Godless Gift' it was called. It was clear that the rebels had gone through a lot of effort in establishing the nursery. There was a question of what to do with the five children we rescued. It was Bishop Sorren who suggested he would care for them and try to see what was so special about them. He had everyone present swear to God to keep the existence of the children a secret. The children were placed in homes. A priest was assigned to monitor them and deliver a yearly allowance to the families caring for them. Their location would be known only to the Church, Bishop Sorren and the Council Chairman. A position I was voted into because of the prior Chairman's death."

Chairman Sumner sat in silence looking at Arbin, who suddenly realized the story was over and the Chairman was waiting for his response. "Are you telling me I was one of those children?" asked Arbin.

"Yes," said Chairman Sumner. "It was you and two sets of twins. A boy and girl in each set of twins."

"My parents were not my real parents?" said Arbin. "Why should I believe any of this?"

"Do you remember Father Sauer?" asked Chairman Sumner.

"Yes, he was a friend of my father. He would visit us once a year." Arbin paused, then said, "Are you saying he was the one who was checking on me?"

Chairman Sumner nodded.

"And he was paying my father to keep me?" asked Arbin.

Chairman Sumner said nothing. He just took another sip from his cup.

"I still cannot believe it," said Arbin. Forgetting his anger at his father, he said, "My parents loved me. I have the same last name. They named me after my mother's grandfather."

"Yes, they loved you," said Chairman Sumner. "Father Sauer made that clear in his writings. I can get you his notes if you want."

Arbin sat there, not knowing what to do. He was on the edge of just getting up and leaving. After a few minutes of silence, he said, "The other kids. You said they were twins."

Chairman Sumner nodded and said, "From what we can tell, all the children in the nursery were twins. Except for you."

"Twins," said Arbin. He paused for a few more seconds, then said, "Like Jayden and Mia?"

"Like Alex and Elizabeth too," said Chairman Sumner.

This was becoming harder for Arbin to cope with. They were in the nursery together, and now, somehow, had been drawn back together. He needed some way to check if this was true. He needed something he could take to Jayden or Elizabeth. "Father Sauer checked on them as well?" asked Arbin.

"Yes," said Chairman Sumner. "But unfortunately, Father Sauer passed away and by the time they named a replacement we had lost track of you, as well as Jayden and his sister. We spoke with your father, who said he had a fight with you and did not know where you were. Jayden's parents said much the same thing. It was then that we decided to keep Alex and Elizabeth a little closer to us, so we accepted Alex into the Seers. The rest I think you know better than us."

"Do you know who our real parents are?" Arbin asked. He was not sure why he asked, or if he wanted to learn the answer.

"No," said Chairman Sumner. "The records we salvaged are not complete. The best we can tell is that they collected the mothers from different countries. All mention of the mothers ended a few months after giving birth."

"You said all the other children, including the ones that died, were twins. Did I have a twin sister?" asked Arbin.

"I am sorry, Arbin. The records show your birth mother was pregnant with twins, but over the course of the pregnancy your twin disappeared."

"Disappeared!" said Arbin. "What do you mean disappeared?"

"Bishop Sorren assures me that this happens sometimes," said Chairman Sumner. "I would suggest that if you want to learn more, you speak with him. Since the nursery, the Church has learned a lot about twins. During the purge, we would kill whole families. Now we only focus on the twins, where the children are a boy and a girl. We have also learned that when it comes to Fades, it's the male twin that is the one we most often need to deal with. We have had a few cases where both twins must be destroyed."

"You knew about Jayden?" Arbin asked.

"It became clear from reading Father Sauer's notes that he suspected," said Chairman Sumner. "But we could not deal with him before he disappeared."

"Deal with him?" asked Arbin.

"The law is clear. All Fades must die," said Chairman Sumner.

"What about me?" asked Arbin. "I am a single child. What about my Talent?"

"Bishop Sorren believes that your single birth is a sign that you are special," said Chairman Sumner.

"Does anyone else know about this?" asked Arbin.

"A few very senior people in the Church, Bishop Sorren and myself," said Chairman Sumner. "Everyone else with me at the nursery has passed on. Oh, and of course, the people who raised you and the others. However, only your father had any knowledge of the nursery. The others were told the children were victims of the war and were asked to care for them. We also asked them not to tell the children anything about their past."

"You mean Elizabeth does not know about her past?" said Arbin.

"We did not see what good it would do to tell her," said Chairman Sumner. "Elizabeth and Alex have parents they love. Now that Jayden is dead, there is no reason to tell Mia, if we knew where she was."

"Why tell me?" asked Arbin.

"I had not planned on it, but I needed to prove a point to you," said Chairman Sumner.

Arbin looked at the Chairman and after a few minutes of silence said, "What is your point?"

"The point is, we have been caring for you most of your life," said Chairman Sumner. "We had always intended on doing what was best for you and the others. If things had gone better for you, we would have seen that you found your way into a useful career, probably with Seers, just as we did with Alex."

"The Bishop did not act like he wanted me to join the Seers," said Arbin.

"In his notes, Father Sauer suggests that Jayden was turned to evil shortly before he left home," said Chairman Sumner. "We do not understand what makes a person turn. When we lost track of you for a long time, we needed to make sure the same had not happened to you."

"And now you are sure that I am not evil?" asked Arbin.

"Bishop Sorren does not consider you evil. He feels that because of your past, you lack the discipline and the required moral character to become a Seer."

"I guess that you and the Bishop do not think I am ready to take on the position of Guardian either," said Arbin.

"If you were older, and I had more time to work with you, I would not mind," said Chairman Sumner. "You need to believe that we have what is best in mind for you as well as Alex and Elizabeth."

Arbin sat looking out the sunroom windows, taking in everything that Chairman Sumner had said. "Just out of curiosity, what great plans have you got for Elizabeth and Alex?"

"You know truly little about them. I am sure if you were to ask them, they would say that they have lived a good life so far," said Chairman Sumner. "But if it will help you trust us, I will tell you." Chairman Sumner tried to pour himself another cup but found the pot was empty. He lifted the lid to look inside and said, "disappointing." He turned as if he would call for Jacob but when he saw the expression on Arbin's face he put the pot down and said, "Alex, well, once High Seer Kindermann becomes Guardian, we would promote Alex to High Seer. Bishop Sorren tells me Alex is a man of big ideas and lots of energy."

"And Elizabeth?" asked Arbin.

"You may have noticed that Elizabeth has a special way with Dylan," said Chairman Sumner. "Her presence has been a blessing during this hard time. Dylan wants very much for her to remain a part of his life. Bishop Sorren and I have talked about it and believe the best thing for both her and Dylan would be for her to wed Otis Kindermann once he becomes the Guardian."

"You will force her to marry the High Seer?" asked Arbin. He did the best to hide the anger he felt at the suggestion. "He's an old man. Have you asked her what she wants? What if she wants to be with someone else, like Masimo?"

"Sometimes marriages are for reasons greater than emotions," said Chairman Sumner. "A marriage to the Guardian will make Elizabeth a rich and powerful woman. You might find that she may be more open to the arrangement than you think."

"Last time that I talked to her, she was not too happy about the arranged marriage thing," said Arbin.

"Bishop Sorren has approached her on the idea and assures me that she appears open to it," said Chairman Sumner.

"I cannot believe that," said Arbin. "I would like to hear it from her."

"I understand, but as hard as it is to believe, we have her best interest in mind. Just like we do with you. That is why I am asking you to consider refusing the nomination."

"Is that necessary?" asked Arbin. "Councilman Darr said that I do not really have a chance of winning. To tell you the truth, I am only in it because I do not have a way of supporting myself right now and Councilman Darr has been nice enough to pay me to stay in the race."

That answer irritated Chairman Sumner. "If it's money you want, I can guarantee you employment," he said. "In fact, you could do what your father did for us. I can promise you lots of work and travel."

Arbin had to admit that was a very tempting offer. It would get him out of this place and keep him in money. No more sleeping in sheds. No more hiding. He remembered how easy life was traveling with his father. The word father had a strange sound to it. *I do not know what I should call him now,* Arbin thought.

Chairman Sumner watched Arbin thinking over what he had just said and taking it as a good sign, decided to sweeten his offer. "I applaud your concerns for Elizabeth," said Chairman Sumner. "I am prepared to make you an offer that may relieve your concerns for her. If you refuse the Guardian nomination, I will promise you she will be free to marry whoever she chooses."

Arbin thought about it for a few seconds and asked, "Is it okay if I have some time to think it over?"

"I will give you until sunset tomorrow," said Chairman Sumner. "After that I must lift my hand of protection from you and leave you to your own resolve."

Arbin nodded and said, "That should be enough time."

Chairman Sumner pulled on a cord attached to a pillar behind him. Jacob soon appeared holding a new pot of tea. He placed it on the table and as he picked up the empty one said, "This way Mr. Adean."

Chairman Sumner smiled at Arbin and said, "I look forward to your decision. The sooner we resolve this issue, the sooner everyone can get to work doing what is best for the country."

Arbin stood and reached out his hand to the Chairman but saw that he had returned to reading some documents in front of him. Almost as if he was not there. He heard Jacob say again, "Mr. Adean, please." Arbin left the Chairman to his work and followed Jacob.

As he headed down the hallway toward the front door, Arbin heard Jacob say, "This way, please." He saw Jacob standing in front of the hallway that led toward the kitchen area and the back door.

Arbin let out a small laugh and said, "I should have known."

ARBIN STOOD ON THE step to the back door and looked around. The afternoon was comfortable, and he stood there feeling the warmth of the sun. What the Chairman had told him left him in a kind of daze. For some reason he felt there was a truth in what he had heard, even though it upset him to think about it. It was the comments about his twin and the fire that haunted him the most. All those nightmares growing up and the feeling that he did not belong. He could feel a shiver run through him despite the warmth of the sun. He closed his eyes and did his best to push back the tears that wanted to rise. He opened his eyes and stared at the scene in front of him, trying to think of something else. In the distance were the vineyards. He watched as the workers moved around it, thinking how peaceful it looked. It was while he was admiring the view that he heard his name.

He turned and saw Elizabeth and Dylan standing about thirty feet from him. They were walking on a path which he imagined led back into the woods he had spent some time in. The voice he had heard calling him was Dylan, who appeared both surprised and happy to see him. Elizabeth's expression was more guarded.

"Dylan," Arbin said, "It's nice to see you. I wanted to thank you for the nice gift you sent me."

He turned to Elizabeth and said, "it's nice to see you too, Miss Keller."

Elizabeth just nodded in return and placed her hands on Dylan's shoulder as if to stop him from running to greet Arbin.

"I'm glad you liked it," said Dylan. "I wanted to take it to you myself, but Miss Keller said you need more time to heal. What are you doing here?"

"I came by to speak with your Grandfather," said Arbin. "I think he wants to offer me a job."

"A job," said Elizabeth. "What happened to your nomination for Guardian?"

"That has become a little complicated," said Arbin. "I would like very much to talk to you about it."

"Now is not a good time," said Elizabeth, pulling Dylan closer to her.

"Actually, now is the time that I really need to talk to you," said Arbin. He really needed to speak to her and was almost pleading when he said, "it's important, and affects you in some ways."

"Me?" asked Elizabeth.

"I would not ask if it was not important," said Arbin. For the first time, she held eye contact with him. "Please," he said, looking back into her eyes.

Elizabeth sighed, looked down at Dylan and then back to Arbin and said, "Dylan, I need to talk to Arbin for a little while. Would you please go on into the house? Maybe you can find another story to read."

Dylan looked at Arbin who said, "it's important. Oh, before I forget, I wanted to thank you for saving my life the other day. If you did not fire your gun when you did, I might have been in real trouble."

"I worried you might be mad at me for shooting you," said Dylan.

"You have nothing to worry about," said Arbin. "As you can see, I am up and around. The wound was not that bad. It will probably leave a great scar that I can brag about."

Dylan smiled and said, "Okay," and headed into the house.

Arbin turned back to Elizabeth and said, "Can we walk a bit. I do not want anyone to overhear what I have to say."

Elizabeth nodded her head, and they headed back up the path she had just arrived on.

After a few minutes he said, "I did not know you could read."

"Is that what was so important that you had to talk to me?" said Elizabeth.

Arbin could feel Elizabeth's anger growing. He put his hand to his head and took a breath to help deal with the slight dizziness.

Elizabeth looked at him and asked, "Am I too close to you?"

"What? "asked Arbin.

"I know now that I have an affect on you and I just wanted to know if I am too close," said Elizabeth.

"No, you are fine," said Arbin. "I think I am getting used to you. It only really bothers me when you get upset."

Elizabeth nodded.

"First, I want to tell you I gave your drawing to Captain Eustace when he dropped by to see me. He was most impressed," said Arbin.

"I was happy to help," said Elizabeth.

"I have also discovered the person in the drawing was killed the other day," said Arbin. "Captain Eustace will use your picture to confirm his identity."

"Killed, who did it?" asked Elizabeth.

"We do not know," said Arbin. "They stabbed him in the back. My guess is it had something to do with the man he met on the bridge the other day. The one who did not look happy with him."

"Well, that is a relief," said Elizabeth. "Both Henry's killer and Jayden are dead. I am sure that Captain Eustace will hunt down the rest of the group. Does Chairman Sumner know?"

Elizabeth's mention of Jayden threw Arbin for a second. He now wished he had not mentioned the picture. He knew he would need to tell her the truth soon, but he needed a better time and place.

"I'm sorry about Jayden," Elizabeth said, mistaking that his silence was over Jayden's death.

"I do not have time to talk about that right now," said Arbin. "I need to talk to you about the meeting I just had with Chairman Sumner."

"Okay," said Elizabeth, who was a little confused at his response. "Was it about the nomination?" she asked. "Dylan said Chairman Sumner was really upset with your nomination."

"Yes," said Arbin. "Basically, he asked me to refuse the nomination."

"What did you say?" asked Elizabeth.

"I told him I needed to think it over. That I wanted to speak to you about it first," said Arbin.

"Me! Why me?" asked Elizabeth.

"Do you remember talking to me about how much you disliked the idea of arranged marriages?" asked Arbin.

"Yes," said Elisabeth. Surprised at the change of subject, she shifted her weight a little away from Arbin and stood with her arms crossed in front of her.

"Chairman Sumner told me both he and Bishop Sorren think it's a good idea for you to wed High Seer Kindermann once he becomes the new Guardian. Have you heard that?"

Elizabeth took a few steps away from Arbin and then after a few seconds turned and said, "Bishop Sorren said something that suggested he was thinking about it." When she saw the concern on Arbin's face she quickly added, "He hasn't spoken to me formally about it yet,"

"Well, it sounded like it was a done deal. Chairman Sumner also suggested that you would not be opposed to the arrangement."

Elizabeth said nothing but continued to watch Arbin.

Her lack of response surprised Arbin. *Maybe the Chairman was right.* He thought. He looked at her standing there, as calm as could be. If she was upset at the idea of marrying the High Seer, it did not show. *No, it must be something else. I know I am right about this.* After a few more seconds of thinking about it he said, "The Chairman also said that if High Seer

Kindermann became the Guardian, Alex will become the new High Seer. Did you hear anything about that?"

Elizabeth nodded and said, "Bishop Sorren said that would be a possibility."

"Is Alex's promotion tied to your agreeing to wed the Guardian?" asked Arbin.

"He did not say it directly, but it would not surprise me." said Elizabeth.

"Are you thinking of going through with a marriage to High Seer Kindermann for your brother's sake?"

"I don't know," said Elizabeth, crossing her arms again.

Arbin could see she was becoming uncomfortable with the conversation.

"I don't understand how who I marry is any of your business," said Elizabeth. "I told you before. I don't have the same freedoms that you do."

Elizabeth turned as if she would walk away but stopped when Arbin said, "I have a way to give you that freedom." Elizabeth turned back to him and gave him a strange look.

"Chairman Sumner told me that if I refused the nomination, he would make sure you had a choice in who you married," said Arbin. "The problem is, I promised Captain Eustace that I would accept the nomination. Plus, being Guardian could help me find Mia."

"Captain Eustace thinks you should try?" asked Elizabeth

"Yes, when he came by yesterday, he said that he did not want High Seer Kindermann anywhere near Dylan," said Arbin. "He plans on calling in some favors and is sure that with that, and the backing of Councilman Darr, I would become the Guardian. As the Guardian, I could keep the High Seer away from Dylan and use the resources of the Sumner family to help locate Mia."

"You are willing to give that up so I have the choice of who I will marry?" asked Elizabeth.

"I never wanted to be a part of this whole thing," said Arbin. "I have thought many times about just leaving. The problem is, I worry about what will happen to the people who have been caught up in this. I think Dylan will be okay as long as Captain Eustace is looking out for him. Your brother will be okay too. You are the one I am most worried about."

Elizabeth looked away from him but said nothing.

"So, I need to know. Do you want to marry Otis Kindermann?" asked Arbin. "Please, let me know what to do. Do I stay in the race or get out?"

Still looking away, Elizabeth said, "I want to do what is best for Dylan."

"I think it's time you did what is best for you," said Arbin. "I am sure you will be in Dylan's life even if you do not marry Kindermann. Captain Eustace said as much."

Elizabeth ran her fingers through her hair. She took a deep breath, then walked back toward the house.

Arbin watched her as she walked away, not sure what to say next. He quickly caught up to her and followed along beside her. "I have until sunset tomorrow to give Chairman Sumner your answer," said Arbin.

She stopped at the door, turned around as if to say something, but nothing came out.

It was then that Arbin saw a person walking past the kitchen hallway, heading toward the sunroom. A thin person with a long ponytail.

"Who is that?" he asked, pointing behind her.

Elizabeth turned, but the person had already passed out of sight. "I didn't see anyone," she said.

"It was a thin man with long blond hair," said Arbin. "I think he had something in his hair."

"Oh, that must have been the courier used by Chairman Sumner," she said. "He is here a few times a week. Why?"

"Just for a second he looked like the man I told you about," said Arbin. "The one I saw talking to the killer."

"Him?" asked Elizabeth. "You must be mistaken. He has worked for Chairman Sumner for a long time. I think he even does some work for Bishop Sorren."

"He has the same thin frame, long blond hair in a ponytail, "said Arbin. "He was even wearing nice clothes."

"Lots of people wear their hair like that," said Elizabeth. "When we first met, you had long hair."

"I guess you're right," said Arbin. "I think it's time for me to go. Remember, I need your answer before sunset tomorrow."

Elizabeth looked at him for a few seconds, then turned and went into the house.

Arbin started walking towards the gate but could not get the thin man out of his mind. *I need to get a second look at that man,* he thought.

Arbin stopped and looked back at the house. *I could either sneak around to the sunroom and look in or wait around outside for him to leave.* It was late afternoon, and there was plenty of sunlight. The idea of sneaking around the grounds where there were bound to be armed guards did not sit well. Arbin looked out beyond the fence line and saw that there were no real places where he could hide and wait. His only choice was to go back in the way he came out.

Arbin headed back to the kitchen door and knocked. He was not sure what he would say. He was glad when the woman who was working in the kitchen opened the door and stepped aside, allowing him back in.

Arbin was hoping Elizabeth would still be here, but she was nowhere in sight. *She must already be with Dylan,* he thought.

"I was just here meeting with Chairman Sumner," said Arbin. "Can you tell him I need to speak with him again."

The woman walked over to the wall and pulled a rope hanging there. She gave him a smile, pointed to a chair and then returned to the work she was doing. After a few minutes, Arbin wondered if the rope really did anything.

He was thinking about speaking to the woman when he heard someone shouting, "Alarm, Alarm! To the sunroom!" Soon there was the blast of a whistle, much like he had heard a few days ago. He put his hand to his wounded arm and looked around. He heard more blasts of the whistle and saw a Shadow Guard heading toward the sunroom. Arbin followed as quickly as possible, not sure what he could do.

Arbin found two Shadow Guards and Jacob standing around a figure on the floor. As he got closer, the guards looked up. One of them said, "It's the Chairman. I have sent someone to check on Dylan. I need you to check outside." Arbin saw that the door to the backyard was open. Without thinking, he headed that way. He could not help from looking down at the Chairman's body as he passed by. It was slumped on the floor in a pool of blood. The shawl he had been wearing had partly covered it, but Arbin could still see the hilt of a knife, the blade of which had been driven up under the Chairman's chin and into his brain. Arbin almost stumbled when he saw it. *Jayden! Why?*

Chapter 20 - Clean Slate

THE SUMNER HOUSEHOLD was in a state of confusion and grief, with people doing their best to be helpful or at least look busy. Captain Eustace arrived about a half hour after the murder with what looked like every available Shadow Guard.

Shortly after returning from checking the backyard, Arbin had been told to stand by the back door until someone called on him. While outside, he had thought long and hard about running, but for some unknown reason went back into the sunroom.

From his waiting spot, Arbin had watched as Captain Eustace examined the Chairman and pulled the knife from him. Arbin had to turn away at that point, and his mind had not completely returned to normal since. Arbin had seen a dead body before, but never one of someone he had just been with, and never one killed with a knife belonging to him. He watched as Captain Eustace studied the knife like it was a valued gem. Every time the Captain looked his way, he felt guilty. He was sure the Captain knew it was his knife. *What was Jayden thinking?* he wondered as he watched Captain Eustace wrapped the knife in a cloth. *What am I going to say if he asked about the knife?* He was still thinking of what to say when he realized that the Captain was talking to him.

"Arbin, Arbin, did you hear me?" asked Captain Eustace.

Arbin heard the Captain but could not focus. He looked at the red-colored sheet covering the Chairman's body, then back to the Captain.

"Arbin, I need you to focus. I was told they sent you to the backyard. Did you detect anything?"

"What?" said Arbin. "You mean like a Fade?"

"Whoever did this had to sneak in unnoticed. That means we are dealing with another Fade or someone on the inside," said Captain Eustace.

"A Fade? No. I detected nothing," said Arbin a little too fast. "Look, I know what this looks like, but I did not do it. I do not know how my knife got there. Honestly, you must believe me. He was alive when I left him. You can ask anyone."

"So, it was not a Fade," said Captain Eustace, completely ignoring the rest of what Arbin had said. "And you did not see anyone outside?"

"No." said Arbin, looking back at the covered body. "I cannot believe this. I was just talking to him. He offered me a deal. What am I going to do now?"

"A deal?" asked Captain Eustace.

"He said that if I refused the nomination, he would make sure that Elizabeth was not forced into an arranged marriage and he would give me a job," said Arbin.

"Did you agree to this deal?" asked Captain Eustace.

"He gave me until sunset tomorrow to decide," said Arbin. That's when I left him and went outside to talk with Elizabeth.

Captain Eustace turned to one of the Shadow Guards near him and said, "He is no good to me in this shape. Send him home." He turned back to Arbin and said, "I want you in my office tomorrow around noon," and waved his hand to signal the guard to escort Arbin out of the sunroom.

"I had nothing to do with this," said Arbin, looking back toward the body of the Chairman. "You need to believe me."

"We will talk tomorrow. Bring the knife Dylan gave you to the office with you tomorrow," said Captain Eustace.

Arbin walked back into the center of the house, not looking at the covered body of Chairman Sumner, and headed for the front door, hoping the carriage that brought him was still there.

As he walked out the door, he saw Elizabeth and Dylan just getting into the carriage. He walked up to them and said, "I am sorry, Dylan. There was nothing I could do. I looked for the attacker but could see no one."

Dylan nodded and Elizabeth said, "Thank you, Arbin. I am taking him to stay with me for a while."

"Elizabeth, I really need to talk to you," said Arbin.

"I think you do not have to worry about the deal anymore," said Elizabeth.

"This is not about that anymore," said Arbin. "This is a lot more important. I really need to speak to you about something."

Elizabeth looked at him and after a few seconds took a breath and said, "Okay, we can meet tomorrow in the park around noon."

"It has to be earlier than that," said Arbin. "I have a meeting with Captain Eustace in his office at noon and I really need to speak to you before that meeting."

"10 o'clock then," said Elizabeth. "Will that work?"

"Yes, at the place where we last met," said Arbin.

Elizabeth nodded and then turned to the driver and said, "Let's go!"

The carriage lunged forward and Arbin had to jump back slightly to avoid the wheels. He watched them head down the road and thought, *I need to tell her the truth before I leave.*

THE FOLLOWING MORNING Arbin got up early. He packed a bag in preparation for leaving. He was not sure if he would bring the bag to the meeting with Elizabeth or come back for it later. He decided it would be best to take it with him. He had one last good meal and wrote Masimo a friendly note thanking him for his hospitality. Then he sat on the couch and waited for the time to go by. He looked around and felt sad. He had not been here long and was surprised at the sadness he was feeling now that he was leaving. *I need to go,* he thought. *I do not know how many people will be out today, and I want to get to the park before Elizabeth does. It would have been nice to actually see the Unification Ceremony. I have heard so much about it.*

While he made his way toward his meeting place, he listened to the chatter of people as they walked by. It surprised him he heard nothing about the death of Chairman Sumner. *I wonder how long they can keep something like that a secret.*

As he got closer to the memorial section of the bridge, he could see that the work on the stands was almost complete. There were more people in the park than he had hoped, but he found an empty bench near the statue of Princess Hanna and Prince Carl. He sat in the middle and placed his bag on the bench to make sure no one joined him before Elizabeth showed.

He did not really have any way of knowing the time. He knew he was early, so he sat looking out over the river, thinking of what he would say to Elizabeth. He was in the middle of a good argument when he felt her presence. That meant she was probably not in a good mood. He would need to take that into consideration when he talked to her.

He took a deep breath and said, "Hello Elizabeth," without looking back. "I'm glad you came."

"I told you I would be here," she said. "But it looks like you will not be here much longer."

Arbin moved over and put his bag between his feet and said, "That really depends on how you react to what I have to say."

"Okay, if I sit?" she asked, pointing to the bench.

"Yes, I can tell that you are a little upset, but I can handle it," said Arbin.

Elizabeth took a seat, straightened her dress and sat with her hands on her lap looking out at the river. They both sat in silence for a few minutes until she said, "I'm here, what is so important?"

Arbin had planned out his entire conversation with her in advance, but now that she was here, he was not sure where to start. He wanted to hold off the real reason for their meeting as long as possible. Before he knew it, he blurted out, "I had nothing to do with Chairman Sumner's death, no matter what you may have been told."

Elizabeth looked at him and said, "I know that." When she saw that he was serious she asked, "What would make you think I would believe that?"

Arbin's face turned a little red. He was already starting off wrong. "I was a little worried what you would think when you found out that Chairman Sumner was killed with a knife that looks just like the one that Dylan gave me,"

Elizabeth looked at him, started to say something, then stopped.

"The problem is, I do not know where my knife is," said Arbin

"What!" said Elizabeth. "What do you mean, you don't know where it is?"

He could feel her emotions start to rise. He mumbled, "I gave it to someone."

"Why would you do that?" said Elizabeth.

"It was a kind of payment for something," said Arbin. "I really did not have a choice."

"Who did you give it to?" Elizabeth asked.

"It would be better if you did not know," said Arbin.

"What kind of answer is that?" said Elizabeth. "You ask me here to tell me something and now you give me a stupid answer like that!"

Arbin could feel her anger growing. He had to stand up and step back a few spaces. He put his hand on the back of the bench to steady himself.

Elizabeth stood up and stepped back a few steps as well. "I'm sorry," she said. "I forgot that my, what do you call it, Talent, makes you uncomfortable."

"It's okay. I just need a minute." said Arbin. "The longer I am around you the easier it gets. A little dizziness I can handle."

Elizabeth smiled. "I remember the first day we met. You kept throwing up and could barely walk. Just like Jayden." Elizabeth's face went white. She opened her mouth to say something, but nothing came out. She sat back down on the bench and stared at Arbin as if she saw him for the first time. Finally, she said, "That can't be. My brother said you are a powerful Seer."

"That's what I wanted to talk to you about," said Arbin. Elizabeth slowly shook her head back and forth as if saying no. "Your brother is right. I am a Seer." Arbin paused. He knew he had to go through with this. He took a deep breath, turned his head slightly and squinted like he was getting ready to be hit and said, "I am also a little like Jayden. I do not know why, but I have both Talents."

Elizabeth continued to stare at him.

"I think Chairman Sumner may have given me the answer to that question last night."

"Chairman Sumner knew about you?" asked Elizabeth.

"He suspected that there might be something special about me, but he wasn't sure what. He told me about how you, Alex and I were all rescued from a nursery run by rebels about twenty-seven years ago."

"What? That is not true," said Elizabeth. "Why would you even say something like that? Please, for once, just tell me the truth."

Arbin understood how she was feeling. He had felt the same during his meeting with the Chairman. He knew it was going to upset her, but he had to continue for his sake as much as hers. He needed to know if it was true. "Do you know a Father Sauer?" he asked.

Elizabeth did not answer, but he could tell he had her attention.

"Chairman Sumner said that after he rescued us from the nursery, he placed us in homes, and it was Father Sauer's job to check on us. After Father Sauer died, Chairman Sumner had you brought to the city so he could keep an eye on you and Alex."

Elizabeth had stopped looking at him. Arbin could tell she was thinking about what he had said.

When Elizabeth said nothing, he continued. "The Chairman said the nursery was filled with children, all twins except me. He said somehow the place caught on fire, but they could only save five children. Two sets of twins and me. Jayden and Mia are the other twins."

"How does that make you like Jayden?" asked Elizabeth.

"Chairman Sumner said they gathered the mothers from all over," said Arbin. "That means there was something special about them. The Chairman said that after the nursery they learned that sometimes twins have Talents. That nursery was full of twins. You, Alex, Mia and Jayden each have a Talent. Somehow, I ended up with two Talents. I think the people who ran the nursery knew we would end up with Talents."

"That's crazy. Do you know what you are suggesting?" asked Elizabeth. "That kind of talk can get you killed. I cannot believe Chairman Sumner would have suggested that. You must have misunderstood him."

"How do you explain that all the children that survived the nursery have Talents? All of us, including Mia and you. The Chairman said the rebels called their work the Godless Gift. That must suggest something," said Arbin.

"No!" said Elizabeth, shaking her head. Arbin expected her to put her hands over her ears next. "People are not born that way," She said without looking at him, "Fades are the way they are because demons possess them. Just like God blesses Seers."

"What about me? Am I evil?" asked Arbin. "Please, believe me. That demon talk is not true. You have been around me and must know it's not true by now."

"Every time I trust you, I discover another lie or secret," said Elizabeth. She looked at him and said, "That's both evil and hurtful."

"You are right," said Arbin. "I have kept secrets from you, but it was because I was afraid. If anyone found out about me, it would be my death. It might also be the death of anyone that supported me."

"So, you lied to me for my own good," said Elizabeth.

"Yes, I mean no. When you say it that way, it sounds stupid," said Arbin.

"Yes, it does," said Elizabeth. "Now tell me again how you differ from Jayden."

Arbin could feel her anger growing again. He picked up his bag, expecting the need to run any minute.

"I did what I did because I thought it was the right thing to do. At first, I was just protecting myself. Later it was because I wanted to protect you."

Arbin held his bag to his chest, waiting for Elizabeth to yell for the guards. After a few seconds of silence, he sat down, but as far from her as he could. When she did not get up, he said, "Jayden enjoys being what he is. He was always trying to get me to join him in the things he did. I think he was a little jealous of my Talents and looked for any opportunity to show me up. He would always take more and more chances, and I could tell he was enjoying the danger that came with it."

Arbin put his arm on the back of the bench with his hand near Elizabeth, but not touching. When she did not move, he said, "My Talents have caused me nothing but grief. They have turned everyone I care about against me. I have been in hiding for years, hoping never to be forced to use them again. The only time I have ever been able to use them for good was when I was using them for you and Dylan."

Arbin felt Elizabeth's anger weaken.

"Believe me, sometimes I wish I was still hiding in my little town," said Arbin. "I think it might have been better for everyone if I had left earlier before I got caught up in this tragedy."

Arbin knew he had said the wrong thing when he felt Elizabeth's anger rise again. She looked at him and said, "And that is why you are here with a bag ready to leave town? Now is when you decide it is time to leave this 'tragedy', as you say, behind? Is that what we have become to you?"

"No, it's not like that," said Arbin, looking at Elizabeth, who was no longer looking his way. "I do not know how much longer I can keep this a secret," said Arbin. "If anyone finds out about it, I'm dead. Leaving may be the best thing for everyone, but I did not want to leave without telling you the truth."

Elizabeth put her head in her hands, and Arbin was not sure what she was doing. After a few minutes she looked up at him, and he could feel the anger. It was so strong he had to stand up and take a few steps back. He stood there clutching his bag to his chest as if it would protect him from her anger.

She wiped her face on her sleeve and said, "Why do you always do this to me? I was thinking I was wrong about you. That you were someone I could trust and now you do this."

"I'm sorry," said Arbin.

"You are always sorry," said Elizabeth. "My life was so simple before you got involved in it. One minute you tell me you'll sacrifice your future so I can be free to marry who I want. Next you say you want to run away, leaving me holding a secret that could get me killed. I don't understand why you do the things you do, or if you're even telling me the truth?"

"I wanted to tell you the truth, that is why I asked you here today," said Arbin. "I did not tell you before because I was scared. I was not sure how you would react. I knew how you felt about Jayden and I was worried how you would act toward me when you found out."

"If you did not trust me then, why do you trust me now?" asked Elizabeth.

"Because I decided that you deserved the truth about me and about the nursery. Even if it was the last time I got to see you. I have always tried to do the right thing with you, but I still needed to protect myself," Arbin said, looking down at the bag he was clenching. "What I told you the other day was true. Do not forget I put my life on the line to protect Dylan because that is what you asked me to do."

Arbin felt a little embarrassed at that last remark and said, "I didn't mean for that to sound like you owed me. I am sorry..." he cut his apology short, remembering what Elizabeth had just said. He looked out at the river again. Right now, he felt like just jumping in. When he looked back at Elizabeth, he saw that she was watching him. He lowered his bag and looked her in the eyes and said, "I am supposed to be meeting with Captain Eustace shortly. I do not think it will go well and I had decided to leave after I spoke with you."

"We've talked," said Elizabeth. She did not look away, but he felt she was trying to decide something when she asked, "Are you going to run away or stay?"

"I would like to stay if that is okay with you," said Arbin.

Elizabeth continued to study him but said nothing. After a few seconds, she turned her gaze back to the river. Arbin did not feel a rise in her anger, so he took that as a good sign.

"If I stay, I do not know if I will be able to see you again," said Arbin. "I do not want to put you in any more danger."

"This was always one of my favorite places to sit and think," said Elizabeth as she looked around the park.

Arbin was not sure if she heard him or was just ignoring him. "This has become one of my favorite places too." he said.

"When is your meeting with Captain Eustace?" asked Elizabeth.

Arbin shifted his bag from one hand to the other. "Now, I guess."

"You're going through with it?" Elizabeth asked.

Arbin studied Elizabeth's face for a few seconds, "Now that we talked, it would be the right thing to do."

"You can't walk into his office carrying that bag," said Elizabeth.

"Yeah, I had not really thought that far ahead, I guess," said Arbin.

Arbin thought he saw Elizabeth, give a slight smile. After a few seconds of silence, she said, "Leave it here. I am going to spend some time here. You should plan on making it a short meeting."

Arbin placed the bag on the bench. He stood looking at Elizabeth, who did not look back. He said a quiet thanks and trudged back up the path toward the Bridge of Sorrows memorial and the Government Building.

Chapter 21 - Let's Talk Knives

ARBIN ASSUMED HE WOULD find Captain Eustace's office in the cluster of buildings near the Shadow Guard barracks in the northern square. What he discovered was that while there was a space there that Captain Eustace used for meetings, his office and apartment were on the fourth floor of the old palace.

He had no trouble finding Captain Eustace's office, with the help of a Page. After a few pleasant words with the guard sitting at a small desk, he signed a logbook and took a seat. He watched as several people visited the guard, dropping off and picking up items. Each one making his mark in the logbook. Arbin was not in a hurry to meet with the Captain, but with each visitor he became more and more aware of the passing of time. Soon his fears about meeting with the Captain were replaced with a worry about Elizabeth. *This is taking too long,* he thought. *I wonder if she is still waiting.*

The meeting with Elizabeth had not gone as planned. He figured he would be heading out of town by now. Instead, somehow, he ended up here in the place he most wanted to avoid. He tried to remember if it was his idea or hers. He was not even sure where he stood with her. Her talent told him she was upset with him, but she had not called for the guards and had agreed to wait for him. Mia had been so easy to understand. Elizabeth was full of contradictions, a complete mystery to him. He was glad to be rid of the burden of keeping his Fade secret from her. He knew he had to tell her about Jayden soon. He was not sure if it would be better to say something now, hoping she would appreciate his not wanting to keep secrets, or if it would be better to wait for her to calm down some more. Arbin was mulling over his choices when the guard signaled that Captain Eustace was ready to see him.

The Captain's office was not what Arbin was expecting. For one thing, it was small, maybe twenty feet from end to end. Also, the room ran left and right of the door he entered through. Across from the door was a simple oak colored desk with two simple oak chairs in front of it. The desk and chairs sat on a large oriental rug.

Behind the desk was a portrait of a man in uniform. It was not Captain Eustace, but there was some resemblance. Arbin guessed the portrait was close to life size, but it was set in a very large golden ornate frame that made it look much larger.

The wall that held the painting was light, almost pastel green, while the others were a slightly darker green. The trim around the high white ceiling was a very dark green with gold floral designs scattered through it.

The room was lit by three windows. One on each side of the painting and one at the right end of the room. Since it was on the top floor, the full-length windows were narrow and curved at the top. None of these had drapes, but flagstaffs flanked the one on the right. One had the National flag and the other the Shadow Guards flag. The wall to the left had a single door which Arbin guessed led to an apartment.

On the walls were weapons of all kinds. Built into the walls under the mounted weapons were drawers that ran almost the full length of the walls, from the windows to the walls at each end. Placed around the room were stands with uniforms on them. The place looked more like a museum than an office.

The two things that seemed most out of place were the two paintings on either side of the entrance. The one on the left was of a lone military figure on a horse studying what must have been a field of battle shortly after the battle had ended. The one on the right was a painting of a couple sitting under a tree near a river having a picnic. The peaceful green of this painting was in stark contrast to the red, black and gold of the other one.

When Arbin entered, Captain Eustace was sitting at his desk. He stood and directed him to one of the two chairs in front of the desk. He noticed Arbin looking around and said, "My hobby is collecting specialty weapons, I also have a few trophy items from engagements."

Arbin looked up at the painting and Captain Eustace said, "My father. He was a famous Army officer." He smiled and said, "His presence still makes an impression on visitors."

Arbin nodded in agreement.

"Now, let's talk," said Captain Eustace as he sat back down at his desk. "You told me last night that you did not kill Chairman Sumner and I must let you know that I have ruled you out, but I have not ruled out your knife. Did you bring it as I asked?"

"I do not have it anymore," said Arbin.

"Where is it?" asked the Captain, sitting a little straighter in his chair.

"Do you remember me telling you about a friend that was helping me find Arron Schilling?" asked Arbin. When the Captain nodded. Arbin said, "I gave it to him as a kind of payment for his work."

I asked you not to go looking for more trouble," said Captain Eustace. "What is your friend's name?

"Hugo Winters," said Arbin.

Captain Eustace wrote the name down and said, "Get in touch with him and get the knife back. If you do not, I will have to hunt your friend down."

Arbin agreed then said, "It does not seem to bother you too much that I could not prove that it was not my knife that killed Chairman Sumner."

"Let me show you something," said Captain Eustace. He walked to one of the drawers built into his wall of weapons. He took out a key, unlocked the drawer and returned with two boxes. He placed them on his desk. Still standing, he opened one box and took out a knife identical to the one that killed the Chairman.

"Is that...?" started Arbin, but he could not finish his question.

Captain Eustace nodded and said, "This knife killed Chairman Sumner." He opened the second box and pulled out another knife, just like the one already on the desk. He placed it next to the other knife and said, "We found this when Jayden dropped it after struggling with you back at Noor Point."

"They are the same," said Arbin.

"I suspect that it's an assassin's trademark. It is not uncommon in the east," said Captain Eustace. "I still do not know if the knife that killed Chairman Sumner is the knife that Dylan gave you."

Arbin looked at the knives, let out a breath and muttered, "Jayden, you said you had nothing to do with the rebels."

"What was that?" said the Captain. "When did you talk to Jayden?"

Arbin had not realized he was speaking out loud. He froze for a few seconds, knowing there was no way to take back what he said.

Captain Eustace placed his hands and his desk and leaning forward and, in a voice, quieter than he expected said, "When did you speak with Jayden?"

Arbin leaned back in his chair, trying to put some distance between the Captain and himself. "The day after the party. He wanted my help." Arbin stopped there, hoping that would be enough.

"Your help with what?" asked Captain Eustace.

"He said that supporters of the Adelist Movement had kidnapped his sister and her children and were using their safety to force him to do things for them," said Arbin. "He wanted my help in finding and rescuing them."

"And what did you tell him?" asked Captain Eustace.

"I told him I have no idea where they were, or how to find them. He also told me about how he got his instructions. His last message told him to go to the Capital and wait for more instructions. It also said to make sure he did not hurt Dylan."

"Dylan!" The Captain stood up straight as he said the name. "The instructions mentioned Dylan?"

Arbin nodded and said, "Jayden got the idea of kidnapping Dylan and holding him to force the release of his sister and her children. I disagreed, and he left."

Captain Eustace stood, eyes narrowed, and arms crossed while one hand pulled at his beard. Arbin started to worry. He expected the Captain to explode with anger at any moment. It surprised him when the Captain calmly put the knives back into their boxes. When he finished, he looked at Arbin and asked, "Is that why you went to the Sumner Estate that night?"

"Yes," said Arbin. "I saw Elizabeth and Dylan leaving after your shooting practice and followed them. When I got close to the house, I knew that if I could do it, so could he, so I waited."

Captain Eustace tapped the fingers of his right hand on one of the knife boxes while he studied Arbin. When the tapping stopped, he said, "You should have told us."

"I was more afraid of you than him," said Arbin. "I believed him, that Mia was in trouble, and I wanted to help her. I thought I could convince him to change his plans."

Captain Eustace picked up the two boxes and returned them to their place. As he was locking the cabinet, there was a knock on his office door and Hans put his head inside. He looked at Arbin and then back to the Captain and said, "Sorry, Captain, but it's important."

"Report," said Captain Eustace.

"High Seer Kindermann is dead," said Hans.

"What?" asked Captain Eustace. "How did he die?"

"It looks like he choked on something he was eating. It happened about a half hour ago," said Hans.

"Half hour ago! Why am I just finding out about it now?" said Captain Eustace.

"I am sorry about that Captain," said Hans. "I secured the area and sent runners to Bishop Sorren and to you." Hans looked down and said, "The man I sent to you is new and returned to ask if he should bother you because you were in a meeting. That's when I came myself."

"Understood!" said Captain Eustace. The sound of disappointment in his voice was clear. "Is there anything else?"

Hans said, "No, sir. I left the new man with the body. I would like to return to the scene, if it's okay, sir."

"That's fine," said Captain Eustace. Arbin could see that the news bothered the Captain. As Hans reached the door Captain Eustace said, "Hans, High Seer Kindermann was Bishop Sorren's man. Make sure your men stay out of his way. That includes letting the Seers handle moving the body. As soon as the Seers arrive, our people can leave. Understand?"

Hans signaled his understanding and left.

"That was a surprise," said Arbin. "What happens now?"

Captain Eustace was deep in thought and did not respond right away. When he realized that Arbin had asked him a question, he said, "I am sorry, what was your question?"

"What happens with the whole Guardian thing, now that the other candidate has died?" said Arbin.

"In the end, the Council makes the final decision," said Captain Eustace as he rang a little bell on his desk. When his assistant entered, the Captain instructed him to reschedule all his appointments for the day. When his assistant left, Captain Eustace turned back to Arbin and said, "I think it would be proper if I was present when Bishop Sorren arrived to recover Otis's body."

Arbin said, "Okay. So, we are all done?"

"There is still the matter of your knife," said Captain Eustace.

Arbin stood, made his way to the door and said, "I will get it for you, sir," and stepped out.

Great, what do I do about that knife? he thought. Just when I thought things were getting better, my past gets in the way.

Arbin quickly headed back out to the park, hoping that Elizabeth would not be too upset. He found the bench he left her at empty. He was relieved to see that his bag was gone as well. Not sure what to do, he decided to just head back to Masimo's home.

Chapter 22 - Pulling at Loose Ends

THE CITY OF LEABORO had once been two cities separated by the river. The cities were joined long ago through a royal marriage where the properties of both houses had merged. The city was not called Leaboro then. That name would come at the end of the civil war that started because of disagreement on the redistribution of lands resulting from the royal marriage. The unified city would eventually take its name from the Blessed Friedrich Von Leaboro, a hero instrumental in the defeat of the Fades and ending the war.

Being two cities resulted in some duplication. One of which was the operation of two cathedrals. On the south-western side of the city was St. Benno, the oldest of the two cathedrals. The eastern side had St. Hildergard. It was in the north-eastern section of the city. The campus of which also included a school and the neighboring National Library. Bishop Sorren's family had donated some land for St. Hildergard, and he had a family home nearby. The Bishop was responsible for both cathedrals and the chapel on the island that belonged to his Order. He had an apartment and office in the old palace but spent most of his time at St. Hildergard. He enjoyed the large grounds, which included several gardens and a walking maze. Recently he had made it a habit of spending a few hours in the early evening alone in the walking maze. This evening, however, he was not alone. Curt Bergman walked along with him while several of Bergman's men took up positions to react to uninvited visitors if needed.

"I was a little surprised when you asked to meet with me here," said Bergman as he did his best to walk beside Bishop Sorren along the narrow pathways. "It is not my way to talk about business out in the open?"

"I have always enjoyed the view from here at sunset, and I can assure you, we will be given our privacy, despite the efforts of your men. I have made it clear that I am not to be disturbed during my time here." said Bishop Sorren. "Besides, Captain Eustace has started an annoying requirement of logging everyone that enters the Government Building and certain offices, mine being one of them."

"That would be a problem," said Bergman. "However, I am still curious, what is so urgent that we could not find a more appropriate place."

"Captain Eustace is becoming more and more difficult to handle," said Bishop Sorren. "After he found another of your knives at the scene of Chairman Sumner's death, he has become convinced it was the work of a mercenary group. You promised me professional work."

"I had what I thought was a good person assigned to that project," said Bergman. "When I had not heard from him for a few days I handled it differently."

"I must admit, I was getting a little concerned," said Bishop Sorren. "However, when you took action it was sloppy. It was stupid of you to leave the knife at the Estate."

"Time was of the essence and I didn't think Captain Eustace would take that much of an interest in it," said Bergman. "And I would ask that you keep our conversation civil, please."

"My apologies," said Bishop Sorren. "It is just that you have made things a little difficult for me to handle."

"I understand," said Bergman. "This has been a challenging assignment. I must admit, I was a little surprised at your request, what with your close working relationship with Chairman Sumner."

"I had no choice," said Bishop Sorren. "Chairman Sumner was becoming consumed by his plan. He was acting more and more like a man near his end. The answers to each obstacle he faced were becoming ones of violence. He was also becoming careless, acting without letting me know beforehand. I did what I did to protect both the Church and our nation."

"Interesting idea," said Bergman. "Violence for the sake of peace. Sounds more like the words of a statesman or a warrior."

"Since we are speaking of obstacles, our problem Guardian candidate has been doing some talking with the good Captain. He has even provided him with a sketch of a late employee of yours." said Bishop Sorren.

Bergman stopped walking. It took Bishop Sorren a few seconds to realize it, and when he turned to look back, he could see that Bergman was quietly thinking. "Now that is an interesting bit of information," said Bergman. "Do you know how he learned the identity of that person?"

"The reports from Noor Point said that Arbin was chased out of a building by your former employee," said Bishop Sorren. "He could not give a good identification at the time. It appears Arbin's memory improved when he saw your employee speaking with a thin, blond haired man on the Bridge of Sorrows."

"Is that the extent of his description of this second individual?" asked Bergman.

"As of now, yes," said Bishop Sorren.

"That is something to think about," said Bergman. "If I'm not mistaken, Arbin was at the Estate the same time I was."

"There was a meeting," said Bishop Sorren. "The Chairman said he knew how to handle the Guardian issue. Funny, it was the one time I wished he acted on some of his more aggressive suggestions."

"That's amusing," said Bergman. "I wonder if he would have succeeded, if he lived."

"It was not needed," said Bishop Sorren. "We had what we needed to get the High Seer appointed. I told Chairman Sumner that it was just getting the waters muddy."

"Does Captain Eustace have any other leads we need to worry about?" asked Bergman.

"He mentioned the name Hugo Winters," said the Bishop. "But I am not sure what his involvement is."

"Hugo Winters," said Bergman slowly. "I don't think I know that name." He used his finger to call over a man who had been following, almost out of hearing range, behind them. He was obviously in charge of a small group that was doing their best to ensure the privacy of the meeting.

"Mr. Mueller, does the name Hugo Winters mean anything to you?" asked Bergman.

Konrad Mueller stepped closer to Bergman and said, "He showed up a few days ago wearing one of our knives. Said he took it off someone in a fight. He expressed an interest in a certain kind of work, so we have him standing by for evaluation."

"Well, that explains what happened to the person I assigned to the Chairman," said Bergman. "Thank you, Mr. Mueller."

Mueller nodded and returned to his former position.

"Another loose end!" said Bishop Sorren. "I am becoming concerned. These types of mistakes are not what I expected from you. It may be time to think about how best to speed up the completion of our plan."

"With the High Seer's death, that would leave you without an acceptable Guardian candidate," said Bergman.

"My temporary position on the Council has been accepted, thanks to the letter Chairman Sumner gave me," said Bishop Sorren. "With the other Family Chairs against Arbin getting the position, I believe they would welcome the suggestion that I act as a temporary Guardian until we can find a better solution. I do not expect any objections."

"It looks like you are making the best out of the situation," said Bergman. "Do you have any suggestions on how to bring this plan to a close?"

"We need to clean up loose ends," said Bishop Sorren. "Our problem Guardian candidate for one. It is also important that the public view the Shadow Guards as the force that defeated the rebels."

"That will mean casualties and will be very expensive," said Bergman. "Are you ready for that?"

"My new position will give me access to more money," said Bishop Sorren. "Will you be able to put together a group that the Shadow Guard can defeat?"

"That will not be a problem," said Bergman. "It appears the movement had more supporters than expected. Our Mr. Winters is an example of that."

"Good," said Bishop Sorren. "Once they defeat the rebels, you will be heavily rewarded."

"Our former employer always saw to it we had a little something before the work at the start of a new assignment," said Bergman. "Employee incentives you understand."

"You will get paid," said the Bishop. "Besides the quick resolution of those two assignments, I would like you to do something about Councilman Darr. At one time I thought I could counter his influence on the Council using our Fade. However, with his death and the interference of Arbin, I think it's time to act in a manner that will insure the removal of any threats to the voting rights of the Family Chairs."

"When you say clean up loose ends you mean it," said Bergman. "What do you want done with our special guests?"

"Those children are very important to the future of this nation," said Bishop Sorren. "I will contact my seniors and arrange for them to be taken off your hands. Until I get instructions, you will have to keep them for a little while longer."

"You only mentioned the children. What about the mother? She has been helpful in controlling them."

"It is the children I am interested in," said Bishop Sorren. "I do not want to tell you how to do your business, but I need the children kept safe until I have someplace for them."

"That is much like the advice I got from your partner. However, I must insist that we receive payment for that activity in advance. There are expenses, and this work requires more senior employees."

"I had expected as much," said Bishop Sorren. "I have a package ready for you to pick up at my office."

"That's good, but I will need you to double the amount," said Bergman.

"Double! I told you this was for the good of the Nation."

"And I told you there were expenses," said Bergman. "You have said that the plan needs to end. That means there may be extended times where we cannot communicate as easily as now."

Bishop Sorren stopped walking and looked at Bergman. "I cannot do that until I have access to additional funds. That might take a few weeks. Take the money I am giving you now and then get back in touch after the Unification Ceremony."

"I'll give you one week," said Bergman.

"That may not be possible," said Bishop Sorren.

"Like I said, I have expenses and we are dealing with some of my most senior employees," said Bergman.

"I thought you were a man capable of handling difficult people," said Bishop Sorren. "At least that is what Chairman Sumner always said."

"I consider myself an excellent manager and can be very persuasive, but a delay of more than a week will bring more trouble than this contract is worth. If you understand my meaning," said Bergman.

"My dear boy," said Bishop Sorren "Let us not forget that you are speaking to the head of a Holy Order. My work is God's work. Your cooperation will bring you rewards greater than heavy pockets."

Bergman studied the Bishop. His lips tightened for a second before he relaxed into a more casual expression and said, "Your meaning is clear, your Excellency."

Bishop Sorren smiled, then said, "Good. Now if you will excuse me, I am going home. My dinner will be waiting. You might find more time in the maze good for improving your concentration. I will leave you with a word of warning. Captain Eustace is young, but he can be incredibly determined. Give him a loose thread and he will pull on it until the whole thing comes apart."

Bergman smiled back at the Bishop and said, "We will do our best to cut off any loose threads."

As Bishop Sorren turned and walked away, Bergman signaled for Mueller.

"You need something, sir?" asked Mueller.

"For now, please have two of your men see that the Bishop makes it home," said Bergman. "Tell them to keep a watch on him. I do not trust him."

"He is a Bishop," said Mueller.

Bergman smiled and said, "Exactly." He watched the Bishop as he headed toward his family home and said, "I don't like the way this job is going. I should never have taken it on to begin with, but it was such an interesting challenge. Our prior employer's motives were clear, and we could rely on his discretion. I suspect the Bishop does not hold us in the same regard. I feel he is not as committed to our wellbeing as I would like."

"Do you really want us to shut things down?" asked Mueller.

"Like the Bishop said, there are too many loose ends. I worry we may be too exposed by now," said Bergman. "We need to understand what is known about us, and how many people know it before we can start cleaning things up."

"So, what do we do about the Bishop's requests," asked Mueller.

"We go ahead with his request to take care of Arbin before his memory improves. I like the idea of the Shadow Guards and the rebels. We can deal with a few of our own problem people that way, and it will stop anyone from looking for us."

"And the woman and her kids?" Mueller asked.

"I do not know what makes them so valuable," said Bergman. "I do not trust the Bishop to treat us fairly on this deal. I think we will contact his seniors and try to broker a deal ourselves. If we dislike where it is going, we sell them through the normal methods."

Mueller nodded, "What about Mr. Winters?"

"A very loose end. Place him in the group that we will let the Shadow Guards deal with," said Bergman. "He wanted work. Let's give him a chance for a hero's death."

"And Councilman Darr?" asked Mueller.

"Let us hold off on that. The Councilman is the Bishop's problem, but he is not ours yet. Besides, we might need another investor when this whole thing blows over."

Mueller nodded, "It's done." As he walked away, Bergman called him back.

"Have one of our special people ready," said Bergman. "I really did not like the way the Bishop talked to me. Depending on what your men report, we may want to end our relationship with him a little sooner."

Mueller nodded and walked away.

Bergman looked around at the maze, took a deep breath and said, "This is a beautiful view. Maybe the Bishop is right about walking this thing. Besides, it's always good to score points where you can."

Chapter 23 - Careful What You Wish For

ARBIN HAD NOT HEARD from anyone for several days. No notes from Jayden and no visits from Alex. He was sure that Elizabeth was mad at him for leaving her stranded in the park for so long. When he had returned to Masimo's home, he found his items laid neatly out on his bed and the food in his bag returned to the pantry. It was like he never left, but the place was painfully empty of people. That had been four days ago.

Arbin did not know how to get in touch with Jayden and was not sure where Elizabeth and Alex lived. While he knew where Alex worked, he was not sure how it would look if he just dropped by and asked where he lived so he could spend time with his sister.

After a few days of waiting, he could not take it anymore. Arbin knew he needed to do something. He figured the easiest thing would be to speak to Councilman Darr. He made good time getting to the Councilman's home, but his luck was not the same once he knocked on the door.

"I'm sorry, the Councilman is not available," said the man who answered Councilman Darr's door.

"It's important that I speak with him," said Arbin. "He said someone would meet with me about the Guardian nomination, but they never did. I want to make sure I did not misunderstand him."

"I know nothing about that, sir," said the servant as he stepped back from the door.

"How about Simon? Is he here?" asked Arbin, putting his hand against the closing door.

"He is with Councilman Darr at the meeting. Now, please excuse me, I have a lot of things that I need to take care of."

"Meeting? What meeting?"

"They are at an emergency meeting of the Governing Council," said the servant with a smile as he successfully closed the door, leaving Arbin standing there staring at it.

Great! I guess the best thing to do is see if I can get into the meeting, he thought as he started the long walk toward the Government Building.

Arbin was a little worried that he might have some trouble getting past the guards at the Government Building, but they only asked him to sign in. With the help of a young Page, he was soon standing outside of the Grand Council Meeting Room.

When the Guard asked his business, Arbin stood up as straight as he could and, in what he thought was an impressive voice, said, "I am the candidate for Dylan Sumner's Guardian, and I am here to attend the meeting."

The guard pointed to a logbook which Arbin quickly signed. Once it was confirmed that Arbin had signed on the right line, the guard said, "I am sorry, sir. This is a closed meeting. No guests allowed."

Arbin stood looking at the guard, not sure he heard him right. "No guests? I am not a guest. Maybe you did not understand what I said. I will be the Guardian of Dylan Sumner. If you check, you will find that they are probably meeting about me."

"I apologize, sir."

"That's okay," said Arbin, in what he felt was a comforting voice.

"Now, if you could just present your summons for me to review, I would be happy to send you right in," said the guard with an outstretched hand.

Arbin muttered to himself all the way back down to the courtyard where he stood for several minutes trying to think of what to do next. "Well, since I am here, I guess I should visit Alex." He headed to the northern end of the compound where he knew he would find the Seer barracks and offices. He wasn't sure which building Alex would be in, so he asked a passing Seer, "Where can I find Alex?"

The Seer gave him a strange look. "High Seer Keller is in his office." He pointed toward the Administration Building, where Arbin had met with High Seer Kindermann a few times.

"High Seer Keller? When did that happen?" asked Arbin.

"The day after the old High Seer died."

Arbin thanked him and made his way to the entrance of the Administration Building for the Seer Core. The person at the desk had him sign a log and asked him to wait while he let the High Seer know he was here.

Alex appeared a few minutes later with a big smile on his face. "Arbin, I am glad you came by. Come on in. I want to show you my new office."

"I heard," said Arbin. "Too bad about High Seer Kindermann, but congratulations on the promotion."

"It has been a busy week. I am sorry, but I just did not get the chance to let you know."

As they walked down the hallway, Alex said, "The whole thing happened so fast. One minute I was taking the test for First Class and the next, I was in Bishop Sorren's office accepting the position of Acting High Seer."

"That was fast," said Arbin. "Funny. Now you are the person you complained about back at Noor Point."

Alex smiled, "I told Bishop Sorren I would only accept the position if they allowed me to make some changes. It surprised me when he said as High Seer, I could make any changes I wanted as long as I did not violate the Charter of the Order. Changes at that level would need more senior approval."

They stopped at a flight of stairs that led to the upper level where Arbin had met with High Seer Kindermann. Alex saw Arbin looking up the stairs and said, "I did not want his old office. I wanted mine on the ground floor. It's at the end of the hall."

Before they could start walking again, a First Year that Arbin did not recognize called, "High Seer! Wait, please." He presented Alex with a message and then left. Alex looked a little embarrassed, "It still takes some getting used to."

"Well, it looks like, from the smile on your face, you are happy with the new job," said Arbin.

Alex nodded. "I already made some changes based on suggestions from Elizabeth and you."

"Me? I do not remember making any suggestions."

"Well, Elizabeth made them, but she said she got the ideas from you."

"All right," said Arbin. "What grand ideas did I have?"

"That Seers could exist at two levels," said Alex. "One with more abilities than others, kind of like you."

"I don't remember saying that, but go on, what else did I say?"

"She showed me some drawings from the early days, along with a diary that Dylan has been reading. She suggested I form two groups. One to fight Fades and one to support the fighters."

"She got all of that from that diary?" asked Arbin.

"She always was a lot smarter than me," said Alex with a smile. "Anyway, that is what I am doing. It will solve the problem of Seers that cannot pass the testing or do not want to fight. I will put them in a support group. I can take advantage of their enthusiasm and skills without calling out any that might not be able to verify their gifts."

"Sounds like a perfect solution," said Arbin. "Glad I thought of it," he said with a smile.

Alex stopped at a large double door with the nameplate of "High Seer Alexander Keller" on it. "Wait till you see this place," he said as he pushed open the doors.

The office was much nicer than the prior High Seer's office. Less clutter, for sure. It was long, and there were several windows down one side that filled the room with light. It was divided into two sections. The front section was set up for meetings with a long table and chairs. Past that was a railed banister that blocked off a smaller section that was obviously Alex's work area. There was a large wide bookcase built into the wall on the side across from the windows that ran the length of the section. At the very back was a wall with the beginnings of a large mural.

Alex's desk sat in front of that wall and faced the entrance. There were two simple chairs in front of it.

"What's with the painting at the back of the room?" asked Arbin.

"Oh, that's another suggestion from Elizabeth. It is a copy of the drawing she was working on. She pestered me until I agreed to put it there," said Alex. "I must admit, now that I see it, I am starting to like it."

"Very nice, Once again, congratulations."

"That's not all," said Alex. "They gave me an apartment in the palace!"

"Wait, you will live here, on the island? What about Elizabeth?"

"I will still keep my old place until I am settled in," said Alex. "Elizabeth has been spending a lot of time with Dylan. It is my understanding that they will offer her a position as Dylan's nanny."

"That is great," said Arbin. "I am sure that will make her happy."

"Yes, she will probably stay there until she gets married. After that, I am sure she will live somewhere else. I know Masimo is family, but I am sure that as a newlywed he will want some privacy."

"What!" said Arbin, staring at Alex. It took him a few seconds to remember to breathe and when he did, he asked, "Did you say she was going to marry Masimo? When did this happen? She said nothing to me about that."

"I just found out myself," said Alex. "I spent the morning meeting with a representative of Lady Casandra. He was here to speak to Bishop Sorren and myself about Masimo's request and about the Bride Price."

"You agreed to her marrying Masimo?"

"I had always hoped she would end up with Lubin, but Masimo is an agreeable arrangement. He is a decent guy with the ability to support her in the manner she is accustomed to. It will let her stay close to Dylan. Plus, as a distant family member, her children have some rights to the Family Chair. I am sure she will be happy with the arrangement when I tell her. After all, look how much time she spends with Masimo now."

"No one has asked her yet?"

"Don't worry. We are still working out the details, but I will tell her soon. Please do not spoil it for me. I really want to see her expression when she finds out."

"Me too," said Arbin, almost to himself. "When is all of this going to happen?"

"Lady Casandra's representative said she would be well enough to travel in a little over a month. Masimo should be back by Unification Day. I am sure that Lady Casandra will want to be here for the wedding ceremony and will not want it competing with any other social events. I guess maybe in six or seven months."

"So soon," said Arbin, looking out through the windows into the courtyard.

"Things are happening a lot faster than I ever expected," said Alex. "It's funny, even during all this turmoil, we all are getting what we wanted."

"What?" said Arbin, looking back at Alex. "Getting what we wanted?"

"I get the chance to make the changes I wanted to the Seer Core," said Alex. "Elizabeth can stop complaining about not being married, and she will have something she can feel passionate about. You will finally get to go back to the life you have been asking for."

"Elizabeth complained about not being married?" asked Arbin.

"She has often complained about the uncertainty of her future and Bishop Sorren's resistance to discuss it," said Alex.

"That I can understand," said Arbin. "What did you mean about me getting what I wanted."

"Ever since I have known you, all you have said was you wanted nothing to do with the Seer Core. You said several times you wished we had left you where you were," said Alex.

Arbin nodded, "I have been through a lot since I got here."

"Well, one thing that Bishop Sorren agreed on was that you no longer need to join the Seer Core," said Alex. "I would really like to have your knowledge, but since the death of the Fade things have changed. Bishop Sorren said you are free to leave town. He has also asked Captain Eustace to close the investigation into the death of Chairman Sumner and laid it at the feet of the rebels."

"That was fast," said Arbin.

"The Bishop is a lot easier to work with than I thought," said Alex. "I am sure my position has a lot to do with that. He is more open to telling me things now. He even told me about my parents."

"You know about that?"

"After Elizabeth told me what you said, I confronted Bishop Sorren. He told me the complete story. I must admit I was a little upset that the truth was kept from me. When he explained the reason, I had to admit that I might have done the same thing myself."

"You are kidding? You would have kept a truth like that from a child?"

"Yes," said Alex. "Bishop Sorren did us a big favor. Our lives would have been much different if people knew we were children of rebels."

"That is what he told you?" asked Arbin.

At that moment, a Seer knocked on the office door. Alex waved him over. "This is Seer Kimble. He is my new assistant."

Seer Kimble smiled and shook Arbin's hand, then said to Alex, "Mr. Surowiecki is in the lobby. He wants to talk to you about pledging his son Astin."

"Thank you," said Alex. He turned back to Arbin and said, "Duty calls."

"I understand," said Arbin. "We can talk more later."

Alex put his hand on Arbin's shoulder, and with a smile, pointed toward the office door.

Arbin congratulated Alex again on his promotion and left the office.

His conversation with Alex had left his mind spinning. He wandered around without thinking about where he was going and ended up sitting on his favorite bench in the Memorial Park.

"Could I have been so wrong about Elizabeth," he said, looking at the statue of the loving couple. "I was sure she did not want to be forced into marrying someone. I wonder if she would marry Masimo if she had the choice."

Arbin noticed that the people walking by were looking at him. He gave them a polite smile and thought, *Do I have the right to interfere? After all, I was not really a part of their lives until I was forced to be.* Alex's words, 'We all got what we wanted,' kept playing repeatedly in his head. *What do I really want?* he asked himself. *I really do not know anymore. I could just take off like Alex said, but where would that leave me? Hiding from the world until I got caught again.* Arbin looked around the park, took a deep breath and whispered, "This is really a pretty place. Of all the places I have been since I arrived, this place has the best memories."

He thought about the other times he had been here. He soon realized that the best times, even though they might have been stressful, were the times he was here with Elizabeth. He remembered how she had reacted when she learned who and what he was. Hiding his secret was hard, and he was tired of it. He had to admit it felt good to tell her. It allowed him to feel freer, a little like old times. It reminded him of how he felt when he spent time with Mia and Jayden. There were problems back then, but Mia and Jayden had made him feel like he was part of their little family.

A tear came to Arbin's eyes, and he had a powerful urge to cry. *I will not spoil this place with bad memories,* he thought. Arbin got up, looked around and decided that he would have to talk to Elizabeth. He headed off toward the east side of town. The walk to the Sumner estate was a little longer using the northern bridge, but it would have less traffic and he felt like being alone right now.

Chapter 24 - Snake in the Grass

IT WAS LATE AFTERNOON as Arbin approached the Sumner Estate. The walk had taken him longer than he had expected, but he used the time trying to plan out what he would say to Elizabeth. The main gate was guarded. Arbin studied the three men as he approached. He was a little surprised that two of the men were dressed in the uniforms of Duke Henry's men. The third he recognized as Hans.

"Hello Hans," said Arbin, as he did his best to walk casually past.

"Just a minute!" said one of the Duke's men.

"Sorry," said Arbin. "I was just going to speak with Miss Keller."

"Do you have an invitation?"

"Invitation?" asked Arbin.

"I'll handle this," said Hans as he signaled for Arbin to follow.

"But Bishop Sorren left orders that —" started one guard who was interrupted by Hans saying, "He's my guest."

Arbin watched as Hans stood looking down at the guard, who lowered his gaze and took a few steps back toward the gatepost as if it would protect him. Hans turned and walked up the path, not waiting for Arbin to follow, which he did as quickly as possible.

"What is going on here?" Arbin asked as he followed close behind Hans. "Why are Duke Henry's men here?"

"Things have changed," said Hans without looking back. "Do you want to speak to Miss Keller or not?"

"Yes, thank you," said Arbin as he followed behind the big man. He was a little confused when they started heading toward the side of the house instead of the front door. "Where are we going?" he asked, looking back at the front door.

"Gazebo. "That's where you will find her, but I don't know for how much longer."

As they rounded the side of the house and into a backyard which he was starting to know all too well, he could see Elizabeth sitting in the smaller of the two Gazebos, the one at the far end of the yard and closer to the forest line. It was almost the only sunny spot in the yard at this hour. He was taken at how pretty she looked sitting there. Her eyes closed, her hands folded in her lap and the sun resting on her face. She looked so peaceful, but he had a feeling something was not right.

Hans cleared his throat, and Elizabeth opened her eyes. She sat there for a few seconds looking at the two men coming her way, then she glanced over to the sunroom as if to see if there was anyone nearby who could see them. Elizabeth stood as they reached the base of the Gazebo and Hans said, "A visitor for you, Miss Keller. If you don't mind, I will wait near the sunroom door."

Arbin had expected to feel some kind of anger from Elizabeth, but he felt nothing. This was the first time he had been so close without her Talent making itself known.

Elizabeth said, "Thank you Hans," and she looked at Arbin, pointed to a chair, and sat back down.

As Arbin sat, he could see that she had a slight redness to her eyes. Even though she appeared surprisingly calm and greeted him with a small smile, there was something off about her. It upset him to see her this way. He thought about what he would say to her on the way over here by the only thing that came out was, "Where's Dylan?"

"Taking a nap, I hope," she said, looking up toward the second-floor windows.

Arbin followed her gaze to the second floor balcony and when he looked back, he found himself staring into her eyes. When she raised her eyebrows slightly, he realized he was not talking. He looked down at his hand and then back up. Elizabeth's expression had changed somewhat from when he had first sat down, and she felt more like the girl he had known in the park. That thought reminded him of how he had abandoned her on that bench. He took a breath, "I'm sorry I took so long with Captain Eustace." He realized as soon as he said it, he was saying he was sorry again.

Elizabeth put up her hand. "I didn't wait. I knew you would be long, so I dropped off your things and went home."

Arbin let out a small sigh. "Well, that makes me feel a little better."

"Still, it would have been nice if you tried to make your apology a little sooner," said Elizabeth. "It would make it a lot easier to believe."

"I am sorry," said Arbin. "I wanted to talk to you, but I was not sure where to find you. Plus, I was not sure if you wanted to see me again."

"I am glad you're here to deliver your apologies, but right now might not be the best time for it."

The words 'glad you're here' made Arbin smile, but he could see that she was nervous. He looked around. "What's wrong?"

"Bishop Sorren had a talk with me yesterday. He said he did not want me speaking to you anymore. He also said he did not want you around Dylan as well."

"He never liked me," said Arbin. "When I become Guardian, I will make sure he has nothing to do with you or Dylan."

Elizabeth looked at Arbin with an expression of concern and sadness. "You don't know, do you?"

"Know what?" Arbin asked.

"The day after High Seer Kindermann died, there was an emergency meeting of the Executive Committee, and they accepted Bishop Sorren as the temporary Guardian until a permanent appointment can be made."

"Executive Committee, who are they? What happened to all that talk about me being nominated?"

"The Executive Committee is made up of one Family Chair, one elected Noble, and one elected Guild Member," said Elizabeth. "They normally decide on issues of critical importance in situations where a full Council is not available. From what I hear, Bishop Sorren acted as the Family Chair."

"How could Bishop Sorren do that?" asked Arbin. "The Chair belongs to Dylan."

"Dylan has not been seated yet. Chairman Sumner still holds the Family Chair until the full Council can meet and do that. The power of attorney Chairman Sumner gave Bishop Sorren is still in effect until then."

"There was a full Council meeting today. I tried to get in but was told it was a private meeting."

"That's what I heard as well," said Elizabeth. "Bishop Sorren has stopped all visitors, so I am only hearing things from the guards." She looked over at Hans, who was leaning up against the wall of a planter.

Arbin looked at Hans as well, "I hope he does not break that thing."

His comment brought a smile to Elizabeth, and Arbin was happy he said it. *How can I say something so simple and make her happy when everything else just seems to get her upset?* he thought.

"I talked to your brother, the High Seer today."

Elizabeth smiled. "How is he? I have not seen much of him since they appointed him. He hasn't been staying at the house and I have been spending a lot of time here."

"He seems thrilled," said Arbin. "He told me about the nanny position."

Elizabeth nodded. "I agreed to act as nanny until Lady Casandra can return. As far as moving in, I have not agreed to that. They have moved Dylan into his Grandfather's room and want me to stay in Dylan's old room."

"The one he shot me from?" said Arbin, looking up to the second-floor landing and holding his shoulder as if begging for sympathy.

Elizabeth gave him a quick smile and said, "It's nice being nearer to Dylan, but I don't want to surrender my freedom."

Elizabeth's mention of freedom reminded Arbin where he was going with his conversation. However, he was not ready to get there yet, so he decided to put it off a little longer.

"Your brother said something kind of interesting to me today," said Arbin, trying to think how best to say what he wanted to say.

Elizabeth waited, and he hesitated for a few seconds until she urged him. "Go on, I'm listening."

"He said that it was funny how even with all the turmoil we all got what we wanted," said Arbin, looking down at his hands.

When Elizabeth said nothing he continued, "Before I came here, I was sitting in the park thinking about that. When I first got here, I was sure of what I wanted, and that was not to be here."

Arbin looked up and saw that Elizabeth was still sitting there quietly watching him. He looked back down at his hands. "Captain Eustace once called me a selfish man, who would stand by and watch a man die if I thought it would help me go unnoticed."

Elizabeth shifted in her chair but still said nothing. The less she said, the more he could not stop from talking. "I asked myself today what it is I really want." Arbin looked up. "I'm tired." Just saying it felt like he had released a great weight. His face felt flush and he could feel the urge to tear up raising. He could feel Elizabeth watching him. *No, not now. What will she think of me if she sees me crying?* He squeezed his hands tightly to help get control again. He looked back down to hide any glint of tears in his eyes and continued, "I'm tired of hiding, I'm tired of living in fear. I'm tired of not trusting people, I'm tired of being that selfish man that Captain Eustace talked about." Arbin finished but was afraid to look Elizabeth in the eyes so he stood, took a deep breath and looked over at Hans.

"I'm still waiting," said Elizabeth to his surprise.

Arbin turned back and saw her calmly sitting there with her hands in her lap. *How can she be so calm?* he wondered. "Waiting for what?" he asked.

"It sounded as if you were going to tell me what you wanted out of life," she said.

Arbin rubbed his shoulder again, and after a few seconds sat back down. "Didn't I just say it?"

"No, you spent a lot of time saying how you feel, but you didn't say what you want."

Arbin stared at her for a few seconds. He really could not keep his thoughts straight when he was around her. He thought he had shared everything, but it was clear from looking at her he had not. He closed his eyes and thought back to the park. He felt the emotion swell up in his throat and quietly said, "I do not want to be alone anymore. I do not want to live just for myself anymore." Arbin paused before he opened his eyes. "What I really want is to be with you."

"Now, that wasn't so hard, was it?" said Elizabeth as she stood. She took a quick look toward the house. "I need to go check on Dylan." She gave Arbin a quick smile then walked toward the sunroom, leaving him sitting there and staring after her.

As she passed Hans, she stopped and said something to him. Hans smiled a thank you in response and headed over toward Arbin.

Arbin looked up and said, "Did you know about Bishop Sorren becoming the Guardian?"

"I hope you got the chance to say everything that you needed to say because I don't think Bishop Sorren will let you see her now that she is engaged."

Arbin stared at Hans. "She knows?"

"She was told this morning. She has been sitting at there most of the day. Now if you follow me, I will ..." Hans stopped in mid-sentence. Arbin looked up to see that his eyes were looking past Arbin's shoulder, but his head was still tilled down.

"What is it?" whispered Arbin, resisting the urge to turn around.

"We are being watched," said Hans. "Don't turn around. Do you sense anything?"

Arbin relaxed the best he could and reached out to detect the presence of anyone, Fade or Seer.

"Nothing. Where is he?"

"The forest edge behind us," said Hans. When I say so, we will charge him. You go to the left side; I will take the right. Don't go too far. Ready, one, two, now!

Hans was off running before Arbin even had a chance to refuse. He followed Hans into the forest, looking for the watcher and hoping he was not running straight into another knife fight.

The thickness of the trees caused the late afternoon sunlight to splinter through their leaves, making it a little difficult to see into the shadows of the bushes. Arbin slowed his advance, not wanting someone to jump out from those shadows.

Arbin could hear Hans thrashing to his right but could not see him anymore. He pushed ahead and then decided his best option was to Fade. He needed protection in case the watcher was armed. He found a small amount of cover, closed his eyes and focused on pulling the Fade around him. When he was sure that he had the Fade in place, he listened for the sound of movement, much like when he had hunted deer when he was younger.

The sound of Hans thrashing died out, and he was not sure if he had turned back or was still searching. Arbin slowly made his way forward, pausing every few yards to wait and listen. About twenty minutes had passed, and he was feeling the fatigue caused by putting so much concentration into keeping up such a strong Fade. He decided that if he found nothing in the next few minutes, he would turn back.

It was then that he came to the edge of the forest. It emptied on to a large grassy landscape with the river far off to the right. This must be somewhere beyond the orchards he had cut through the last time he was on the Estate. There were no homes around, but there was an old building, possibly a warehouse, about another hundred yards ahead, just at the edge of the forest. The surrounding high grasses partly hid it from view.

Arbin was studying the area when out of the corner of his eye he saw a figure slipping through the tall grass about twenty feet from him. Arbin froze in place, forced himself to relax and focused on his Fade. The man, which Arbin guessed was the watcher, did not slow his advance.

Arbin did his best to follow unnoticed, looking for people around the building. He knew he had a better chance of being discovered by someone further away than by the nearby watcher who now appeared to be completely under the influence of his Fade.

When the watcher was about forty five feet from the building, he let out a strange bird call which was answered from some place in the tall grass. At first one man stood up, then there were two more. The watcher waved, and they returned the wave. The watcher then moved at a more normal pace toward the building and was met by a man that appeared in the doorway.

The fading sunlight prevented him from making out the faces of the two men. The hour of the day did not require there to be any extra lighting, but he could smell a cooking fire. He could see lights coming from what he guessed was a barge on the river that was a good seventy-five yards away, but it looked like the barge was tied up at a nearby dock.

Arbin continued to advance in the tall grass. He was hoping to get close enough to get a good look at the watcher and the person he was talking to. If he got close enough, there might be a chance he could hear them talking.

He also wanted to get close enough for his Fade to protect him from any other guards lurking in the grass.

He got as close as he dared and could just make out bits of conversation. The man that came out of the house was upset with the watcher. Arbin could just make out the faces of the two men but had never seen them before. He studied their faces, hoping he could describe them later. It was then that he saw a familiar face, as a thin man with a long blond ponytail walked out the door and started speaking to the two men. Arbin thought he saw a glint of silver in the man's ponytail.

Bergman, Arbin thought. He had learned the courier's name and was honestly glad to know that his suspicions about him being no good were right.

Bergman listened as the two men in the doorway talked. Both pointed occasionally toward the Sumner Estate.

The watcher appeared to be trying to defend himself. Arbin watched as Bergman calmly placed his hand on the shoulder of the watcher and said something. It looked like whatever he said ended the discussion. The watcher turned to walk away, and Bergman put a knife in the watcher's back. Bergman used his hand on the man's shoulder to help direct the body as it fell forward into the tall grass. He then turned and walked back into the building.

Arbin fell face first, back into the grass, trying to make himself as flat as possible. He laid there barely breathing, trying to process what he had just seen. He slowly looked back up at the building. He was close. Much closer than he wanted to be after what he had just witnessed. Arbin knew he needed to relax, or he would lose his Fade. He took a few deep breaths and tried to calm himself. It was then that he got a strange sensation. One that he had not had in a long time.

He cleared his mind and reached out for the presence, and this time found one. "Mia!" he said in an almost breathless whisper.

Chapter 25 - Matter of Timing

ARBIN RAN THROUGH THE dimly lit forest, paying little attention to the surroundings. He stumbled painfully to the ground several times, but the excitement of finding Mia kept him moving forward. It reminded him of running from the killer and his friend back in the forest of Noor Point, except this time he was sure he had not been seen, and he was not worried about being found by the Shadow Guards. He only hoped he could get them heading back to rescue Mia before something happened to her and the children. He was not sure if Mia had detected him, but he hoped she had. It would make it easier for her to prepare for the rescue when it happened.

A startled guard looked up as Arbin stumbled out of the forest into the backyard of the Sumner Estate. "I found them, I found them," shouted Arbin as he hurried toward the guard.

The guard stared as Arbin approached. He knew who Arbin was but was not sure how to handle his sudden reappearance. The guard froze for a few seconds, then fell back on the old standby that had been drilled into the head of every military man and shouted, "Halt, identify yourself!"

"Go get Hans! It's important," Arbin shouted and paused for breath as he reached the guard. "Where is he? I found Mia and the rebel hideout." As the confused guard turned and pointed back toward the house, Arbin shouted, "Hans, Hans, I found them, where are you?"

"What's wrong?" Arbin looked up at the balcony and saw Elizabeth with Dylan at her side.

"I found Mia!" he shouted back. "She is being held in an old building at the far end of the Estate near the river."

"I told you not to run off. You're worse than a kid," he heard Hans say as he walked out of the sunroom. "Now, who is holding who?"

"Hans! Boy, am I glad to see you. I found that guy we were chasing. I followed him to an old building where he met up with a group of men. That is where they are keeping Mia. I also witnessed that courier, Bergman, kill him."

"Bergman?" came a voice from behind Hans as Bishop Sorren stepped out of the sunroom. "What's this about Bergman killing someone?"

Arbin paused, partly leaning over and signaling with his hand that he needed a second as the excitement and the running had caught up with him. He took a few beep breaths, then stood straight and looked at the Bishop. "I just saw him kill the man that Hans and I were following. He just stabbed him in the back!"

Bishop Sorren turned to Hans, "What is he talking about?"

"There was someone watching the house a little while ago," said Hans. "Arbin and I followed him into the woods, but I lost track of him."

"I found him and followed him to that old building," said Arbin. "I saw the man talking to Bergman and just as he turned to walk away Bergman stabbed him."

"You must be mistaken," said Bishop Sorren. "Bergman has been a loyal employee of Chairman Sumner and myself for years. The man is no killer."

Arbin turned to Hans and said, "I saw him. It was Bergman. After seeing him, I am convinced he was the man I saw meeting with Duke Henry's killer, twice."

"You said you did not get a good look at that person," said the Bishop. "What makes you decide now that it's Bergman?"

"I was closer this time," said Arbin. "I am sure now Bergman was the person I saw meeting with Duke Henry's killer both in Noor Point and on the bridge the other day. I also know I saw him here when Chairman Sumner was killed. The same thin frame, the same long dirty blond hair in a ponytail and something else. I remember now seeing something in his hair each time, like jewelry."

"How close were you?" said Hans.

"Close, maybe twenty feet. There were people hiding in the grass around the building, keeping watch. I got as close as I could without being noticed."

"You are mistaken!" said Bishop Sorren. "I do not know what you saw, but I can guarantee that you did not see Bergman kill someone. I know this for a fact because Bergman is out of town on an errand for me." Bishop Sorren turned to Hans. "Have your men return to their stations."

"I can prove it!" said Arbin. "Just follow me back to the building."

The Bishop turned back to Arbin. "Honestly, I have no reason to believe you based on your claim that your memories suddenly and miraculously improved. I will speak to Bergman when he returns. Until then, you need to stop making any more of these terrible accusations with nothing more than your word as proof."

The other guards headed toward the house but stopped when Hans asked, "How many people were there at the building?"

Arbin closed his eyes and pictured the building. He counted off the men he saw and where he saw them. When he opened his eyes, he noticed that everyone was watching him. It made him feel nervous. "There could be more, but that is what I remember."

"Twelve armed men, maybe more," said Hans. "I only have two Shadow Guards and a Seer. Plus, the four guards from Lady Casandra. Too few to go after a group in an easily defended building."

"So what? We just let them go?" asked Arbin. "Hans, Mia is there. I know it. We have to do something."

Hans turned to Bishop Sorren, "I feel it's important to investigate Arbin's story. If there is a group of armed men this close to the Estate, it could pose a threat to Lord Dylan. We may need to relocate. No matter what we do, I will be required to include the incident and our actions in my report to Captain Eustace."

Bishop Sorren said nothing, but it was clear he was uncomfortable with Hans' request.

After a few minutes Hans said, "I can send one of my people to get more men."

Bishop Sorren looked at Arbin and then back to Hans. "No! I will send someone. If there is a threat, I would prefer you stay here."

"I can go!" said Arbin.

"No!" said the Bishop. "My man can go by carriage," and headed back into the house.

Hans stood watching the Bishop leave. Arbin could see there was something on his mind. "How long will it take for someone to get here?"

Looking back at Arbin, Hans said, "Captain Eustace is out chasing down a report of rebels, so I am not sure how many people are still at the barracks."

"You believe me right, Hans?"

"Your description of the building and the men convinced me you were there, and you were close. I am not sure about Bergman and you haven't told me how you know your friend Mia and her children are with them."

"More of a girlfriend than a friend," said Elizabeth as she joined them.

Arbin blushed, looked at Elizabeth and then said, "Mia is in the past."

Hans looked at Elizabeth and then back to Arbin. "I need to make sure my men are back on post," He then turned and walked away.

Elizabeth walked over to the Gazebo and sat down. The slight dizziness he felt when she had joined him said she was not in a good mood. He followed her and stood near the Gazebo.

"You are upset," said Arbin. "I can feel it."

"Good!" said Elizabeth. "At least this Talent is good for something."

"Mia was a long time ago. She is not someone I want in my future, but I owe it to her to help."

"About that," said Elizabeth. "You've said that a few times. Why do you owe it to her?"

Arbin paused and looked down. He was not sure what to say but could feel Elizabeth's anger growing.

"I abandoned her," he mumbled. "I made a promise to take care of her, but when things got bad, I abandoned her."

Elizabeth looked him in the eyes as if judging if he was telling the truth. The longer she looked at him, the more uncomfortable he felt.

"Mia and Jayden were the first persons I ever met with Talents. I thought there was something wrong with me until I met them." Arbin sat down, took a deep breath and looked at Elizabeth. "It was a few years after my father disowned me. I wandered around for a while doing odd jobs until I met up with Mia and Jayden. Mia attached herself to me right away." Arbin felt Elizabeth's anger rise. "Sorry, I never had someone like her in my life and I enjoyed the attention," Arbin said apologetically.

He paused for a second to study Elizabeth, and when she said nothing, he continued. "We kind of wandered from place to place until I found us jobs working for a man name Hahn. I was a clerk in one of his warehouses. Mr. Hahn was a collector, and books were his chief interest. One day I was doing an inventory of his collection and discovered an item that belonged to my family. It was a needlepoint that my mother had made of my favorite story character, 'The Little Green Mouse'. I planned on asking Mr. Hahn if I could buy it, but the warehouse foreman took it from me. When he would not give it back to me, we got into a fight during which he fell and hit his head on something. I thought I killed him. I panicked. I told Mia what happened, and that I had to leave. She begged me to take her with me, but I told her no. I told her I was cursed, and wherever I went, trouble followed. I said I was doing it for her own good, which at the time I believed."

Elizabeth shifted in her seat but continued to look at Arbin.

Arbin knew it was too late to stop, so he continued. "I used my Talent to hide until it was darker. Then I went to the docks, where I planned to steal a small boat. Jayden found me. He told me that the foreman did not die but was seriously hurt and the authorities were looking for me. Jayden said Mia sent him to find me because they were also leaving. She wanted me to go with them. I do not know why, but when I refused, Jayden became violent. We fought, and at one point he pulled a knife on me. I knew he could not swim, so I jumped in the river to escape him. I can still remember him yelling how he would hunt me down and kill me for what I did to his sister."

Arbin watched Elizabeth. She was studying him as if she were trying to decide something. Finally, she said, "Thank you for telling me the truth."

"But you are still mad at me," said Arbin, sensing no real change in his dizziness.

"Yes, I am, but I feel you are telling me the truth and that's a start. It helps me understand who you are a little more. I'm still not sure if you are someone I want to get to know better." There was a moment of awkward silence until Elizabeth said, "The Little Green Mouse, I don't think I know that story."

Arbin smiled, happy to have something more pleasant to talk about. "I think my mother made it up. It is about several families of mice living in an old hollow tree. One of the young mice goes out to play in the freshly cut grass and comes back stained green. The rest of the mice laugh at her. When the stain does not come off, the father says she will grow out of it, and her mother says she still loves her. One day an owl lands in their tree and the mice cannot go outside to get food. The little green mouse could sneak out without being seen and collect food for the families. After a while, the owl tires of waiting and flies away. The little green mouse ends up being a hero. End of story."

"That's a cute story, I am sure Dylan will like it. I would have loved to see the needlepoint your mother did."

"It was the only thing I took before I left. It was my only link to my mother." Arbin took a deep breath and said, "I lost it in the fire back in Noor Point."

Elizabeth watched as Arbin's eyes watered. "We can work on making you another one."

Arbin looked at her, not sure what to say next. He gave her a smile. "I wonder how long we will have to wait before we get help?" Looking back toward the house, he noticed Dylan standing on the balcony of his room watching them.

"We're being watched," said Arbin with a simple wave toward Dylan.

Elizabeth looked back and smiled at Dylan. "He thinks you are a hero. Someone he wants to be more like. Demon hunter, he calls you."

"He should be more like Captain Eustace than me," said Arbin. When he looked back up at the balcony, Dylan was gone.

"I only told you that so you would know how others see you," said Elizabeth.

Arbin noticed that his dizziness had decreased. He smiled and was about to say something he thought would impress her when he heard, "Are you going after the rebels or not?"

Arbin turned and saw Dylan standing at his side. Seconds later, a Shadow Guard joined them, doing his best to catch his breath. It was clear Dylan had left his room without the guard noticing.

"Yes," said Arbin. "As soon as more men get here."

"Soon it will be too dark to go looking for them," said Dylan.

Arbin looked around and then said quietly, "I am starting to think that is what Bishop Sorren wants."

"Then we need to do something now." Dylan turned to his guard and said, "Go get the rest of the men and report back here."

"Yes, my lord," said the guard as he turned to obey the instructions he had been given.

"Impressive," said Arbin. "You are getting the hang of this lord thing really fast."

"Uncle Jessup has been giving me some advice," said Dylan, smiling. Arbin could see that he was enjoying showing off his authority.

A few minutes later, a group of seven armed men and a Seer were standing in front of Dylan.

"I was told you wanted to see us, my lord." said Hans. Arbin could see that Hans was a little upset with being summoned.

"I have decided that we are going to investigate the warehouse," said Dylan.

"It would be best if we waited for the additional men to arrive," said Hans. "I do not want to be outnumbered in a fight."

"I agree," said Dylan. "That's why we will investigate and confirm that there is a group there. We leave the Seer here to let the extra men know where we are. That way when they arrive, we will know how best to make our attack."

Arbin was a little surprised that Hans did not argue with Dylan's plan.

"Do you still remember the way?" Dylan asked Arbin.

Arbin nodded and Dylan said, "Show us."

Arbin led the way through the woods, stopping once they had approached the edge of the forest. Hans, Dylan and Arbin went on ahead to the edge of the forest while the rest waited in cover. It was early evening, but there was still enough light to see the building and the grass area that surrounded it. There were no lights or the smell of campfires in the area, including the river's edge. Arbin reminded them about the men that had been hiding in the grass. They studied the building and surroundings for several minutes until Dylan asked, "Where are they?"

"That is a good question," said Hans. "Is that trail of crushed grass where you crawled?"

"Yeah, I think so," said Arbin. "I was focused on not getting spotted."

"I don't see any other trails. I think it would be best if you followed your old trail while we watch, since you were so good at it before. If there is a problem, we will come to help."

Arbin looked over at Dylan, who excitedly gave him a big smile. Arbin took a deep breath and started crawling forward.

After a few minutes of crawling, Arbin looked back and when he could not see Hans or Dylan, he let himself slip into a Fade. He moved forward slowly, stopping every few feet to listen for movement or talking in the weeds. Before he knew it, he could see the top of the building's roof. He did not remember getting this close last time.

He paused and checked for Mia. He reached out, hoping to detect her presence. A feeling of dread rose in him when he got nothing. He relaxed more and tried again. Still nothing. The truth sunk in. Mia was not nearby.

Arbin pushed up to the very edge of where the grasses thinned. He was laying flat but had a good view of the area around the building. He tried to detect Mia, but again got nothing.

The door to the building was just a few yards away and the place where he had last detected Mia was just on the other side. Arbin could not stand it anymore. He stood up and ran for the door which he found unlocked. Arbin rushed in expecting to find a room full of men but found nothing. He stood in the room looking around. There was some evidence that people had been here, but it was empty now. Walking back outside, Arbin waved for Hans and Dylan. After a few minutes, he saw the entire group heading his way through the grass.

Arbin stood in the door, in the same place he had seen Bergman, and looked out at the sea of tall grass surrounding the building. It was hard to believe that this was the same place he had seen just a short while ago. There were several trails through the grass toward the river. It was easy to guess who made them. They seemed to disappear as the grass thinned several yards from the riverbank near a small boat dock. Something was different about the river, but he could not place it.

"Someone was here," said Hans as he joined Arbin. "They're gone now. It looks like they left in a hurry."

"So is Mia," said Arbin. "They took her and the children with them." Arbin leaned against the frame of the doorway and fought back tears. "I lost them again."

"Over here," said one of the men in the group.

Hans joined the man, but Arbin leaned back against the building wall, looking out at the river again.

"Arbin," shouted Hans. "Over here!"

Arbin forced himself up straight and slowly walked over to where Hans was standing.

"Blood," said Hans, pointing at the ground. "Lots of it, but no body." Hans looked out at the trails in the grass. "They probably dumped it in the river."

"That proves he was telling the truth," said Dylan as the group started their walk back through the woods to the Estate.

"It proves someone was killed, and someone was using the building, but it's dangerous to say anything more than that," said Hans.

As the small group came out of the forest into the backyard, Bishop Sorren met them. With uncharacteristic anger he said, "I gave instructions for you to wait for help to arrive."

"We were following Lord Dylan's instructions," said Hans, who stopped and signaled the rest of the guards to continue.

"We found blood and proof that someone was in the building," said Dylan as he joined Hans.

"Go to your room, Dylan!" said Bishop Sorren.

"Arbin was right," said Dylan. "We need to tell Uncle Jessup so he can find them again."

"We can continue this conversation in private, but for now I need you to go to your room." The Bishop looked at the guards standing there. "Back to your stations." The group moved slowly but found a burst of energy when Bishop Sorren shouted, "Now!"

Dylan turned and looked at Arbin, who nodded. Dylan walked toward the sunroom, not saying anything else.

Hans turned to leave, but Bishop Sorren said, "Not you!"

Hans stopped and looked back at the Bishop. It surprised Arbin when Hans calmly asked, "Did you have any luck with the reinforcements?"

Arbin could see that Bishop Sorren was thrown off by the question. He watched as Bishop Sorren took a few steps toward Hans, who was several inches taller. Somehow, the Bishop took on an air of authority that made him seem as large as Hans.

"You placed Dylan's life in danger," said Bishop Sorren.

Arbin saw Hans' shoulders lower slightly as he responded, "I was following orders."

"He is a child," said Bishop Sorren. "You are an adult, and I am his Guardian. Your orders come from me. You are dismissed! I will speak to Captain Eustace when he returns, and I will see to it you are never allowed anywhere near him again. Do you understand?"

"Yes sir," said Hans as he turned to leave.

"And take this person with you," said Bishop Sorren, pointing to Arbin.

"That's it?" asked Arbin. "You will do nothing about this? Why won't you accept that I was right?"

"The Sumner Family is my responsibility now, and I am doing what I need to protect them. Which is why you two are leaving and will have nothing to do with Dylan again." Bishop Sorren turned to leave but stopped, turned back to Arbin and said, "If I find out you have made any more of these false claims about Mr. Bergman to anyone else, I will have you arrested. Is that clear?" Not waiting for Arbin's answer, Bishop Sorren walked away and soon disappeared into the sunroom.

I am really starting to hate this place. Everything good seems to go bad here. Maybe I am cursed! Arbin took a deep breath and muttered, "What do we do now, Hans?"

When he did not get an answer, Arbin looked around and saw that Hans was well on his way toward the gate. He ran and caught up with him but could not get a response when he asked him again about what they should do next. Arbin quickly gave up trying to talk to him and just followed along behind.

This will be a long walk home, he thought.

Chapter 26 - Unexpected Help

"ARBIN, YOU AWAKE?" asked Masimo. "I'm making breakfast. You want some?"

Arbin sat up on the couch, rubbing his face with his hand. "What time is it?" he asked.

"Breakfast time, you want some?" said Masimo in a cheery voice. "You know you should really try sleeping in the bed. I've heard everyone's doing it now."

Arbin smiled and said, "Funny. What's for breakfast?"

"Whatever I can find left over in the pantry. I figured I better cook up what's left before we get more."

"Yeah, sure," said Arbin as he stretched. "Thanks."

"You tossed and turned a lot last night. Bad dreams?" asked Masimo from the kitchen.

"Sort of. I have something on my mind, and I cannot work it out."

"How about a nice cup of calming tea? That always works for me," said Masimo.

"Thanks," said Arbin, without even thinking about it. He really did not like tea, but he found it hard to resist Masimo's hospitality.

Arbin had been home for a few hours when Masimo got there last night. He was a little surprised to see him. Alex had told him he would return but thinking about him coming back and him being here were two different things.

Masimo was actually happy to see Arbin, and he kept him up late telling him about Casandra, the attack, and finally about his plans to marry. Masimo's excitement was obvious, and Arbin could do nothing but listen.

Even when he talked about marrying Elizabeth, Arbin could not stop himself from congratulating Masimo.

Soon Masimo had dragged the events of his absence out of Arbin, who really did not want to talk about it. Arbin did his best to hide any mention of his visits with Elizabeth.

"I heard about Chairman Sumner's death," said Masimo. "Casandra had promised to introduce me. Now there was a man that would have some splendid stories to tell. I heard you got to meet him. What was he like?"

"He was not what I expected. But it appears I was everything he expected."

Masimo was not sure how to respond, so he said, "I also heard you were up for the Guardian position. Better you than me."

"What do you mean?" said Arbin.

"I am the closest male relative after Dylan. Despite the issues of citizenship, I was a little worried that they might appoint me. The money would be nice, but it would really impede my work,"

"I did not really want the position either," said Arbin. "So, things kind of worked out for the best. I have some serious concerns about Bishop Sorren's appointment, even if it is supposedly a short time solution."

Masimo studied Arbin for a few minutes and in an obvious change of subject said, "I was glad to hear about Alex's promotion, even if it was because of a tragic event. I never met the prior High Seer, but I understood he was not an easy man to deal with."

"You have no idea," said Arbin. "Alex and I do not share the same vision for my future, but he always treated me fairly. I am sure Alex will make a much better High Seer. Last time I saw him, he was like a kid with a new toy."

Masimo studied Arbin for a few minutes and sounded a little embarrassed when he said, "When you saw Alex, did he say anything about my marriage offer?"

Arbin paused, not sure what to say. He could see the concern on Masimo's face, so he forced a smile. "Alex mentioned it. I do not think he was against it."

"That is a relief," said Masimo. "I am still waiting on their final decision." He paused, then said, "Elizabeth can be a little particular about things. I was getting a little worried. I just might take a chance and visit her brother today."

"He might be a little busy today," said Arbin. "I am sure he has lots to do getting ready for the Unification Day Celebration."

"That's true," said Masimo. "I've waited this long. I guess I can manage a few days more."

Arbin took a long sip from the teacup and set it down. It had gone cold, and he was really looking forward to both the tea and the conversation to be finished.

"You'll come to the wedding, of course. I know Elizabeth would want you there."

Arbin had not expected or even thought about that question. He looked at Masimo's smiling face and to his surprise said, "Sure, if I can. When is it?"

"It will be several months still. Lots to do and Casandra will want to be here for the planning."

"Months," said Arbin. "I might not be here then."

"Really, what happened?" asked Masimo.

"Both the Seers and the Council have no need for me now. They have made it clear I can leave any time," said Arbin. "I have appreciated your hospitality."

"When are you leaving?" asked Masimo.

"Soon. but I have something important to do first."

"Well, you are welcome to come back anytime," said Masimo as he returned to the kitchen. "Any friend of Elizabeth is a friend of mine."

Arbin could hear Masimo humming as he worked in the kitchen. Normally, his humming did not bother Arbin. However, today the reason for Masimo's happiness caused a sharp pain in his chest. He decided he could not sit around here any longer.

"I have changed my mind about breakfast," said Arbin as he started getting dressed. "I have a lot to do today and need to get started. I will get something from a street vendor but thanks anyway."

"That's probably for the best," said Masimo. "The mixture of what I found in the pantry is not really working. Give me a second and I will join you."

"I'm heading to speak with Captain Eustace," said Arbin in a heavy voice, hoping it would discourage Masimo tagging along.

"That's okay, I will walk with you as far as the gate. I need to go shopping. I will make something better tonight. We can have a celebration."

Arbin realized that he would not get out of having Masimo's company. At least it was only to the compound gate.

While Masimo was locking up his front door, Arbin looked around. The morning traffic had already started, and there were several people making their way toward the business district. Out of the corner of his eye, Arbin noticed a man sitting on the curb. He was not sure, but he thought he saw the same man sitting there when he came home last night.

"Arbin, you coming?" said Masimo.

"Yeah, sorry, just daydreaming," said Arbin.

"A pleasant morning walk is just the thing to get those cobwebs cleared," said Masimo.

Arbin caught up to Masimo and as they walked toward the compound. He could not stop thinking about the man he saw sitting on the curb, and the entire way to the Eastern Gate he fought the urge to look back over his shoulder.

"I'M NOT SURE HOW LONG Captain Eustace will be in today," said the Captain's assistant. "He just arrived back from a successful attack on an Adelist rebel camp. He is probably exhausted."

"I understand," said Arbin as he signed the logbook and took a seat. "If you could please tell him it is important."

The assistant knocked on Captain Eustace's door and it surprised Arbin to see him step out a few minutes later and signal for him to go in.

Captain Eustace was sitting behind his desk looking at some paperwork. His uniform jacket was hanging on one of the chairs by his desk, partly hiding a stack of logbooks. Arbin could see he was tired. This was the first time Arbin had ever seen the Captain out of full uniform and felt like he was intruding.

Captain Eustace looked up and pointed to the empty chair. Once Arbin was seated, Captain Eustace leaned back and said, "I know why you are here, Mr. Adean. I have already had a conversation with Hans, and I am quite disturbed by what he has told me."

Arbin let out a sigh of relief. He had been worried about how best to bring his concerns to the Captain.

"I know you are going to ask me to take some action and I assure you I will take appropriate action, but it may not be when or how you are expecting," said Captain Eustace.

Arbin sat up straight and was about to say something when Captain Eustace raised his hand.

"I have known Bergman for some time and your accusation is serious. Hans believes that there was a death at that old warehouse, but without a body, and you as the only witness, it is too early to arrest people."

Arbin sat back, "He is the person I saw speaking to Arron Schilling, both in Noor Point and on the Bridge of Sorrows. I also know Mia was in that building."

"Yes, Mia," said Captain Eustace, leaning back in his chair. "On that point, Hans said you were positive she was there, but it is not clear how you knew that."

Arbin took a deep breath and knew he was in dangerous territory. He stared at the Captain, not sure what to say.

"If you want my help, you need to tell me the truth."

Arbin nodded and whispered, "I sensed her."

"You what?" said Captain Eustace, leaning forward. His head turned to one side as if trying to hear something. "I don't think I understood you right."

"Mia is a Seer," said Arbin, watching the Captain's expression closely.

Captain Eustace sat back and Arbin continued, "I sensed her just like I would any other Seer."

"I have been told that women cannot be Seers," said Captain Eustace. "You know what you are saying, if true, puts you and this Mia on dangerous grounds with the Church."

Arbin nodded, "That's why I have told no one."

"Perhaps you are mistaken. Maybe it was the taint that the late High Seer Kindermann referred to. After all, she grew up with a Fade for a brother."

"She is a Seer. There is no such thing as a taint caused by being near a Fade."

"Both Bishop Sorren and the late High Seer Kindermann said otherwise. Why should I believe you?" asked Captain Eustace.

"Since I have been here, I have heard a lot of things that are not true," said Arbin. "They were wrong about fighting Fades. They are wrong about many other things as well. I do not really care if you believe me. I know that if you find Bergman you will find Mia and her children."

Captain Eustace said nothing but continued to study Arbin for a few minutes. "I am sure you have heard that the Shadow Guard attacked and defeated a sizable group of rebels."

"I just heard about it," said Arbin.

"The battle resulted in losses on our side, including Sergeant Gruber," said Captain Eustace. "The rebels were taken by surprise. They fought almost to the last man. Some were well trained, almost professional, the others died early in the battle. Overall, their forces were not what I had been led to expect."

"You almost sound sorry for winning."

"It is clear you do not understand warfare," said Captain Eustace. "But back to your earlier comments, it was Bishop Sorren that gave us the details on the rebel camp."

Arbin was not sure how to respond, so he just looked at the Captain.

"Bishop Sorren said he got the information from a trusted source. Want to guess who gave Bishop Sorren that information?"

Arbin suspected he knew who that person was but did not want to say it. He continued to stare at the Captain.

"Bergman gave him the location. Bishop Sorren never explained how Bergman came by the information, but the location was accurate."

Arbin felt his hopes for help slip away as he let that information sink in.

"Now," continued the Captain. "Can you tell me why the person you say is a leader of these rebels would give their location away so we could slaughter them?"

Arbin leaned back in his chair and said, "No."

"Neither can I," said Captain Eustace. "Now if you excuse me, I have more work to do."

Arbin stood, and just before he turned to leave asked, "Can you tell me why no one came to assist us yesterday?"

Captain Eustace looked down at the logbooks in front of him, "Hans asked me the same question. As I said, I have more work to do."

The Captain rang a small bell on his desk, and his assistant opened the office door.

Captain Eustace stood, "I know you will not stop looking. If you find something, please contact me before you take any action. I would also follow Bishop Sorren's advice and not make any more public accusations."

ARBIN LEFT CAPTAIN Eustace's office, not sure where he stood with him. The Captain expected him to keep looking for Mia, but it was also clear that he would get no help from him or anyone in authority. That left him with the same problem of no help and no idea of where to look. The only thing it had done was make him more suspicious of Bishop Sorren.

Thinking about all this was giving Arbin a headache. His dreams had kept him awake all night. There was something he was missing. He decided that the best thing to do was to return to the last place where he knew Mia had been. Maybe there he could find a clue. As Arbin left the compound using the Eastern Gate, his stomach reminded him he had eaten nothing yet. He looked around for a street vendor and noticed someone familiar. It was the same man that he had seen outside of Masimo's home this morning. This was no coincidence. Arbin now knew he was being followed.

If he used the north route to return to the old building, he would be too exposed and easily followed. He decided to cross over to the west side and use the busy streets of the city as a cover and hope he could lose the man.

Arbin stopped at a street vendor close to the Bridge of Sorrows. Partly because he was hungry, but mostly because he wanted to see what the person following him would do. Halfway through his meal, Arbin confirmed that the man was still there, but he was quite a ways back.

The Bridge of Sorrows was busy, as expected. Several people were gathered around the Memorial area, and the park was packed. Both the Government Building and the grandstand out in front had black drapes hung to honor Chairman Sumner. As he passed through the area, he heard people talking about how the Shadow Guard had finally defeated the Adelist rebels.

Arbin ducked behind a few pillars in the Memorial Section and let himself go into a Fade. When he returned to the bridge area, he peeked back and saw that he was still being followed. He had to guess that the man was just outside of the effective range of his Fade. *It is almost like he knows to do that,* thought Arbin.

Arbin released the Fade and hoped to lose his tail by weaving in and out of the foot traffic. *This is not working,* he thought. *The streets are too crowded. I cannot get enough distance from him.* As Arbin neared the end of the bridge, he thought. *I will have to make a run for it while he is still tied up in the crowd.*

The road along the river through the dock section would be the best route to where he wanted to go, but he would reach it too soon and the person tailing him would see him heading that way. Arbin decided he would walk a little further, turn and run, then cut back over toward the river when he could. He hoped this would let him lose his tail.

Arbin weaved from side to side as he reached the end of the bridge and pretended to be looking over the edge. He took one last look to see how far the man was behind him. Arbin could not see him, but was sure he was there, so he followed his plan.

When he left the bridge, he kept walking straight until he reached the next intersection, where he did a quick right and ran as fast as he could, making his way through the crowd. After a few blocks, he turned right again and could see the river. The street ahead of him was clear of traffic, so Arbin made a dash as fast as he could. He felt sure his plan would work now. All he had to do was make a left once he reached the river road and keep going.

Arbin took one last look behind him as he approached the river road to make sure he was not being followed. When Arbin looked back to where he was going, he saw the man that had been following him just a few feet in front of him. The two ran into each other and both tumbled to the ground.

His 'tail' was faster to recover and stood up holding a knife. The same kind of knife used by the Adelist assassins. Arbin tried to scramble to his feet, crawling away from his attacker as he did, all the time expecting to feel the point of the knife. He tripped and rolled onto his back. As he looked back toward his attacker, he was surprised to see the man just standing there looking at him.

"Sorry," the man said, putting away his knife. "Force of habit." The man extended his hand as if to help Arbin up, "You really gave me a scare. Now, we really need to go."

Arbin took his hand and stood up and stepped back from the man, not sure if he should run or not. He finally managed to say, "Go? What do you mean go?"

"Mr. Winters wants to speak to you, Mr. Adean."

"Mr. Winters," said Arbin, exhaling a quick laugh. "Are you kidding me?"

"This way," said the man walking north along the river in the same direction Arbin had intended on heading.

"Wait," said Arbin as he watched the man walk away. "You mean you are not here to kill me?"

The man looked back, "Like I said, Mr. Winters wants to talk to you."

"You could have just said that earlier instead of following me around and scaring me half to death."

"Just because I wasn't here to kill you don't mean that someone else wasn't trying to do so," said the man. "In fact, I dealt with one person already."

Arbin looked confused. "You mean you killed someone that was trying to kill me?"

"We don't have time for this," said the man. "Please hurry. We need to get out of sight before you are discovered again."

At the next intersection, they turned and Arbin followed the man as they did a zigzag course through the city until they were in what he guessed was the northernmost section of the docks. The area was littered with warehouses. The man finally knocked on the door of a warehouse and when it opened, he pointed for Arbin to go in. The man remained outside and closed the door behind Arbin. It took a few minutes for Arbin's eyes to adjust to the low light, but when they did, he saw Jayden and two other men inside.

"About time you got here," said Jayden as he walked over to Arbin, putting his hand on his shoulder and directing him away from the small group.

Jayden leaned close to Arbin and said, "You need to call me Mr. Winters here. Do you understand?"

Arbin was still a little confused by what was happening but nodded as he continued to look around. "Where have you been?" he asked. "I really needed you!"

"I will explain it all to you when we have more privacy," said Jayden, signaling with his hands for Arbin to speak softer.

"I found Mia," Arbin whispered.

"Where is she?" asked Jayden, holding on to both of Arbin's shoulders. His voice was loud enough to get the attention of the other two men in the warehouse who made their way over to them.

"I do not know where she is now! I found them, but by the time I got some help Bergman took off with them. He has them."

"Slow down," said Jayden. "You are not making sense. Where did you find them, and what does Bergman have to do with it?"

Arbin was going to explain when the man that had been following him stepped into the warehouse and said, "He is safe now. I had to kill someone to get him here." He walked over to Jayden and held out a knife. "I took this off someone who was stalking him."

Jayden looked at it, "That's one of ours."

"He's been marked," said the man. "That means there will be more."

Jayden pointed to the man holding the knife and said, "This is Wagner. The older gentleman there is Schwartz, this warehouse belongs to his family. The skinny kid next to him is Braun." Each man nodded as Jayden said his name.

Jayden turned back to Arbin, "It's time for you to tell me what's going on."

The group gathered around as Arbin told the story of finding the building with Mia in it and Bergman killing someone. He also told them about the fight with Bishop Sorren and his delay in getting help.

"Who is Mia?" asked Schwartz.

"My sister," said Jayden. "She and her children were kidnapped, and I have been looking for them."

Wagner sat on a nearby crate and slowly rubbed the stubble of his beard.

"Something got you worried, Wagner?" asked Jayden.

"You didn't say you were making a move against Bergman," said Wagner. "I only agreed to help your friend because you said he could make it worth my while. If Bergman is after him, he is as good as dead."

"You know Bergman?" said Arbin.

"Never spoke to him personally, but I spent time near him. Also did some special work for him," said Wagner. "I mostly dealt with Mueller, his number two."

"Do you know where he took Mia and her children?" asked Arbin.

Wagner ignored the question and pulled out his knife and carved on the wood crate nearby.

"Do you know anything about where my sister is?" asked Jayden as he moved to put some crates between him and Wagner.

"Your friend mentioned Bishop Sorren. There was a meeting between the Bishop and Bergman where a woman and her children were discussed. It sounded like a lot of money would be made off some deal involving them," said Wagner.

"I knew it!" shouted Arbin. "Wagner, you need to come with me to tell Captain Eustace what you know about the Bishop and Bergman."

Arbin's outburst surprised both Wagner and Jayden. Wagner laughed and said, "Why would I want to do something like that?"

"Because Bergman was responsible for the death of Duke Henry." Arbin looked at Jayden and saw that he was still wearing the knife he took from him. He felt a big relief and said, "I now believe he is also the one who killed Chairman Sumner."

"That's possible," said Wagner. "But I will not be the one to turn him in."

"You cannot trust him," said Arbin. "He kills the people that work for him. Look what he did to the person at the old building. He also killed someone named Arron Schilling."

Wagner laughed and with a smile said, "Bergman did not kill Arron."

"What about the rebel camp?" said Arbin. "It was Bergman and Bishop Sorren that gave Captain Eustace the location so they could be attacked."

The group was suddenly quiet.

"What's wrong?" asked Arbin.

"We were part of that group," said Jayden. "Originally the group was told they would cause minor problems. Hitting supply trains, stuff like that. But shortly after I joined, they received orders to just sit and wait for additional supplies and recruits. After a while I got tired of just sitting around."

"That is when Mr. Winters talked us into scouting out the routes for the supply wagons," said Braun. "Plus, we identified some nice rich homes to hit once we got the okay to start up again."

"We were gone for one day," said Wagner. "When we got back, we saw that the Shadow Guards had attacked the camp. It looked like they killed almost everyone. All their bodies stacked up like kindling, waiting for the Shadow Guard to burn them. My brother was one of them."

"I find it hard to believe that Bergman was behind the attack," said Schwartz. "It also does not explain why he is after you."

"That's easy," said Jayden. "He can tie Bergman to the murders of Duke Henry and Chairman Sumner. He can also link the Bishop to the murders and the Adelist supporters." Jayden studied the faces of the group, then said, "I'm done with the Adelist. You can do what you want, but I need help hunting down this Bergman and saving my sister and her kids. Will you help me?"

The three men were quiet and looked at each other. After a few minutes Wagner said, "You're sure Bergman is behind the attack that killed my brother?"

"Yes, Captain Eustace told me himself," said Arbin.

"I wonder what would happen to us if we tried to rejoin Bergman?" said Braun.

"You become a loose end," said Jayden. "If he had no problem ordering your death before, what makes you think he will let you live now?"

Wagner put away his knife. "Okay, I will help you find the people responsible for my brother's death. After I kill them, we part ways."

Schwartz and Braun nodded in agreement.

Jayden turned to Arbin and said, "Do you have any idea where Bergman took Mia and the children?"

"I was on the way back to where I saw them last. There is something about the place that has been bothering me. I was hoping to pick up their trail."

"All right, you know the way so lead on," said Jayden.

Schwartz opened the warehouse door and looked out. As he did, Arbin saw a barge going by. "Wait!" said Arbin, pointing toward the river. "That is what has been bothering me. I think I just figured out where she is."

"What is it?" asked Jayden.

"The barge," said Arbin. "The first time I was at that old building there was a barge tied up at a dock nearby. When we went back, the barge was gone, and we found trails leading through the grass to the river. That is where they are. On the river."

"The river is a big place. They could be long gone by now," said Braun.

"I do not care," said Arbin. "If there is a chance of finding them, I will take it. Even if I have to do it myself."

"There is one slight problem with that," said Jayden. "You're a marked man. If you go wandering around by yourself, you will end up dead."

"Here, this might help," said Wagner, handing Arbin a knife and belt. "I took this off the person who wanted to kill you."

Arbin looked at it. The knife was just like the ones he had seen in Captain Eustace's office. He called Jayden closer and whispered, "Do you really think I will have to use it? You know I was never any good with these things."

"No one else knows that," said Jayden, patting his knife. "A person will always think twice about attacking someone with a weapon. That may be all the time you need to get away. Besides, this is a very special knife."

"I know," said Arbin. "It's just like the one Dylan gave me. It is also like the one that killed Chairman Sumner. I think the best thing to do is give them to Captain Eustace so he can prove you are not a killer."

Jayden looked back at the small group of men and moved Arbin further away from them and whispered, "Keep that to yourself," as he looked back toward the small group. "I used the knife to get into the graces of the Adelist. They think I earned it, just like Wagner did. The status that comes with this knife is what gives me any power in this group. I am not giving up my knife. I told you before. I will do whatever I need to do to protect my sister and her children. I don't care if it causes you a problem."

Arbin saw how serious Jayden was and said, "Calm down. I was only trying to protect you. If I do not give Captain Eustace the knife that Dylan gave me, he will hunt you down and take it."

"Then give him the one we just gave you," said Jayden.

Arbin studied the knife he was holding. It looked just like the one that Jayden had. "Okay, that could work," he said. "Now, can you do me a favor?"

"What's that?" asked Jayden.

"Can you show me how to wear this thing?" asked Arbin, holding out the belt and knife.

Chapter 27 - Best of Intentions

"WELL, WHAT'S THE WORD?" asked Jayden as Arbin entered the warehouse door.

"Narrow minded idiot," said Arbin, slamming the door behind him. He walked over to an empty section of the warehouse.

Jayden looked back to Wagner, Braun and Schwartz, who were sitting on some crates. He signaled for them to wait and walked over to Arbin.

"What happened?" asked Jayden, watching Arbin as he paced in small circles. When Arbin did not answer him, Jayden grabbed him by the shoulder and demanded, "Are they going to help us or not?"

Arbin looked up at him, "Oh, they will help us, but it may not be in the way we wanted."

Jayden let go of Arbin and said, "What's that supposed to mean?"

"I thought he was more open minded than the others. At least that's how he acted all the other times I talked to him."

Jayden grabbed Arbin by the arm, "Tell me what happened."

Arbin pulled his arm loose. "Both Captain Eustace and Alex welcomed the information that Bergman and his men might be on a boat or barge. They will start checking the docks today."

"So, what's the problem?" asked Jayden.

"Alex is the problem. He spoke to me after the meeting. He asked how I knew Mia was in the old building and I told him."

"You what!" said Jayden loudly. The other men turned to look, expecting there to be trouble.

"I thought he would be different," said Arbin apologetically while putting his hands in front of him. "He has accepted so many other things I have told him."

"You fool," said Jayden. He shook his head as he turned and took a few steps away from Arbin. Jayden spun, walked up to Arbin and grabbed him by the front of his shirt. "This was a stupid idea. I should have never let you talk me into it!"

"Please calm down," said Arbin, stepping back slightly, and breaking Jayden's grip on his shirt. "You know we do not have enough people to search everywhere and if we found them, we could not fight them."

"Yeah, but why would you ever tell them about Mia? You know what they do to women who claim to be gifted."

"Keep your voice down," said Arbin, looking over at the three men who were watching them. When he looked back, Jayden was pointing his knife at him. He could see the anger in his eyes.

The two stood staring at each other for a few seconds, waiting for one or the other to make the first move when they were interrupted by Wagner saying, "Everything okay, Winters?"

Jayden continued to stare at Arbin. "If anything happens to her, you're dead this time." He turned quickly and walked toward the other two men. "Time to check the docks. Thanks to our friend here, the Shadow Guards will do the bulk of the work for us. We watch them and then we will figure out what to do once they find Bergman. Remember, my sister and her children should be with them."

"What about him?" said Wagner, pointing back toward Arbin. "You still want me babysitting him?"

"No!" said Jayden. The anger in his voice was unmistakable. "The genius can take care of himself. Wagner, your job is to make sure you kill that bastard Bergman."

Wagner looked over at Arbin and smiled. "I was hoping you'd say that."

Arbin watched as the group exited the warehouse. Jayden was the last one out. He stood in the doorway with his knife still in his hand. Arbin wanted to say something but stopped when he saw Jayden shake his head and step out, leaving the door open behind him.

ARBIN STOOD IN THE warehouse doorway, not sure what to do next. Jayden had made it clear he did not want his help. *I am not going to be able to rescue Mia alone,* he thought. *I might get close enough to detect her, but Bergman knows who I am. That will make it harder to hide from him.* That was one of the reasons Arbin visited Captain Eustace and Alex. People were used to them walking around town. He hoped Bergman would not panic if he saw them on the docks.

He had also hoped Alex would have the Seers help search for Mia. Alex made it clear he would search for her. Arbin was afraid to think of what Alex would do now if he found her.

"How could I be so wrong about him?" he muttered angrily. "I wonder if Elizabeth could talk him out of it." Arbin shook his head. "That's another awful idea. I would just get her in trouble as well."

Arbin leaned against the doorway and looked up at the sky. *It must be well past midday, already. With the Ceremony only a day away, I am sure the streets will be packed. I guess I could use the crowds to hide in. I cannot just sit here and wait for something to happen.*

Arbin made his way through the crowds, stopping occasionally to search for any evidence of Mia. It surprised him how quickly he reached the Western Gate to the Government Compound, where he found a group of Shadow Guards gathered along with a few Seers. Lubin was one of them. Arbin did his best to pass by unnoticed, but soon heard Lubin calling his name.

"Hello, Lubin," said Arbin as he walked back over toward him, putting out his hand. "Are you going to be part of the search party?"

Lubin accepted Arbin's hand, "I thought you would join us, Arbin?"

"No, I was just out for a walk," said Arbin, "Alex made it clear that this was to be Seer Core only."

Arbin could see that Lubin was uncomfortable with him referring to the new High Seer by just his first name.

"I am sure the High Seer has an excellent reason," said Lubin. "He will join us in a few minutes if you want to speak to him again."

"No, I think I will follow his advice and stay out of your way."

Lubin patted Arbin on the shoulder, "I'm sure that will be the best thing."

It disturbed him how fast the two people he thought were on his side had become so narrow minded. They were quickly becoming an obstacle to his saving Mia. He could not just walk off saying nothing, so just after he turned to walk away, he turned back and said, "Do you want me to ask Masimo if you can come to his wedding?"

Lubin said nothing, but Arbin could tell he hit a sore spot. "Good hunting," he said as he continued to walk toward the Bridge of Sorrows. By the time he reached the bridge, he was feeling depressed and useless. He decided to go sit in the park for a while. It was the only place he could really call his own. As he walked toward the park, he started to appreciate the name of the bridge.

Arbin stopped at the memorial section and looked at the stages set up near the Government Building. They soon would be full of music and speeches. A celebration that would last for a week, and if things did not change, would be a constant reminder of his failure that would haunt him each year.

Arbin's normal seat was taken, so he made his way down to the water's edge and sat on some boulders. The lapping of the water helped to drown out the noise of the crowds. He looked out and watched as a few boats floated by, wondering if Mia might be on one of those. He watched them continue down the river as far as he could see. He had seen boats like that floating past Noor Point but never thought about where they had come from. Braun was right, the river is big and there are lots of little places on it just like Noor Point.

Arbin remembered riding through two towns on his journey here. The first was not really a proper town, more like a rest stop. The other one, named Tobin, was not far from here. He could probably see it if he strained his eyes. *Not a bad little town,* he thought. *I think I could even enjoy living there. I think I even saw a few warehouses and docks. Now that the Guardian thing will not happen, I could always give my old line of work a try.*

After a few minutes Arbin sat up straight and said, "Warehouses and docks!" Arbin strained his eyes trying to see the docks from here. "I need to find Jayden."

He started walking back towards the bridge and then stopped, remembering the anger in Jayden's eyes. How would he react if Arbin sent him on a wild goose chase? He decided it would be better if he checked it out by himself.

Arbin had traveled through Tobin using a road that ran along the eastern shore. He was not sure if he could get there from the west side of the river. He knew that walking would take some time, so he decided he would try to pay someone to take him. It took a lot of begging and several coins before he found someone with a cart that would give him a lift.

He knew he was going faster than by foot, but the pace of the cart was driving him crazy. It took him about twenty minutes before he reached the town of Tobin. It did not have much of a business area, but that was where he had the cart drop him off. After a few minutes of searching, he found the docks. The Capital had its docks on the west side, but to his surprise Tobin had docks on both sides. It did not have a bridge but had a ferry that carried traffic across the river.

There were a few small boats on both sides of the river, but there was also a good size barge on the western side. It was too far for him to sense Mia. He thought about taking the ferry across, but they said he would need to wait for more people or pay the full price, an amount which he did not have after renting the cart. So, the only thing he could do was to stand on the eastern docks and watch for any signs of Bergman and his men.

He did not have to wait long. A young boy came out of a hatch and started running toward the ramp. A man standing by the ramp grabbed him, picked him up and looked back toward the hatch as another man came out limping and rubbing his shin. The first man shoved the boy back towards the limping man, who then picked up the boy and carried him back below deck. The entire thing was over in just a blink of the eye. Arbin continued to stare, hoping he would see something else, but the scene on the boat appeared as peaceful as before.

Arbin did not know what Mia's children looked like. Jayden said she had twins. A boy named Mika, and a girl named Flora. Jayden said they were about six years old. The boy looked like the right age, and it was clear he did not want to be on that barge. That was all he needed.

He studied the barge and shore, trying to get a good count of enemies. He knew there were at least two on the barge. He had seen three men standing outside a nearby building smoking. There was also someone walking back and forth to the barge with supplies. Too many for him to fight. He needed to go get Jayden.

Arbin made his way back to the road and looked around for a ride. Unable to find one and worried about the vanishing daylight, Arbin prepared himself to make the trip back on foot. He ran when he could and walked when he had to. By the time he had reached the Bridge of Sorrows, he was out of energy and the sun was getting lower. He was not sure where to find Jayden but guessed the warehouse where they had been hiding would be the best bet. Arbin made his way through the crowded streets, aware of how much time was being wasted. He let out a sigh of relief when he spotted Schwartz standing outside the building. Arbin ran the last few feet to the door, pushed past Schwartz and shouted, "Jayden, I found them," as he entered the building.

Wagner was talking to Braun when Arbin entered, but he did not see Jayden. "What are you shouting about?" asked Wagner.

"Where's Jay ...," Arbin paused and then said, "Mr. Winters?" Arbin took a breath, "I found his family."

"He just stepped out for a few minutes," said Braun. "Nature calls," he said with a laugh.

"Something funny?" said Jayden from the warehouse door.

Braun looked away as Jayden entered.

"I found them," said Arbin, turning and walking toward Jayden. "But we have to hurry. I think they are getting ready to leave."

Jayden walked over and put his hand on Arbin's shoulder, "Are you sure it's them?"

Arbin continued to catch his breath, "I saw the boy. They are in the next town. I had to run to get here."

"Next town," said Jayden. How long will it take to get there?"

"Thirty minutes by cart. Longer by foot," said Arbin. "We need to go now."

"Okay, we will," said Jayden. "One of you, go get us a ride."

Schwartz said, "I'm on it."

Jayden turned back to Arbin, "How many guards?"

"There were two on the barge, and a few on shore by a nearby building," said Arbin. "I also saw someone taking items from that building to the barge."

"All right, as soon as Schwartz gets back, we go!"

Chapter 28 - A Little Fresh Air

CAPTAIN EUSTACE AND three Shadow Guard, all armed with pistols, were sitting on horseback watching the flow of traffic at the western entrance to the Bridge of Sorrows when Arbin and his cart approached them. There was no way to cross the bridge without going past them.

"Good afternoon, Mr. Adean," said Captain Eustace. "You and your friends appear to be in a hurry."

"We are just doing our best to escape this maddening crowd," said Jayden. "I do not know how you can stand the noise and the stink."

Captain Eustace studied the group in the small cart. Arbin had been under that stare before and noticed how the Captain's eyes took in that everyone was armed. The longer the Captain was quiet, the more nervous Arbin got. "This is Mr. Winters, Captain," said Arbin, a little louder than he intended. "We talked about him before. I am sure you remember."

"Ah yes, Mr. Winters," said Captain Eustace, nodding to Jayden. "So nice to finally meet you. I see he has returned your missing knife."

Arbin reached down and touched his knife without thinking.

"I guess Bishop Sorren was right to close that investigation," said Captain Eustace.

"Arbin has told me you are looking for his friend and the men that kidnapped her," said Jayden, looking calmly at the Captain.

"That's correct," said Captain Eustace, looking at Jayden for a few more seconds. Turning back to Arbin he said, "I am sorry to say we have had no luck yet."

"That's okay," said Arbin, a little too quickly. "I know you are doing your best." He gave Captain Eustace a smile.

"If you'd excuse us, Captain," said Jayden. "We would like to be on our way before it gets too late."

Captain Eustace pulled his horse back a few steps, "Of course, Mr. Winters. Where were you going again?"

"Tobin," said Arbin. "Not far. I was there earlier today. Nice little town."

"Good. If we find your friends, we will know where to find you."

Arbin thanked the Captain, and soon they were on their way.

As Arbin and his cart disappeared into the bridge traffic, Captain Eustace turned to one of his men, "Get two more units. I think it's time we got some fresh air for ourselves."

THE FERRY DID NOT TAKE long to cross the river, but Jayden did not enjoy any part of it. They had agreed that as soon as they arrived, they would ride past the area of the dock and would park the cart where it could not be seen. It was late in the day, almost early evening, but there was still plenty of sunlight left and it took them a while before they found a suitable place to leave the wagon. Next, the group made their way to a spot where they could sit and watch what was going on around the barge.

"Okay," said Arbin. "Any ideas?"

"First we save Mia, Mika and Flora," said Jayden. "Bergman can come later."

"The only reason I'm here is to get revenge on Bergman," said Wagner.

"I promise you, once my family is safe, we will go after Bergman," said Jayden.

"If I have the chance to get Bergman, I am going for it," said Wagner.

"Wow," said Arbin, putting his hands up slightly. "I guess I should have said do we have a plan on how to do those things?"

"I think it is pretty clear," said Jayden, looking at Wagner. "I go for Mia on the barge and Wagner can take care of Bergman and his men in the barn."

"Agreed!" said Wagner.

The group looked back to the warehouse where they now counted five men standing in the doorway smoking.

"We will need something to keep those guys from coming out of that building once I go for the barge." said Jayden. "Any ideas?"

"The cart," said Schwartz. "We get the door closed and block it with the cart. It won't hold for long, but it should keep them busy for a few minutes."

"Okay," said Jayden. "I guess we can try to use that to our advantage." Jayden turned to Wagner, "If Bergman is busy with you, it will be easier for me to get Mia. Schwartz, you're with me."

Schwartz asked, "Why me?"

Jayden turned to the others and asked, "Who here can swim?" Schwartz and Arbin raised their hands. "That's why." He turned to Wagner and said, "You get Braun."

"That's fine with me," said Wagner. "At least he can handle a knife."

"What about me?" asked Arbin.

There was an uncomfortable silence, then Jayden smiled and said, "You get to use your special talent and act as scout and lookout,"

Arbin glanced over to the warehouse and the five men standing outside, "Not again."

"It will be fine. Just like in the good old days,"

"I do not think we are talking about the same old days," said Arbin. "Let's hope Mia remembers what to do when you give your signal."

"I'm counting on it."

"Then, I guess closing the door is my job," said Arbin.

"Okay, sounds like we have a plan," said Jayden. "Wagner, you and Braun get the cart. Schwartz and I will get ready to rush the barge. Arbin, you scout. If there is an issue, you walk away. We will hold off until you give Wagner the signal. Everyone got it?"

There was a slight pause and Arbin was relieved when Wagner slapped Braun on the shoulder and they both headed back toward the cart. Jayden and Schwartz started moving toward some cover closer to the barge. That left Arbin staring at the buildings he was to scout.

Arbin waited a few minutes to give Wagner time to get the cart. Then, he let himself go into a Fade and walked casually toward the group of buildings. There were two buildings connected to each other. The farthest to his right was the warehouse that the rebels were using. The building door, that was his assignment, was still open, but fortunately the smoke breaks were over. Unfortunately, he could not see inside from where he was. There were some crates and barrels against the wall near the spot where the two buildings met each other. He walked up to them and did his best to look like he belonged there. They did not give him a lot of cover, but it was something. Arbin took a deep breath and made sure he was in a Fade. He did his best to control his fears while watching the building door.

In the old days, when Jayden was pulling one of his jobs, Arbin would act as a lookout. Mia would find a place nearby where she could act as a distraction if needed. When he was ready, Jayden would go into a Fade which both Mia and Arbin could detect letting them know he had started his job. If there was a problem, Arbin would go into a Fade warning Mia who would make a scene, giving Jayden the distraction that he needed to get away.

Today, it was a little different because Arbin was already in a Fade and he was well out of Mia's range. He was not sure how it would work this time. Arbin understood Jayden's reference to his talent. Now, all he had to do was to get the door closed and somehow signal Wagner. Jayden would use that distraction, go into a Fade hoping Mia would remember to start a distraction on the boat giving Jayden the chance to attack. He figured he would stay in the Fade until he closed the door but needed to drop it to signal Wagner.

Arbin was not sure how things were going with Jayden, but he did not see Wagner or Braun anywhere. He was not sure how much longer the door would be clear. *What now?* he thought. *I cannot wait here forever. I am sure they are outside of my Fade range. We are running out of time. I need to check out the building.*

Arbin stepped out from behind the boxes and took a stroll toward the warehouse entrance. As he walked by, he looked inside and was dismayed to see at least fifteen men. Some were standing, others sitting on boxes, but there were many more than he had ever imagined. Arbin continued to walk past the door. He turned around and headed back to a spot where he could close the door. It was time to signal Wagner, but he was nowhere to be seen.

My Fade must be preventing them from seeing me, thought Arbin. *I have no choice but to drop my Fade.*

Arbin positioned himself at the door and started to close it as he dropped his Fade. Shortly after that, he heard a cart approaching. He looked up to the frightening sight of Wagner and Braun heading his way at high speed. He froze for a few seconds, the door not even halfway closed, trying to decide if he had time to close the door before the cart arrived. The problem was, some men in the building also heard the cart and stepped out to see who was coming. It was hard to tell if they were more surprised by the charging cart or Arbin standing just a few feet behind them trying to close the door.

The men by the door ran a few feet either way to make room for the fast approaching cart. One yelling, "Watch where you're going, you stupid idiot." Anything else he had to say was cut short by Wagner, who jumped from the seat of the cart and drove his shoulder and blade into the man, knocking him to the ground.

Wagner regained his footing, turned toward Arbin and yelled, "You were supposed to close the door!" Arbin yelled back, "You were supposed to wait for me to close it!" The rebels now knew they were under attack and that Arbin was one of the attackers.

The man nearest to Arbin took a swing at him which he dodged, but the second man hit Arbin in the stomach knocking him to the ground. He looked up and saw that both men had left him alone to avoid the horse of the cart that Braun had driven through the small group of men, stopping just short of where Arbin lay on the ground.

Braun jumped from the cart to help Arbin up and was attacked by the two men he had just chased off Arbin. Braun grabbed one of his attackers while Arbin pushed the other away, causing the man to stumble backward. Arbin heard Braun yell, and he turned to see the man he was struggling with stab him in the side. Arbin watched Braun crumple to the ground. He could see Wagner using his knife more successfully on the other side of the cart. He also saw several men come out of the building door like ants.

Braun's killer advanced on Arbin from his right. Arbin took a few steps back and was thinking of where he could hide. The thought of abandoning Wagner embarrassed and angered him.

Arbin startled himself when he yelled as loud as he could and ran straight at Braun's killer. Arbin pushed him with all his strength, driving him backwards and onto his back. Arbin did not stop, but ran past the fallen man, putting some distance between him, before turning around to face the next man who he was sure would be close behind him.

No one followed Arbin. Instead, the small group of men had stopped what they were doing to look at the group of charging horses coming from the direction of the ferry. Arbin also found himself frozen in place, staring as Captain Eustace and what looked like ten or twelve Shadow Guards on horseback, charging towards them with swords out.

There was a sudden sound of thunder, and wood cracking as Arbin saw a man near the building doorway drop and parts of the wood wall near him splinter. Arbin looked back at the charging men and saw a cloud of gray smoke and knew they were firing guns. The area around the door exploded with activity. Not from gun fire but from men running to get away from what was coming.

Arbin felt the panic that had scattered the others, even though he knew they were not coming for him. He stood there watching, unable to move. He saw Wagner moving with the others away from the charging horses. Soon Arbin, the cart and the building exit were surrounded by men on horseback. Some rebels tried to fight back. One rebel stabbed a horse, causing the rider to fall, but was quickly cut down by a guard on horseback behind him.

Through the chaos, Arbin saw a familiar thin blond hair figure trying to make his way toward the edge of the fighting. *Bergman! He is getting away.*

Arbin found himself moving toward Bergman. He knew if Bergman saw him, he would not stand a chance. He let himself go into a Fade, hoping the fighting would keep him unnoticed. The closer he got to Bergman, the faster he ran. At the last second, Arbin pulled out his knife and yelled, "Bergman!" thrusting it at him.

To Arbin's surprise Bergman stopped and turned, causing Arbin's knife to miss. Bergman's reflexes were fast, and he delivered a punch into Arbin's left arm as he passed by him. The pain surprised Arbin, and he lost his balance, falling and rolling on to his back. He looked at his arm and saw blood. He looked back at Bergman but did not see a knife. What he saw was the look of recognition come over Bergman's face.

Bergman said nothing, but Arbin saw a frightening smile of satisfaction grow on his face as he headed toward Arbin, now with knife in hand. Arbin knew he could not get away in time, so he just held his own knife out in front of him as if he expected to scare Bergman off with it.

Arbin heard thunder again and saw Bergman's expression go from one of surprise to one of pain. Bergman dropped to his knees, dropped his knife and then fell face forward with his head just a foot or so from Arbin.

Arbin looked up and saw Captain Eustace on horseback with his pistol pointing toward where Bergman had been standing.

"Is he dead?" asked Captain Eustace as he steadied his horse. Arbin gave Bergman's head a couple of kicks with his foot and nodded.

"Too bad. I wanted to talk to him. Maybe if I had let him kill you, he would have surrendered." Arbin just stared at the Captain, not sure if he was kidding.

Another Shadow Guard soon joined the Captain. Because of the armor, Arbin almost did not recognize him. Captain Eustace turned and asked, "Where do we stand, Sergeant Faber?"

"We're holding a few that didn't make it out of the building in time. We killed five and about six or seven took off when we arrived." Hans paused, "There were some minor injuries. We lost one horse and two others have injuries."

Captain Eustace said nothing, almost like he had not heard. Instead, he looked back at Arbin and without turning away said, "Send a unit to recover as many as you can. Kill any that resist."

Arbin got back to his feet and looked around at the scene of the brief battle. It was hard to believe it had just happened. He was looking at the body of Braun when Captain Eustace asked, "Where is the girl?"

In the middle of the battle, Arbin had forgotten all about Mia. He looked back towards the dock and saw that the barge was gone. He looked down the river and could just make out the outline of a boat heading downstream. "She's gone," he said.

The Captain followed Arbin's gaze down river. "And Mr. Winters?" asked Captain Eustace.

"Gone as well, I guess."

"Captain Eustace," said Lubin as he rode up next to the Captain.

Captain Eustace turned towards him, "Yes, Seer Lubin. You have something to report?"

Lubin looked at Arbin then said, "Captain, I am sure I detected a Fade for just a few seconds."

Captain Eustace turned to Arbin and asked, "Can you detect a Fade here?" Arbin closed his eyes, took a deep breath. He opened his eyes and said simply, "No."

"You said Mia had children, twins I believe," Captain Eustace said in more of a statement than a question.

"That's right," said Arbin. "A boy and a girl."

"Is there any chance that the boy could have been a Fade?" asked Captain Eustace.

"I would not know. I never met her children."

Captain Eustace turned back to Lubin, "Check the area just to be safe. Have Arbin help you."

"I am sorry, Captain," said Arbin. "But Bishop Sorren has made it clear that I am not good enough for the Seer Core. Plus, as you can see, I am wounded. If you will excuse me, I would like to go home."

Captain Eustace looked at Arbin for a few seconds, then said, "We need to have a serious talk about this."

Arbin nodded and as he turned to make his way to the cart, he heard Captain Eustace say, "Seer Lubin. There may be a possibility that Mia and her children escaped on a boat. When you finish checking the area, I want you and your unit to check the neighboring towns."

"Shouldn't I do that first?" asked Lubin.

Arbin stopped, turned and looked at the Captain who, to his surprise, was still watching him.

"If the boy is a Fade it will not matter," said Captain Eustace as he studied Arbin's reactions. "If he is not, they should be traveling slow enough for you to catch up with them."

A feeling of panic came over Arbin and he was about to say something but stopped when Captain Eustace said to him, "Don't you have someplace to be?" The Captain did not wait for Arbin's reply but turned and rode over to where his men had a group of rebels sitting on the ground, held at sword point. Arbin did not recognize anyone in the group.

Arbin made sure that the Shadow Guard knew that Braun was not one of the rebels. He did not know who his family was, so he accepted the Shadow Guards offer to handle his remains.

During the crossing, Arbin looked down the river wondering where Jayden, Mia and her children were. Once he was safely across, he looked back at the scene he had just left. He thought about just heading south but decided that there was only one place he wanted to be now, so he headed his cart back toward the Sumner estate.

Chapter 29 - Where Leads the Heart

ARBIN FOUND IT A LITTLE difficult to climb with the pain in his arm, but soon made it to the balcony outside of Elizabeth's room. He had used his Fade several times on the way here. He knew it would be useless once he got closer to Elizabeth. He fixed his bandage as he sat down to catch his breath and thought about what he would say. Arbin could feel Elizabeth nearby. She seemed to be in a good mood. He took a deep breath and tapped on her window.

"What are you doing here?" asked Elizabeth as she opened the window.

Arbin stepped in, "Right now, hiding?"

"You can't just come into my bedroom," she said. "It's fine if we meet in the park or someplace public like that. Now get out," and pushed him toward the window.

Arbin winced in pain. Elizabeth stopped, looked at the blood on her hands and said, "What is this? Are you hurt?" She did not wait for a response. Looking back at her hands said, "What happened? How bad is it?"

"Bad," said Arbin. "That's why I'm here."

"Sit, I will get something to bandage it with," said Elizabeth, looking around the room.

Arbin looked at his arm, "No, not this, I just came from a fight and think I reopened my old wound. I already wrapped it."

Elizabeth stood staring at him for a second. "Another fight? You really need to get better at fighting if you're going to keep this up." She gave a worried smile but could see from Arbin's face that there was more he was not saying.

Arbin gave a slight smile, "I'm not the only one that got hurt. I really want this to be the last time."

Elizabeth looked at him for a few seconds, saying nothing. The serious look on her face and the silence worried Arbin. "What's wrong?" he asked.

"Who did you kill this time?" she asked quietly.

"I did not kill anyone, but we found Bergman and rescued Mia and her children," said Arbin with a deep sigh. He shook his head and said, "I can finally put that burden to rest."

Elizabeth was quiet as she walked over and sat on the far edge of the bed. She folded her hands in her lap, "And now, you are here to say you're leaving?"

"I had to use my talents during the attack, and I think Captain Eustace is on to me. He wants to speak with me tomorrow. You know how hard I tried to keep my curse a secret. This time, I had to Fade in front of others. It was the only way I could save Mia and her children." Arbin smiled and looked up at Elizabeth. The smile left his face when he saw her expression. He could also feel her anger rise.

"Where will you go?" she asked quietly.

"North," said Arbin as he moved to stand in front of her. "The Church has less power there."

"So, is this how you did it with Mia?" said Elizabeth, not looking at him. "Get her to fall for you and then run off, leaving her to deal with the mess you made."

"No," said Arbin. He reached out his hand to take hers, but she pulled it back.

"Did you promise to come back for her?"

"This is not the same. I love you. I want you to come with me."

"Did you ever tell her that?" asked Elizabeth as she stood and walked to the other side of the room.

Arbin did not answer right away. He looked at the ground, "I did not really know what love was until I met you."

"Nice words," said Elizabeth. "How do I believe anything you say after you lied about Jayden?"

Arbin stared at her. He opened his mouth as if to say something but closed it again. After a few seconds he asked quietly, "How long have you known?"

"How long were you going to wait before you told me? You say you love me, but you are still keeping secrets from me!"

Arbin rubbed his face with one of his hands, took a breath and said, "This is not going the way I wanted it to."

"What, did you think you could sneak in here, flash your smile at me and have me follow you like some kind of puppy?"

"I hoped you felt the same way about me as I do about you. I hoped you would leave with me," said Arbin. "I can feel your anger. I think I may have misunderstood your feelings about me."

"My anger should tell you how I feel about the way you are treating me. Not if I have feelings for you."

Arbin looked at her, trying to understand what she just said.

"Really, you are the most selfish, ignorant man that I have ever met. Do you even care about what I want or need or are you just thinking about yourself?"

"I care about what you want," said Arbin shyly.

"Then what do I want?"

Arbin could feel her anger getting stronger. He was not sure what to say, so he just said the first things that came to his mind. "You want to be comfortable. Taken care of. That means someone that can provide for you in the manner you are accustomed to. I am also sure you want a family to care for."

Elizabeth sighed, "Where is the person I met in the park?" She went to the window and lifted the curtain. "It's time for you to go. Have a nice life, wherever it is."

"Please wait," said Arbin. He looked at her, "I'm not used to being honest with people. I have always said what I thought people wanted to hear so they would leave me alone. Please, I do not want to be alone anymore."

Elizabeth put her arm down, letting the curtain fall back.

"I know you want someone you can trust," said Arbin, "Someone that hears you. Someone to stand by you in the dark times. A person who will enjoy your successes and someone who will not lie to you when you are wrong. A person who will give you the freedom to grow."

Elizabeth stepped away from the window, "Did you read that someplace?"

Arbin shook his head, "No, I just told you what I want. I hope you want the same thing."

"You understand what you are asking us to give up here?" Elizabeth said.

"If you want me to, I will stay," said Arbin. "However, I do not know how I will protect you if I do. I am not even sure if I can protect myself."

"I'm worried about Dylan," said Elizabeth, looking toward his room.

"Captain Eustace will take care of him. He treats him like he was his own son."

Elizabeth nodded, "Lady Casandra will be here soon. I am not sure what our relationship will be like after that."

"Come with me and you will have children of your own to take care of," said Arbin.

Elizabeth gave him a look that made Arbin realize he should not have said that.

"I haven't said I was going with you,"

"I understand," He walked over to the window and surprised Elizabeth with a quick kiss, then stepped out onto the balcony.

"I will come by tomorrow with a horse and cart," said Arbin. "I will wait until noon. I am sure Captain Eustace will send someone to look for me if I wait any longer."

Elizabeth did not answer him.

Arbin took one last look into her eyes and then left.

Elizabeth watched him as he slipped into the forest. When she was sure he was gone, she walked over to her new favorite chair and flopped down in it. She stared up at the ceiling for several minutes, then looked around the room she was making her own and cried.

Chapter 30 - A Man of Tradition

ARBIN WOKE EARLY TO the familiar smell of straw and horse dung. For a few seconds, he thought he was back in Noor Point until he opened his eyes and saw the unfamiliar roof of the Schwartz's warehouse. He had been too afraid to go back to Masimo's house after his talk with Elizabeth, so he chose the only other place he could hide. A quick glance around showed that he was still the only person using it. Arbin was becoming concerned about the others. He did not expect Wagner to come back, but this was Schwartz's place. He hoped their absence did not mean they had been caught or killed.

Even though it was early, he heard activity outside. Today was the start of the weeklong Unification Celebration, and people were out early. Arbin decided he better get an early start and did his best to clean up and tend to his horse.

The Sumner Estate would normally be a ten-minute ride from the warehouse, but today the streets were full of people dressed in colorful outfits heading in the opposite direction. The business districts would be littered with vendors and food merchants. It would be like someone had turned the entire city into one big marketplace.

Arbin parked his little cart across the street from the entrance to the Sumner' Estate. When he did not see Elizabeth come out, he knew he might be in for a wait, so he did his best to make himself comfortable.

A few hours later he was still waiting and was getting worried. He had gotten a few looks from the guards at the gate, but they had left him alone. He was mulling over the possible good reasons Elizabeth had for taking so long when he had a terrible thought, *I do not remember if I said I would meet her here or at her house.*

He pictured the events of last night in his head, but as hard as he tried, he did not remember what he had said. *What do I do now? I still do not know where her house is. I cannot go to her brother, and I doubt if the guards know. I could ask Dylan. That is, if they let me.* He remembered the Bishop's order for him to stay away. He was sure the guards would also remember.

As he sat there hating himself for being so stupid, he saw a small carriage arrive and pull up to the front door. It looked like the one he had seen coming out of the Government Compound the day he had been shot. Before the driver could reach the door, Elizabeth stepped out.

She was wearing a long, short-waisted light green dress with light golden puffed sleeves done in a floral pattern. The front from the waist up was a mixture of red and green with gold embroidering. She had a dark black wrap around her shoulder fastened in front by a strap holding a large broach and hanging pearl that brought his eyes to a display of more cleavage than he was comfortable with. She spoke to the driver, then looked across the distance at Arbin and walked towards him.

Arbin was so taken by her appearance that he forgot to get out of his cart. He just sat there staring at her with his mouth partly open.

She stopped a few feet from the cart and swished her skirt back and forth, "Do you like it?"

Arbin quickly got out of the cart and took a step toward her. "It is breathtaking." He did his best to keep his eyes fixed on hers.

Elizabeth gave him a slight smile when she noticed how nervous the dress made him.

Arbin looked down at his outfit, "That does not look like traveling clothes."

"This is what I am wearing to the celebration," said Elizabeth. "I will be on stage with Dylan when they present him as the new holder of the Sumner Family Chair."

"The presentation. That will be late this afternoon," said Arbin. "We have to get going before then."

"I thought all night about what you said, and I have decided that I am staying here."

Arbin felt like someone had punched him in the chest. It was like all the air went out of him. He placed his hand on the cart to steady himself. "Not going?" he said. "I do not understand. I told you how I felt, and I thought you felt the same way."

"I care about you very much," said Elizabeth, touching him lightly on his arm. "But I have just met you. I am not sure if I can trust you with my life yet."

"Of course you can trust me. I will protect you. I promise!" said Arbin, putting his hand on top of hers.

"I am talking about more than defending me," She took a small step back, holding her hands in front of her. "I worry that if I follow you and things get tough, I could end up all alone in a shack with a dirt floor in the middle of nowhere."

"I will not let that happen." Arbin took a slight step towards her.

Elizabeth placed her hands on both of his arms, looked directly into his eyes and said, "Then prove it to me!" She let go of his arms. "Look how much effort you put into finding Mia. Look at the risks you took for someone you say does not matter. Prove to me you care that much about me. Prove to me, you will take those kinds of risks to keep me in your life. If you care about me, show me!"

Arbin stood looking at Elizabeth. He did not sense any anger, but the volume of her voice rose as she talked to the point where he became concerned that the guards at the gate would get the wrong idea and feel the need to save her. Thankfully, Elizabeth stopped talking. He was still thinking about the guards when she stepped forward, took hold of his hands and fixed her eyes on his. He realized with a bit of panic that she was waiting for his answer.

Arbin squeezed her hands, "I care about you and I will not leave you, but I am not sure how to show you that."

"If I asked you to stay here with me, what would you do?" asked Elizabeth, still looking straight into his eyes.

"I worry about Captain Eustace and what he will do," said Arbin.

Elizabeth let out the breath she was holding and looked down. She took a small step back, letting his hands drop from hers.

Looking at her, Arbin understood he had just failed his first chance to show her how he felt. "The last time I was worried about the Captain you stood by me and nothing bad happened," He said. Elizabeth continued to look down and Arbin said, almost pleading. "I will stay. Please give me another chance. What else do you want me to do?"

"Fight for me the traditional way." She looked up at Arbin and could see he was not sure what she was suggesting. She gave him a smile, "If you want me, you have to win me." She could see that Arbin still had not understood her. "Go to my brother and tell him how you feel. Convince him you are the best choice for me."

"Masimo is rich," said Arbin, a little stunned at what she was asking.

"And you are famous," said Elizabeth. "Use that to better yourself in his eyes, even if you have to join his Seer core. He knows you have valuable knowledge." She took his arm and walked with him toward the entrance of the Estate. "You might even try doing what your father did. You have some friends on the Council that would like to have you owe them a favor or two. I could even talk to Dylan about it. However, I will not use my influence with him until you have taken the first step and talked to my brother."

They stopped at the entrance, and as Arbin thought over what she had said, she squeezed his arm, gave him a smile and just before walking away said "Show me."

Chapter 31 - An Impossible Choice

ARBIN DROVE HIS CART back to the warehouse and found it still empty. He wondered what had happened to Schwartz and Wagner. He had seen Wagner run off as Captain Eustace and his men attacked. He hoped he had gotten away safely. He wanted to speak to Schwartz to make sure Mia and her children were safe.

So, she wants me to take risks, thought Arbin. *I guess the best thing to do is get the biggest risk out of the way first and go see the Captain.*

He left the cart and horse inside the warehouse and made his way toward the western gate of the Government Compound. He was not sure how much longer his use of the warehouse would go unnoticed.

It did not take long to reach the western gate since all the traffic was heading in that general direction.

The Government Building was still being guarded by the Army. They were not as formal as the Shadow Guard. Arbin could hear the crowds enjoying themselves nearby. It was obvious that the guards would rather be with the crowds then dealing with Arbin. They were so involved in their talk about the upcoming celebration events that they never asked if he needed a guide.

Arbin made his way to the Captain's office where he signed in and soon discovered that Captain Eustace was not in. The guard seated outside his office said, "He is out patrolling for the Unification Celebration. He will be out of the office for a week. The soonest you can see him will be in two weeks." Arbin thanked the guard, happy that the meeting had been delayed. *I can still tell Elizabeth that I took a risk,* he thought. As he was getting ready to leave, the guard pointed to a young Page that was sitting nearby and said, "This lad has been waiting here all day for you. Hey, Page, here is your man."

The young boy looked up, jumped from his chair and scurried over to Arbin. He held up a piece of paper with Arbin's name on it. "Is this you, sir?"

"Yes, that is me," said Arbin, looking at the guard who just shrugged his shoulders.

"If you would follow me, please. Bishop Sorren would like to speak with you."

Arbin followed along behind the Page, doing his best to remember the way back. They stopped before a door that Arbin recognized. It was the entrance to the Grand Council Meeting Room.

The Page peeked inside the room and then opened the door for Arbin. Bishop Sorren was standing on the platform that Alex had used behind a small podium. He smiled when he saw Arbin and welcomed him in. The Page eagerly accepted a few coins from the Bishop and ran out. The door closed behind him with a loud click that echoed through the room.

"I find this a perfect place to practice speeches and as you know I have an important one soon," said Bishop Sorren as he used his arm in a sweeping motion toward the empty room.

Arbin kept his distance and his silence. He did not trust the man anymore. He could not prove it, but he believed the Bishop was involved with Mia's kidnapping and the murders of Duke Henry and the Chairman. He had hoped that he would not have to deal with the Bishop again, but Elizabeth had said she wanted him to take risks. That was the only reason he followed the Page here.

Bishop Sorren gathered and folded the papers before him and slid them into an inside pocket. He ignored Arbin's silence and said in the same pleasant voice, "I had hoped you would visit with Captain Eustace or High Seer Keller today. To tell you the truth, I was starting to think maybe you were on your way back to Noor Point."

"There is nothing left there for me now!" Arbin was surprised that the words slipped from his mouth. The empty room made them seem louder as they echoed back to him.

"Like I said, a splendid place to make speeches," said Bishop Sorren with a slight smile as he stepped down off the platform.

Arbin took a step back, still watching the Bishop. Arbin did not think the Bishop would attack him, but his pleasant demeanor worried him.

"Actually, it is to both our good fortune that you are still here. I have something that belongs to you. You have saved me the trouble of hunting you down to give it to you." Bishop Sorren pointed to a satchel, much like what a messenger carried, sitting on a nearby table.

"You want me to deliver something for you?" asked Arbin.

"No, it is for you," said Bishop Sorren with a chuckle. "A thank you from the Council. The bag was my addition. After all, you will need a way to carry all that money."

Arbin walked over to the satchel and discovered three bags of money inside, plus an envelope containing a letter and a ring.

"What's this for?" asked Arbin, still looking inside the satchel.

"The money is a reward, of sorts. It comes from each of the Family Chairs. Their way of saying thank you for ending the threat to their lives and helping to find Henry and Chairman Sumner's killers."

Arbin let out a short, quick laugh and shook his head. "That's funny, and the ring?"

"That's the best part," said Bishop Sorren, taking a few steps toward Arbin. "That ring belongs to me. With it, and the letter, you can go into any Cathedral and collect an advance on your annual allowance."

"Why are you giving me an annual allowance?" Arbin dropped the letter and ring casually back into the satchel.

"Because as of now, you are working for me," said Bishop Sorren as he straightened his cassock.

Arbin stared at the Bishop, not sure what to say.

Bishop Sorren smiled, "It is a job that will require a good bit of travel and may take some time to complete."

Arbin picked up the satchel and hung it from one shoulder. He turned back to the Bishop. "That will not happen. I will take your reward because I can use it to start my new life with Elizabeth Keller." Arbin took the letter with the ring and tossed it onto the desk the satchel was sitting on. "I think it is time for me to leave."

"You will not marry Miss Keller," said Bishop Sorren. "In fact, I have decided that she will never marry."

Arbin looked at the Bishop and could see that he was serious. "What makes you think you can decide who we can marry?"

"The law, the Church and tradition give me the right to decide who she will marry, and I have decided that it would be safest if she did not marry."

"Just a few days ago, you had no trouble with her marrying Masimo. Besides, I think her brother has a say in this," said Arbin as he walked toward the door.

"A few days ago, I did not know that she had a 'Talent' as you call it," said Bishop Sorren.

Arbin stop and turned to look at the Bishop, who smiled when he saw the concern on Arbin's face.

"I read in the reports from Captain Eustace and High Seer Keller about your claims that Mia had the Seer gift. I had always suspected that all the children from the Nursery were different. I wasn't sure about Miss Keller until your reaction just now."

"Elizabeth does not have a Talent!" said Arbin, his voice echoing in the empty room. "You already tested her."

"You are right. But I believe it is time to take another look. Dylan is very fond of her and would be devastated if we lost her."

"I tell you, she does not have any Talents," said Arbin. "Ask her brother, or anyone around her. They will agree with me. She is not a Fade or a Seer."

"I am sure I can find people that would be willing to say she has some ability," said Bishop Sorren. "You understand the penalty for someone charged with practicing witchcraft."

Arbin stood looking at the Bishop. His eyes narrowed, and his fists clenched. "If you try to hurt Elizabeth, I will..." he stopped short of finishing his sentence.

"What happens to Elizabeth is really up to you. As I said, I am offering you a job. Complete the assignment within six months and Elizabeth will be safe. However, I will never allow her to marry."

"Why? I do not understand why you would not allow her to marry."

"It would be more correct for me to say I cannot allow any of the children from the Nursery to have children of their own," said Bishop Sorren. "That includes Alex and yourself."

Arbin laughed, "You are a little late with that plan. Mia already has two children."

"Yes, I know," said Bishop Sorren. "Twins, a boy and a girl. The reports on your struggle with Mr. Bergman said there was a Fade in the area. That leads me to believe that Mia's children have Talents. We did not do so well dealing with the last Fade. Last thing we need to do is repopulate the world with an enemy we are not prepared yet to fight."

Arbin shook his head, not sure what to say next. *I wonder if he would change his mind if I told him I was the Fade they detected*, he thought. *I think I can get away if I do. He might still hurt Elizabeth. I do not think I could get her away tonight. Mia is gone, so that is not my main problem.* He knew he had no choice. "What do I have to do to keep Elizabeth safe?"

Bishop Sorren walked over and picked up the ring and letter and handed them to Arbin, who grudgingly took them and put them in his satchel. The Bishop took a few steps away from Arbin and then said, "It's simple, really. I want you to find Mia and her children and bring them back here."

Arbin felt like his legs would collapse. He leaned back against the nearby desk. He wanted to say something but could not find the air to speak.

The sound of music could be heard softly from the front of the building. The Bishop looked in the music's direction. "That is my cue. Walk with me, Arbin. It will give you a chance to see Miss Keller before you leave. She will be on stage with Dylan as they introduce him as the new holder of the Family Chair and me as his Guardian. She will be so proud that you found employment as my messenger."

Arbin just stood there watching the Bishop as he headed for the door. His mind whirled, while he searched for a possible way out.

"Arbin, if you try to run or warn Miss Keller or anyone else, things will not go well for her. I never approved of Mr. Bergman's methods, but a missing finger proved to be a powerful motivator. Time to show me you care for her."

The Bishop left the room as Arbin followed mechanically behind him. As they headed downstairs, Arbin studied the Bishop. Here was the man responsible for hurting Mia and her children. He must be behind the deaths of Henry and Chairman Sumner. Arbin realized that the Bishop could and would kill Elizabeth if he did not do what he wanted. *What am I going to do? If I bring back Mia, he will kill her and the children. If I do not, he will kill Elizabeth.* Arbin felt a hate for this man unlike anything he had felt before. *I could attack him. That will not work. I am no good with a knife. If he lives, Elizabeth and I will not.* Before he knew it, he was out in the courtyard at the foot of the stairs that led to the stage. He watched as the Bishop climb the stairs and stood next to Elizabeth, who gave Arbin a discrete little wave, which he returned with a weak smile.

Most of the presentation happened in a blur. Arbin could not concentrate. He focused on Elizabeth. She was so pretty in her dress and looked so happy. He smiled when she smiled and wanted so much to be up there with her. His anger grew and his fists clenched each time Bishop Sorren spoke to her. The idea of the man that wanted to cut off her finger being so close made him want to vomit.

Before he knew it, the presentation was over, and Elizabeth was coming down the steps followed by Dylan and the Bishop. Arbin did his best to keep a smile on his face as Dylan asked how he looked on the platform. He went on about how high it was and how far he could see. After a few minutes, Elizabeth told Dylan that she wanted to talk to Arbin before they left for the fireworks.

Elizabeth took Arbin by the arm and they walked about twenty feet away from the stage. Arbin looked back and saw that Bishop Sorren was watching them.

"Bishop Sorren told me the good news," said Elizabeth, smiling as she looked up at him.

"Really, what did he say?" asked Arbin.

"He said you are working for him now. He also said the Council gave you a large reward."

"That's true. But I will have to be away for a few months and will have to leave tonight."

"I know," said Elizabeth sadly. "He said it was important Council business and you could not talk about it."

"Did he say anything else?" asked Arbin.

"He said something about Masimo, but I could not really understand him because of the crowd."

Arbin took Elizabeth's hands, "I want you to know how important you are to me. I told you I would do anything to protect you and I will."

Elizabeth gave him a smile, "I know."

Arbin reached inside his satchel, "Look, here is the reward money." He lifted out one bag to show her. "I wanted to give it to you before I left," he said, but as he started to remove the satchel, she stopped him.

"What am I going to do with this now?" asked Elizabeth. "I cannot walk around with this. You hold on to it until later. You should give it to my brother as the Bride Price."

"As soon as I can," said Arbin with as cheerful a smile as he could. "Look, I need to go now. If I stay any longer, I will start crying."

This time she surprised him with a quick kiss on the cheek. "See you when you get back." She walked away to join Dylan and the Bishop. The three of them soon disappeared into the crowd.

Arbin looked around, trying to decide where to go next. He had a few things at Masimo's house that might be useful, but he did not feel like seeing him or fighting the crowd to get there. He headed back to Schwartz's warehouse. He would need the little cart for his journey.

He took his time walking. He touched his cheek and thought about both Mia and Elizabeth. Two people he cared about. Both of their lives would be ruined because of him. *Just when things are going well, that old curse shows up.* Before he knew it, he was at the warehouse. He opened the door and noticed that a lantern was lit. He was trying to remember if he had left it burning when a familiar face stepped into the light. "Wagner! I am so glad to see you!"

Chapter 32 - Good and Bad of It

WHEN BISHOP SORREN woke, his head hurt. He tried to reach for it and found that he was in a chair with his hands and feet tied. He also had a gag made from cloth in his mouth. Arbin stepped into his view, "I was a little worried I hit you too hard. I have not done this before. I was also a little surprised how easy it was to get to you. I expected your home would be guarded like the Chairman's. It was almost a waste of a perfectly good shadow."

Arbin reached over and pulled the gag from Bishop Sorren's mouth and let the loop of cloth hang around his neck.

"Do you understand how much trouble you are in?" asked Bishop Sorren as he tried to look around him at the dark interior of an old building. A single lantern placed on a crate was the only source of light. "Have you gone crazy, Arbin? Let me go now or I will have you executed for kidnapping a member of the Governing Council!"

"Do you recognize where you are?" asked Arbin, ignoring the Bishop's threat.

The Bishop started yelling as loud as he could for help. Arbin stood and watched until the yelling stopped.

"Yelling will do no good. We are far from anyone who can help you."

"If you wanted more money, you should have told me," said Bishop Sorren. "Ransom will take a long time and afterward, we will find you. Release me now or when the ransom is paid, I will arrest Elizabeth and charge her as an accomplice."

Arbin walked over and picked up the lantern. He held it higher so that more of the room was lit. He returned the lantern to its crate. "You are in the old building where Bergman held Mia and her children prisoners. This is also the place where Bergman killed someone." Arbin walked up to the Bishop, looked him in the eyes and said, "This is a place of pain, sorrow and death!"

Bishop Sorren was silent as he studied Arbin. "You would not dare harm a Bishop of the Church. You would be committing an unpardonable sin. You would be damned for all eternity."

"A few minutes ago, you were just a member of the Governing Council," said Arbin with a slight smile. "Besides, according to the Church, I am already damned."

Bishop Sorren stayed quiet. Arbin could see the confused look on his face.

"I have struggled my entire life with the concepts of good and evil," said Arbin, walking toward the Bishop as he talked. "Can an evil person change by doing good or are they cursed, destined to do bad? Thanks to you and Chairman Sumner, I think I have an answer I can live with. You both talked about the Nursery you found me in. You also talked about all the others there. All those twins and me. Something about that has bothered me until you gave the answer."

"We saved you and the others," said Bishop Sorren. "It is true, one of you fell prey to the curse of the devil, but the others, including you, escaped that curse. God has blessed you with a special gift. This is no way for you to behave. Maybe you are just ill or confused. Release me and I will get you the help and guidance you need."

"That is kind of you, Bishop, but hear me out, please. You said that each of the children rescued from the Nursery have a Talent, correct?"

Bishop Sorren nodded and Arbin continued, "The Chairman told me at one time I had a twin, a sister I am guessing, who 'disappeared' before I was born. I believe that my twin sister must have had a Talent as well." Arbin paused to make sure the Bishop was following him. "I think somehow she gave that Talent to me. That is the only thing that can explain who I am now." Arbin looked directly into the Bishop's eyes, "You see, I have both the Seer and the Fade Talent. As a Seer, you say I am destined to do good. As for my Fade side, people expect me to do the work of the devil."

"I think you are confused," said Bishop Sorren, staring back at Arbin. "I am sure I can help you understand what–,"

"Please!" said Arbin, raising his hand, interrupting the Bishop. "I do understand! I realize now that I am the way I am because of my parents and not because of a curse or a blessing. The Godless Gift, I think the Chairman called it. I cannot express how liberating it is to discover I have the freedom to do good or bad for my own reasons," Arbin paused as if he was done speaking. Once again, he looked into the Bishop's eyes, "Today, I have decided to do both."

Arbin could see a look of understanding in the Bishop's eyes, followed by a look of fear.

"I want to introduce you to someone," said Arbin. "His name is Wagner. You might not know him, but he knows you."

Bishop Sorren jumped in his chair as Wagner reached out from somewhere behind him and firmly grasped the Bishop's shoulders.

Arbin smiled when he saw the fear in the Bishop's eyes. He stepped closer. "He also knows that you are the one responsible for the death of his brother. Introducing him to you is the good thing I will do."

While Arbin had the Bishop's attention, Wagner grabbed the Bishop's hair tightly and slid his knife blade across the Bishop's cheek. The cut was not deep, but the suddenness and the pain caused Bishop Sorren to cry out. The wound bled more than Arbin had expected. He watched as Wagner wiped the blood from the blade on Bishop Sorren's smock. Arbin continued to stare into the Bishop's eyes and said, "You might be correct. I might not have the tenacity to kill you, but I can make you suffer. I only wish I had the stomach to make you suffer the way you had Mia suffer."

Wagner released the Bishop's hair but remained behind him. Even though he was out of sight, the Bishop could still hear him breathing.

The Bishop stiffened when Arbin put his hand on his shoulders for a few seconds. Arbin quickly pulled the gag back up and into place. Made sure it was secure and stepped back out in front of Bishop Sorren.

"I know that hurt, I am sorry to say that was not the bad thing I am going to do," said Arbin. "The really bad thing is I spent some of the reward money you gave me. I gave it to Wagner. He insisted he would kill you for free, but I had him promise to do to you the bad things that I could not."

Arbin looked at Wagner, then back to the Bishop. "I am going now. I will take your advice and leave town for a while. I might even collect on that advance you promised me. After that, I will return here and do my best to live the traditional life with Elizabeth, whatever that is. With that said, I now leave you in the talented hands of my associate."

Arbin looked back toward Wagner, who with the nod of his head toward the door, made it clear it was time for Arbin to leave. Without looking back to the Bishop, Arbin left the warehouse, and once outside pressed his back against the closed door as if he were preparing to keep the fear and anger on the other side from escaping. Looking down, he saw that his hands were shaking. Around his feet the dim reddish light of the warehouse's lantern seeped out under the door, along with the sounds of the Bishop's muffled protests.

Arbin quickly stepped forward as if stepping out of a puddle. The adrenaline running through his body kept him moving forward through the tall grasses until the sounds and light of the warehouse were replaced by the soft gentle sounds of the river and the croaking of frogs. Arbin stopped and took a deep breath. As he let it slowly out, he felt a tension start to leave his body. He took a few more steps forward and stopped. The cool darkness of the night surrounded him like that old blanket of his mother. He took a few more deep breaths, letting each out slowly. As he let out each breath, he could feel the shackles of his past start to fall away. Like his fear of an imaginary curse that left him living alone, afraid, without a future. With every deep breath he took, he felt more and more relaxed, almost peaceful. He felt more and more like a new man. Not one determined by clothes and money, but a man that no longer hated himself. A man with the chance of a future and a chance at love.

Arbin looked up at the sky and was surprised at the display of brilliant stars in the moonless night. As he stared up into the heavens, he realized it felt different tonight, larger, grander, almost overwhelming. A smile came across his face and he said in a clear and surprisingly cheerful voice, "Such a beautiful night." With that, he headed off to collect his cart and make his way to a new beginning.

Don't miss out!

Visit the website below and you can sign up to receive emails whenever Jeffrey Crosby publishes a new book. There's no charge and no obligation.

https://books2read.com/r/B-A-LIRL-ZMYJB

BOOKS 2 READ

Connecting independent readers to independent writers.

About the Author

Thank you for reading my book.

I comes from a family rich with creative and talented people. I did not get the bug to be creative until I retired and was looking for a new hobby.

I plan to make writing my new adventure and hope that you enjoy the trip as much as I do. If you would like to read more about the characters in this book please let me know.

Jeffrey Crosby